ASIM'S

EXTRAORDINARY

JOURNEYS

BOOK 1
ALL FOR THE CHILDREN

Written by

Tommy Lee Davis

(Page intentionally left blank)

ABOUT THE AUTHOR

TOMMY LEE DAVIS was born in Hertfordshire England, where he first become interested in writing poems and short stories. He later moved to the United States. He lived in Texas, Missouri, Illinois, and Ohio before stopping in Nevada. Tommy and his wife, April, now reside in Las Vegas, this is his third book in the series of Asim and his warriors. (full bio on Amazon Author page)

GLOSSARY

Name	Pronunciation
Asim	Ace-sim
Apora	A-poor-a
Boben	Bow-ben
Duf	Duff
Exim	Ex-em
Garronas	Gar-own-as
Jubly	Jube-lee
Lanee	Lan-e
Langel	Lan-gel
Larby	Lar-bee
Leham	Lee-ham
Pantra	Pan-tra
Radel	Ray-dell
Theon	T-on
Tonas	Toe-nas
Toya	Toy-ya
Tyron	Tie-ron
Yuby	You-bee
Zabin	Zay-bin
Zollo	Zol-low

TABLE OF CONTENTS

(Page intentionally left blank)

INTRODUCTION

It seemed like just yesterday but was a long, long time ago," said Saon Jestin, teacher of children in the small but quaint village of Tress; he sat there with a large book sprawled across his lap. "I will tell you all about life back then!" Saon spoke intently to the class of village children between eight to sixteen years of age.

"It was back in an evil time," he said, "where at an early age, boys turned into men and girls into women."

The class snickered at the thought.

"Stepping back into an early age in time," he started again, "where wicked kings, dragons, and monsters ruled over everything! It was at a time when an evil veil seemed to shroud everything living throughout these lands.

"The stories I'm about to tell you are of a band of warriors, comrades united together, standing for strength and bravery in those perilous times. A group of warriors that set out to right all the wrongs. It was their courage that helped make what we have today.

"We are drifting back to when village life seemed so simple and ordinary. Their small houses were made of wood and straw, sitting erect away from pathways of dirt. Clothes hung on a rope to dry. The smokestacks whispered curls of smoke up high in the air before they slowly faded away. It was not by any means a wealthy community. Let's say the village people lived an adequate life. The villagers ate, drank, and lived their lives without much worry. Crops were plentiful and the stock kept mostly full. The village was nestled deep in the southern area of Prostatos, close to the vast forests of Trespason. Children could run, laugh, and play their games in the village square with no fear—or so they thought…"

Chapter 1

THE NIGHTMARE

Tonas, a relatively large man to look at, was in his forties. Some say he was a kind but strange person who had taken charge of the village after the death of Elder Johan Sabitt. His curly brown-and-gray hair drifted down his neck. Having keen brown eyes and a broad smile, he stood all of five feet ten inches tall. His waist would be considered stout but without fat. He was a pleasant man, for sure, but he had never married.

The village of Tress nestled between the Great Forest of Trespason. In an area called Prostatos, it lay between the vast forests, rivers, and small rippling rivulets, all close to the magnificent backdrop of the high mountains that stood an excellent two-day walk from Tress, depending on how fast you wanted to travel. That one mountain range stretched all the way back to the rolling hills of Byrnea to the east.

Tress was a beautiful and tranquil place for two hundred or more village men and women and an ample number of children who played happily on the dirt paths and in the village square during the day when not laboring in the fields or doing their chores, which were taken care of early at sunrise.

Just like any other ordinary day between dusk and dawn, a fire burned brightly in the village square. Children always played games in the early evenings using the light from the flames that burnt brightly.

This night, there was a loud rumbling in the distance. It was unyielding, the kind that you could feel rippling under your feet.

Each of the children panicked, and some were already running home, unsure of what was happening.

The rumbling was growing louder now. Adults of the village stepped out of their houses; some ran in from the barns to see what could be happening in their village.

Mothers were outside waving and screaming for their children, still left by the fire. "Run home," they shouted.

Suddenly, out of the dark sky, through the outlying bushes surrounding the outskirts of the village, the people saw a small army on horseback riding in! The glowing light from the fire made the silver buckles strapped around their magnificent steeds shine like mirrors. The harnesses on these horses sparkled as the bright silver cascaded from the light of the flames, so brilliant that some of the villagers had to cover their eyes.

These were menacing-looking soldiers dressed in black, sitting high as they rode through the village. Tucked on their sides were their shields and large spears. The polished silver of their armor and helmets gave the impression that their heads were on fire.

Following just behind them was a wide, covered cart with bars, the kind used for hauling prisoners to jail. The wooden wheels clunked loudly. Sitting at the reins was a strange-looking man, very tall and thin, toting a long beard, long silver hair, and a large pointed hat that sat firm on his head. Pulling up at the village square, he stopped close to the fire.

The villagers found out later that the riders were the king's guards from a faraway kingdom in the north called Nordak, and they were there to steal their male children!

The soldiers were showing no regard for the villagers' lives, just fulfilling their quest, using their spears when necessary to either move or skewer anyone stepping in their way. Loudly, the village bell was rung, alerting everyone to the present danger. Chaos was evolving amid the shrieks, shouts, and the screams. The thunderous noise of the horses added to this dark and ominous sight. The men of the village were coming out to fight for their young boys, who were now carried off against their will by the soldiers. Alas, the village men were no match for their armored-clad foe, who overcame them and struck them to the ground. The young boys were plucked out of the grasp of their mothers, who were left screaming! The soldiers were taking only the younger boy children and tossing young girls to one side. On finding each of the boys, they would load them into the cart. Some soldiers were setting fire to the houses, forcing more children into the open. They continued to fill the old cart with the younger boys until it was full; now, they stopped and were ready to leave. The village itself was in turmoil; homes were burning in the night.

Bleeding bodies were lying on the ground; some were dead.

And as quick as they came, the soldiers left through the surrounding bushes into the forest, back to where they came.

Tonas, whose head was still spinning, was trying to grasp the reality; he looked at the devastation, the noise still buzzing in the air. Crying women were tending to their men on the bloodstained ground, those that were still alive. The flames from the fire painted a horrific sight. Through the blood, the dust, and dirt, slowly the screams and shouts were at last slowly fading.

A nightmare, he thought, as bodies lay on the ground, with some strewn across fences. Smoke filled the surrounding sky. The heat was blowing in a light breeze, and the houses were still slowly burning. Some villagers had set out for the stream nearby, filling their buckets to put the fires out.

This night seemed the longest they had ever endured as they all worked relentlessly. Now, the sun was slowly creeping up in the sky. They had survived through the night. The wounded were cared for and bandaged up. They had loaded the dead bodies onto carts to be buried nearby. And the fires were put out!

Tonas rang the bell, calling a meeting of all who were still able. Gathering everyone in the middle of the village square, he looked at the men and women standing in front of him.

Tonas spoke about the terrible, devastating happenings of the night before. "We can never forget," he expressed. A quick chill suddenly went through his spine as he gave a quick thought to the nightmare they had just endured. The shouting, screaming, and other noises were still fresh in his mind and dulled his ears.

"It was pure evil," he said again. "To be taken by surprise by those evil cowards. Now our boys are gone, stolen from our homes, every boy child over the age of five. They murdered countless of our friends and burned our homes. I cannot—no, I will not rest until we bring them back again. We cannot let them do this and leave!" He was staring out at the people's tired-looking faces, still filled with horror and disbelief at all they had faced.

One of the women in the crowd shouted out. "How can we fight an army?"

At first, Tonas did not answer, but with a tear in his eye, he said, "I am asking you not to take stock of what has happened. We have lost a lot of loved ones. I am asking every one of you to stand with me."

"Again, how can we fight an army?" the woman shouted.

"I will fight anyone I must," proclaimed Tonas. "I will gather help somehow to bring our boys back. I will ask for volunteers. And although there are a lot of able women, I must request that only men volunteer. I also need our builders to stay. I know this village must be put back together."

One villager spoke out. It was Yuby, a slender man in his thirties with short grayish-brown hair and rugged features, standing five feet eight inches tall. Yuby had lost no child. "I will gladly fight with you to save the boys." As he volunteered, he walked toward where Tonas was standing.

Boben was a good-looking young man of twenty years old, having a slimmer and more muscular physique. Standing six feet tall with shoulder-length blond hair, he stepped forward to volunteer. "I lost my young brother. Therefore, I will go, too."

Gad was tightly bandaged and had great difficulty standing up to volunteer.

Tonas was looking intently at him. "Your injuries need to heal. I'm sorry, we cannot take the wounded either. I know your heart is heavy, and I feel your pain."

Senso, a lad of twenty-five, standing six feet tall, with bright red hair to his neck and a muscular build, also spoke out. "I have lost no one close, but I will join you." He approached Tonas in the village square. He tripped and fell to one knee on the ground, causing a small ripple of laughter in the crowd. Tonas helped him up and smiled. "Thank you. At least we can still laugh over the pain."

Then there was Spen, an overly portly man in his fifties. He stood five feet six inches tall with a belly larger than it should be, not just due to age but his regular consumption of food and mead. Tonas looked at Spen and asked him if he was sure.

Spen responded, "As best as I can recall at this moment." He had a very large flagon of mead hanging around his neck; raising it to his lips, he took a sip.

The conversation went silent. Then, one of the women stood up again and shouted, "Most of the villagers were wounded or were too scared to fight! You could wait for some of our men to return from the other villages."

"That might take days or weeks," said Tonas.

"You know you will battle an army?" she shouted again.

"And I only see five standing!" another woman yelled.

Tonas answered, "I have made my vow. Even though we are few and we may not make it back alive, we will die trying."

"God be with you then!" the woman shouted.

"I hope so," he agreed.

They all stood together, Tonas being the leader of the other four. He indicated to them that their hearts would make up for any shortage and instructed them to load up their weapons and be ready to leave on their journey.

"Wait!" cried Yuby. "I know we are short on people, but I have heard of someone who may help us!"

"And who would that be?" Tonas asked.

"His name is Asim, and from all accounts, he is a great warrior from afar. He may just be the fighter we need. I have heard that he helps people in need, and I know where we can find him," said Yuby. "We will have to travel through the valleys of Panchal and the vast forests of Trespason. The only problem is it could be a little unsafe in that part of the forest, so we would have to be careful as we could journey through dwarf territory. Some dwarfs are not as welcoming as others. But I believe the risk will be worth it to seek Asim's help."

"What if we do not find him?" said Senso.

Tonas agreed and had a concern that the extra journey through dwarf territory could be a waste of their time, not to mention dangerous.

"Let's stop and think about it," asked Yuby. "There are five of us. Between all five, not one of us are warriors. We all own a sword, but do any of us have any skills with one? To rescue the children, we must fight the king's army, who fight for a living. Do you think if we knock on the castle door and tell them we would like our children back, they will turn them over to us? We need help!"

"But we have no money or gold," professed Tonas. "We cannot pay anyone."

"I have heard that this man, Asim, helps people in distress and does not ask for payment in return."

"It makes no sense," scoffed Tonas, "that he would do this for nothing in return. But again, I say, what if we cannot find him?"

"That would be a chance we take," said an eager Yuby.

"I must agree you make sense. I believe our hearts are racing ahead of us. We need help, and if we find this Asim, we should pray that he will help us."

"I think he sounds too good to be true. Are you sure you heard this from a reliable person?" asked Senso.

"I know who told me, and he is reliable, or I would have said nothing."

"Well," said Tonas. "We have to prepare to leave. We will look for this Asim in the hope that he will help. We will meet back here as soon as possible. Be ready to leave."

Chapter 2

THE SEARCH BEGINS

The sun was still transitioning over the mountaintop as they left out of the village. Traveling through the bush area heading west, they could see the large oak trees approaching, the leaves swaying lightly in the breeze as they entered the forest. Only a short distance away, the trees appeared to be growing strangely closer together, giving the appearance of no clear path into the now darkened forest. They became a little skeptical of the whole journey, scared they could walk in circles and would not find Asim, added with the thought of being killed by dwarfs on their minds. Still, they traveled deeper into the forest. Lost in thought, Spen pulled out the flagon he had carried with him for the journey and took a sip.

Tonas turned, asking Yuby, "Have you any idea in which direction we should go?"

"We need to keep going straight. I have a feeling it will take us closer to where Asim could be." He was hoping Asim would present himself to them.

"You mean like he is waiting for us?" scoffed Senso in his doubtful voice again

Yuby never answered him.

As night fell upon the forest, they decided it was time to rest. Dusk had already settled itself around them. "We will need to camp here," Tonas said to the others, sending two to collect wood for a fire, "We have food to cook and eat for nourishment before settling down to rest." After they ate, they slept until sunrise the next morning.

The men awoke to pack up and start back in their search of Asim, waiting for Senso to extinguish the fire, making sure it was out.

Suddenly, they found themselves surrounded. A small man wielding a giant sword stood behind Tonas, placing his sword to his neck with great conviction. Tonas's heart was pounding in his chest, crying out in pain as the blade of the sword put a slight nick on his skin. The other four stood, afraid of being in the same predicament, as what seemed a multitude of small dwarfs kept them from moving.

The strongest among them, standing taller than the rest, spoke, telling them, "Stand still." It was Swank, leader of the dark dwarfs, making it known to Tonas that he was not playing!

None of them wanted to challenge this grumpy, sandy-faced dwarf with a large nose. He stood all of four feet eight inches tall, although, in Swank's mind, he thought himself to be at least ten feet. He was as sarcastic as he was offensive. Standing out in front of them all, with anger in his eyes, he howled at them, "What are you doing in my forest?" Swank demanded, laughing cruelly at the look of fear on their faces; his men laughed with him. "We will not just shed drippings of blood. We may have a bucket filled with the intruder's blood." He laughed again. "First, we will relieve you of your coin."

Tonas, not knowing what to say but fearing for his life, tried to explain they had no money and what had happened to them two nights ago, how the king's army had ridden into their village, killed, burned, and stolen their boy children.

"Hmm," said Swank. "Sad, yet not my problem." He laughed again. "We will take your coin, and we may even let you live. If you compensate us enough, that is."

Tonas stated again that they had nothing. "All we have is what you see."

"No coin!" shouted Swank. "Well, we will just have to kill you!" They all laughed again as he told them. He was sure they would not be missed.

Suddenly, there came a voice from behind them. "Withdraw your blades," said a good-looking young man standing behind Swank. The dwarfs were feeling the steel at their necks now and obliged without a fuss.

"Asim," shouted Swank, "stay out of our business."

"I don't believe this is good business." Asim was in his mid-twenties, a suave man standing six feet tall, exceptionally attractive, with blondish hair to his shoulder and a rugged, athletic, muscular-looking body. He was staring intently at Tonas, with his sword still drawn toward Swank's neck.

"What are you villagers doing in the forest of Trespason?" Asim asked Tonas.

"I think we are looking for you," mumbled Tonas, his voice trembling. "Are you Asim?"

"I am. What dealings do you want with me? And it had better be good, or I may let the dwarfs keep you!" This changed the cringe on Swank's face to a quirky smile.

By this time, four more of Asim's men had stepped forward.

Stone was in his late twenties, a ruggedly handsome man, six feet tall, with long brown hair and a very muscular build.

Theon, somewhere around thirty, was six feet tall, with thick brown shoulder-length hair, rugged features, and a slim physique.

Lube, in his early twenties, was five feet ten inches tall, with long brown hair, perfect features, and a robust and muscular build.

Zollo, a young man in his late teens standing six feet tall, was extremely good-looking, with long black hair and a healthy, athletic, muscular body.

All were now awaiting Tonas's answer. Tonas explained to Asim of the king's army, the decimation of their village, and the stealing of their young boys. "We were hoping you will help us to return them home."

"Any reason why I would?" Asim asked, looking at his eyes.

"I was told you were a good-hearted man that helps people in distress."

"I do a lot of things." Asim smiled.

"I am afraid we have no valuables to pay you," Tonas stressed. "We want to have our children home. Will you please help us?"

"No coins," sneered Swank. "Who cares about children? You would be a fool to go."

"Shut up!" shouted Asim to Swank's face. "I'm sorry about our dwarf friends here. They have no compassion. However, my heart goes out to you and your plight. You have not only found us, but we will make ourselves available. We will help you, although I am unsure about your men." He looked at Spen, who gingerly took a sip from his flagon.

"Do you know where the army came from?"

"We think they are Nordaks, from up in the farthest northland," Yuby told them.

"I believe I have heard of them," replied Stone. "It sounds like something they might do. Ruled by an evil king named Brayon or something like that? In the lands of a wizard or warlock, I think? So I heard."

"In the lands of Perogia?" asked Asim.

"Yes, I believe so."

"Where did you come by all this information?"

"In one of the taverns," chuckled Stone. "You know how people like to talk."

Asim thought for a second. "You are more than welcome to come with us, Swank, but I'm sure you would try to murder us in our sleep!"

"I do not have a quarrel with any king," snarled Swank, "only people in my forest. You will all pay soon enough. We will leave."

"Move out of here," Asim sounded annoyed, "before I lose my patience with you and your ugly brood."

Tonas seemed happy now. "I am glad they have gone."

"Well, I'm sure we could see them again, so we must stay alert. But for now, we need a plan to bring your children back! I know you are all feeling brave, and I feel it my responsibility to tell you that you all could be in grave danger, and some could lose their lives on this journey. So, take a while to think about how much it means to you. Know that anyone of you will show no shame in returning home." It was silent at that moment.

"I am with you," said Tonas defiantly.

"Me too," said Senso.

"Count me in," said Boben.

"Me too," added Yuby.

Spen was silent for a brief time, sipping from his flagon again. "Count me in." He tripped and bungled forward, Asim putting his hand out to stop him from falling over.

"I can see you will be the fun one." He laughed. "For your safety and ours, I will expect you all to learn basic bow and sword skills that we will teach you along the journey. We will be going up through the forest to the river. Prepare yourselves for a long trek."

Setting out through the woods that day, they traveled until the sky turned dark as it started to rain. It was a substantial rainfall. Everyone was walking through the now-gathering puddles, their vision a little blurred as the large raindrops splashed on the leaves as the rain fell around them. Asim, leading the pack, stopped a moment as he wiped his brow. "We should camp here. The rain is slowing us down, and we need cover. Besides, it will be nighttime soon."

Finding an area where the bushes gave them sufficient cover, they made a camp. The fire was more challenging to complete in the rain, yet some of the villagers still managed to sleep under the circumstances. Asim had Stone and Lube stay on guard that night, just in case.

They woke up early the next morning, just as the sun was rising. The rain had gone. Only a few smaller dark clouds had hung around. Setting out again, they were shaded by the large trees from the sunlight. Soon, they were approaching a dense area in the forest.

Swish, thud! Asim reacted to an arrow striking a tree close to his head. "Down!" he yelled to the others as two more whistled in close to them. Asim was shouting for them to "Stay back behind the trees. Lay as flat as you can."

Senso had felt a sharp pain and looked to see blood trickling down his arm. It was only a small gash from one of the passing arrows catching his shoulder, tearing his jacket and shirt on the way. He slid behind the closest tree to avoid another strike.

Asim signaled his men, having them circle in each direction.

Tonas moved close enough to check Senso's wound. "What is happening?" he asked.

"Dwarfs," whispered Stone. "Keep your head down."

"I was hoping they would leave us alone."

"Not Swank!" whispered Stone, wiping the sweat from his face.

The overcast sky was back, the clouds drawing in again. The sun became a distant memory as the rain started. The drops were light at first, more of a pattering on the leaves, then turning to larger drops splattering as they hit them. They were trying to cover their eyes now; the rain had become more of a challenge.

"Can we move him?" asked Asim to Tonas.

"It's just a graze," said Senso. "I will be fine."

"Let's move back. Keep your heads down. I have my men circling to stop them." They moved back as the arrows seemed to have stopped. "I am afraid," said a shivering Boben as he looked at Asim. Reaching out his hand, Asim placed it on Boben's shoulder.

"We all are," he assured him with a slight squeeze, making Boben feel a little less insufficient as they continued to edge backward.

Spen gasped as his head backed into what he figured to be a tree. Looking up, he saw the rain-drenched face of a dwarf with his bow pointed at his skull.

Asim saw the danger, drawing his dagger and hurling it at the dwarf. It plunged deep into his chest. Not moving a muscle, the dwarf fell backward. When Asim realized there was another. This time, taking his sword, he dove, and with one swift strike, he stopped the dwarf's blade from striking Boben. Asim rolled and swung; his blade sliced the Dwarf's neck, splattering blood on everyone close.

Lube and Zollo had made their way behind two more of the dwarfs and were quick in using their swords to strike them down, using swift and precise strokes. Now, there were four dead lying in puddles filling with their blood; the rain was slowly washing it away in the downpour.

"Let's keep moving now," said Asim. With the thought of more dwarfs close by, he had Theon and Lube stay behind. "They will catch up later." The rain slowed down again, but already soaked, they did not seem to care. Spen had slipped in a mud puddle, landing square on his backside. "I am all right," he shouted; his face was a little flushed.

"Is your face red from embarrassment or the mead hanging around your neck?" Asim laughed.

Spen just gave a wry smile on his now mud-dappled face.

"I know this is difficult, but we must keep going."

The rain stopped, making their visibility easier while they continued sidestepping around the puddles. They were taking a careful look as they passed the trees and bushes surrounding them, not knowing if the dwarfs had gone!

Lube and Theon returned.

"We killed three more of the dwarfs," said Lube. "And we have not seen any more signs. A small hunting party, I believe."

"Are we safe now?" asked Tonas.

"One step at a time," said Asim, smiling. "Hmm, I see no arrows. That's always a good sign."

"We are for now, but as long as we stay in the forest, we are never safe from dwarfs. We hope they went in the other direction."

The clouds broke up; the sky lightened again, and sun rays crept through the trees. Stone and Zollo went on ahead, making sure they were not attacked. Everyone seemed warier now, looking for dwarfs as they continued forward. They were making up valuable time in their trek through the forest. They met a few chirping birds and the odd wolf, but otherwise, it was uneventful.

Stone returned. "We see a dwarf camp up ahead. I'm unsure of which one yet. I left Zollo to move in closer! I don't think they are dark dwarfs. We have moved too far to the north now!"

"You mean there are more kinds of dwarfs?" asked Boben.

"Yes!" said Stone. "Some are good, and some are bad."

"You mean they won't try to kill us? How can you tell the difference?"

"The good ones don't shoot arrows at you," said a smiling Stone. "Let's hope these are the good ones. Never take anything for granted."

"So far, all we are seeing are smoke trails rising in the air."

Moving closer to the top of the hill, they could see the thicker smoke from the fires as they walked toward the camp. Asim was smiling as they met with armed dwarfs who were making sure no one was sneaking into their camp. Recognizing Asim, they stood aside to give them an entrance. Looking around, Asim could see Zollo sitting by the fire.

"My friend," shouted a dwarf as he came out to meet them. He was grand looking, a little portly, with a finely aged face, standing all of three feet six inches tall, not including his tall hat above his curly gray hair. His clothing was more impressive, bright, shiny red and blue.

"Bendo, my friend," he shouted.

"Friend indeed," replied Bendo, now close enough to shake hands and hug, Asim having to bend to reach around the dwarf.

"I heard you ran into our enemy on the way here. What is young Zollo telling me about this journey you are on?"

"True," Asim said. "We are on a quest to retrieve children stolen from this man's village." He introduced Tonas. After Bendo welcomed them, they all gathered around a large fire, taking the chill from their bones after a long walk in wet clothing.

"You were lucky to still have your lives from a surprise attack from Swank's men," said Bendo. "I know those sneaky dwarfs. I am glad you are all safe. But knowing Swank could be in the area, I will double my guard tonight." He gestured to one of the other dwarfs, who left to take care of his order.

The wood crackled in the fire, popping from time to time as the active flames gave them the warmth they needed. Bendo passed around a large furry pouch filled with a mead substance. Spen smiled as the pouch reached him. They all took a sip.

"Oh my," gurgled Spen, "this is so good." He took another gulp.

"Slow down!" shouted Tonas. "We want to make sure everyone stays sober."

"Ha-ha," Bendo laughed. "Glad you like it. There is plenty more where that came from. I will even fill your flagon before you leave."

This brought a large smile to Spen's face.

"You will stay the night here with us. We need to feed you for your trip abroad."

"How can I thank you," said Asim. "We accept your offer for food and shelter. We shall be safe tonight. Before we settle, we have a little teaching to do with these village people anyway."

"You are always welcome for all you have helped us with in the past," said Bendo. "And we will be glad to help you train as well."

Later, after dark, when training was over, they all gathered back around the large fire again, talking about swordplay, the journey ahead to the northlands, and some of the difficulties they may face while filling their bellies with food and mead. Later, they drifted off to sleep.

Chapter 3

DWARFS AND FEMALES

As they woke up, sunlight slowly crept through the clouds. They rose early this morning. As they packed up to leave, Bendo approached Asim.

"I understand your plight very well," said Bendo. "I am very aware of the Nordaks, as I mentioned last night and their evil king. I can plainly see you are short on men, so I want to send with you ten of my best warriors. I know you will need the help."

"You are generous," expressed Asim. "And your gift is pleasing, yet I cannot commit to making sure all would come back alive."

"I understand. That's why all my men have volunteered. Not to put pressure on you, they are all aware of what could happen, and they may not return." He made a gesture with his hand as ten dwarfs came up from behind to stand in front of Asim.

Anson was a larger, solid-looking dwarf standing four feet six inches tall. He was notable, with a strong, brawny frame and a handsome, etched face that was just starting to show a few years. He had a long brown beard and no hair under his helmet.

Larby, his cousin, stood four feet four inches tall. He had a solid frame with flowing red hair hanging past his neck, and very noticeable.

Benson stood four feet and one inch tall, slightly heavier, with a muscular build and a younger, fresher, innocent face. His light brown hair covered his head, but his nose was a little larger than the rest of them.

Dooly, Sooly, Wooly, and Pooly—all four brothers were robust, athletic-looking. All had long brown beards and hair, all with large noses, each standing at three feet eleven inches tall, except for Pooly, who was only three feet seven inches. It was hard to tell the other three apart.

Jig had short blond hair and a short blond beard. He was a portly but not fat dwarf with an infectious smile, standing three feet eleven inches tall.

Mup was the youngest of the dwarfs, with sandy hair on his head and a baby face, always looking happy. He had a solid build, standing four feet tall exactly.

Tig, last on the list, stood four feet one inch tall. He was a young, vigorous, burly man with long brownish-blond hair.

"Anson will be your lead," smiled Bendo, feeling proud.

"We will give our lives," shouted Anson to Asim.

"I hope it will not be necessary," he said.

Jig smiled back at him. Asim had to smile, thanking Bendo once again for all his help as they were leaving.

"We will be here at this camp on your return," Bendo declared.

"I like your confidence," said Asim.

When they left, the sun was now shining brightly through the trees. The heat was drying up the puddles from the day before, making it easier for them to walk. Asim instructed Stone, Benson, Zollo, and Mup to scout ahead in case Swank was still around the area.

Tonas walked with Asim and Anson, expressing how much stronger they were now the dwarfs had joined them.

"Better," he replied. "We still don't know what to expect."

As they continued traveling toward the river, Asim started to explain to Tonas how they must remain careful. "On this side of the river, there are a lot of strange ferocious giant beasts that live on this side of the mountain, such as a flying serpent or burus in the water."

"What are they?" Tonas asked in a quizzical voice, looking confused.

"Well," Asim laughed, "the buru, I hear, are real large fish, more massive than four houses, found in the rivers around these parts. They are at least twenty lengths long or longer, with a mouth the size to easily swallow you whole and teeth like razors that could cut you in half! Not to mention the serpents that fly in the air. I have been told they stay close to the mountains and around the rivers."

"Is it like a dragon? I have heard of them," Tonas quizzed.

"Not so much; it does not spew fire and is not as large. The worst part, I hear, is their spit. If it hits you, it can turn your body to rock."

"I hope we don't encounter these things." Tonas was quite perturbed.

"We will know as we draw closer to the river. There are a lot of strange things on this mountain, things I hardly know about and some I have never heard of. We must stay aware. We will have to cross the mountain or go through it." Asim smiled.

"If we cannot find a way, this will be bad." Tonas shivered. His voice lowered, and a slight tremble came to his lips. "I think I am going to be afraid."

"I will let you into a secret," Asim professed. "We will all be afraid if we see one, so put on a happy smile for the journey ahead." He was smiling at him.

Spen, in one of his more alert moments, had been walking close enough to overhear Asim and Tonas talk about the serpent.

"Are you sure about these things?" he asked Asim. "I mean, about turning you to rock?"

"I have only heard of this. I am not anxious to meet one to find out."

Spen looked shocked. "I think I am with you on that one." He took a sip from his flagon.

"We will all have to be watchful on this journey. Soon, we will be heading into the fairy realm before we arrive at the river." Spen looked puzzled at the talk of a fairy realm.

"It is an area in this part of the forest that fairies, along with their queen inhabit as their own. So if you see anything strange flying around, well, stranger for you anyway—"

"Should we fear them?" Spen asked, taking another sip from his flagon. A small drop of mead dripped down from his bottom lip to his chin; his voice sounded a little slurred as he wiped his mouth with his sleeve.

"It depends," laughed Asim. "If we upset them or not by going through their land. It is the quickest way. Stone is up ahead. He will let us know, and don't worry; he is very good with them."

They continued to move through the forest when they started to see large, lily-like, pure white flowers growing in a patch on their own. They were the perfect white to the dull brown trees as their backdrop.

"Just breathe in the beauty of what's in front of you." He was breathing deeply. "Sights like this you will never see in a lifetime," Spen swore he could see fairies on the petals. Asim was not sure what he was seeing. The ambience was broken abruptly when Zollo returned running back to them.

"There is a problem ahead in the forest," he blurted out. "Dwarfs are fighting with someone. I think it could be a hunting party. Stone is gathering Benson and Mup to scout for more information, as we don't see dark dwarfs this far out."

"Let's move forward slowly and quietly," replied Asim. "Someone will be back with another report soon."

Tonas shouted loudly. "Are we going to fight?"

Asim stared at him. "This will be a real possibility if you don't stay quiet."

Mup came in from the side. "Seems they have trapped some women behind a set of trees ahead. At least one, maybe more?"

"If that is so, I need Lube, Theon, Anson, Pooly, and Dooly to go with you and cut around the back on the far side to join the others. I need Zollo and Sooly to come with me. Everyone else stays here and stays quiet." He glanced at Tonas. "Let's start moving to see if we can help, although if it is who I have in mind, I'm sure they are far from in trouble!" Asim smiled. "I was contemplating going around until they mentioned a woman." He laughed. "Spread out to the left, Zollo, and you the right, Sooly. We can catch these dwarfs off guard. The others will take them from the rear. We have the element of surprise this time."

Soon, they heard the zing of arrows through the air and the heavy thud when hitting a tree, the snarling shouts barked out by the dwarfs. Asim motioned for the group to stay quiet, reaching for his bow. They were moving closer when a familiar voice rang out.

"Face us like a man, you coward," a woman yelled.

"We will kill you all," shouted a dark dwarf.

"Come and try it if you're man enough," the woman yelled.

Then, there was a fierce exchange of arrows between the dwarfs and the woman. Asim was now close enough where he could see ten to fifteen of the dwarfs behind rocks and the tall oak trees. Figuring he had given Mup enough time to carry out his order, he stood with Zollo and Sooly to shoot at the dwarfs, taking them by surprise! Their arrows found their targets. Three of the dwarfs fell dead to the ground. Reloading to shoot again, Asim struck one sitting high on a tree branch; he landed on the ground with a thud, all before the dwarfs could return a shot. Mup, Stone, and the others had moved in behind, coming up shooting. Their arrows scattered the dwarfs in all directions. The dwarfs were trying in desperation to run away to elude the trap set for them.

"Retreat!" one was shouting. They were running for their lives; arrows continued to strike them as they fled.

"It is treachery," another of them screamed as he ran away. Stone, Mup, and Benson chased after them, making sure they cleared the area. Asim, Zollo, and Sooly checked the bodies lying close to the trees where they fell; they were all dead.

A jubilant female voice shouted from behind him, "Asim!" He turned to see Lanee, a female huntress from the forest. Her long, flowing black hair was lightly swaying in the breeze. She stood five feet nine inches tall with a slender but muscular body. Lanee was in her late twenties, with the face of an angel, but she was one strong lady.

Asim turned the rest of his body to face her as Lanee put her arms around him and placed a kiss on his lips.

"Thank you for rescuing a lady in distress." She laughed as she looked deep into his face. "You know we could have handled this little skirmish."

"I know so well," said Asim. "We were passing, and we owed them one anyway. You know me, I can't resist a fight." They both laughed.

"Where have you been?" she asked. "It has been such a long time since I have seen you."

He told her that they had been deep in the southwest.

"What are you doing here?" she asked, "and why do you have all the dwarfs with you?"

Asim told her about the quest they are on and about the Nordak's army and the villagers' stolen children.

"Sounds like a death mission even for you?" She looked shocked.

"I know, but these people needed help. I could not find it in my heart to turn them away."

"Now that's the Asim I know." She laughed. "Let me talk to my girls." She walked back to the tall trees.

Asim sent Lube back to have the others join them. Lanee and her girls were walking back to where Asim was standing. There were four more stunning ladies.

Toya, with a healthy, strong, agile body, stood five feet nine inches tall, with long blonde hair, a stunning beauty in her early twenties.

Pantra, the tallest of all of them at six feet, with medium length brown hair, was substantial but not fat, beautiful, with a vigorous and muscular body in her thirties.

Jubly, the shortest of them, at five feet six inches tall, had long, flowing red hair, with a slim and agile body, and a beautiful smile. She was a very strong and spirited young lady in her twenties.

Radel, who was darker skinned, standing five feet eight inches tall, was muscular and stocky, with shorter black hair, was pretty, with a more distinguished look. She was the oldest of them all, in her late thirties.

They were thrilled meeting back up with Asim and his men. Lube was back and had the others with him. Stone, Mup, and Benson had returned from chasing the dwarfs; everyone was there now.

Lanee had gathered the girls, explaining the journey that Asim had taken in joining the village people to rescue their children. Not taking long, the ladies decided together they would be willing to join him. They stood in front of Asim as Lanee told him, "We are all going with you."

To which he reminded them, "No guarantees. You already know there's a chance we won't all come out of the Nordak castle alive, even if we make it inside."

"We are all aware of what can happen." Lanee was smiling.

Asim smiled back. "Well, all I can do is welcome you." He hugged Lanee and then the other four women, accepting a kiss from each.

Tonas was feeling very pleased now. "Are these ladies called Amazons?" he asked Stone, who was close to him.

"No," said Stone. "And I would let none of them hear you say that."

"Oh," said Tonas, now feeling silly he had asked.

"I will tell you this," added Stone, "these women are warriors and some of the best fighters you will find, just what we need for this journey."

Tonas smiled.

Asim made sure they were all ready to leave. "I need scouts," he shouted. "Stone, go straight ahead. Jig, to the left and, Lube, to the right." He asked Zollo and Benson, "Follow up at the rear." They started their journey again, continuing through the forest. After they had trekked for a distance, dusk settled, and the sun disappeared behind the mountains. "It's time to find shelter." Asim was looking at the surrounding area.

Stone returned, telling him of a small clearing ahead that looked safe. They camped for the night, utilizing their scouts for safety.

28

Chapter 4

FAIRIES AND SERPENTS

Bright was the sun as it dazzled down through the treetops. Morning had arrived. It was time to stretch and pack their belongings, heading out again. Asim changed the scouts for the new day, using Larby, Wooly, Sooly, and Tig.

Still feeling secure from the day before, Tonas's face was sporting a broad smile. He saw their numbers increase again, and he asked Asim, "Do you think we have a chance now?"

"First, we must make our way there to see what we are facing!" Asim replied. "And then I will let you know."

"Fair enough," said Tonas. Asim turned to include Lanee in the conversation.

"You know we are being spied on?" he told her.

"Yes," she said, looking at him, "I had that feeling. I was going to ask."

"Not seeing anything," said Tonas, looking around.

"How did our scouts not see?"

"Maybe they did," said Asim.

Out of nowhere, appearing majestically in front of them was such a breathtaking and stunning vision in all her radiant glory, with gossamer wings that dazzled in the sunlight, rising in the colors of a rainbow, sitting on the reddest of birds you would ever have seen. She was eight inches tall when standing. Her bright silver hair cascaded down her body from under the bright neon blue hat she wore to the bright neon blue boots. She was dressed in gold and white. This was a magnificent sight.

Spen looked, rubbing his eyes. He looked again, taking a quick sip from his flagon. "Is this an apparition?" Spen exclaimed. "Or have I drunk too much today?"

"Sober up!" Lube frowned. "The fairy queen herself is here."

"How do you know?" Spen was still unsure of what he was seeing.

"Tin-Tina in her glory. Can you not tell? She is a magnificent sight!"

Spen muttered a feeble "Yes."

"Your Majesty Tin-Tina," Asim said. "You are looking beautiful today," He could see her face now turning the color of the bird she sat on as she rode to them. Fairies flew in from all directions, surrounding them on both sides.

"We come in peace," Asim said again.

"We are at peace with you, Asim."

"You remember my name."

"You always flatter me." She smiled.

"I tell the truth."

"We are here to help you. You are entering an area ahead full of hunters' holes just outside my realm. I informed your scouts, but we were not quick enough to warn your red-headed dwarf. We have tried to keep you safe since your run-in with the dark dwarfs. But I could see you needed no help. And we know of your journey."

"How is that?" Tonas spoke out.

"We know things," added Tin-Tina. "We will take you to your dwarf." She disappeared.

"I think I must slow down on this stuff," slobbered Spen, clutching his flagon.

"Maybe you should stop!" growled Radel, who was raising her eyebrows at him as he took a small sip. "Not today," he slurred. "Perhaps slowing down will be good for now?" She shook her head and walked away from him.

Two fairies were there to lead them to the hunter's hole while making sure they stepped carefully. Asim looked over into the hole; he could see Larby facedown, his blood-soaked body impaled on the sharp wooden spikes at the bottom of the pit. He was about to ask the fairies about the hole, but they had disappeared too.

Asim apologized to Anson. "We did not want to lose anyone, especially this way, but we must move forward. We have no time to regain his body."

"I understand, said Anson."

"The hunters will fill the hole. They will be back before nightfall," said Asim. "We will move on in the forest; only this time, we will be more careful. Stone, Lube, and Jubly take the scout this time. Lanee and I will stay to the rear. We will change early." It was a somber mood as they continued the journey. This time, it was more uneventful, and they walked until late before they camped.

When they started out again early the next morning, the sun was in trouble as an overcast sky was approaching.

"I was hoping to make it to the river today," said Asim. "I cannot be sure we will. Look at the darkening sky?" Leaves were falling and fluttering around them. Now, the wind swirled through the trees, blowing in the darker clouds.

"I hope it's not blowing in anything bad," said Tonas.

Theon had returned, telling Asim he could see a lot of serpent activity ahead.

We're probably near the river, thought Asim. "Are they staying in one area? If so, maybe we could go around?"

"It seems they are for now; I am not sure how long they will stay that way. Jig and I can trek to the east to find a safer route for us to travel to the river."

"We will stay here then for now. Go see what you can find out." Everyone was patiently waiting for Theon's return.

Zollo returned and walked into the midst of the camp. He approached Asim. "There is no trouble to report. I did see some serpents in the sky up in front of us. That could slow us down. I will keep my scouting closer for now until we reach the river." Asim had noticed that Radel had not returned, as they were still waiting on Theon and Jig.

"I do not like just waiting here," Asim stressed to Lanee. "We are too vulnerable." As the morning clouds had dissipated, he felt even more open to a serpent attack.

"I don't think we have a choice right now," she said. Asim was looking agitated at this point.

Theon and Jig returned later that day. "We traveled a safe distance," said Theon, "where we can move away from the serpents, hopefully! We think we also found the right place at the river to cross, although there is a thick mist rolling slowly off the water now, and with this wind, it could stir it up, leaving us without too much sight."

"We will see when we arrive there. Did you see Zollo?"

"Yes," replied Jig, "on our way back. He was on his way here as well."

Before they were ready to leave, Lanee spoke to Asim, "I am a little worried about Radel. She has been missing too long."

Asim touched her arm as he walked over and talked to Zollo and Benson, telling them, "Head west to try to find Radel. Tell her of the change in direction."

Starting to head east, they continued their journey, moving across to the outer path before traveling up toward the river again. Asim noticed the slow swirling mist was thin at first, staying low to the ground above their boot tops, but as they drew closer to the river, it thickened, starting to drift higher as they continued their trek.

"We seem to have moved away from the serpents for now," said Asim, noticing the open sky above them.

"Not too much further up in this direction," said Theon, "although it's hard to tell anymore." The mist was continuing to rise.

"This seems a bit scary," said Yuby, looking up at Asim.

"A little." Asim smiled. "It will, for sure, stop us crossing this river until morning. It's too thick to see where we would be going. This river will be hard enough to cross when we can see!"

"What river?" asked Yuby, looking outward.

They looked around on hearing a loud roar but could not tell from where. Stone hoped the noise was coming from in the mountains.

"We may be too close to the river. We will be better off moving back towards the trees again, just in case," said Asim. "At least until we know what's making that noise." Another loud roar filled the air. This time, it was a lot closer. "I am still not seeing anything in the sky."

Two large wolves rushed by them, almost running into Tonas in the thick mist.

"That's not a good sign," shouted Lanee. "Something is coming and coming fast."

The roaring sound had now turned into an ear-pounding screech!

"This is a lot scarier," uttered Yuby, holding his hands to his ears.

Spen looked at Asim, clutching his flagon tightly. The sky had turned to a strange, deep blue color, and the sun would soon be waning over the mountains.

"They must have followed us," said Theon, looking up through the trees into the sky.

Asim's vision was a little impaired with the vast number of branches above. Still, he could see nothing, as the ground was veiled with a dark shadow from above, casting over them with the deafening screech above their heads. "Down," he yelled.

They all dropped below the mist to the ground, still clutching their hands to their ears to stop the deafening noise. Looking up in the sky, this time, he could make out the massive figure of a serpent. Its wings spanned at least five lengths on each side of its massive elongated black-and -gray body. The sky had darkened as it passed over. Then, there was another dark shadow as a second serpent as large as the first passed over. They will come to know them as a cockatrice.

This time, Asim could see this one's oversized rooster-shaped head with a large beak-like mouth; although he was not able to look at its teeth, he was sure they were in there. "Stay down," Asim ordered. "I don't think they will see us through the dense mist. They are looking for food. Let's make sure it's not us! Be very careful of its spit. I have heard it can turn your body to rock."

"What? To rock?" said Spen, whose mind was a long way away, sipping again from his flagon.

"I don't think they come out too often unless they are searching for food or water," Asim said again.

"Just our luck," uttered Spen, taking another sip.

"Be careful, Spen. You will need to be ready if we have to move fast," said Asim.

Spen was thinking and staring blankly at Asim. "Do they eat the rock?" he asked.

"No, why do you say that?"

"How do they eat if they turn everything to rock?"

"That is just a defense."

"Defense," Spen thought out loud, looking up as if the thought had drifted over his head.

"If they wanted to eat you, they would tear you to pieces with their giant teeth, I would imagine," Asim said again.

Spen lowered himself even lower to the ground, both hands clutching his flagon like a hurting baby.

"They seem to be flying lower this time around. Do you think it's possible for the beast to smell us?" asked Lanee.

"Please say it's not so," exclaimed Spen. "We—"

"It's not," Lanee cut him off. "It's the mead." She smiled. Spen shut his eyes and lay flat, still clutching his flagon.

"We need to move back," Asim suggested. "We need to be in the forest, using the trees for cover. Try to crawl back towards the rocks." As soon as they did, one of the cockatrice spit a projectile, hitting a tree close to Lube's head, turning a patch of the tree to rock as it hit. The cockatrice spit again, this time landing closer to Spen, who still had his eyes shut, hitting the ground making a small pile of rock just inches from his feet as it flew off.

"They may be back, so let's make it as difficult as we can for them to see us," shouted Asim. "Move back to the thicker trees." They heard a voice.

"Asim," the voice shouted. It was Zollo.

No one had seen the cockatrice turn back from the mountain.

Asim stood up and shouted, "We are here! But there are serpents. Come down from the rocks." The cockatrice was returning.

"We didn't see them!" Zollo yelled. "But I do now. Down!" he cried. Benson and Radel had joined him on the rocks as the cockatrice flew over the top of them. "Let's go!" he shouted, jumping from the rock to make a run for the thick trees. Sensing their movement, the serpent took a short turn, returning straight for them.

"Dive," yelled Asim as he stood there watching, trying to make the jump for them in his head. The cockatrice was flying low, and as they were trying to jump down from the rocks, the cockatrice, with one giant foot, clawed Radel by the head in midair. Her hair and face seemed stuck between the creature's talons and toes.

She yelled and screamed with the pain! It held her tight as it flew away.

With all the shouting and screaming, at least it meant she was still alive! Asim thought. As it flew straight up in the air, he grabbed his bow, as did the others. Shooting arrows at the cockatrice as it flew over, they were careful not to hit Radel, still hanging from its foot. Most arrows were striking the beast and deflecting off its hard-skinned body. Now downhearted, no one had realized the second cockatrice had been following close behind. Flying over, it turned its head to spit a projectile. Everyone dived as the liquid hit the surrounding ground, just missing each one of them.

"That was too close," shouted Lanee.

How the spit missed each one, they were not sure. Everyone was nervous as they gathered together, looking up into the sky, back at each other, then into the sky again. The cockatrice had landed close to the river. The other one had followed.

Zollo and Benson had arrived back now. "We didn't see them," shouted Zollo in anguish.

Asim grabbed his shoulder. "We need to see if we can bring her back."

"I'm ready," shouted Lanee.

"Wait! We must do this, right? It doesn't seem our arrows hurt them. They glance off their body. Let's try the neck and head this time. It may be more vulnerable. That's if we have the chance?"

"Zollo, Stone, Pantra, and Jubly, go left around the back of them. Your job will be to grab Radel when you can. Lanee, Toya, Benson, and Theon, go with me. We will approach from the right. Let's hope they stay there and she is still alive! Lube, keep everyone calm and their heads down in case everything changes."

Both groups left in different directions, with the same objective. As they arrived closer to the river, Stone could see the two cockatrices had stopped to take on water. The force of their mighty wings and their size had caused the mist to dissipate from the riverbank, making both them and the river more visible now. He saw the body of Radel lying sprawled out on the side of the bank. He could not tell if she was unconscious or dead. Stone could see a blood ring around her head. "We must slip in closer," he whispered.

"They will see us if we do," whispered Pantra, "now the mist has gone."

"We don't have time to wait." Now Stone could see Asim had arrived on the other side. He was gesturing to Stone, although he was not sure what he was trying to say.

Asim was motioning for them to stay and grab Radel on his mark; knowing Stone well, he hoped he would understand. Turning to the others, he said, "We will run straight at them, shoot our bows at both. Aim for the neck. Shoot as many arrows as you can. The plan is to startle them so they fly up and leave Radel. Stone and the others can grab her. Keep your fingers crossed that the beasts take flight, then you run and hide as quick as you can."

Now, both cockatrices were busy drinking in the water, lifting their heads, only to screech that deafening noise that they all were trying hard to ignore.

"Oh," said Asim without his usual vigor, smiling at Lanee. "I forgot to tell you this part of the plan. We will run in the opposite direction to draw them away if in case they dive back down."

She looked at Asim, puzzled. "This is your plan?" she said while shaking her head.

He could only shrug his shoulders with a wry smile on his face. "It will be as easy as one, two, three for us. Let's go," he shouted as they shot arrows at the two cockatrices, running forward, striking the beasts in the neck and head. "One," he shouted. This did startle the cockatrice, even though the arrows deflected again off their rough skin. They both rose in the air.

"Two," he shouted to Lanee as the cockatrice dived back down toward them.

"Run," cried Asim to Lanee as everyone else scattered.

With all this commotion going on, Stone and Zollo had run to the riverbank and grabbed Radel's body. Not having any time to see if she was alive or dead, they moved her into the mist, back into the forest. Pantra and Jubly kept their bows at the ready the whole time, willing to shoot if the beasts came back in their direction. They could see they were heading the opposite way as they turned and ran behind Stone and Zollo, carrying Radel.

As luck would have it, or maybe not, the cockatrice turned, heading straight for Asim and Lanee, who were running to the right side of the river as fast as they could.

Toya, Benson, and Theon scattered as a beast spit a projectile, missing Benson by a hair and hit the ground just in front of him. He tripped over the rock, landing headfirst on the ground. Blood was now

trickling from his nose, and Theon and Toya dived into the thicker mist.

Both cockatrice had sensed Asim and Lanee's running and were heading toward them. A projectile of spit flew past Asim's head. "Three," he shouted. "I think they are following us!" he yelled. "We need to split up now. You take the river." She turned away and headed in that direction. Asim ran toward the forest. The thick mist around them was now blown away from under the giant wings of the cockatrice flying close to them.

Lanee, now close to the river, knew to dive in. It would be her only chance. She could feel the wind from the cockatrice behind her. "Why did they follow me?" She dived straight into the water, feeling the water twisting her body around. Realizing the cockatrice had also entered the water, Lanee continued to swim underwater until feeling her lungs would burst. Then she had to return to the top for the air she desperately needed, not knowing what she would find as she emerged from the water. She choked and gasped for the fresh air, which filled her lungs again. She looked around, and to her surprise, she could see the cockatrice a little way away from her. *What a relief*, she thought, twisting around and seeing only one. *They must have split up, and the other followed Asim.* It looked as if this one was waiting for her to come back up in the water. She swam around in a semicircle. Thankfully, Lanee knew she was far enough away not to be seen as the mist swirled. *It's good*, she thought, smiling, and an even greater feeling of relief came over her. But then, thinking about Asim, worry soon struck, knowing she could not help him at this point. She was wondering how long she would have to stay in the river, at least until the beast flew away.

Asim had continued to run toward the forest, the cockatrice following and spitting projectiles that could have split him in two had he not continued to change directions. Then another landed too close to him; he looked up, seeing the trees, still running as if his life depended on it, which it did. "Yes," he sighed in relief, reaching the trees and hiding behind the first one. He heard the thud as the tree shook violently; a projectile from the cockatrice had hit it hard. Asim, poking his head out to one side of the tree, could see it flying back in the air. He slid out into the open, taking his bow in hand and waiting for it to fly back around; shooting his arrow fast, he struck the beast in the throat. The arrow hit with a glancing blow. It seemed to put a small gash in its neck. The cockatrice screeched loudly, turning around in a speedy circle. Holding his ears, Asim dived behind the tree; again, the beast spat a projectile, hitting close to the tree and him! Swooping down, it dug its claws deep into the tree as if it knew he was there. It thrashed its wings powerfully to pull the tree out of the ground.

This is great, he thought. *I have made it mad now*. He was sliding himself back toward the tree behind him, hoping the beast was too busy trying to pull this one up from the ground. He could see roots stretching from the ground, knowing he better move fast. Suddenly, the roots ripped out; the tree was pulled up high. Asim scrambled behind the next one. The beast, looking down, did not see him, even now that the tree had gone. It let go of the tree with power; it struck the tree Asim was behind, bending it backward. Branches whipped around, slapping and scratching his face and body, knocking him to the ground.

The cockatrice was taking to the air again. *At last*, he thought, dragging himself out of the branches to his feet and rubbing against his scratched-up face. *I can go and find Lanee*. Then it hit him, knowing that Lanee had to have the other cockatrice chasing her.

I must find her, he thought. He was running toward the river, close to the bank, when he heard the screech; he had hoped that he had escaped! Looking back, he saw the ominous figure of the beast heading toward him and thought maybe he needed to dive into the water. His mind was swiftly made up for him as the cockatrice spit a projectile that ripped past him. Just enough of it glanced off his shoulder, but even a glancing blow was forceful enough to knock him off his feet. He rolled and slid down the bank into the river, not feeling his arm, only the numbness. Asim was hurrying to slip down below the surface, swimming away, hoping the beast would leave.

He stayed submerged as long as he could. Then, feeling the need for air and unable to wait any longer, he ascended to the top, thinking more in the hope the beast had gone. But his luck promptly changed.

From the depths, a giant eel, known to the village people as a garpy that lived in some of these rivers, sensing the movement of Asim, latched itself around his body, wrapping itself tight as he struggled to swim to the top to breathe. For a second, his head was above the water, choking, trying to inhale as much air as he could. Being pulled back under, he now realized that the garpy's body had trapped both his arms, and he could not reach for his sword or dagger. The creature was tightening its grip as he rolled with it through the water.

The rolling stopped as they approached larger rocks. The garpy swam by close enough to where Asim was able to catch his feet on a jutting rock; using all the strength left in his beaten body, he tried to stop its progress, confusing it long enough to struggle and pull them both into an upright position. In one motion, he pushed both feet as hard as he could, as if on a spring, from the rock, forcing them both rapidly toward the surface. The creature reacted, swiftly continuing the motion, adding lightning speed, causing them both to soar upward. They emerged high out of the water.

The garpy, with its head well above him, opened his enormous mouth, ready to strike. Asim could see the massive teeth bearing down on his head as saliva dripped on his face, knowing he was helpless. Then, in an instant, he found himself and the garpy suddenly ascending faster and higher in the air. A deafening screech! The cockatrice had seized the head of the garpy in midair. Its mighty talons squeezed hard around its head, causing it to release Asim, who found himself rolling over and over, unraveling himself from the garpy's body. He descended into the river with a heavy splash, emerging with just enough strength to see the beast flying off in the distance with the garpy hanging from its foot. Then everything went black. He passed out.

It was night when he awoke to Lanee pulling on his body, struggling as she was dragging him up the riverbank.

He coughed, spitting out river water. Lanee now realized he was still alive. She turned him over and lifted his scratched-up face to hers.

"All right?" she said, looking at him.

"Yes," he choked out, still coughing up more water.

"One, two, three," she quipped, looking in his eyes. "Easy as one, two, three." She shook her head while affectionately squeezing his face; he tried a wry smile. He needed help from Lanee standing up as he discovered how sensitive his body was from the slapping of the branches to the face. He had numbness in his shoulder where the rock had hit, and the painful grip that the garpy had around him had bruised his ribs. He felt like he had swallowed half the river, too.

Using Lanee as a crutch, they ambled back to the others, making sure nothing more was in the sky. Both were soaking wet from the river. They laughed through the pain, which severely hurt as they talked about what happened to them both. They were happy they were still alive.

"No more one, two, three, please," she said.

They were hoping everyone was still there; they had been gone a long time. Lanee's fears subsided when she saw the camp close to the forest. They both could see Radel laid out while Jubly and Toya were comforting her, both smiling at each other.

Theon, Stone, Lube, and Pantra came out to greet them. They could see Asim was in pain. Theon and Stone took over from Lanee to help him walk to the camp, and Pantra and Lube helped Lanee.

Asim asked about Radel.

"Beaten yet alive." Theon was holding his nose. "Do you realize you have an overpowering odor, like a dead fish or something?"

"It was a long story. I will tell you later—how I had the life beaten out of me by an eel, then saved by a serpent."

Theon looked shocked. Pantra grabbed Spen's flagon and gave them both a sip. Jubly and Zollo came over to tend to both Asim and Lanee, who were now sitting at each other's side against a tall tree.

Chapter 5

A FISH STORY

The sun was shining brightly in the sky. Asim considered this to be a beautiful, cloudless start to the day; he was feeling a lot better after a night's sleep. Although things were still a little tender, at least the feeling was back in his shoulder again. He wandered over to talk to Radel, who was still a little groggy.

"My head feels like a fire burning! But I'm alive and glad of it." She thanked him.

"It was everyone," insisted Asim.

Lanee was also on her way over. "Will you be able to walk?" she asked.

"I believe so, although I may need a crutch. I'm sure Pantra won't mind." Radel tried to laugh, but the pain stopped her.

"Don't overdo it." Asim smiled. "You will need a lot more strength to cross this river today."

Asim sent Stone and Theon out early to make sure there were no serpents to stop their crossing today and find a place where they could cross. They were starting out later. Asim was hoping the mist would dissipate in the sun. They packed up, ready for Stone's report. "All clear." He smiled on returning. They all followed behind him to the spot where they would cross, seeing the early morning mist burnt off by the sun.

Asim was gazing across the river. "This looks good," he said to Stone. "I'm sure we will need to swim at some point, but it seemed somewhat narrower here." They both were trying to figure out the best way for everyone to cross.

Then appeared a host of fairies. As before, it was a beautiful and mesmerizing sight with the shimmering gossamer colors dazzling, bursting off the water in the morning sun. Tin-Tina was in the middle, this time carried on a chair of gold. She was wearing clothes of the brightest blue you would ever have seen, from her head to her boots; she had the most beautiful smile on her face as she approached them.

"Hello, Asim, it's a good day," she said. "I am hoping it will not be full of the disasters of yesterday. We are sorry we could not help."

"Good morning, Your Highness," he said. "You are looking as beautiful as ever. We hope for a better day too. We need to cross the river and head for the mountains today."

"My fairies can help you with the river and where to cross. It will be less of a current if we travel a little farther, although we cannot guarantee what's in the river."

"I found that out the hard way." Asim was rubbing his ribs.

"We will also take you to the mountains and keep you aware of any danger."

"You are sweet," replied Asim. "Going out of your realm for us." He blew her a kiss, which brought out an even broader smile and a slight blush on her cheeks. She moved back with the other fairies. They flew a little further up the river. Asim and the others followed, walking along the bank. When the fairies stopped, Asim knew this was the place they would cross.

"Is there any way we can go around the mountains?" asked Lanee.

"I don't know this area well. We never venture this far out, but I'm sure it would be dangerous!" replied Tin-Tina.

"I figure," said Asim, "going through the mountain could be less dangerous. I'm sure some caverns and passages go through to the other side. We may have to put up with any drawbacks."

"What drawbacks?" asked Tonas. "Not like what we saw yesterday, I hope!"

"Well, there is always the possibility of serpents if they are hungry. But we could see goblins, even trolls, and maybe an ogre or two," he said, smiling. "The one thing we don't want to run into is the tiki."

"What is that?" asked Tonas with an uneasy look on his face.

"It's a large albino ape that inhabits caves in the north, so I have heard."

"What does that thing do?" he asked, looking quizzical.

"It sucks blood."

"Whose blood?" he asked with a little tremble in his voice.

"Why, anybody's it wants." Asim smiled.

"Do we have to go this way?" Tonas asked, still with a quizzical look.

"Now, Tonas, don't tell me this worries you?"

With a grimace, he gave a quiet "No,"

Asim laughed.

The fairies flew in a line across the water, showing where they should cross.

"It all seems too quiet," said Stone.

"I was thinking the same." Asim had been looking around. "Not even a screech! How about you go first?"

"I swear I heard Zollo volunteer." Stone was laughing, knowing Zollo was nowhere close. Stone waded in; it was shallow, close to the bank. "Oh, it's chilly water," he said, turning with a slight grimace on his face.

"Go," said Asim. As Stone was moving out, the bottom suddenly sank. To what depth, he did not want to find out, swimming, the rest of the way across.

Asim shouted, "Can everyone swim?" It was quiet at first, then they mumbled among themselves. "I figure some don't," he said. "Those who don't swim, we will tie a rope around you and help you. Line up for me here."

Stone had now swum to the other side, jumping up and down to warm himself.

Asim took the rope and tied Boben, Spen, Yuby, Senso, Pooly, and Dooly together. Pantra tied herself to Radel on a separate line as she was still not feeling up to doing this herself and needed the extra help. Pantra put her hand under Radel's chin. "Looking after my baby," she said in a motherly voice. Everyone was laughing. Pantra laughed with them, seeing the funny side.

"Let's go," he shouted. "I need my swimmers to help these people across."

Tin-Tina had sent fairies that now hovered over each one to help as they were crossing; Asim was leading them. Stone was swimming back to help as Lanee and Boben stayed on the bank, keeping a watchful eye on them all. When Spen's head disappeared under the water, the fairies swiftly gathered, lifting his head while he swallowed water. Looking pale, he tried to cough it back out.

"If this were mead," Lanee shouted, "you would be in paradise." She and Jubly both laughed.

Spen could not answer, still busy trying to keep his head high. Lanee swam out to him. "Keep your head afloat and grab the rope," she encouraged him. Seeing he was fine again, she swam back to see how Radel was. Lanee looked at the bandage as blood had trickled down her face, mixing into the water.

Pantra had a strong arm around her. "I will keep her close," she said. They had just swum out together.

"I am a little worried about the blood," Lanee told her. Now, a small trail had floated down the river.

"It will be all right. We will soon be across," Radel replied.

They had left later than the other non-swimmers, for whom the other side could not come fast enough.

"Look at this little band of courage," said Asim as they approached the other side.

Stone was out to help, pulling each one into the shallow water. Untying themselves to walk to the bank as relief showed over their faces. Different from the terror showing before, Asim and Stone both laughed. "Well done," they both said as more of the swimmers arrived.

Pantra and Radel had reached the deeper water. As they crossed, the waves steadily increased.

"Maybe a little faster if you can," Asim yelled.

It seemed like slow motion. From nowhere, a serpent reared its ugly head high above the water, heading toward them both as they floated in the middle of the river.

"I knew it was too good," shouted Asim, gnashing his teeth, trying not to show his anger.

Pantra looked around, still holding Radel as tight as she could. She turned to see the creature's massive green eyes staring at them both. With its large glistening head and spear-like tongue protruding from its mouth, it reared its enormous fleshy white body rising against the backdrop of the river. The fairies rallied close by, flying high above the beast, showering arrows at its head, making little difference, appearing to make it angrier. The serpent dived deep under the water.

"Oh god," cried Spen, taking a sip from his flagon upon seeing what was happening.

Lanee and Boben swam out toward Pantra and Radel. Asim and Stone were still on the bank, reaching for their bows. Senso, Yuby, and Pooly had also come forward, pulling off their bows and loading arrows.

"Shoot when you see it," Asim yelled as it emerged high beneath Pantra and Radel. Lanee and Boben had just arrived. The serpent, trashing up out of the water, pulled all four up in the air along with it. They found It was a hard landing back in the water again. Pantra was still tied to Radel; both landed awkwardly together.

"Untie us," Radel shouted at her. "It's this blood. We are a target together. You can use your sword. I will be all right."

"Not if this thing comes back again," shouted Pantra, treading water.

Asim and the others could only manage a couple of shots; they were more worried about hitting one of the women or Boben. They watched the arrows deflecting off its skin. The beast dived back under again. Both Asim and Stone dived in to swim out to them. The serpent was turning, its eyes fixed on them. Radel and Pantra still seemed to be its target, not realizing Lanee had landed away from all three, adjusting her senses from her hard landing in the water. She was now swimming back toward them.

Pantra grabbed her sword, cutting the rope attached to Radel.

"I will protect you," she shouted, knowing Radel had no weapon.

The serpent was heading straight for them. Those on the bank shouted a lot of directions, but the arrows were still not penetrating its skin. The fairies were shooting from above the creature with similar results; the arrows seemed to bounce off. Nothing seemed to be stopping this beast.

Pantra could see the spear-like tongue was heading for Radel; she swam out to head it off. Boben, also sensing the predicament, swam to her. Pantra rose, her sword was high, striking it down hard on the beast's tongue, cutting it deep; blood appeared right before it reached Radel. It dived deep again. Within seconds, it came back up fast, hitting Pantra, Boben, and Radel, pushing them into the air again. This time, they all three landed hard into the water. Seconds later, Lanee arrived close to help Radel.

Asim and Stone had left the bank with their daggers at the ready. He could see Pantra was floating on top of the water just a short distance from the others. With great urgency, the fairies were there trying to help her move. Both Asim and Stone were swimming vigorously to her aid. Just before they reached her, the serpent, circling underneath, wrapped its massive tongue around her body and pulled her into its mouth. The fairies flew back sharply before they were sucked in as well, continuing to shoot arrows at the beast in the hope it would drop her, but to no avail.

Asim was close enough now to strike at the serpent with his dagger but not close enough to hurt it, catching his blade on the side of its belly. A small gash appeared, but not enough to stop its progress. Stone arrived as he also struck at the beast; it dove back under the water again. They could hear Pantra scream for a second as she struggled. The serpent had plunged deep. It was painfully quiet until it emerged a short distance from them.

Asim could see Pantra still struggling, not able to reach her sword. Its tongue held her tight against its teeth. They all were in a panic, swimming fast, trying to reach the creature. The fairies flew hovering above, still shooting more arrows at its head, but there was no stopping the creature.

The serpent now stayed there, not moving; it was as if it was taunting them all. Asim and Stone swam, reaching the beast. They changed from daggers to swords. They brandished them, thrusting hard, trying to cut into the creature in the hope of releasing Pantra.

They could still hear her screams from the pain shooting through her body. Her cries were softer now as the air was leaving her body. Their swords, covered with blood, continued slicing and piercing the creature as its welts flowed with blood. The beast just turned its ugly head, rearing back as it slammed its mouth shut. There was a loud cracking as Pantra's bones snapped. Letting out one harsh scream, she felt nothing; everything went blank. Everything was silent. A trail of blood dripped from the creature's mouth. Asim continued to strike the beast, plunging his sword deep into its side. Pulling away like nothing happened, the beast slithered off down the river.

Everyone's faces dropped in disbelief. Those standing on the river bank were in shock. The fairies were horrified at what they witnessed. Asim still could not believe his sword and the blades of the others did such little damage to stop the beast.

Radel was screaming, crying, and pulling her hair as Lanee swam out to console her. "It's my fault," she screamed. "It's all my fault."

Asim also swam to them and grabbed her. "It's not your fault," he said, trying to calm her down. "She only wanted to save me."

"This could have happened to any of us. Don't blame yourself."

"It was my blood it wanted!"

"We don't know that," he said, holding her tight until she calmed down. He put his arm out to Lanee. "This is sad, but it was no one's fault." Asim pulled them both closer to him in the water. Radel had settled down; now, they slowly started to swim back to join the others on the river bank. Everyone had huddled together, trying to understand why they could not kill the serpent. They had lit a fire so they could all dry out; it was a quiet time for them all. Asim was visibly upset, knowing there had to have been sorcery involved but not knowing why.

Deciding not to venture further that day, they stopped and made camp.

Chapter 6

GOBLIN PROBLEMS

If nothing else had gone right for them, at least the weather had cooperated; the sun was shining brightly in the sky, although the loss of Pantra had dampened everyone's spirits.

"Let's pack up everything," shouted Asim. "Hopefully, we can make it to the mountains today. We have a long way to travel."

Tin-Tina came to him. "We will continue to scout for you," she said. "We are all still upset about the river. We know this to be an evil thing. It had to be sorcery."

"We did everything that we could have done," Asim replied.

"We were not prepared for dark magic!" she said, saddened by what happened to Pantra.

"Thank you for your help." She disappeared. Everyone continued talking among themselves along the way.

Jubly was talking to Lanee, "I was proud of her. She helped me many times."

"She was a great warrior," said Lanee. "I know we will all miss her."

Toya and Radel were consoling each other. They had trekked for a while and now through the forest, rocks, and large brush, and now the trees seemed to thin out.

Tin-Tina flew back as she said to Asim. "You are approaching the rolling hills of Byrnea. We're not too far from the first mountain range. These are larger hills, some with small rivers and caves. Sometimes, hunters can be found in this area. But it's mostly goblins that inhabit here. They go in hunting parties. It could be safer to go around. You never know where they are. And even going around, we still may run into them, and you will lose another day. We can scout and protect you as best we can, but they are sneaky. We will all need to be careful."

"I will send Stone and Zollo out ahead," he said, "as we go through the hills."

"You must be careful. They know these hills well, although you are a larger party, which could help. We will reach that area soon."

Asim reached out his hand. He lightly squeezed her arm. "I know you and the goblins do not see eye to eye!"

"That's one way to put it." She chuckled. A broad smile came on her face.

"I would ask you not to travel any farther. I would not want it on my conscience if anything were to happen to you. or the other fairies. I know they would try to kill you first."

"We are not shy of a battle with that old oaf of a leader, Garronas. He is a pig that we should stuff. We said we would go with you to the mountains. We never go back on our word."

Asim let his hand fall. "I know," as she disappeared again. They continued their trek toward the mountains, just a lot of thick brush; they were traveling out of the thick of the forest. Tin-Tina had said the trees would become sparse when they reached the hills. "We have not heard from Stone or Lube, so all must be well so far." He smiled. "Let's keep alert as we move into the hillside." He had not seen any of the fairies since Tin-Tina came to him earlier. "Spread out a little," he said. One of the fairies flew toward them.

"Follow me," she said, and they all followed her. Asim could now see in the distance the body of Stone lying motionless on the ground. Lanee ran as soon as she saw him.

"He is still alive!" she cried out.

Zollo was returning from a westerly direction. "What happened?" he asked, rushing up to Stone, kneeling close on the ground.

"I thought you two were scouting together?" Asim asked him.

"We heard noise west of us. I went to see. Stone was going to stay here."

Tin-Tina flew in on a small bird. "We knew when Zitty did not return something was wrong. We were scouting west and east. I sent her to look in on Stone and Zollo."

Checking him, Lanee found a large welt on his head. She took water from her pouch and splashed it on his face. "He is coming around." He was still struggling to focus. "What happened?" she asked.

"I was struck hard on the head by something, is all I remember." Stone was feeling around in his clothing. "Someone went through my pockets. My small coin pouch is gone. I saw nobody."

"Goblins." Lanee frowned.

"I told you they were sneaky," said Tin-Tina. "I am surprised they did not kill him. I have a feeling goblins could be spying on us now. Hmm…" she was thinking. "Maybe that's why they didn't?" Having her fairies spread out, flying upward past the trees, she disappeared again.

Stone was back on his feet, still rubbing his head.

"Lube and Theon," said Asim, "go find two large oak trees to the west and east. Let's see if we see anything out there." Both clambered up the trees. Close to the top, they had a clear view of the surrounding land. Lube looked to the west side, far into the distance, while the clouds seemed to billow around the mountaintops, casting a dark shadow toward him. He raked his eyes back across the rocks and bushes in the direction they would be heading, not seeing anyone or anything moving or hiding. Theon, looking to the east, at first could see nothing but hills and large rocks, but then a large bush caught his eye. At first, he thought it was the wind that moved, but then he realized there was no stiff breeze. His eyes stayed fixed on the bush, "Yes!" There, he saw it move again. Now, they were both climbing to the ground.

"Out to the right," said Theon. "There is a large bush. I saw it moving, more than a breeze would do. Close to the large rocks ahead."

"I saw nothing moving in the opposite direction," replied Lube.

"Could it be an animal?" asked Asim.

"No, I don't believe it was?" Lube insisted.

Asim scratched his head. "I guess we should take no chances."

"All right, this is what we will do. Lube, Zollo, Theon, and Toya start out to the left. On my signal, work back across so you come in behind the large rocks to see if there is anything there.

"Lanee and Jubly, we will go to the right. Stone, I want you—" He stopped for a second. "Are you all right?"

"Yes," said Stone. "I was checking my head. I'm ready."

"That's good news. I want you to act normal going forward as if we know nothing and we may not. Be careful, maybe spread out a little." Now, he could see Tin-Tina flying toward him; he waited for her.

"We see something moving in the east." She hastily stopped.

"We do, too," said Asim.

"I will send my warriors from above."

"And we will work our way around on the ground."

She disappeared again.

"How does she do that?" asked Lanee, who looked into the air, mystified.

Asim could only shrug his shoulders. They all left, walking close together. When they were not too far from where Theon had seen, the bush move. He signaled for Lube and the others to go; they moved out to the left.

"Lanee, Jubly, let us move in from the right." Working their way around through the shrubs and scattered trees this side of the large rocks, they could see ahead, drawing their swords as they continued.

Stone and the others carried on walking ahead. Soon, they reached an area of bushes and high rocks. Just to the side of them, close to the pathway they were walking on, four goblins were standing in their way.

The goblins stood a little over three feet ten inches tall. All had sizeable muscular upper bodies and were armed with swords. They were standing and leering at them, with their scraggly black hair and greenish brown faces, half hiding under their tall brimmed hats, with their large noses, boggle eyes, and oversized mouths.

"What do we have here," sneered one of the goblins. "Where do you bunch think you're going?"

"To the mountain," answered Stone.

"Trying to be smart, are we," he sneered again.

"You asked where we were going," answered Stone. "We're going to the mountain."

"Give us all your coin, or we will kill you and take it all,"

Stone grabbed his sword; before he could clasp his hand around the handle, three arrows thudded down by his feet. As he looked up, he saw several goblins, bows at the ready, standing on top of a rock wall, arrows aimed at each of them.

"Well," said Stone, turning back to the others, "these men want our coin. Little do they realize they are about to die."

"What did you say," sneered the goblin, walking toward him.

Asim, Lanee, and Jubly had moved in behind the rock wall and could see the goblins standing on top. "We need our bows," he whispered, giving a quiet motion with his fingers.

Lube, Zollo, Toya, and Theon had worked around to the back of the four standing goblins on the pathway.

The goblin raised his sword toward Stone. "What—" he started to say, *swish* and then *flump*! He fell heavily at Stone's feet, an arrow sticking from his back. The other three gasped as three more arrows struck instantly; in the same fashion, they fell.

Hearing the arrows and seeing their friends fall, the goblins on the wall were unsure how to react. Asim, Lanee, and Jubly shot their bows, striking three more as they fell from the rocks. The goblins were startled and confused, not knowing what was happening. In a panic, they ran. Asim was fast to reload, shooting again, striking another down from the rocks.

Lube now running in behind them, shooting down another before they all had time to jump from the wall, scampering back behind the rocks.

Asim, Lanee, and Toya had moved around toward the rock face to find the goblins; he could see thirty more of them. It looked like they had set up a small camp inside the rocks.

On a broader rock farther up stood a grotesque-looking goblin. From head to toe, he was all of four feet three inches tall; this was tall for a goblin! He was as round as he was tall. The long silver hair from under his broad-brimmed hat was covering some of his dark brown and greenish looking face. His large hands and feet looked out of place, and he was dressed all in black.

"Garronas!" a voice shouted from above them.

Looking up, Asim could see Tin-Tina. "Garronas?" he asked.

"Yes! King of the goblins! This is a hunting party we need to stamp out."

Asim, moving closer, caught the eye of the goblins from behind the rocks as they rushed out toward them. Swords were flashing in the air. He and Lanee released two more arrows before they reached them. Tin-Tina shot down another before she disappeared. Both Asim and Lanee swapped their bows for swords while Jubly moved wide around the outside, looking for a shot at Garronas.

The clash of steel was loud; the two warriors were too quick for the advancing goblins. Although they could handle a sword, they were defeated, struck down with a few slices of Asim and Lanee's skillful blades, and the other goblins started to run back.

More goblins started to slide out from behind the rocks, but once they saw what happened, they were quick to squirm back again. Lube and the others had found a way around the high rocks and joined in the fight.

Garronas let out a shriek, jumping down from the rocks. "Curse you! Curse you all," he was shouting.

Knowing they were no match with a sword, the goblins were quick to run back behind Garronas, taking up their bows again.

The fairies were high above the rocks, shooting arrows at the goblins, who were shooting back.

Asim looked at Lanee with no more goblins to fight, knowing they all were hidden back behind the rocks again.

"We must draw them out of there." He was watching Lube lunge forward, striking another of the goblins, trying to crawl back up from the ground. Stone also had moved forward toward the rocks.

Asim could see Garronas pick up a strange-looking bow that seemed to sparkle, as did his arrows. Shooting one, it flew up and then down, sliding across. As the arrow hit Stone, it shone, and he collapsed. Asim's eyes fixed on Garronas as he watched him shoot again, this time striking Benson, who also collapsed.

It was as if he could not miss with this magical bow. Again and again, he shot the bow, each time hitting its mark. They could hear him laughing and dispatching his arrows.

"I don't believe this," shouted Asim, seeing his warriors collapse. "We have to stop him!" He moved closer to the rocks.

Lanee grabbed his arm from behind. "Don't move too close, or you will be next," she shouted.

Jubly, who had worked her way around to the back side, had Garronas in her sight; she shot her arrow, hitting Garronas squarely in the arm, causing him to drop the bow.

The goblin cursed. They guessed as he screeched something loud, grabbing his bow with his other hand. "Retreat," he yelled with the arrow still stuck in his arm. The few goblins left ran back through the rocks with him.

"Great shot," shouted Asim.

"I was aiming for his head," she shouted back.

"Oh…well, it worked," he shouted back to her, not knowing what else to say.

The fairies took off flying after the fleeing goblins as they ran. Lube, Theon, Zollo, and Boben had also given chase through the rocks. Asim, walking over, looked down at Stone and the others lying on the ground. He was not sure if they were alive or dead. Lanee knelt beside Benson, who, like the others, was struck down by an arrow from Garronas.

"He is alive!" she shouted to Asim, who was quick to check on Stone, kneeling and lifting him.

"This is strange." He was shaking him. "I saw the arrow hit him. Now there is no arrow?" He shook him vigorously again. "He is alive but will not wake!" Asim started shaking him harder.

"Stop," Lanee yelled, "before you do, shake the life out of him! Benson is in the same shape." She went to Yuby and then Pooly. They were unconscious, but again no arrow, and they were alive. Pouring water on their faces and shaking them was not working; nothing was waking them. She looked around, seeing Dooly, Wooly, Mup, Jig, and Senso all in the same condition.

Tonas was kneeling next to Senso. "This must be sorcery," he said, shaking his head.

"I am thinking the same," sighed Lanee, looking at all the unconscious bodies.

Tin-Tina returned from chasing the goblins. "We lost them down a large hole close by. They know these hills too well. I would have loved to have pinned Garronas's hide on a wall. Maybe next time," she exclaimed. "What has happened here?"

"It seems we won the battle, but we lost the war!" said a dejected Asim.

"He was using some enchanted arrows," she said. "They are not dead."

"No," replied Asim, "they are all alive, but we cannot wake them."

"They are all under a sleeping spell. They will never wake!"

"Sleeping spell? What can we do?"

"Only a magic antidote will break the spell. And you will never find Garronas. He would have been happier to have killed them," she said. "Now he will go into hiding. He lost a lot of his men today, so he must regroup. Although…" She paused, thinking. "There may be one other way. There is a witch that lives in the mountains not too far from us, I believe. Not sure exactly. I believe she is close to the direction we are heading if we can find her?"

"A witch?" Lanee seemed confused.

"Yes," said Tin-Tina, "she is a white witch. I remember meeting her once a long time ago. She is a good witch, and maybe she will help you. Her name is Apora. Finding her will be the problem."

"We have too many good men down now." Asim was a little discouraged. "I cannot leave them like this. We must try to find her. Can we carry their bodies close to the mountain where we can camp? We are not too far away."

"I don't think you're that close." Tin-Tina frowned a little. "We can help with your men to carry them there. Garronas will not be back."

Fairies were carrying Dooly, Sooly, Wooly, Pooly, and Mup as Asim lifted Stone. He put him over his shoulder. Zollo carried Jig, Lube carried Senso, Theon carried Yuby, and Boben carried Benson. The journey to the mountain was a lot further than he had first thought, and with Stone's weight, it seemed to make it even longer. As the mountain came into view, a smile came on his face. Soon, they found a place to camp close to the mountain wall where the fairies had taken them.

Chapter 7

THE WITCH HUNT

It was later that day, when they set up camp, each of the sleeping bodies was laid down neatly next to each other.

"Everyone will need to settle in. We don't know how long this will take," Asim declared. "We will try to find the witch with the antidote so we can have them swiftly back on their feet again."

"What if she will not help and tries to kill you?" stressed Boben.

"Maybe she is nice?" Spen slurred in, taking a swig from his flagon, which was still hanging around his neck.

"Well, there is only one way to find out," replied Asim. "I will leave Radel, Jubly, and Anson in charge to make any decision together while we are gone; I hope it will not take us too long."

"I will try to stay," Tin-Tina added. "We also can help to watch over those that are asleep."

"That's why you are sweet."

She blushed and again disappeared. A host of fairies settled in the trees close to them.

"Zollo, Toya, Lube, Theon, and Lanee, you will join me as we go to the mountain. We will try to do this as fast as we can. As soon as we find the witch, we will return."

"I will drink to that," slurred Spen, taking one more swig.

"Is that a never-ending flagon?" Asim asked.

"No, I'm almost out," he replied with a sad, reddened face.

"Well, be careful and take it slow. You never know when you could be needed to keep everyone safe."

"I'm always ready," slurred Spen, trying to smile.

Asim shook his head. "Somehow, I don't know why, but I believe you. Everyone, stay alert."

Spen flopped down on a rock, and of course, he missed, sliding down onto his bottom on the hard ground. "I'm all right."

Asim just shook his head.

"We will need all the daylight we have left," insisted Lanee.

"Do you think this is a good plan?" Toya asked Asim.

He looked at her. "Honestly, no, but it's the only one we have at this point. We must find the witch."

"We may need a bit of luck, and so far, none of it seems to be going our way." Lanee smiled, punching him on the shoulder.

"What was that for?"

"Frustration, I feel better now."

"I was feeling a lot better until you punched me." He smiled, rubbing his shoulder. They both had a laugh.

The overwhelming mountain loomed large above them; its sheer size was astounding, and the striking red-and-black coloring of the mountainside heading up into the sky gave it a look of being majestic and magnificent. But there was an eeriness surrounding the dark shadowy clouds that gripped onto the peaks, which made you believe it was a doorway to enter into a whole new world.

"We must find a way in," said Asim. "The sheer wall is not helping. Keep looking. We may end up having to climb."

They moved around the mountain base, checking every space for a cavern entrance, a split in the rock, or something that would help them.

"Finally, a break, I think," said Zollo. "Look, there seems to be an entry."

Asim looked to where Zollo was pointing. He could see there was a sharp split in the mountainside that seemed like it could lead upward into a crevice.

"Good eyes! Not sure how we will climb up there," said Asim.

Looking intently, Zollo made out what he thought looked like a hole just above a large crack leading inward between the rocks.

"I think I can climb up with a little help," exclaimed Zollo. "Give me a rope and hoist me up to the first ledge." Climbing on Asim's shoulders, he found he was a little short but close to being able to grab ahold of the ledge. "A little higher."

Asim tried to push him.

"A bit more."

"What do you think I am?" Asim asked, straining his whole body.

"Just a bit more." He was on his toes, having one foot on the top of Asim's head as he pushed himself up to grab his hand onto the edge of the protruding rock. "Made it," he shouted, pulling himself up onto the small ledge.

Asim stood rubbing his head, relieved, watching Zollo scaling the wall and pulling himself up on the top of the ledge to where he could enter the hole. Zollo felt he had achieved the climb with ease. He turned around and walked into what he could see was a cave. It was dark, damp, and a little musky. He was thinking it could have been the rain from the other day. He did not want to go too far with the fading light from outside, but he saw nothing that would stop them from entering the mountain. It did not look inhabited by any animal. He knew he needed to report back so he could help the others climb the rope to the cave.

"I can't see too far. It's too dark. It looks deserted except for a few bird droppings on the wall." Zollo rubbed his arm on his pants. Asim had to smile.

Dropping the rope from his back, Zollo tied it around a rock, throwing the other end down to them. Asim pulled hard on the rope to make sure it would hold them, keeping the tension as Lanee climbed up first, scaling the line with some ease. Toya, Lube, and Theon followed suit. Asim climbed up last as they all stood at the top of the ledge. Asim turned to Toya. "We will need the torch if we want to see where this takes us. Let's hope we are on the pathway we need to be traveling. At least we know who we are looking for."

Toya was holding the torch as she led them into the cave. "My, it's dark," she said.

"Watch out for the bird—oh, too late." Zollo had seen her arm rub against the wall. He was trying hard not to laugh. The walk was slow as they came across a lot of rocks and cobwebs. At first, they wondered if it was leading them anywhere. As they continued up the passage, they found a blackish-gray feather in a crack stuck between two tall rocks. It was enormous, over a length and a half long.

"I hope we don't run into the bird this belongs to," Toya stressed, looking back at Asim.

As the cave twisted and turned, Toya noticed it was becoming lighter.

"I think we may be coming to somewhere," she said, smiling.

Good, Asim thought while they continued to walk the darkened passage. They arrived at a vast and open area inside a cavern, the light being a lot brighter. Looking up at the shaft that went to the top of the mountain, Asim could see all the sides of the cavern extended upward, opening to the sky above. As he looked forward, he could see a usual dilemma ahead; there were three caves, each looking like they took different directions.

Toya looked at him and giggled.

"Glad you find it funny."

"It's that we have found nothing to be straightforward on this journey." She giggled again.

"Well, we will need to split up! I don't want to do that as we don't know what we could be facing, but there is no time to check each tunnel together."

"Toya, go with Zollo."

"Gladly," she said, smiling at Zollo.

"Lube goes with Theon and Lanee; we can stay together. We want to make this as quick as we can. If you find the witch, ask her to come here. Or at least secure the antidote."

"We will all meet back here to see what we have found out. Toya and Zollo take the tunnel to the left. Lube and Theon take the middle. Be careful. Remember, time is not on our side."

Taking a torch each, they left for their respective tunnels. Toya and Zollo were heading for the one to the left; it was dark as they walked along the passageway. It seemed to them to be an extraordinary amount of large rocks they had to climb over along the way, which made their trek more difficult.

Zollo could not help but laugh when Toya tripped on a rock and hit her knee; she sprawled on the ground.

"Very funny," she said, glaring at him.

He was trying not to laugh as he helped her back to her feet. She punched him hard.

"Ouch, that was uncalled for."

She was rubbing her knee.

"Are you all right?"

"I will be if it doesn't stiffen up. Let's keep moving."

He had to have one more laugh to clear his thoughts. Continuing, they stayed silent for a while.

Eventually, Zollo turned to her. "I'm sorry, you looked so funny when you fell. Is your knee all right?"

"Yes," she had a thin smile, "if it wasn't for the pain!" Both were hearing a loud noise in the distance.

Toya was busy listening. "What does that sound like to you?"

"It seems like it could be a serpent. No, maybe a bird because it was more like a squawk!"

"That would be one big bird."

"Remember the feather?" Zollo said.

The noise was becoming louder.

"Better take our swords out, just in case." He made ready.

"I think we may have found another shaft to the outside." She shrugged. It looked that way as the ceiling was rising again. Ahead of them, they could see a lot of bones, fragments, and fur scattered around the rocks. The ground itself looked darker.

"That could be blood, and I hope that's animal bones?" He was hesitant about the find.

"We could be in trouble."

"We could," he replied. On closer examination, when they reached the bones, he figured some of them to be cows and a wolf or two. That means whatever had been eating these animals was very large.

"Do you think we should go further?" She was looking a little hesitant.

"Well …" he thought for a second. "We haven't gone far?"

"I know, but with all these bones, we need not add to them!"

"Ha-ha. I think we should at least look at where the shaft goes now all the squawking has stopped." Zollo walked on ahead.

"All right," she said, "just a quick look then." They both looked up at the shaft as it elevated into the sky above.

"Look." He pointed to the pathway that ended about five to six lengths past the shaft and looked over the edge. Toya could see it went a long way down; she was not able to see the bottom.

"Well!" she said. "We couldn't go any further anyway, and we never found the witch!"

They were both feeling downcast as they walked back to the cave opening again.

Then, there was a loud, deafening squawk and a sudden wind which almost pushed them forward off the path. Holding on to each other, both turned at the same time to look back.

"What's that?" she shouted as a giant bird landed with a loud crunch, its long talons sticking out from its oversized feet on the pathway close to them. Its massive wingspan almost blew them over before it stopped.

"Large bird," he yelled, looking as it stood five lengths high with its enormous black head, sunken red eyes, and its beak over a length long. The fat black-and-gray feathered body was a good four lengths long, with a large white tail. "It's a giant," she yelled through the loud squawking. "Can we outrun it back to the cave?"

"We will try," he yelled back. "We sure don't want to be dinner!"

The bird was heading straight for them with a loud squawk, its beak wide open. Zollo could see teeth inside, heading right at them.

"Faster!" he yelled. He turned back again, not realizing he was running faster than Toya. Not able to slow down to stop himself from running into her, they both stumbled. It was hard to keep her footing, but somehow, she stayed on her feet.

Zollo fell, landing hard on his left shoulder, striking the ground first. His athletic body helped him to roll as he landed upright on his feet again. It had slowed them both down enough for the bird to catch them. Its beak stabbed at Toya, knocking her to the ground before she reached the cave entrance. Seeing this, Zollo grabbed his sword to help. The bird was trying to stab her as she was rolling and dodging, moving from side to side, causing the bird to miss each time, as its beak continued striking the surrounding ground.

He lunged his sword at the bird, striking one of its chubby legs. It threw back its head with a shrill squawk, hopping backward a quick step. *This was their chance*, he thought, with just enough room for them both to slip into the cave. A few steps, and he was at the entrance, grabbing and pulling Toya back in with him out of harm's way.

"Are you all right?" he asked, breathless.

"I may need a new coat." She showed the tear where the bird's beak had split it.

"How are you?"

"My shoulder's numb, but I'm feeling good."

"Grab your bow. I'm mad now," she shouted. "You don't ever tear a girl's coat! We will take a few arrows to this thing before we leave."

They had moved back a little deeper into the cave. As they stepped forward, they could see the bird had moved inside, close to the entrance, using its large beak to stab at them again.

They both shot arrows in quick succession, but they deflected off its chest.

"It must be made of metal!" she shrieked.

"Aim for the neck," he shouted. The bird was still squawking as they both shot again, only to see their arrows glance from the top of its breast; he figured the neck was too hard to hit with its head down; grabbing the burning torch from the ground, he edged closer to the bird.

"Where are you going?" she shouted at him.

"I need to run this thing out of here. I have to make it raise its head."

"Well, wait for me!" Toya shouted.

He was forcefully swinging the torch backward and forward at the bird's head, staying out of the range of his enormous beak. The flame seemed to work as the bird was moving backward. He continued swinging the torch as he inched himself forward. He thought of taking his sword in the other hand, but he was not sure about the strength of his shoulder not being left-handed. The bird continued stabbing at them. They had now reached the cave entrance. Knowing he had no more room, he threw the torch at the bird's head, missing but having the desired effect as the bird reared back its head.

My chance, Toya thought. Her arrow flew from her bow to the bird's neck, this time piercing into its fleshy skin under the feathers. The bird squealed and squawked again. This time, it sounded sharp. Toya, twisting away, shot once more, missing its neck with an awkward shot; the arrow glanced off the side of its head.

Zollo's sword was out, aiming for its belly; thrusting the blade, he stabbed it deep before withdrawing, his blade covered in blood. Staggering back a step, the bird flew off as its massive wings hoisted it in the air.

"I don't think that bird will be back for a while."

"I hope not," Toya said, picking up the torch as they walked back into the cave. They collapsed next to each other.

"That was exhausting."

"Let's rest for a while, then go back." She sighed.

He smiled at her as he laid his head back on the wall. She leaned her head on his shoulder.

Chapter 8

THE WITCH HUNT 2

Lube and Theon had taken the central tunnel. They both were sure it was the darkest of all the caves, so they lit a torch, trying to see in the murky light.

"Can you smell that odor?" said Lube as they continued along the passageway, walking with his nose in the air.

"I'm glad you said that. I was hoping it wasn't you." Lube broke out in laughter, proceeding to lean over to sniff him as they both laughed. They continued walking, their eyes fixed now on the drabness of the cave: no bones, debris, spiderwebs, or anything other than a few rocks.

"That's strange," said Lube, "this passageway seems empty."

Theon shrugged.

Continuing straight, other than the smell, which appeared to worsen, the darkness was fading. He felt they had walked a long enough distance inside this cave.

Stopping, Theon asked him, "What's wrong?"

"We have walked and walked and have seen nothing. I don't want to give up, but how much further should we go with this smell?"

Theon thought to himself. It was a quiet moment.

"What's that," Lube asked.

"What's what?"

"Quiet." Lube was listening in the distance.

 Theon stood silent but could not hear anything.

"A drumbeat. I hear it," said Lube. Grabbing Theon's arm, he pulled him farther up the passage. He stopped again, holding his fingers to his lips. They stood silent when, in the distance, Theon thought he heard what sounded like a drum. It was muffled and unclear, but there seemed to be a regular beat. "I do hear something." He continued listening.

"Should we follow the sound?" asked Lube.

"Asim said not to go too far."

"What is too far?"

"Not finding the witch, I guess."

"Let's go a little way down to see where it ends," said Lube.

"All right, we will try to locate the drum if that is what's making the noise."

The beat was a lot louder now, and the smell seemed to be worse. The passageway was twisting toward the right.

Lube could hear the drum sound clearer as they rounded the curve. On the pathway, there were rocks scattered everywhere. Now, they both could see smoke drifting around ankle height toward them.

"Witches burn fires," Lube exclaimed.

"You know, this smells terrible…unless the witch is cooking something nasty that died ages ago."

Both drew their swords when they rounded the corner. Lube saw an opening leading out to a bridge; the smoke seemed to float up from underneath the pathway. The drum was beating loud now.

"This stench will burn my nose hair off," said Theon, putting one hand over his nose and mouth. "Maybe my beard too!"

"You don't have a beard."

"Oh no! Is it happening already?" He laughed.

Lube just shook his head with a smile.

As they were approaching the end of the cave, there were sounds of the drumbeat, a commotion from below them, and a sudden warmth they were feeling from the smoke, which seemed to be thickening. They both heard a scream that sounded like it came from under the path.

"That scream sounded almost human!" shouted Lube.

"You're right! We need to find out what is going on here."

"The fire is under this bridge," shouted Lube to be heard above the continuing noise. "The scream came from down there, mixed with this smell and the smoke. It's sweltering in here." He was wiping his sweaty face.

"I hope I'm not going to be sick," Theon rasped. "I don't know what this is, but I have a bad feeling in the pit of my stomach."

"Wait," shouted Lube, "I have an old rag attached to the back of my quiver." Taking it off, he found the cloth, tore the rag, and gave half to Theon. "Tie this around your face. It will help stop some of the stench so we can find out what's down there."

Lube was now standing at the start of the bridge, peering into the smoke, trying to see the ground. "I see nothing. We will have to look down over the side here." They both bent down on their hands and knees, looking over the top. Theon figured they were about forty or so lengths up from the ground; the billowing smoke from several fires below wafted upward. Seeing they were in a shaft, he noticed the sky, looking up at a small vent through the haze above them. The smoke and the smell continued to drift around them, creeping up the slick mountainside, fogging its surface to give off a dull reflection. Still trying to focus through the smoke from below, he was able to make out people moving around, some lying on the ground, some with paddles stirring large pots sitting over the fires; they appeared to be cooking something.

"Maybe that could be food?" whispered Theon.

"I'm not sure what that is. I know it stinks." Lube was adjusting his rag.

"I've heard there are a lot of unusual things on this mountain. Maybe it's some strange tribe," Theon said. He could see the people were skinny and withdrawn, dressed in rags for clothes. The foul and pungent odor seemed to be hovering around them. Theon patted Lube on the shoulder. "Look in the corner." Lube fixed his eyes there, making out what looked like meat remains through the smoke. The way it was stacked, it looked like it could be rotting animals. It was hard to tell as they shoveled it up, dumping it into the pots over the fires.

"This is where the smell is coming from," Lube whispered. "Glad the rags on our faces seem to help."

"Look again," whispered Theon. "Is that a head?"

Lube took a second look. "My lord, it looks like a human head. And could that be a foot? Maybe we should slip back out of here. If this has anything to do with the witch, I don't believe we want any part of it!"

Still, with his eyes fixed on what was happening below, Theon noticed one of the men looking back at him.

"I think we have been seen."

"We!" whispered Lube. "You're the one with your head stuck over the side."

"Well, we need to go." They heard a crash. The beat became louder and more deafening; the shouts sounded like "Mamba-mamba." Feeling he had to look one more time, Theon saw them squirming around. "I hope they can't climb up here."

"I would not put a wager on this one," shouted Lube.

His eyes fixed below as he saw a tall figure of a man who looked like he had come up from a tunnel below the ground. *He must be the leader*, he thought to himself. He was extremely skinny and taller than the others. It looked like his enormous head was too big for his body. Theon snickered. Was it a tuft of hair standing straight up on his bald head? He was shouting out orders to the others. Theon did not understand anything he was saying. He only pointed with a large, bony finger and looked toward him.

Lube grabbed Theon's shoulder. "Let's go."

"I have seen nothing like it, not even the Lugit tribe we saw last year." Still unsure of what he was seeing, and taking another last look, he shook his head. "That is one strange man."

Seeing them climbing the walls, Lube was aghast. He watched them use their hands and feet.

"They're like spiders. How are they climbing like that?" Lube asked.

"I don't want to find out. Let's go." They both turned to leave back down the cave. Two of the people had already climbed up and were blocking the entrance.

"I refuse to believe they crawled up a wall that fast," shouted Lube.

"We could be in trouble. These people look crazy. With their eyes glazed over, how are they even seeing us?"

Each of the men, who was only five feet tall, was moving their bony frames and bald heads toward them, each carrying a large bone as a weapon!

"That looks like a heavy leg bone."

"Human?" gasped Lube.

I need to vomit, thought Theon.

The two men still heard the shouts from below, "Mamba-Mamba." The people reacted to the chanting as the men ran at them. Both were twisting their bodies to dodge them, running past as Lube, wielding his sword, turned and sliced deep into one of the men's backs; a line of blood appeared where the sword cut. Theon then thrust his sword blade into the other man's neck on his quick turn. Both lay dead on the ground.

"Let's leave," shouted Lube.

Unfortunately, more of the men had entered onto the bridge, and some had clamored to the entranceway.

"Here we go then!" shouted Lube as he spun forward to stab the first man approaching him. One jumped on his back, another swinging a bone at his head. His sword hand was still free as he drove his sword hard. Blood gushed from the man's chest. Another was still grasping his back when a wild swinging bone caught him with a sickly thud on his shoulder. Feeling the pain shoot through to his brain in agony, he fell back, landing with the man on his back and crushing his head into the ground. Lube turned his head. Groggy, he lay on the ground for a second, trying to focus.

Theon was kicking one man off the bridge. Making his way to Lube, he swung his sword when another of the men jumped at him, slicing the man's neck. Grabbing Lube's hand, Theon pulled him to his feet again. Lube rubbed and shook his head, helping him focus, barely aware as he thrust his sword deep into another of the men rising from the ground. As more started toward him, he was seeing almost a blur of arms swinging the heavy bones! Another then came another. It seemed there were more and then more. The men were no match one-on-one with the warrior's swords, but sheer numbers had given the strange men favor.

Theon moved back toward the entrance, determined to make way for an escape, to stop them from blocking it again.

Lube was fighting at the foot of the bridge. He continued to strike down everyone within the length of his sword, and blood-spattered, knowing he was not letting them move too close. The bloodstained bridge had become a sea of red.

Theon was battling at the cave entrance, now overrun with the men. He was wielding his blade, taking satisfaction in cutting them down. Swerving his body, he did not notice one of the men had clasped onto his leg, holding it so tight it caused him to stumble; another of them jumped, grabbing his head. Twisting and squirming, he used both his arms to throw him off, wrestling to remove the man from his leg. A bone hit his neck with force. There was sickening pain, and he lost his composure. With one now biting and pulling on his leg, he fell back hard to the ground, more in shock from the throbbing, trying to regain his senses. He fended off the man locked to his leg by kicking him hard. He plunged his sword into another, but another swinging bone struck him, this time in the face. Theon was knocked back. His head seemed to burst on fire in pain. He was oblivious when a large hand grabbed his head. Bony fingers wrapped around his face. He could feel the large man from below pulling him upward. Theon swung his sword hard toward him, and his blade caught another close by, sinking into his body, stopping it from reaching the large man. When another of the men delivered a severe painful blow to his head, pain again ripped through him. The grip on his face was tightening. He felt like his head was about to explode, and he was in trouble. He tried shouting out for Lube, who was locked in a battle, striking down the men at the bridge. Hearing a muffled cry through the noise, Lube glanced back and saw Theon in trouble.

Lube knew he had to be there.

Pivoting, he kicked one of the men to the ground as another grabbed his leg, trying to bite him. Stumbling but kicking the man off left Lube off balance, and he fell crashing to the ground. Two more came swinging their bones toward him. One caught his arm, and he shrieked with the pain he felt. Still, he was trying to focus with one eye on Theon. Pain shot through him again from a glancing blow on his back. He rolled over and twisted himself on the ground, still swinging his sword at anyone close to him, slicing hard into the leg of one man standing in front, who screamed and hopped off over the bridge. Lube kicked another hard between his legs as his sword cut deep into another. He scrambled to his feet, still kicking, punching, and thrusting his sword.

The large man had grabbed Theon's shoulder with his other hand as Theon was trying to shout out the agony that he was feeling. Two more of the men had wrapped around his body, biting into his flesh. The man's large, bony fingers, which were still covering his face, were not only stifling his voice but also making it hard for him to breathe, pulling his shoulder down to leave Theon's neck exposed. Lube was still fighting his way to him, now only witnessing from afar, knowing he would not reach Theon in time. He grabbed his dagger, reaching back and throwing. It hit the large man, sinking deep into his ribs. He squealed with pain, but it was not enough to stop him from biting deep into Theon's neck, who now had stopped struggling and blacked out. His head pulled back; the large man ripped the flesh from his throat as blood spurted out.

Lube could see the blood dripping down the large man's face as Theon's flesh was hanging from his lips. Kicking another of the men to the ground in his way, he cried out loudly, grabbing his sword tighter, striking another man down on his left, the return swing catching another man on the right side. Knowing he had to be there for Theon, he used his sword mightily. He sliced down another of the men, kicking another out of his way, now reaching the large man who had now dropped Theon's body. Lube could see his friend's body jerking as it slumped on the ground.

The large man was now looking wildly at Lube, the dagger still sticking out from his ribs; he had grabbed Theon's sword and was holding it out toward him.

Looking at Theon's blood-covered face enraged Lube. Taking his sword, he sidestepped and plunged his blade deep into the large man's stomach, twisting the blade hard before pulling it out. Squealing again, the man dropped the sword from his hands; he fell to his knees. His enormous head fell forward. Lube dispatched a hard blow from above his head that sliced deep down into the top of his skull, parting it down the middle. The man fell in a bloody heap to the ground.

He did not stop, seeing three more of the men still on Theon's body, biting into his flesh. In his rage, he grabbed hold of one of them, kicking him so hard he toppled over the edge of the path to the ground below. Then, grabbing hold of another, he used his blade to plunge it deep into his heart, twisting again as he pulled it out. Pulling the last one up from Theon's body, he sliced and sliced at his body, releasing his anger and creating an eruption in blood; he dropped the bloody, lifeless body on the ground. He could see Theon lying there covered with more blood, knowing he, too, was drenched with the same blood, feeling himself sweating profusely.

The men, knowing their leader was dead, crawled back down the wall. What a relief he felt as his body ached, looking through the blood and sweat on his face at the dead bodies. Seeing two were still alive, he plunged his sword one by one deep into both their hearts. As he stood again, Theon's lifeless body lay there; blood had pooled around his neck. Dropping to his knees, Lube whispered, "We did it!" He lifted Theon's blood-spattered head to his chest, his fingers closing Theon's open eyes, feeling tears welling up in his own.

"I'm sorry, I should have been here." He pulled him tighter, knowing his friend, his brother in arms, was dead. He noticed the rag had fallen from Theon's face; he found it close by and wrapped it back, covering his nose again.

"There." He sat back, holding his friend for a while to let it sink in he had died. Standing to his feet, he lifted Theon's body, taking him back into the cave and laying him close to the rocks. Searching, he found as many rocks as he could use to cover his body.

"You were a great warrior, my friend. I wish you were continuing this journey with us. I will say goodbye." Finding Theon's sword, he plunged it into the rock pile as a marker. He picked up the torch and walked back down the passageway, wiping a tear from his eye and sweat from his brow. His clothes were sticking to his body from the drying blood; he was slowly making his way back to join the others.

Chapter 9

THE WITCH HUNT 3

Asim and Lanee disappeared down the passage to the right, lighting the torch before they left, encountering the usual darkness of the cave. The two started out straight before the pathway veered hard to the right.

"That's strange," said Lanee.

"I hope that's the only strange thing we find on this journey," Asim replied.

After walking a fair distance, they noticed the cave was coming to an end; seeing the passageway leading out, it was a short ending, nothing but a ceiling that opened wider. Asim could see nothing but steep walls.

"I was hoping we would at least see the sky if we looked up," she shouted, "not a tunnel that is leading us to another cave."

"Well, I'm sure there are hundreds of tunnels in these mountains, not all ending in good places."

"Let's hope we find the one that does." Lanee laughed. The passageway was widening as they moved into the next cave. Both had noticed it was lighter than the last one. Still, they had to use the torch.

"I wonder how the others are doing," Lanee thought out loud.

"Good question! I hope someone has already found the witch. All we have found are caves!"

The ground was rising as the passageway led upward and veered hard to the right again, "We will be back where we started," Asim said, "if we keep heading to the right." Although it seemed to level off, he hoped it was not taking them to the top of the mountain. He had noticed on the ground there were a lot of small bones scattered around. *Most likely birds*, he thought. "Bird bones," he said, like he had seen something of value. Lanee nodded and carried on walking; they could see the cave was ending, and it was becoming a lot lighter. This time, the shaft went upwards; they could see the sky.

"Fresh air," Lanee shouted. "Too musky in here." She turned her nose up, looking at the opening.

"It looks like this one goes to the mountaintop." Looking ahead, he could see another cave entrance.

"Do we keep going?" she asked. "We seem to be going from cave to cave, not finding anything."

"I guess we will go through this one. If we find one more empty cave, then we will go back."

Upon entering this cave, the first thing they noticed it was not dark at all, and there were more bird bones scattered on the ground. Asim did not remark this time.

"I think they could be bird bones," she said to him.

He looked at her, a little subdued, shaking his head. They had not walked too far when they smelled smoke from a fire.

"Feels like a fire," he said; they could see the light up ahead. They both were feeling the warmth moving through the passageway of the cave, then saw a small trail of smoke. *It had to be from the fire*, he thought. Ahead, there was an opening, and it looked like it might be a door, only it was wide open. Stopping, Asim stuck his head in first. It seemed like a small den, and there was a bright fire with a large cooking pot hanging over the top of the flames.

Asim beckoned Lanee forward, and they could hear what sounded like singing and humming coming from the back of the den. They could not see back there; it was blocked off with a large rock. But they could see chairs, a small table, and blankets piled in a corner. There was a wall with lots of small and large bottles containing various powders and liquids. He was unsure if he saw something crawling inside one of the bottles. You could smell cooking in the air, but not like anything he had ever smelled before. Lanee turned her nose up and looked at him with a cringe. There was a cat fast asleep in the corner, curled up in a ball. It was an overfed white cat.

"I think this could be the right place," he said, smiling.

But before Lanee could answer, a medium-built black-skinned lady around forty-five appeared around the corner. She was wearing an exquisite white dress matching her beautiful features and flowing black hair. She was dancing; her perfect white shoes skipped over the floor. She was singing in full voice.

Her eyes caught sight of Asim, and she screamed and stopped. Before he could say anything, she made a quick sign with her fingers and cast a spell on him.

Asim went missing. As Lanee looked around, she noticed another cat had appeared. A large, brownish-furred cat was standing by her feet.

The lady turned and looked at her.

"Wait!" Lanee screamed, knowing it would be her turn next. "I believe we have been searching for you. Are you the witch?"

"I am," said the black-skinned lady. "I am the white witch of the mountain."

"But you are black?"

"I assure you, I am white!"

"No!" said Lanee. "Your skin is dark."

"Oh!" She laughed. "My name is Apora, so what are you doing inside my home?"

"We are sorry for entering. My name is Lanee, and this…well, was Asim." The cat was now trying to gain Lanee's attention.

"Do you want me to change him back?"

She thought for a split second as the cat meowed loudly. She laughed. "Yes, I need him."

Apora made a sign. Asim was back again.

"Wow! That hurt." He was rubbing his head with his hand.

"Well, don't come in someone's house unless invited," Apora replied.

"I will remember in future," he rubbed his head again.

"I'm sorry, but you scared me. Are you Asim?" asked the witch.

"Yes, I am."

"I have heard of you. You are a great warrior."

"Well, if it is what they say."

"And handsome, too." She smiled as Lanee brushed herself up closer to Asim.

"Why are you here?"

"We are looking for the white witch."

"I am the white witch."

"But you're—" Lanee kicked him, "—beautiful. I was going to say." He glared at Lanee. "We need your help."

"Help!" said Apora, who was leaning back as she took a drink from a large flask on the table and then passed it to Asim. He took a sip; it seemed to take his breath away for a second.

"Woo, this is powerful!" It went down smoothly. Lanee took a sip. She found it to have the same effect.

"My," exclaimed Asim. "It is good." He told her about the battle with the goblins and how Garronas had used an enchanted bow.

"The arrows, when they hit my men, put a hex on them, and now they cannot wake."

"Sounds like a sleeping spell."

"Yes, and we came to see if you have an antidote to wake them. Tin-Tina was the one who sent us to look for you."

"Ah yes, the fairy queen. I like her, for she is a beautiful little creature. I have met her." She took another drink.

"Garronas, he is a nasty piece of work." She grabbed another bottle close by and took another drink. She offered the bottle to them, but they both declined this time. "More for me." She laughed, taking another drink. "Where were we?"

"Garronas," he said.

"Oh yes, a nasty piece of work. Ugly, too." She laughed out loud; it was an infectious laugh. Asim could not help but laugh with her. She took another drink. "I have an antidote, but you must take me with you." She laughed and drank again.

"Does she remind you of anyone?" asked Lanee quietly to Asim.

"She must be related somehow." He laughed.

Apora stood up. "Let's take another drink," she said.

"One more only," he said. It was as powerful as the first one.

Apora sat back on a rock behind her but then slid off, landing on the ground. "I'm all right," she said as he helped her to her feet. She laughed again. "You must think I'm awful."

"No, no." He smiled.

"I don't go out much anymore."

"Well, we would love for you to come with us so you can help."

"I will," she replied, smiling and clapping her hands to express her excitement. "I am an open casket," she announced.

Lanee shook her head. "I don't know what that means," she whispered to Asim, who shrugged his shoulders in bewilderment.

"We must have one more drink before we go," she told them. She stood up and grabbed a large pouch this time. They all took one more drink as she went around the house, putting things in a bag she had placed over her shoulder. "I may need these things," she said. Hitting the corner of the table, she toppled forward, almost falling on the cat, who screeched and ran out.

"A friend of yours?" he said sarcastically.

Lanee helped her regain her composure as she grabbed her pouch, took a drink, and threw it over her shoulder.

"I'm ready," she announced.

"Are you all right to travel?" asked Lanee.

"Never better."

"Are you leaving the fire?"

"It's fine. I have a new spell: boiling. It will be all right."

"Let's go then." The cat was running back into the den as they walked into the passageway back to meet the others. Asim had a broad smile at this point; this was one journey that had gone right. *We have an antidote*, he smiled. They arrived back at the open shaft, hoping to find the others.

No one was there. "We are the first to arrive back!"

"Well," said Apora. "With all this walking, I need a drink."

"I hope the others are back soon," said Lanee. "We never put a limit."

"I know it would be hard to do." He thought to himself, *We have the witch, so they could not find her.*

"I hope they did not go too far or find any trouble."

It was not long before Zollo and Toya walked back out of the cave. Both Asim and Lanee went to meet them. Zollo told them about the run-in with the giant bird.

Apora overheard them. "That's an egit."

"It was enormous. It attacked us."

"This is Apora, the white witch," Asim said.

"But she is—" Zollo started to say.

Asim cut him off. "We have been through this. She is the white witch." Zollo smiled.

"Have a drink?" she said, offering her pouch to Zollo and Toya.

Zollo, who took a sip, was motionless for a second. "This is a

drink. It lit a fire in my mouth, yet I feel wonderful now."

Toya was nodding her head in agreement.

Apora smiled. "It affects everyone differently." She smiled as they all continued to wait. Asim paced up and down. It seemed a while before Lube made it back, walking out of the cave alone. Asim was first to him. He looked disheveled and covered in dried blood.

"My god." He was holding him. "What happened?"

Lube looked at him, his eyes still dazed and red from rubbing the tears away. "He's gone," he said. "It's my fault. I was not there when he needed me, and I was not able to save my friend. Now I am here, and Theon is not!"

Asim now found himself with a tear for Theon as the reality of what Lube said settled in him. He wrapped his hands around Lube's face as Zollo joined, placing his arm around Lube's back.

"It is not your fault." Asim was looking into his eyes. "I know you, and you would not let Theon down. You would have done everything you could to save him."

"We knew when we started this journey it may not end well for any or all of us. It was not your fault." Asim hugged him.

Lube explained all that happened. Zollo was now putting his arms around them both. Lube told of the tragedy they faced as Lanee and Toya joined them.

Apora came over with a small bowl. "Please drink," she asked.

"No." Lube shook his head.

"Please," she insisted as Asim also encouraged him. Apora said something as he took a drink. He coughed as it went down.

"There is a warmth entering me. I feel calm. What is this?"

"A drink from Apora," said Lanee, "to make you feel better."

"Those flesh eaters are a scourge on this mountain," Apora sneered. "I am glad you killed their leader, but another will come to take his place. It's been this way for years. I had trouble with them once. Now they know better than to mess with me." She took another drink. "Here." She let Lube take another.

He took another sip; it put a smile on his face.

"We need to travel back," said Asim. "People that need us are waiting." Arriving at the cave entrance, they were relieved to see the rope was still hanging there. Lanee climbed down first, followed by Toya.

"All right. Apora, you will be next. Apora?" There was no answer; he looked around, and she was nowhere in sight. "Did anyone see her leave?" he asked.

"I don't remember her standing here," replied Zollo.

"Strange! All right, all of you go down. I will look for her." He went back down the passageway when he heard shouting from below. He walked back and looked over the edge. Lube was at the bottom of the rope. Asim looked at everyone. Apora was standing with them. He scratched his head and grabbed the line, lowering himself to the bottom.

He looked at her. "How?" he asked.

"I took the steps." She smiled. "I don't do rope."

"Steps?" He had a puzzled look on his face.

"Yes."

"Why didn't you tell us there were steps?"

"Well, for one, you didn't ask, and two, you all looked like you were having fun." She smiled, feeling amused. She walked off humming to herself.

Asim shook his head as they all followed, making their way back to the camp. They found the others patiently waiting.

"Finally, we're back!"

He could see while they had gone, they had built a shelter for the bodies and put a roof over it. "You have all been busy."

"Where is Theon?" Radel asked, noticing he had not returned.

"He is not with us anymore. It is a sad day. We lost him up there. I will explain everything later. We must give the antidote to all these sleeping people." He introduced Apora to them.

"Here is the white witch of the mountain, Apora, and before anyone says anything, again, this is the white witch. She is wonderful, and she has an antidote."

She walked around the camp, checking the bodies lying on the ground. She took her pouch from her shoulder and took a drink.

Spen looked at Asim. "Why do I like this lady?"

"Yes, I believe you both have a lot in common."

Spen gave him a puzzled look and reached for his empty flagon, and tried to take a sip.

Handing her pouch to Asim, she then took off the bag from her shoulder. She fumbled around inside until she found two small bottles of liquid, one red and the other black. She took them, uncorked them both, and put a small amount of each into an empty larger bottle, putting a top on them and dropping the smaller bottles back into the pouch. Shaking the liquid hard, it turned a deep brown. She knelt at each body lying dormant. Stone was the first in line; she took the liquid in the bottle and dropped just one drop on each eye. By the time she was at the last sleeping body, Stone had stirred and opened his eyes. Spen was hopping up and down, excited as he grabbed his empty flagon, again trying to take a sip. Everyone who had been asleep was now awake. They were all rubbing their eyes and standing.

"What happened?" asked Stone. "I must have blacked out again."

"You did more than that, my friend," said Asim, grabbing his shoulder.

He told them all of them what had happened and how Apora had come back with them from the mountain to administer the antidote to each one. Stone walked over to Apora to thank her, as did each one of the others. Walking back to him, Stone asked about Theon. It was then Asim gathered everyone together to tell them about the loss of Theon; there was a deep feeling of sadness at the loss of a friend.

Apora was feeling good after the last one thanked her. She went to Asim for her pouch, and she took a long drink.

"Tell me please," asked Spen as he approached her. He had noticed Apora was drinking from her pouch. "What is in your pouch?"

"It's a mixture I made myself, a mead with a kick." Apora laughed. Spen laughed, too. "Would you like to try a little?" She smiled at him.

"I would love to," he said eagerly. "I had my own, but I ran out." He sipped from the pouch. "Oh my, I think I felt my toes curl!" They both laughed, sitting back on a rock close by, and they drank together.

"It's heartwarming to find someone who loves their mead as much as I do."

"Where are the fairies?" Asim asked Radel.

"They had to leave right before you arrived back. There was trouble back in the forest, and we're off to see what happened. Tin-Tina wished you luck on your journey and said you will meet again soon."

Asim joined Spen and Apora, this time telling her of their journey to the Nordak castle to rescue the children and take them back to their village.

"I wish I could go with you, but alas, it cannot be. I should go back now."

"We need to leave, too," he said. "Will you wait so we can walk to the mountain together?"

"I will." She smiled.

Spen agreed, "We can have a little sip together on the way."

"Ha-ha," Apora laughed. "Here's to the good times." The three of them all took a drink.

"Pack up," shouted Asim. "We're heading for the mountain."

As they were walking, Spen asked Apora about her pouch and if it would be possible to take some of the drink with him. His flagon was empty, and he had to leave it there.

"You silly old man," she said. "I will gladly give you this pouch. But it's not just any pouch. It will fill itself two more times when it's empty. Just turn the top three times to the left and once to the right and say, 'Apora.'"

"You are heaven-sent," he told her. They seemed to laugh all the way back to the mountain.

"Let's hope no more problems arise on the way," said Lanee. Asim just nodded his agreement; it was easy to see his mind was not there. He was deep in thought all the way to the base of the mountain.

Asim asked Apora if she would show them the steps she came down.

She laughed. "Follow me." They all followed her as they reached a crack in the mountainside, leading to the steps going upward on the steeper side, where the mountain divided into two pathways in either direction.

"That was not there before." Asim smiled. Apora looked and laughed.

"Here is where I must leave you," she said. "You, go up," pointing to the path leading to the other side of her. "I must go this way. Just follow the path, and you will reach a cave entrance." Taking the mead pouch from her shoulder, she gave it to Spen, telling him, "Drink well, my friend," and she kissed him on the cheek.

He thanked her, blushing as he continued up the path.

Apora pulled Asim close to her and away from the others. "Even though I cannot be with you," Apora reached deep into her pocket and pulled out a small velvet bag, "I want to give you this." She grabbed his hand and placed the bag there, closing his hand with her fingers so he would hold it tight. "What you have in that bag is more than valuable, but it comes with great responsibility, and therefore, I trust only you," she said. "I only have one of these for your journey to rescue the children. If you reach the point of life or death and there is no other possible human answer, take out the pebble inside the bag. It can work both ways: it can bring life, or it can bring death. Once you choose, it cannot be stopped. Use the pebble wisely and only when it's time. Say my name, Apora, twice. This gift is yours. I know you will do what is right if the time comes. Do not lose it. I wish you much luck to you and your incredible band of people. Come back this way one day."

Asim thanked her, promising he would. She cupped his cheeks and kissed him on the lips.

Thanking her again as he left, he took the bag and placed it in his deepest pocket so it would not fall out. He walked back, passing each one of them, grabbing their shoulder with a small reassuring squeeze as he went past them on his way up to the cave at the top of the path, ready to lead them.

"Will she be all right?" asked Spen as he was passing him.

"I think she is more sober than you." He smiled at him.

"That's good stuff." He beamed as he showed him the pouch.

Asim laughed. "We will need to make it in the cave up ahead." Night was falling on them. The pathway narrowed, and they followed single-file. It continued to narrow, and he soon saw the cave ahead.

"We need to light a torch before we go inside. I don't know how far we will have to travel before we find enough space for us to rest." After a short distance, the path opened up large enough for them to camp, make a fire, and relax for a while. Asim was thankful the dwarfs had brought wood with them.

After a well-needed rest, they started the journey again, grabbing up torches. They all headed off down the passage inside the cave.

"Here we go again!" shouted Lanee.

Chapter 10

A HOP, SLIP, AND A JUMP

Let's be careful," said Asim. "We already have had trouble in these mountains. Be alert and expect anything could happen!" He decided it would be good if they all kept their hands on their sword handles and continued to walk. The cave was dark. Their torches gave them only a minimal light. He could feel dampness under his feet; it seemed the more extensive the passage, the damper the ground was.

"There is a stench coming from this water," said Lanee, turning her nose up as she looked around.

"At least it is bearable," he said as they continued splashing through the now-wetter surface.

After they had walked a distance, they could see the tunnel was gradually becoming lighter.

Finally, he thought, *Not too far off now*. He could see a small light; the passage had widened, although the water was becoming more intense. So far, they could not see where it came from. They finally reached the lighter area where the cave ended, leading to a larger cavern where they could move around more easily.

"I don't believe this," he said, staring at three different cave entrances up ahead, which he was sure would take them in three different directions.

"Oh no, not again," said Lanee, also staring at the three caves.

"I don't want to break into three different parties. Maybe by going a short distance inside each one, we will have a better feel for which one all of us to travel." He sent Zollo down the first one, Lanee down the middle, and Stone down the third, each with instructions not to travel too far. "We only need to get a feel of where it might take you!" Each one left and was back. Zollo was a little behind the other two.

"What were you able to see?" Asim asked.

"It seems like the middle cave goes up," said Lanee. "It could take us up towards the top of the mountain, and I thought while I was in there, I heard what could have been a waterfall, which could explain all this water in the tunnel."

"It seems this cave goes downwards," said Stone. "We would have to be careful of the water and the slope, but it could take us closer to the bottom of the mountain."

Then Zollo said, "This cave veers off to the left, neither up nor down. It could take us to or away from the direction we need to go." Standing together, the three gave their thoughts to Asim.

"All right," he said. "Which way, Lanee?"

"I think we should head down."

"Stone?"

"I agree, down."

"Zollo?"

"It was heading left. It might veer around again?"

"It's too early for us to split. We need to all stay together. Therefore, this time, we need to go right and head down."

Stone lightly punched Zollo on the arm.

"Might veer around?" he said to him and smiled.

Zollo just shrugged and smiled back.

"I'm hoping by being closer to the ground. It could take us out to the Ferroca forest and on our way to the Nordak's castle," said Asim. "We have gone from one battle to the next and lost great people on the way. Now I'm hoping our luck changes." Lanee reached out and squeezed his neck.

"You know," she said, "we will go wherever you say, and we are prepared to fight any fight that is necessary wherever you lead."

"We are heading down in the cave on the right," he announced. "Everyone must be careful of the water on the ground."

"That's a coin you owe me," said Jig to Mup and Anson. "I picked that one."

"Be cautious as you enter. It will be slippery," shouted Stone.

The torches flickered as they started down the steep slope, careful of their steps. Stone went back to help Spen, knowing if anyone could slip, it would be him.

"When we reach the bottom, we will be better off," Lanee told Asim. "Maybe we can make up time? It seems we have lost too much in here."

"This passage is taking us down for sure," Asim said, trying to keep his balance. Everyone was worried about slipping as they continued down. It seemed like an eternity before they reached the bottom. "Well, this seems like the ground." The cave itself had expanded and flattened out. They still hoped for the cave to end, not even realizing it had! Asim looked back, not knowing just how big the entrance was. Unknown to them, they had entered another giant cavern; even in the poor visibility, they still could see without using a torch, thanks to small beams of light from the ceiling pouring down from above in the high cavern. *Holes from the top of the mountain,*

Asim figured. They were all looking across the expanse, only seeing formations of rock large and small. The ground itself was still wet, and in some areas, large puddles had formed.

"I wonder where we are," asked Lanee.

"It could be hell," exclaimed Spen, taking a drink from his newly gained pouch.

"No! I don't think there's enough heat," quipped Asim. "We may be at the bottom level on the ground here in this cavern. The same level as the ground outside. All we need to do is find a place to break out!"

"Finding an opening to the other side of the wall?" Spen pondered, thinking hard. "Wherever that could be!" Giving up the thought, he reached for his pouch.

They all started forward on the wet ground and kept moving but soon lost the light shafts. It became dark again. Having to light the torches, Lube noticed the flames still held up well.

"Keep the torches high," Asim shouted. "Maybe we will see something on our trek forward." Holding the torches as high as they could, everyone was peering into the darkness, trying to make out anything useful in front or to the surrounding sides.

"Looks like the ceiling is dropping ahead," he shouted, "but I can't be sure. Could be an illusion." The gloominess of the dark in such a large area like this made it more mysterious than other directions they had traveled. *Everything seemed a little strange*, he thought, not knowing why.

Zollo thought he heard faint drumbeats in the distance.

"Could that be?" Lanee asked, now listening intently.

"It is something," Zollo said, but it was too muffled. They continued climbing over rocks that were blocking their way. Now, the drumbeat was louder. And the puddles were growing larger.

"I'm sure it's a drum we heard now," said Asim. "It's coming from the darkened area over there beyond those rocks."

"We are too far away from the tribe we fought?" said Lube.

"I think it would be in our best interest to go the opposite way. I don't care to find out what it's all about right now. No point in inviting any trouble we don't need."

They were climbing on the rock and moving away from that area when, out of the darkness, a spear whistled through the air, missing Anson by an inch. With a clatter, it skidded off the ground. Anson, at the back with two of the dwarfs, squealed as it startled him. Everyone was straining to see as another spear whistled through the air, catching Dooly, who was standing close to Anson. It grazed his shoulder.

"Put the torches out!" shouted Asim. They did so with haste. "As fast as you can, jump off this rock and run," he shouted again. Asim stood there to make sure they all ran in the same direction. "Be careful of the rocks." He heard the splashing as they ran through the water on the ground. After a short while, the splashing stopped. Closely following them, he almost ran into Spen, who had made it to the rear of the others. Looking behind him, he could see nothing, and he hoped whoever it was throwing spears could not see them either.

Spen was breathing hard. "I can't," he said, "I have no breath for this old body." Asim stood him up straight.

"All right," he said, putting his shoulder under his, taking his weight as they started. Stone came up on the other side, placing his shoulder under Spen's. Now, both men lifted him; Spen was up in the air now; his feet were dangling as they ran with him. They soon caught up with the others and then dropped him down.

"Do you think we are far enough away?" Lanee asked, peering into the dark.

"I hope so. I don't believe they were following, just keeping us away. Everyone close in. When I call your name, let me know so we are not missing anyone in this darkness."

Everyone was there.

"Good!" he said. "All right, when your breath is back, and your hearts stop beating so hard. Spen when you can stop gasping…"

They laughed.

"It's coming back. Just another quick sip."

"We will all keep together. I don't want to light a torch. Grab hold of one another as we cross here."

"Do you think we will ever go back that way to find out what's going on?" asked Zollo.

"Maybe another day if we return this way? We need to move out of here."

After walking for a while in the darkness, Asim hoped his sense of direction would lead them the right way. Soon, relief flooded his mind as he could see in the distance it was becoming lighter again. Moving closer, they could hear a slow churning and the odd splash as if they were approaching a significant amount of water flowing close to them.

"Seems to be warming up in here," said Lanee as a sweat bead rolled down her cheek.

"Well, it sounds like we are close to the river again. I feel we are going the right way."

"I don't know why it would be so hot?" uttered Anson.

There was a massive rock formation in front. They would have to climb to see the river. Climbing to the top, Asim and Lanee could look across the river as it flowed below, splashing as it hit the rocks in its pathway. It seemed the surroundings were scorching hot. Sweat beads had already rolled down each one of them.

"Is that water?" asked Lanee. "It looks like where the heat is coming from." Now, the others had joined them.

"It looks like river water," said Lube. "But it seems a strange color."

"It could be the light in here," said Asim.

There was a scuffling noise, a shout, and then a loud clank as Spen, who had leaned too far forward, fell over the top. He was hopelessly trying to grab anything on the way over as he headed toward the river.

Stone grabbed the foot of Spen, who was now suspended headfirst over the rock.

"He's slipping," shouted Stone. Lube jumped over to grab Spen's other foot. Using their strength, with a little bit of help from Anson and Benson, they pulled him back. Their bodies were now saturated with sweat.

"My pouch," screamed Spen. "I've lost my pouch."

"Oh, shut up," said Stone, almost breathless. "You almost lost your life." They stood him up straight on the top again.

Asim decided they would climb down and check the river and maybe walk the pathway close by if it wasn't too hot. They all climbed down, sweat dripping from each of their brows. This time, Spen was the right way around. He had joyous relief when he found his pouch.

"There is a God," he said. He took a large drink.

"Steady," said Stone, "you know the mead is what put you in trouble!" But Spen seemed too happy to care at that moment.

Asim, taking out an arrow, walked over to the river and placed it in the water. When he pulled it out, the shaft was black, with burn marks, and the metal head had steam coming off.

"This is why it's so hot here," he said. "There must be a fire in the mountain that entered the river."

"I said this was hell," Spen mumbled.

"Nobody goes too close to the water," Asim yelled. "And this means you too, Spen. We will keep back on the path."

"What is happening?" asked Tonas, who had been behind the others.

"This river may run through a hot area in the mountain or under the ground. It's scalding, and we need to stay away from the water!" said a sweat-covered Asim.

"But I still think our best chance is to follow where it goes for now. I still feel we are going in the right direction." They continued their journey following the river. Now, they could see ashes on top of the riverbank as the pathway was descending.

Asim stopped everyone. "Let's be careful going down this hill. We don't, at this point, know what's ahead. Stay by the river and walk close together."

"Is it me," asked Spen, "or is anyone else's feet hot?"

"You're not alone," said Radel. "This was a steep slope, and the water was making it very hot and slippery."

"My feet are slipping. I'm sliding!"

Stone grabbed Spen's arm as his panic turned into a smile. They were all taking slow and precise steps as they moved down the slope.

"Hope this is taking us out of here," shouted Lube.

"Keep hoping," he said; seeing the river and the pathway straightening back out made him feel better about the slope. He could see the river flow slowing down as they reached the bottom.

"No casualties." Everyone felt a great relief.

In the distance, Asim could see a significant lake; the river split in two directions, one into the lake and the other veered away as if returning the way they came.

The lake stretched all the way across from as far as one could see from one side to the other.

Asim stopped following the river to concentrate on crossing the lake.

"I don't see a way across," said Lanee. "Not if it's hot like the river?"

"Unfortunately, you're right," he said as they were approaching for a closer look. They could feel the ground becoming hot and mushy under their steps and becoming softer as they continued.

"Help," came a voice.

A voice cried, "Help!" again. This time, it was louder. Looking to where the sound was coming from, he could see Pooly, who was sinking into the soft ground!

"Nobody move!" Asim shouted as everyone stood motionless, except for Pooly, who was still sinking.

Asim grabbed Stone, who was closer to him.

"Slowly," he said. They stepped slowly and precisely so as not to sink. They moved as close to Pooly as they felt they could.

"Whoever has a rope, throw it to me," he shouted. Dooly, taking one off his back, threw it to him.

"Stone, are your feet firm?"

"Yes."

"I'm throwing this line to you, Pooly." He could see Anson was the closest to him.

"Anson, are your feet on the firm ground?"

"Yes."

"Are you close enough to help him with the rope?"

"No, I will try to move closer."

"No," shouted Asim. "I hope he can grab it himself."

Pooly was able, with a slight stretch, to grasp onto the rope as Asim and Stone pulled hard. His body slowly emerged from the mire. They continued to drag his body until he was close to them so they could help him stand back on his feet.

"Woo!" said Pooly. "That was too close." He thanked them for pulling him out. "I'm as hot as fire." Anson came over and hugged him.

"I don't think we should go any closer to the lake," said Asim. They all moved back to a firmer area as they all gathered around Pooly, making sure he was good.

"Glad you're fine." Lanee patted his hot back.

"Well," said Asim, "we must find a way across, or we may have to travel back the way we came."

"Maybe it's a sign we should have taken a different cave," Zollo smirked. Stone punched him in the arm.

"Ouch, I was only thinking." He was rubbing his arm.

"Do you believe the lake is as hot as the river?" asked Tonas.

"I think so," said Stone. "The river runs straight into it."

"What about the rocks?"

"There are not enough to make it all the way across, and I don't want to lose anyone. It's too dangerous," said Asim, looking out at the lake.

"As far as I can see, there is nothing around to cross over on." Lanee was looking hard. "It seems like we are in a dilemma."

"Hope we're not stuck here," said Spen. "I'm not just talking about our feet." This brought a giggle from Toya and Radel, who were close to him. Spen, not realizing what he said, just took another small sip from his pouch.

Asim called Stone, Zollo, Lube, and Tonas over. "I need you, Stone, and Zollo to go to the left side of the lake, maybe two to three hundred lengths. Check to see if you can find a way across, being careful of the ground. If you start to sink, come back."

"Lube and Tonas, do the same to the right, and we will see you back here. Good luck."

"What are we going to do if they can't find a way?" asked Lanee.

"We will decide then, but we may have to return the way we came. If we must, we will."

As the four were leaving, he shouted, "Use the rocks where you can and be careful."

Stone and Zollo moved forward using the small rock formations. Only standing on the ground when needed, being cautious after the mishap with Pooly, thinking of where they could cross.

It seemed like the lake had no end, no matter how far they traveled. They had gone at least three hundred lengths, maybe four now. They were sweating, their clothes clinging to them; it was sweltering being so close to the lake. "The ground seems to be soft and spongy," said Zollo, who appeared to be sinking the further they went.

"We have seen nothing," said Stone, "and we are sinking more the farther we go."

"Maybe Lube will have better luck in the other direction?"

"If we had taken the other cave," Zollo said again, followed by a punch from Stone.

"You only did that because you know I could be right."

"We will see." They decided together to return to Asim, being careful as they stepped.

Lube and Tonas had left in the opposite direction, tand like Stone and Zollo, they used the rocks where possible. Being careful when using the ground, being soft in this direction, they tested before putting any weight down. Lube looked over the expanse of the lake, seeing no way to cross, just seeing the water.

"Your eyes are a lot younger than mine. What are you seeing?" asked Tonas.

"I see nothing," he said. "We are heading back towards the river again."

"What if we were wrong?" said Tonas, "And the river turns back to help us? I know it seemed to flow in the wrong direction."

"Always a possibility; if we can make it that far, we will see if it does." It was becoming a lot lighter again as they approached the river.

"At least the light is in our favor." They were trying to pass where the river split, searching for a while until they found a hidden path, taking them underneath the river.

"I don't think we would have seen this path?" Tonas exclaimed, feeling relieved.

"We never came this far, and now, in the distance, we can see the bend in the river."

Lube saw something that caught his eye; he was trying to figure out what it was.

"Do you see something?" asked Tonas, trying to look himself.

"Something, not sure yet," he told him. Tonas was straining his eyes, trying to see what he could be looking at. His old eyes were not as sharp as they once were, only seeing the expanse of the lake.

"Sweat is dripping all over my body," he said, wiping his face off.

"Me too, that's not helping my vision. It's worse around this river."

"I hope you see something soon," Tonas said." I know if they find nothing the other way, we may have a real problem."

"This river bends away as it goes into the lake," revealed Lube. "It was easy to see why Asim took us in the opposite direction."

"There is a small rock formation up ahead, and it seems to stair step across. Cannot tell if it goes all the way or not."

"I am hoping," said Tonas. The ground was soggy underneath their feet. They felt lucky they had traveled this far without sinking. They climbed over another rock to be closer to the lake.

"I feel like I'm melting," gasped Tonas, wiping his brow again. They both were dripping sweat from the heat. They were close to the lake when Lube saw a significant cave opening in the distance on the wall on the other side.

"If these rocks stay close, we can do it." They jumped up on the first one. "I think they may go all the way. The problem will be the distance between them. I will climb to see; maybe you should stay here for now. No point in taking any unnecessary risks. Hopefully, I won't fall." He laughed. Tonas felt a little uncomfortable but gave a nervous laugh along with him.

"I'm sure my feet are sinking," said Tonas, pulling one foot free.

"Stand up on this rock here." Lube helped him. "I'm going up." He jumped to the next rock that was close. Soon, he was almost halfway across the lake. "These are easy," he shouted. "You can do this with ease."

He was close to halfway across now. He continued stepping and climbing. As the distance between the rocks stretched further apart, his jump had to be longer. He still made it with ease. *This could be a long jump for some*, he thought. *Oh well, Asim will figure it out.*

He was on the downward rocks. Still high in the air, these rocks did not stick up as far as the others he had climbed. But they continued leading to the other side; the distance became a little wider on the last few rocks. It was a good jump for him. Looking down, he could see he was four to five lengths above the lake. Making a leap, he could see only three more to go. These last rocks were larger and flattened on the top so he could take a small run before he launched himself. He had to admit these last few rocks would be difficult. Landing on the last rock, he stared at the cave entrance before taking a run and jumping to the solid ground. "I'm here," he shouted, not knowing if Tonas could even hear him or not. He took his time to catch his breath before entering the cave; it was dark. With no torch, he could not see far. Not sure if it was good or bad. *Time to return*, he thought. He returned feeling good, taking his run and jumping, making it all the way back to where Tonas was waiting.

"Could you hear me?" he asked.

"No!" Tonas shook his head. "Only when you were on the top rocks."

"Well, the good news is I made it all the way to the other wall and went inside the cave."

"Good news indeed!" Tonas was smiling. "Although I feel you have more to say."

"The problem is going down the other side, which will be demanding. Hopefully, Asim will figure out a way for everyone to cross. That's if we use this way. Maybe Stone has found a better way."

"When you say 'demanding,'" asked Tonas.

"Let's say it will be difficult for some with the distance between the rocks."

"When you say 'some,' I guess you mean me."

"Well," Lube gulped, trying to think how to be respectful. Tonas laughed, which made Lube laugh, too. He slapped Tonas on the back. "Maybe they found something better." He laughed again. They journeyed back, being as careful as on the way there. Asim was waiting; they could see Stone and Lube had already returned.

"I'm hoping for better news."

"We have some!" Lube said, smiling, which brought a smile to Asim's face. "We have found rocks that go from one side to the other and a cave opening, but it will be difficult. It will require some jumping from rock to rock. Some have a distance between them while none were connected. I know you will think of something to help everyone to the other side."

Asim looked at him, a little puzzled.

"We will see. This is good news. We have a way across the lake!" Asim shouted to everyone. They all cheered!

"It may be difficult for some, so we will see when we arrive there."

"We can do it," shouted Lanee.

"We are ready for anything," slurred Spen, taking a quick sip.

"Well, let's make our way there." Lube led the way, and everyone watched out for the softer ground."

"Especially you, Pooly," shouted Stone. Pooly shook his head, carrying on packing his gear. Walking along the lake was a little harrowing with the softness of the ground. Reaching their destination with no casualties was good. Even Pooly kept safe as they arrived at the rocks where they were to cross.

Lube looked at Asim. "You know climbing down on the other side will be a challenge."

"Let's go to the top so I can see what we will face." Both climbed on the first rock.

Lube headed up to the top, and Asim followed. Both needed to jump and climb. It went fast on the more accessible rocks going up, but looking down the other side; he could see what Lube meant as they both sat on the top, which was large enough to hold them both. Asim had now weighed up the situation, calculating the distance between each rock.

Asim was thinking out loud, "What do you think if we tie ropes to the tops of the rocks?"

"It looks possible," said Lube. "If there are places to tie onto, but do we have enough rope?"

"I'm sure we do! It should help those who cannot jump the distance. It may be the last four rocks that will give us a problem. We will run ropes. We can each take a top to tie off."

"I will station myself on the first, then you on the next, then Zollo and Stone. Let's go back down."

Asim asked Anson how much rope they had.

"We have five."

"That should be enough." He gathered everyone together on the first few rocks. "All right, this is what we will do," Asim said. "Let's tie a rope around anyone who feels uncomfortable having to jump a distance between two rocks."

"Talk to Lanee, and we will be there to help you."

"Stone and Zollo, you will go back to the top to secure a rock. Grab the ropes."

Lanee helped each one to make sure they were tied if they needed to be. The four went back up to the top.

"Jump and tie the rope as you go. Stone, on the last one, Zollo the next. Each of you stays on your rock. Secure the line and help everyone cross."

Toya was first and she had no problem jumping across, not needing a rope. Jubly also made it with no trouble. The dwarfs decided they could not jump the distance across, but they were small enough to where they could slide down the ropes from rock to rock. Senso and Boben also made the jump with no problems. Yuby managed with a little bit of help on the last rock from Stone, who caught him in time to keep him safe. Then came Tonas, Radel, and Spen. Reaching the top where Asim was waiting, Lanee was close behind the three.

He smiled. "Who is first?" He made sure they were all tied together. Tonas went first. "As you step off this rock, I will help you. I'm right behind you. Make sure you have both hands gripped tight on the rope. Use one hand and then the other to move along the line. We will help." Lube came out to meet him on the rope.

"It's easy," said Lube. "One hand after the other."

"It's easy for you to say." Tonas was hanging tight on the rope.

"I'm right here with you," Lube said. He was three-quarters of the way across when Radel started out. Asim was helping her start off; she handled the rope well. Tonas was now starting down toward Zollo, and Radel was at three-quarters of the way over when Spen began. He had a significant grimace on his chubby face as he grabbed the rope, following Asim's instructions. Lanee told him she would be next to him, one hand behind. He had his eyes closed as he went one hand over the other.

"Guess you will need a drink after this," she said.

"I need one now," rasped Spen, "to wash my heart back down from my throat." Lanee laughed as she readied herself to set out on the rope close to him.

"You are doing well, my friend," Asim said.

Tonas was now ready to head toward Stone. Radel was halfway to Zollo when Lube came out to meet Spen.

"I'm slipping," shouted Spen in a tense voice.

"Don't talk like that? Grip harder."

"I'm almost with you," shouted Lanee.

"I can't hold," he shouted, slipping fast.

Lanee grabbed him, but as his hands slipped off the rope, his weight took Lanee down with him. She was holding tight to him, and the line was tied around. Spen was screaming now. Lube, realizing what had happened, kept the rope tight with one arm, stretched, and grabbed Spen's arm. But with so much weight, the rope ripped from his hand, falling. He grabbed the rope attached to Spen and found himself being pulled down with them.

The sheer weight of three on the one rope pulled back Radel and Tonas, starting a chain reaction. The rope attached to Radel snatched her back toward the rock, leaving her slammed against the side of the rock face. Tonas was backstepping and dragged back across the rock top. With quick thinking and a show of tremendous strength, Zollo wrapped his arms around him as they were both pulled back over the rock and the edge, suspended in the air. Zollo gripped the rock hard as Tonas held on to him for dear life! Asim knew he had no time, seeing the blood spurt as Radel hit the rock headfirst. He pulled her over the lip toward them. Asim leaped from the rock, turning almost in midair, diving and grabbing the rope holding all three. The weight was considerable, but with all his strength, his feet locked to the edge, he stopped the line from slipping any further. It was straining every muscle in his body, and his hands felt like they were on fire. Lube found the strength to climb back up the rope.

"Hold on," he shouted to Asim as he climbed to the top. He then, helped with the rope to pull Spen and Lanee back up again. It was tiring; now, they were both on the top. Spen found it hard to catch his breath. Asim rushed to Radel, cutting her free from Tonas and pulling her up. He saw the gash on her head was bleeding freely from where she hit the rock.

"Are you all right?" he asked a still-conscious Radel. "That's a lot of blood."

"That is a good question…" Dazed, she whined, "I ka-keep damaging my head." Lanee came over to help.

Stone had jumped back across now to help Zollo and Tonas back on the rock.

"Well…" Lube wondered what they were going to do now.

"That did not go as it should." Asim was a little discouraged. "We will need to piggyback them."

Asim tied Spen, whose breath was back, to Lube. Radel, bruised on her head, although the bleeding had stopped, Asim tied her to Lanee. Zollo tied Tonas to Stone. Asim helped as they crossed hand over hand. Zollo and Boben were there to help them as they reached the other end.

I should have done this in the first place, he thought. He was right behind Lube and Spen to make sure it did not happen again.

I'm not happy with my first decision, he thought to himself, shaking his head as he was untying and grabbing ropes. Jumping across the rocks and back again, he was feeling a little better now everyone was safe at the mouth of the cave. Lanee and Jubly were attending to Radel's head wound. Everyone else was regaining their strength, ready for the journey to start again.

Asim was now pacing.

Lanee could tell as she went back over to comfort him. "What's going on inside your head?"

"I'm all right. I'm hoping that's the only wrong decision I make. I don't want to have someone killed because of my failure!"

Lanee held his chin.

"It was a good plan! Just one slip, that's all. Everyone is alive and ready to go again."

Asim smiled as he walked over to Spen, grabbing him. "I'm glad you are fine. You had us wondering for a while."

"I'm glad too; thank you." He took a drink, offering the pouch to Asim.

"You know, this time, I will." He took a large gulp as they laughed. Asim was feeling a lot better now as he told everyone to be ready. They were about to leave again.

Chapter 11

THE BANDITS

The cave loomed large in front of them now, dark, extremely warm, and a little damp. Everyone continued to walk along the large passageway leading downward.

"What is that?" asked Lanee as they kept walking. "Does anyone else feel a light breeze?"

"I do," Tonas sniffed. "I believe it could be air, yes, fresh air."

"Let's hope," said Asim. The cave seemed to veer to the right, rounding the bend. In the distance, they could see a small light, although it was still far away. It was giving them hope the cave could end on the side they needed to be.

Fresh air, Asim thought. *This is a good feeling.*

Their movement was now a little quicker as they approached the end of the tunnel. As they reached the cave entrance, it had become smaller. With only enough room for Asim and Lanee to look outside, shading their eyes in the sunlight was painful at first. They could see the large trees in the forest and took a breath of the fresh air. Each of the others crowded behind them for a glimpse of the outside again.

"We have all been in this hot and smelly cave too long," sighed Lanee, breathing deeply.

"It looks like we are about three lengths up, and we are on the side we need to be on," he said with pride. "We need a rope up here." He smiled, tying it to a nearby rock. They all slid down to the ground below.

Spen was jumping up and down as he reached a patch of grass.

"Back on the real ground." He laughed, only stopping to take a quick drink from his pouch.

"Your pouch must be running low," said Stone. "I am sure we are close to Marmalos, the village which has a very nice tavern."

"I remember stopping there once before, but we came in from a different direction. I know it was on the side of the mountain."

"Ha," Spen shouted, "there is a God. First, firm ground and now a tavern." He had the largest smile on his face. "You're sure they have a tavern?" he asked two times.

"Yes," Stone laughed, "if my memory serves me right, they have the largest bar wench I have ever seen."

"She is big?" he asked.

"She is huge. Let's say when she stops, her body keeps going." They both laughed.

"I would love to meet this lady," he said, smiling and rubbing his hands together.

Asim put his arms around them both. "Come on, you two, we still have a forest to go through." They had not realized they had fallen behind while talking.

"Let's keep a watchful eye as we move through the woods," he said. They heard a large squawk coming out of the sky above them.

"It sounds like that giant egit thing," Toya said.

"Yes, like the one we encountered in the caves."

"Well, at least we are moving away from the mountain," said Lanee.

"We never went close to the mountain. The last time we were here, we came from the south. I'm still sure we are heading towards the village."

"The one that wanted to string you up," Lube was mocking Zollo.

"I believe so." Zollo frowned. "But it was a long time ago when I was just a boy. I am a man now."

"Don't jump ahead, big man." Asim was laughing. "It was not long ago."

Stone punched him on the arm. "A man?" he said and smiled.

"I am," replied Zollo, defending his manhood. "Besides, they have probably forgotten all that." He was looking a little uneasily at Lube, who shook his head.

"What's the worst that can happen?" Lube let out a laugh, looking back at Zollo with a smile.

"Oh my," said Lanee. "You must tell me what happened." Toya and Jubly joined them.

"Well," Zollo said with a little bit of embarrassment. "I met a girl, and she was pretty."

"Was she pretty like me?" asked Toya with a jealous tone.

"Leave him alone," asked Lanee. "Go on," she said eagerly.

"Pretty," he repeated. "Well, we went to the stables, and we kissed."

"Did you like it? Was she a good kisser?" Toya cut in again, still in a jealous tone.

"Toya, please be quiet," asked Lanee as she noticed Zollo was becoming embarrassed by her attacks.

"Kissing a little," he started again.

"Is that all?" asked Lanee.

"Well, yes, a button may have come undone on her dress, maybe?"

Toya glared at him.

He continued to tell his story with a smile, "Right before her father and some of the villagers came busting in and caught us together. Her father grabbed me, and they wanted to hang me. If it were not for Lube and Stone breaking it up and pulling me out of there, I'm sure they would have."

"How exciting." Lanee smiled.

"Yes," said Toya, glaring.

"Can't wait for when we are there." Lanee was still smiling.

"Me too." Toya frowned; she didn't smile.

"Maybe we can find people from the village to help us," said Tonas. "It would be better, the more we can have on our side."

"If it's possible," said Asim. "But when we arrive at the Nordak castle, everyone we have will do everything they can to save the children and bring them home. Everyone chose to give their lives for this purpose."

"We are with you," shouted Lanee.

"Don't forget the little people," Anson shouted.

"We are with you, too," Tonas said with a tear in his eye. "I have no way to thank you. You will receive a reward somehow."

"I will settle for returning the children home and coming out alive! And to be sure, Lube, you and Anson go scout ahead. We don't want to run into any dark dwarfs or bandits in the forest. I believe they warned us last time about bandits in this area."

Both Lube and Anson went on ahead as the forest seemed to grow dense; the trees were growing closer together. There were more rocks and bushes around. So far, their trek was uneventful. Asim was wondering why he had not heard from Lube or Anson. Only seeing the odd rabbit and a few birds so far, he was deep in thought.

Lube and Anson continued their trek, looking for any activity ahead.

"We should be in the village soon," he told Anson.

Anson was about to say something when out of what seemed to be nowhere stood a huge man, a giant. Standing up, he must have stood over seven feet tall and weighed between three hundred to four hundred pounds. His arms were the size of people's legs. His long, flowing black hair was stark against his bronzed face, which seemed to shine in the sun, emphasizing his bold and robust features. He was in his thirties. They had never seen a man this size. He had a sword in one hand and a wooden club in the other. He stood there in front of them and stared. Feeling very uncomfortable, they stopped right in front of him.

Anson looked at Lube. "He's like a giant! What should we do?"

"Well," Lube thought for a second, "let's find out what he wants, and if it doesn't sound good, we can run!"

"Who are you, and what do you want?" Lube asked. The large man did not speak and kept staring at them with his sword and club at the ready.

"Is this the time we run?" whispered Anson.

Lube pulled out his sword. "You're not very talkative. What do you want?" he asked again.

Still not speaking, he stared straight at them.

Lube leaned over to Anson, close enough to whisper.

"We still have two choices: we can try to move this man out of the way or we can go back to the first plan and run."

"Let's move back a step and see what happens." As they stepped back, there was a thud as an arrow struck the ground by Lube's foot. They both stopped in their tracks.

"The next one will be in your neck," came a voice from behind them. "Put your sword away and turn yourselves around."

Lube saw a man six feet tall in his early thirties with a rugged, muscular build, longish brown hair, and a mask covering half of what looked like a handsome face. He could tell he was a bold man in a black tunic and pants. His bow was pointed at them.

"I see you have met Duf. He doesn't talk. He's just filled with action." Duf smiled. "Let me introduce Tan," who moved in from the side.

Tan stood about five feet ten inches tall, in his thirties, with sandy blond hair and a muscular physique matching his leader. Tan had made himself known with his bow already.

Next to step out was Wilt, a black man with handsome features standing six feet tall and in his twenties. Aside from short black curly hair, he had a rugged, muscular body to match. His sword was glinting in the sun.

"Who are you two? Before I take your coins."

"I am Lube. This is Anson, and we have no coin. So, just who are you?"

"Why, I am Tyron," he said in a vibrant voice.

Lube thought to himself, *Like we are supposed to know.*

"You are nothing but a bunch of thieves."

"Now, now," said Tyron, "are you trying to put us down? Although I guess we do kind of match that description, a small bit, maybe a little bit. Anyway, surrender your coin."

"I told you we have no coin," said Lube. "We are on a quest. Twenty warriors are behind us and will be here soon, so all four of you need to leave while you can."

"Will the others have coin or gold?" asked Tyron.

"I told you we are on a quest," he said again. "We carry no valuables."

"What is this quest? Is it to steal gold and jewelry?"

"No," replied Lube. He told Tyron about the villagers they joined and how they were trying to rescue their children.

"Noble! I don't think I believe you," Tyron pondered a second. "We will take you back to the others just to see, and we can collect the coin and gold all at once. Do not warn them." Wilt had a sword to Anson's neck.

Tan had now put his bow away but held a sword to Lube's neck, making them walk back through the forest toward where they would meet back up with the others. After a short while, they heard voices; Tyron signaled them to stop. He moved around to have a better look without being seen. Coming into his view was a large group of people walking toward them: women, men, and dwarfs. He moved to a visible area. Asim could see Tyron standing in front of them now. Lube and Anson were held back with swords at their throats, with by far the most enormous man he had ever seen standing at the back, towering above them all.

"What can we do for you?" asked Asim.

Tyron laughed. "Well, you can start by giving me all your coin and gold. I will even accept jewelry."

"We carry no valuables," said Asim.

Tyron signaled for Lube and Anson to step up close, still with the swords at their necks. "I guess these two are with you."

Asim looked and nodded. "Yes, they are."

"Then you won't mind if we kill them. Now, will you change your mind about the valuables?" Said Tyron.

Asim said, "We cannot change our mind on what we don't have. We are on a quest right now."

"I heard!"

"Besides, it would be a poor choice for you," said Asim.

"We need gold! But why would it be a poor choice for us to kill these two?"

Earlier, as they stopped, unseen to anyone, Stone and Toya, who were close to the back, had slithered away from the others when they first sensed the danger. They moved behind, climbing the tall trees on either side of the bandits.

"Well," Asim said, "there are two things: one, you would not find any valuables."

"Number two?" Tyron asked hastily.

"Number two, you have arrows aimed down at your heads."

Tyron looked up, seeing the two warriors in the trees.

"You have me at a disadvantage, it seems. I am impressed. You are a smart man, for I did not see that coming. You must be up early in the morning to do that to me." He looked at Tan and Wilt, who had taken their swords from Lube and Anson's neck.

Asim walked over to Tyron and grabbed his arm; he brought him forward into the bush area.

"Let me propose something to you." He smiled. "We both seem to be smart men." Asim looked him in his eyes.

"I am listening," said Tyron, smiling at his compliment.

"It's known you are not trustworthy, but I also know you bandits have a code you follow about loyalty to each other. I have a feeling! So let me propose this: we are short of warriors. You appear to look like you could handle yourselves, especially the big man. Therefore, if you will join us to the Nordak castle, where we can rescue the children, I would care to say the castle will have more gold than you four could carry."

"Have you seen Duf!"

"We only need the children. Any gold you take is yours."

"You think you can storm a castle?" Tyron asked.

"I did not mention that! But I plan to rescue the children. Your help would be valuable."

"How do you know you can trust us?" asked Tyron. "We don't do our trade for glory, you know."

"I deal in honor," said Asim. "I have to tell you some have died already, and there is no guarantee anyone will come out alive, but if you do, the gold is yours."

"Well, that sounds like a real deal breaker right there," Tyron was talking to himself. "Are you sure they have gold?"

"It is a castle! I have not known one that hasn't."

"Our find is all ours," said Tyron.

"As much as you can carry. We need nothing but the children. Will you talk to your men to see if they would agree?"

"No! They do as I do."

"What would your answer be then?"

"Tell me more about all this gold."

Asim laughed. "I can assure you can have all you want."

Tyron still weighed up in his head the danger versus what's in it for them.

"You only want the children," he said as they walked back to the others.

"Yes," Asim replied.

"Let me think about it," said Tyron. "How would you feel if we joined you?" he asked Lanee, who was standing close.

"I do not think I could trust you," she said.

"I understand your concerns, and you think you're right. You know we only steal money. We don't just kill people! Unless they need it, of course? As strange as that may seem, and I know you don't want to believe it, there is honor amongst us."

Lanee shrugged and walked away.

"How about you, little drunk man?" he said to Spen.

"I agree," Spen said in a scared voice.

"About what?" asked Tyron.

"Yes," said Spen again with a tremble.

"Yes, what?"

"Yes...I do," repeated Spen, taking a swig from his pouch and sweating.

Tyron laughed. "I like you," he said, walking back to Asim. "If you walk about seven hundred lengths that direction"—he pointed east—"you will arrive at the village. We will walk with you as I want to hear more about the gold."

"I will tell you all I know, but you must tell me all about the big man."

Tyron laughed.

"We will not enter the village. I know you understand." They all walked toward the outskirts.

"We will camp on the other side. I will give you my answer in the morning."

"If you're not there?" Asim asked.

"Then you have my answer."

"Fair enough."

Tyron and his men left.

Asim and the others proceeded into the village.

Chapter 12

OLD SCORES TO SETTLE

"We need to find the tavern," exclaimed Spen, who seemed to be in a hurry.

"Why?" asked Lanee, confused.

"I need a drink of ale. I am thirsty."

"Oh, tired of your pouch."

"Sometimes you just need a brewed ale." He smiled.

Lanee smiled back. "I need a bath and a change of clothes."

"I'm sure we all need that." Asim smiled. "We will all meet at the tavern later."

Time passed, and they all gathered in the bar, finding a large table on the side. There was plenty of room; they were welcomed by an enormous serving wench who asked what they wanted to order. Her whole body jiggled when she Leaned over. Stone looked at Spen; they burst out laughing. "Ale for everyone," Asim shouted," and please excuse my friends," looking at Stone and Spen.

The bar itself was not full except for a few gathered together in the front corner who looked like they were villagers. The ale served, and Asim lifted his tankard. "We all need this," he roared. "We will drink, eat, and be merry for tomorrow; we will start again."

"I will toast to that," shouted Spen, who looked as though he had been in the tavern for a while. As he stood up, his ale splashed on him. "More ale," he shouted at the serving wench. The evening was turning into one of merriment as they ate and told stories, laughing off the outlandish trials they had faced already. Lube looked around the tavern; he was feeling someone was watching.

"Drink up, everyone," slurred Spen. "More ale," he shouted, falling back in his chair.

The serving wench made her way over to the table. "You will quieten down," she spoke to Spen, staring into his glazed eyes.

"Keep my tankard full, and I promise I will." He smiled. She walked back to the bar, grabbing a large pitcher of ale. As she returned, she spoke to Lube and Zollo. "Someone on the other side of the bar wants to talk to you," she said. They both were unsure of who she was referring to. He said, "He remembers you."

Lube smiled at her and thanked her. "Why do I know it's you?" Laughing, Zollo punched him.

"Do we have a problem?" asked Asim.

"I believe we may have the same one we had last time."

"The young maiden." Lanee rubbed her hands together. Zollo just nodded.

"Is she here?" asked Toya impatiently, looking around the tavern.

"I thought they would forget," Zollo was hoping.

"Maybe you can talk to them," Asim said. "They may listen."

"I hope we will not fight," said Lanee.

"Oh no! That will cut into our drinking time," slurred Spen.

"Zollo, you and Lube, go see what you can do," said Asim. "If we have upset them today or during our last visit, let me know." Walking over, the two did not recognize anyone sitting at the bar or the tables.

"Did someone want to talk to us?" asked Zollo.

An older man looked up. He was in his late fifties, with a peppered gray hair on his etched-looking face. He was portly but not fat, standing five feet ten inches tall. "Do you remember me?" he asked.

"No," Zollo answered.

"I am Brantil. It was my daughter you were with your last time here. I will never forget your face," he said. "Do you remember Langel?"

"Yes, I remember your daughter. I tried to explain last time, but no one would let me! I was trying to say I was sorry and nothing happened between us. But tempers were too hot that night. I was telling you the truth."

"I understand that now," said Brantil. "I needed to let you know I have forgiven the past as I talked to my daughter, and she told me the truth. She has since died." A tear slowly rolled down his rugged cheek. Taking his sleeve, he wiped it away. "I needed to warn you; my son Baylin is hard-headed and not forgiving.

"He swears you sent back an army to kill us all. I tried to tell him you were not a person in the king's army. He swore he would kill you if he ever saw you again! The army came, killed Langel and some of our friends, wounded Baylin, and took my grandchild and a lot of other young children, leaving our village devastated."

"I am sorry for your daughter, Langel. I had nothing to do with an army, I swear. That is why we are here now. My friends"—he pointed to the table where the others were sitting—"they are with villagers from Tress who also had their children stolen."

"Tell me," Lube asked, "the children, were they all boys?"

"Why yes!" said Brantil. "They were five to ten years old. Nobody knew what to do when they came, taking us by surprise."

"So you say this same army took children from another village? We had eighteen from here, including my grandchild, Leham."

"There were thirty to forty of the king's army on horseback with an old cart driven by a strange-looking man."

"We sent a search party with our healthy people still left. But dragons attacked, and only seven returned alive. The soldiers were long gone. We figured they had a way around the dragon lairs or crossed the river somehow. We figured they came out of the north; people in the south are peaceful."

"My son Baylin was wounded in the fight and could not go. I was thankful, not wanting to lose him."

Zollo told him, "We believe it was the Nordaks from their castle in the far north who did this."

Lube added, "They are in the mountains of Kailash."

The door to the tavern opened. It was Baylin, a large man, six feet tall, in his thirties. He was a good-looking man with broad shoulders, a muscular frame, and long brown hair. His friend was smaller, at five feet eight inches, also in his thirties. He was solidly built with rugged features, muscular arms, and shorter black hair.

The tavern went quiet. Everyone watched the two who entered. Baylin saw Zollo at the bar talking to the locals; hate consumed him. He rushed toward Zollo, grabbing his sword from his side, he yelled, "You serpent! You killed my sister and stole my son." He spewed out the words as sweat gathered on his brow.

"No," shouted Zollo, "you have it wrong."

In his anger, Baylin was not listening, shouting, "We will settle the score with my sister and my son. I vowed to kill you." His sword flexed in his hand as he lifted it high in the air.

Zollo had made his mind up to stand his ground, not moving, still trying to explain, not trying to arm himself.

Baylin's arm twitched as the blade came down toward Zollo's head. The swift rushing sound of the blade stopped with a metal clunk. The flashing blade stopped in midair against another.

At the end of the other blade was Asim, having moved closer to see what was happening with Zollo.

"Don't!" Asim said as Baylin tried to swing again. The sword blade was stopped once again by his blade.

"I will kill him, and I will kill you too," he shouted and glared at Asim. His sword was still held steady against Baylin's, and he used his other hand to grab Baylin's shirt, twisting the material tight around his neck and pulling him closer. He pushed him toward the door. Baylin's friend grabbed for his sword in reaction to his friend, but Stone stepped in and punched him; the man dropped to the ground, holding his nose as blood dripped freely. Back at the door, Asim lifted his right foot, kicking Baylin. He tumbled over from the force, sprawled out on the ground. Baylin tried standing back on his feet, grabbing the sword next to him, and turning toward Asim, who was still standing in the doorway.

"I would not do that if I were you."

There was a clashing of steel as swords struck together. Baylin pushed forward toward Asim, who drove him back. They were both outside the tavern now. Baylin's friend was standing up as Stone forced him out of the tavern. The front of his shirt was now covered with the blood from his nose.

"Don't step up again," said Stone. The man looked at him, then looked away to where his friend was fighting and never removed his sword.

The clash of steel was loud in the night air. It stopped, with Asim dispatching two hard blows to Baylin's sword, which had him down on his knees. His sword was at Baylin's throat. Two of the villagers had drawn their swords and stood by the doorway. Lanee sensed danger and punched one in the mouth, which dropped him to the ground. As blood poured from his lip, the other man dropped his sword and stepped back.

Brantil had now reached the door and shouted, "Stop, all of you." He looked at Baylin. "Go ahead," he yelled. "Die by the sword, and I shall lose another child. You can stay on the ground until you not only hear the truth but understand the truth." He turned to Asim. "Please keep your sword on my son's neck," Brantil asked. "He needs to listen now."

He asked Zollo to speak again. "This is the truth…" Zollo repeated what he told Brantil to the now-captive Baylin.

"Now you have heard," shouted Brantil. "If you still want to kill this man telling the truth, which I already knew and you never wanted to listen to, I will ask this warrior to use his sword on your neck. You would be no better than the person who killed your sister."

"I don't want to hurt you," Asim said to Baylin, "but I will not have you raise a sword in anger against one of my friends." He took his sword away.

Baylin stood up still a little reluctantly as he grabbed back his sword, and brushed the dust off himself, and put it away. Asim put his sword away and slapped Baylin hard on the back, almost knocking him forward.

"You put up a good fight for a village man." He laughed.

Baylin was looking at him. "Are you a bandit?"

Asim laughed. "No, I am more of a hunter." They walked back to the tavern. Spen was smiling now it was over; everyone could return to drinking.

"More ale," he shouted.

"I told you to be quiet," said the serving wench, walking up to him.

"My tankard is out." He pinched her on the bottom as she turned away. She turned and slapped him hard on the side of his face, making him fall straight back in his chair. Everyone in the tavern could not hold back their laughter. Spen scrambled up red-faced as she returned to pour his drink before starting to walk away. Turning, she pinched Spen on the cheek and gave him a wink, which brought out another outburst of laughter from everyone. "I think she likes me!" he said with an embarrassed grin.

After a couple of ales and understanding more about the quest, Baylin talked to Zollo and broke down, telling him he was sorry about all the resentment he had held for him. "It was too much, losing a sister and a son in one night. I had to blame someone."

"I am sorry for your loss too," Zollo empathized with him.

Baylin turned to Asim. "Thank you for not killing me. Your skills are amazing."

"Well," he smiled, "if you want to thank me, give this some thought. Come with us. Don't answer now. We leave just after sunrise. If you do, be there in your village square and be ready. If you want to bring your friend, that would be fine."

"Exim," said Baylin, "Is his name."

"I will tell you as I have told everyone: it could be none of us will come back alive. It will not be easy by any means."

"That sounds fair," said Baylin.

The drinking and merriment went on a while longer that night.

The sun came up like a big ball of fire, chasing the dark sky on its way, flashing light rays through the wispy clouds, one catching Asim as he woke. He grimaced when he realized it was morning. He stretched as he came to his feet.

He thought it was time for an early start today. I would need to wash my body. And an extensive breakfast also came to mind.

Later, after eating, they were ready to leave. Spen was running on his way to the tavern. He beat hard on the door until the tavern owner awoke.

"I must fill this pouch for the trip," he explained. "It has a refill, but I don't want to use it yet."

The tavern owner scratched his head, thinking Spen was crazy. He did not understand a word of what he just said. He opened the door, and he filled the pouch for him.

"You are a good man." Spen was happy.

"An exhausted one." He ushered him out the door. Spen made his way back to the others with a broad smile on his face. He caught up with them as they were leaving.

In the square stood Baylin and Exim. "For my son. The chance I never had. We will give you our lives for the quest," said Baylin.

"Welcome," said Asim.

A voice was shouting from a distance behind them as they moved out. "Wait."

Looking back, he could see it was Brantil.

"I am going too," he said, "for my son and my grandson."

"Are you sure?" asked Asim. "No guarantees on this journey. We all could die."

"I may be your oldest, but don't let a few gray hairs fool you. Fighting, I will hold my own! I want my family back. They are my life."

"Can't argue with that. You are welcome to join us." They all moved out through the forest. Arriving at a clearing in the trees, Asim could see Tyron, Wilt, Tan, and Duf waiting for him. Baylin, seeing them, pulled out his sword.

"Bandits!" he shouted. Exim drew his sword, too. Tyron and Asim laughed.

"I should have told you that Tyron and his gang will also join us."

"Bandits?" Baylin asked.

"Yes." They put their swords away.

"Maybe if you remove the mask, you would scare no one," jested Asim.

Tyron laughed. "Just for you." He relinquished the mask.

"Oh my, I should tell you to put it back on, but I am trying to be good today."

"Ha-ha." Tyron was laughing and smacked him on the back. "Well, we are a strange bunch." He laughed. "How are you today, my little drunk man?" he asked, looking at Spen.

Chapter 13

EXPANDING FORCES

et's go," Asim shouted. The frolicking from the night before had caused a slow start as they trekked forward. Soon, they picked up the pace and were far away from the village, moving through the vast forest. Asim asked Tyron, who had walked up next to him, "How safe is this forest to travel?"

"We rarely head north," Tyron answered. "We should be good for a while if we stay clear of the dragons and their lairs. I don't think you will see bandits." He laughed. "We are here! Thinking that was funny, he laughed to himself. "I don't know of anyone else in this area. What do you know about how safe we are?" shouting to Wilt, who was a little way back, talking to Lube.

"Only old man Rabin and his men," Wilt replied when he moved close to them. "But he works more to the east towards the village of Pallea. We know him well, so he wouldn't give us any trouble, anyway. Maybe a cockatrice or two as we head to the mountains, although they seem to stay west. Oh yes, dragons. And I heard something about dark dwarfs hunting to the north. Don't know if it's true or not."

"Are they in this area, too?" asked Asim, looking over at Anson, who shrugged his shoulders.

"Those rats seem to be everywhere. We ran into them in the forest to the west of here."

"That sounds like Swank and his band of misfits," said Wilt. "I have heard a lot about him, none of it good, a cutthroat."

"Yes," said Anson, "that's Swank."

"Well, I hope we have good fortune on this trek to the mountain."

"We must cross the river first," said Tyron.

"The river!" sighed Lanee, turning her nose up with a cringe.

"Yes." He smiled. "And it's a large one. I will find us a good place to cross. You don't like rivers at a guess?"

"Not too much anymore," she said as they continued to walk around the close-knit trees, making this forest very dense at this point.

"Does it stay this way?" she asked.

"At times, but the trees will thin out. It's the quickest way to the mountains," Tyron replied.

Spen was now a little way behind the rest due to stopping to sip from his pouch. He was trying to talk to Duf, who had stayed back to protect them from the rear. Duf said nothing when Spen asked him anything. He looked and nodded, not a word.

"Does he ever speak?" Spen shouted to Tyron.

"I have never heard him, but keep trying little drunk man," yelled Tyron. "You never know. Just don't make him mad."

"Not a problem there," he shouted back, grabbing the pouch to take another early morning sip. Close in the distance, they could hear loud screeches followed by some loud squawking. Hearing that, Asim asked if that was why they were staying away from the mountains, looking into the distance where the noises were coming.

"That's close to the dragon's lairs," Tyron said. "And yes! I am trying to keep us away until we have no choice." Then, for a few seconds, he saw Tyron lost in thought, and then he remembered, "The north towards where we are heading, there was the talk of a wizard? Or maybe a warlock? Yes, I believe it was a warlock who inhabits somewhere in those Kailash mountains."

"Yes," said Stone, "I figured I heard right."

"Oh," said Lanee, "but maybe he is something like Apora, the white witch."

Tyron laughed. "Apora, I have met her. She is a beautiful lady. Just a slight problem with the pouch." He laughed, but then his tone changed. "No! He is one evil man. So the talk goes. I have never met him myself. I'm not sure I want to meet him."

"Another adventure on our journey, maybe?" She laughed.

Asim cut in, "One we don't want or need! Tyron, if you would, send two of your men with Lube and Stone to check on what's ahead of us."

"Wilt and Tan," Tyron called them, "to go up ahead and scout."

The four left together.

"You don't have to ask me. They know you are leading us now."

"I will remember that."

"Duf, continue to stay to the back and keep a watchful eye."

Duf just looked and smiled. "Oh, and take the little drunk man with you. I like him." Tyron was laughing.

Tonas came to Asim as they were walking. "Can we talk in private?"

"Yes," he said, pulling him aside from the others. "What is wrong?"

"I don't know how to say it..."

"Just say it straight out."

"Are you sure we can trust Tyron? They are robbers."

"True. But robbers have an honor amongst their people, and I am a good judge of individuals. I have a feeling about him that he will be loyal. Which means he will be a great asset to us on this journey. I would not have asked him otherwise, so let me worry about Tyron for now."

"Fair enough," said Tonas, "I felt a little uneasy. I had to tell you."

"It was right that you did."

As they continued their journey, time passed, and Asim and Tyron talked a lot as they led them through the forest. One thing Tyron was eager to hear about was the terrifying exploits they had in the last mountain.

"You know," Tyron said, "we will be going in blind when we enter this mountain you had spoken of. We have no idea what to expect." He grinned. "Maybe your luck will change, or should I say *ours*?" He laughed.

"I am hoping it will help us be able to spy on the Nordak castle," Asim replied. "We don't know what to expect or what we will see when we arrive there. I hope we will gain some advantage."

"We will need some, for sure," said Tyron. "It will not be easy to overpower the king's guards with these few men."

Stone, Lube, Wilt, and Tan were all relaxing, sitting close by the river, having nothing to report on a slow and quiet day. As Asim arrived, Stone stepped forward. "Nothing going on around them, only the odd serpent in the distance."

"Nothing in the air or on the ground. That's good news."

"We don't want to cross here," Tyron said. "It's too wide, and the water is too swift. We will find a better place east of here. It will not be far."

Going a little further downstream, they continued staying close to the riverbank.

"You know, if we could, it would be better to cross before nightfall so we can camp on the other side," Asim asked. "Oh! And is there a chance we could find anything strange living in this river?"

"I believe there could be a few strange things. That's why I am looking for a safer part of the river where the banks are closer together. It will be a good place for this large amount of people to cross."

"Well, so far, we have had no luck at all with the rivers!"

"That could change. Look, just up ahead. I see a better place to cross at the river bend. Both sides seem closer." Asim smiled as he stood on the bank gazing across to the other side.

"I want all the weak swimmers roped up," Asim shouted, "just as we did last time. While you are tying everyone, I will try it out first so we know what to expect."

He walked into the water, followed by Tyron and Lanee; they had not gone too far before the bottom disappeared under their feet, and they were swimming toward the other bank.

"It seems the water flows fast and deep here," she exclaimed, feeling the pull of the water.

"True," shouted Tyron as they approached the middle of the river.

The first thing they noticed was the current was swirling around the center.

"We must be careful here. It seems it's a little intense. We should keep a watch for an undertow." Later, they reached the opposite bank.

"Tyron, you and Lanee stay on this bank. I will go back and help to organize them crossing."

"Just to let you know," Tyron said, "my men can swim."

Swimming back, it was not too long before Asim reached the bank; he could see Radel, Senso, Spen, Yuby, and Brantil tied to each other. On a different rope, the dwarfs were tied together.

"Ah, my non-swimmers."

"Not us! We feel it will be better," said Anson. "It's a long way to the other bank."

"I will need everyone's help to cross. Stone, Lube, Tan, Wilt, and Duf, you need to help the non-swimmers. Watch for the current in the middle here!

"Baylin, Exim, and Zollo help with the dwarfs. You can keep a heads up when we cross. It will be tougher halfway. Boben, Jubly, and Toya stay on this back rope. Let's make this swim across the river as swift and as comfortable as we can." He followed everyone out into the water.

Stone was out in front, keeping the rope tight for Brantil and the others, while Zollo was out in front, holding the rope close with the dwarfs in tow. Jubly, Toya, and Boben were all holding the line steady at the rear. The rest of the swimmers filled in between, trying to keep everyone on the ropes afloat.

"You are all doing well," shouted Asim. "Keep pushing with your feet, just like you are running." They were close to the middle of the river now.

"I think something just swam against my legs," yelled Dooly. "It was big!"

"Keep moving," Asim shouted; he waved for Tyron and Lanee to swim to them. "We will be there soon."

"I felt it too," shouted Anson.

"Me too," shouted Benson, tied next to him. "There is something in here?"

Spen froze as something wrapped around his legs.

"Help!" he shouted with a calm voice. Then he realized no one had heard him as he was being pulled under the water and dragged forward by a giant eel, still tied to the others as the eel yanked all of them forward. "*Help!*" he shouted loud this time.

Tan was first to react, diving under the water with his dagger to cut the rope between Spen and Radel to stop everyone from being hauled under with him.

Tyron responded fast, seeing Spen had not emerged. Diving into the water, he followed the direction where Spen went under, following the river flow.

Asim, Lanee, and Stone followed but they could not see where Spen went. They were following Tyron, hoping he knew, swimming in the same direction as the water flow. Now, all four were swimming to help Spen.

Wilt, Lube, and Zollo were quick to help Lube keep Radel, Senso, Yuby, and Brantil afloat together on the rope again. Baylin and Exim helped those in the river to travel past the undertow as they continued to the opposite bank, making sure they all made dry land. Each of the swimmers had the difficult job of keeping everyone moving and their heads above the water.

Spen was dragged under but found himself back on top again as he gasped for air before the eel pulled him back under the water. The one thing in Spen's favor was his weight, which was slowing the eel down, giving Tyron a chance of catching him and jerking his head up for air. He dove under again as he saw Spen's body twisted around by the eel. He could tell he was gaining on them and was hoping he could grab him. Swimming closer now, he reached out and grasped Spen's shirt, pulling hard. He was able to catch an arm. The eel reeled back, feeling something slowing its progress. Twisting again, it tried to swim away.

Tyron reached for his dagger, snatching it from his belt and plunging it deep into the skin of the eel, causing it to recoil with the penetration of his blade, almost losing his grip on Spen.

Now Asim had arrived, dagger in hand. He stretched forward, stabbing the eel. The continual stabbing caused the eel to loosen its grip on Spen, allowing him to break free. Now Tyron had a much better hold of him as he pulled him to the top of the water. Spen was convulsing as he was choking on the air and water he swallowed. Tyron held him tighter to control his body and help him breathe.

Asim continued his stabbing into the eel's body. Then, in a flash, suddenly, the eel's giant head aimed straight for him. Seeing the large razor-like teeth descending at a rapid pace, Asim swiftly reached out with his hand, stopping its attack and digging his fingers deep into the skin of the eel's neck, pushing with enough strength to make it miss his head. He still stabbed with his dagger, continuing to dodge those teeth, being resilient in keeping the eel at bay. As Lanee and Stone reached him, both helped to strike and penetrate deep into the eel's body. A large pool of blood filled the surrounding water. The eel tried twisting many times, trying to swing its body around to move them. With his continual grip on its neck, Asim could feel its giant head dropping as its life was draining. The eyes that had stared so fiercely were now pale. He had Lanee and Stone stop as he let go of the eel's neck. The dead body floated away on top of the water.

Feeling relieved but sticky with the blood in the water, Asim hoped by the time they reached the bank, the blood on them would wash off. They all swam together as they watched Tyron pull Spen's sluggish body up on the bank. It seemed everyone had made it across the river.

Toya and Jubly were rushing to help with Spen. Plenty of the others were also ready to help. Swimming in, the three of them arrived at the riverbank. Walking up, Asim could see everyone crowding around.

Tyron was busy pushing on Spen's chest and stomach; Jubly came and turned him over, laying his belly on Tyron's legs, and proceeded to slap his back. Tyron lifted his legs up, making it more efficient; on the third hard slap, Spen coughed. A stream of water spewed from his mouth.

"That's it," she encouraged him. "Spit up all that water." Then they pulled him to his feet so he could stand. Spen was still wheezing, coughing, and choking. Tyron struck him with a flat hand in the stomach, causing him to bend and spew out more water with a mixture of digested food. He straightened him back up again. Now, looking closer to death than life, he was pale. His bloodshot eyes seemed to glow.

"Stop," in a very raspy voice. "Don't hit me again. I surrender," Spen blurted out.

Tyron laughed. "Happy to have you back, my little drunk man," he said, slapping him hard on the back. Spen winced with the pain.

"All that water?" said Toya. "You drank all that water!" She smiled at Spen.

"If it had been mead, I would have been fine," he croaked, sneezed and coughed again.

"Spen, you are a fool, but I'm so glad you are all right," she said. Everyone was happy and laughing to see Spen doing well again.

Asim came across Wilt walking up the bank. "Did everyone make it all right?"

"I believe so," he said. "Spen is still alive."

Tyron was walking over to them now. "Yes, and he's even sober." He laughed.

"Now that's a first." They all laughed with him.

Everyone had settled, sitting or lying out on the bank. Most were talking. A few were pale and confused at what had happened. Most were ready to rest.

"We seemed to have found another nightmare in the river!" Asim gave a wry smile.

"Well done saving Spen from the beast," he said, grabbing Tyron's shoulder. "We were lucky today. We lost no one! No more rivers in our future, I hope?"

"No!" said Tyron. "Next stop will be the mountain."

"I hate to tell all these people they need to stand up again, but we need to find cover before we bed down for the night."

"I see what you mean with luck in the rivers." Tyron looked at him. "This journey could be exciting."

Asim went over to visit Spen with Lanee and Stone. He was hunched down, still very far from his old self.

"Spen, my old friend, you took on a little water today."

"Too much," he rattled out. His voice was still raspy.

Looking Spen over, Asim noticed one thing. "After everything you went through in the water, you never lost your pouch."

"Have you tried taking a sip?" Lanee asked. "It could do you some good."

"I'm not sure I can take a drink right now."

"I know now you must be sick." Asim smiled.

"Well, maybe I will try just a small sip."

They all laughed. "Now that's the Spen we know."

Asim said to everyone, "I know you are all exhausted. We still need to move to the forest before we camp."

Chapter 14

MEETING A DRAGON

As they bedded down for the night, most were tired. Some slept well, while others had trouble sleeping. It had been a stressful day for some! Asim had left guards for the night. Everything was quiet in the light of the now-waning moon.

Starting out in the early morning, most appeared to wake fresh and ready to start this day, knowing they would head to the mountains. The morning sky was darker than usual, a little overcast, looking as if the rain could be on its way again. Everyone was quietly packing up to be ready to move out.

Tonas was on his way over to Asim, who was standing looking out over the camp and collecting his thoughts for the day ahead.

"We need to talk again," he said. Asim took him to the side, away from the others.

"What is it?" Asim asked.

"I need to take my words back, everything I said about Tyron. He put his life in danger to save Spen. It had bothered me all night. I said he was a robber and doubted he could be trusted. I wanted you to know my feelings have changed."

"That took a lot for you to admit."

"I feel better about this." Tonas smiled.

"I hope you have a sense of peace now, which I hope is the same for everyone else."

The forest on this side of the river appeared less dense than the other. They found more rocks and large bushes growing. It seemed to be a sign they were close to the mountains.

Asim sent Stone and Wilt ahead to scout.

"We all need to keep alert," said Asim.

Having heard some early morning rumbles and strange noises in the distance, they figured they were coming from the mountains as they continued their trek. The sounds were louder as the mountains came into view.

The mountain itself looked disjointed, part of it incredibly long, jutting out from the base toward them, heading across a distance they could not see, only to return toward them again.

"Dragon lairs," Tyron enlightened Asim. "We don't want to enter on this wall."

"Where would be better?"

"It will be better to go around. It will take longer, but it's a safer journey. I dislike the sounds I hear. Something large is making a lot of noise up there."

"We can cut back through the forest," said a still-optimistic Asim. "There is no shelter close to the mountain, so at least we will have shade from the trees."

They continued their trek. It was late morning. When they reached the thicker trees of the forest, the sun had burnt through the early morning clouds. Shining through the branches, sunbeams seemed to bounce off the leaves to make strange circular shadows on the ground.

Then, a sudden darkness took over the sky, and then there was an almost deafening roar from above. The noise had them covering their ears. It seemed over in a moment; the sound stopped, and the sun was shining.

"What was that?" asked Yuby.

"I believe we have encountered our first dragon of the day," said Tyron.

"Dragon!" he cried out." I had heard of them, but I was not sure it was all true!"

"Oh, it's true," said Wilt. He and Stone had joined back with them again. "What we hope is that it was on its way back to its lair, and it's not still hungry."

"Maybe we should send our scouts out again," said Asim.

Lanee and Zollo went to find out what they could see around the mountain base.

The rest of them continued to trek deeper into the forest before they worked their way across and in front of the mountain, scrambling over a few rocks, which left them vulnerable to any serpent flying overhead. Now, looking back, Asim could see two dragons in the distance. This time, he had an unobstructed view as they were heading toward them.

"To the thick trees," shouted Asim. "Fast!" They saw one giant dragon followed by a smaller one heading their way. Everyone was scrambling for the trees, diving, running, and crawling for cover. The first dragon spewed a fire, reigning down, scorching the leaves and branches of the trees close around them. As Wooly's jacket caught on fire, Anson and Benson rolled him on the ground, smothering the flames.

"That was too close," shouted Asim. Looking at Wooly, he asked, "How are you doing?"

"I'm hot, but all right," he said, smiling.

"Let's be ready if they circle again. Use the cover of the trees as best you can. Bows out. Let's show these things; we're not happy to see them either!" Asim was slipping the bow off his back.

The giant dragon did not circle, but the smaller one did, heading back toward them, flying low over the trees where they were hiding.

"Shoot," Asim shouted. A flurry of arrows headed skyward toward the smaller dragon. Some missed, and some just deflected off its scales. But Asim's arrow hit the dragon just above its chest and into a little soft spot in its neck. The dragon screeched a sharp cry, different this time; its wings stopped flapping as it seemed to drop in pain. It was desperately trying to fly back up but could only ascend a short distance. As its wings stopped, again it fell. The larger dragon appeared from nowhere. It swooped down underneath the small one, who landed on its back as they flew off together toward the mountain.

Lanee and Zollo had hurried back. "That was close!" she gasped. "There was no time to warn you." There was a cheer as everyone seemed happy; they felt they had killed a dragon, everyone except for Jubly.

Asim saw a tear roll down her cheek. "What's wrong?" he asked.

"I don't know, my heart hurts. It feels like a mother's pain in losing a child."

"I'm not sure what this could be," Asim said quietly. "Are you going to be all right?" He put his arm around her as she cried on his chest. He beckoned Lanee over to them.

"I don't know what is happening to Jubly."

Lanee took over, holding her as she talked to her, soon joined by Radel and Toya.

Asim moved away. "Not sure about what had happened."

"We need to go now. The danger seems to have gone. We need to continue."

"Is everything all right?" he asked them.

"I think so. She has compassion for the dragon! I have not seen her this way, only when we lost Pantra. But she is ready."

"Good," he said, thinking how strange that was. "Let's go." They all moved forward through the forest again.

"What do you think?" Asim asked Tyron. "Could it be safe to cut back now, or should we go on a little further?"

"It should be safe now."

The giant and the smaller dragons were back on the mountain, although a more massive dragon was flying above them on the mountaintop.

"We will head back towards the mountain to see if we can find an entrance along the wall. These trees will give us cover for a while, so we're not too visible from the air."

Making sure the surrounding sky was clear, they continued moving closer to the mountain. The forest itself seemed to run out of trees. There was an actual vast undeveloped area about fifty lengths before they could be back into the trees again. There were a lot of jagged rocks, most of them small. A few bushes and brush had grown higher than most.

"What is this undeveloped area?" he asked.

"I am sure at one time there used to be a small river that flowed through here," said Tyron. "It will extend all the way down. I think we should be good to cross here."

"We have seen a lot of dragons today, but it won't leave us vulnerable for too long!"

"Maybe we should all run then." Tyron smiled.

"I think that could be a problem with some of our people."

"We can keep going, but it would take us away from the mountains and checking on the castle."

"All right then. Everyone, tighten up all your weapons to your body. Make sure you can move as fast as you can. We need to run across this area to the cover of the trees on the other side. We may have no problem. But remember, if you see anything above you, don't stop. Head for the shelter of the trees. We will do our best to scare off anything with bows this end."

The sun was shining brightly on the mountaintop, making it difficult to see anything in that direction.

Stone, Lube, Wilt, Zollo, and Lanee were ready to cross with some slower-moving people. Duf, Tan, Toya, and Boben would back them up in case of attack.

"Tyron, we will stay back, too, in case of trouble."

"Try to run together if you can," he shouted. "Don't worry if you fall back a little. Just make it to the trees!"

Spen, Brantil, Tonas, and the dwarfs were the first to leave. Everyone was running as if their life depended on it, and for a good reason, they thought it might be. They were over halfway there now.

Shading his hand over his eyes, Tyron was looking into the sun. "Not seeing any dragon activity."

"I believe it could be time for us to leave then," Asim said, looking at Tyron. They both were unaware of the giant dragon from the mountain flying in toward them; the sun had blocked their vision. Without warning, the surrounding air became heated as a now whipping wind blew hard. They saw the flames and smoke close by as the bushes and brush were burning.

"Don't stop! Whatever you do, don't stop!" He was screaming at them now. Asim and Tyron had only traveled one-quarter of the distance when he looked at Tyron.

"We must go back. We won't make it."

"I'm with you," Tyron shouted, who was already sweating profusely.

There was a loud scream. Asim spun to see Jubly, having tripped over a rock, lying on the ground, clasping her ankle, unable to scramble to her feet. She was close to halfway to the other side as the heavy, whipping wind rushed at them. Hearing a loud thud, they looked to see the giant dragon had landed close to them.

They both looked at the scorched patch, then back at Jubly, then back at each other again. Asim was wiping the sweat from his brow. He could see the others had now made it to the other side. They, too, turned to see what had happened, seeing Jubly sprawled out and clasping her ankle as little flames danced across the ground close to her. Smoke was billowing out of the Dragon's large nostrils.

Asim could see the bright yellow hazed eyes of the dragon staring with vexation from its enormous head. Its elongated teeth stuck out from its broad but tapered mouth. They were thick and pointed, only slightly smaller than the giant talons that now dug into the barren ground.

It was a fearsome, monstrous sight. The sun bounced off its silvery scales, giving it a somewhat majestic look, but they knew it was far from that!

"Run, run," he shouted at Jubly, sweating and frustrated, knowing she couldn't. She was trying to crawl, dragging her leg, not putting any weight on her ankle.

He could see Lanee was about to run back. "Stop," he yelled, raising his arms. She did as he asked. Each of the warriors on the other side had taken their bows to defend her.

Asim looked at Tyron. "I must go." He took off running toward Jubly. He thought for a second the dragon was breathing hard, but then he realized Tyron was running right along with him. "You know, we could end up as ashes!" Tyron shouted, almost breathless.

"We must try," he shouted. "Besides, who wants to live forever." He laughed.

Must be nerves, Tyron thought. *Nobody laughs in this situation.* They both dived down next to Jubly.

"Are you two mad?" she shouted at them.

"That's not exactly the response we were looking for," said Tyron as they wrapped their arms around her. A flurry of arrows flew at the beast from the warriors on the other side; none could penetrate its large scales. The dragon, turning its head in their direction, spewed out a flame, which had everyone diving behind the trees. The fire hit the brush and shrubs around, causing several fires close to them.

The dragon turned its attention back to the three of them, who had only moved a few steps as they scrambled to lift Jubly from the ground. Its large eyes continued staring at them.

Asim could see through the dying flames some of the others were burnt from the fire and were receiving attention. He looked back at the dragon's eyes, both still fixed on them. It was not moving, although he could hear it sucking in the air.

Here goes, he thought. *It's ready to burn us to a crisp.*

They were almost dragging Jubly, being careful of her ankle and trying to hurry as the dragon was still watching. Its eyes seemed to follow every move they made.

As they made it across, the trees loomed large in front of them. Lanee, Stone, Zollo, and Radel came to help grab all three, pulling them behind the trees.

Every single one of them was staring, amazed the three of them made it past the dragon.

"Pinch me," said Tyron. "I need to know if—ouch!" he shouted. "You pinch hard."

"You told me to do it," Asim said, laughing, and he was unsure why.

"Well, I know, but it hurt!" He had to laugh, too.

"How in the stars were you three not burnt up?" asked Lanee, looking more in disbelief.

"I don't know how to explain it," he said. "It looked at us and let us pass."

"I think I felt something with the dragon," Jubly said.

"You probably felt pain in your ankle," said Tyron, still laughing and not knowing why.

Asim looked at Tyron, and then they both looked at Jubly.

"Are you all right?" he asked as the giant dragon took off.

"How is your ankle?"

"It hurts a lot."

"I will put a splint on her ankle," said Lanee. "I sent Radel for wood."

"Are you sure it wasn't the pain you felt?" Asim asked her.

"This was different. I had never felt it before. It was as if it was giving us a warning yet asking for help."

"I think the pain went to your head." Tyron was smiling at her.

"Well, I feel all three of you were fortunate," said Lanee as she wrapped the wood around Jubly's ankle. The dragon had looped back around again as it flew over the top of them. Turning fast, it spewed a line of fire well to the side of them before flying toward the mountain, leaving in its wake more burning bushes and grass as the flame hit the tree bark, lighting it up like litmus paper.

"What was that?" Not sure of what just happened.

"I think it was a warning," said Tyron, looking through the trees at the devastation.

Asim looked around at everyone. Some chose no bandage; he could see the red burn marks left from the first flames. "I hope everyone is all right?"

"You know he could have burnt us all up if he wanted to," said Jubly.

"Well, I'm sure glad he was having a good day," slurred Spen while sipping from his pouch. Toya was wrapping a rag around his burnt arm.

"I think everyone is fine," said Tan, rubbing the redness on his arm.

"We need to go again. I want to be on the front side of this mountain before nightfall. I am sure the dragon went back to its lair."

Asim was surprised at the speed with which they were ready to move out through the forest. Duf carried Jubly, so they lost no time in reaching the mountain before nightfall. They made camp on the edge of the forest, a short distance from the wall base.

"Well, we're here," said an enthusiastic Tyron. "And no more attacks! I feel better now. How about you?" He looked at Asim. They both had to smile over the craziness of the day.

"It will soon be nightfall. I want no fire, just rest, and we will have a short distance to enter the mountain in the morning, bright and early."

Chapter 15

LET'S VISIT THE DRAGON'S LAIR

It was almost dark now; they were all in the camp. Jubly hobbled over to where Asim was standing.

"I need to go to the dragon's lair," she told him. "Their baby's hurt and dying."

"Ha—" He was about to laugh, then he realized Jubly was serious. "We have no time for that. It would be foolish! We need to go to the Nordak castle. You know the dragons will kill you!"

"I must go!"

"What about your ankle?"

"I will hold no one up; I will go by myself."

"Let me go with you," said Tyron, who was close by and overheard what they were saying.

"This is a little unexpected," Asim said. "So let me understand this: because we were not burnt up today, you want to follow the dragon back to the mountain so you can be burnt up there?"

"That was not what I had in mind. Although it sounds like it could happen," said Tyron.

Shaking his head, Asim called Stone over to them. "I will leave you in charge. Tyron, Jubly, and I will go to find the dragon's lair."

"You are going with us?" she said, surprised.

"I can't let you two go off like that."

"Have you three been at Spen's pouch?" asked Stone. "You will go to look for the dragon?"

"Well, when you put it like that, it does seem a little strange," said Tyron. "But in short, the answer is yes!"

"If we are not back at first light," Asim grabbed his arm, "I want you to gather everyone together. You must find an entrance into the mountain and work your way towards the castle. Observe and use what I have taught you, and keep the quest as you must rescue the children and bring them home if I do not return!" Stone pondered on the question. "I have taught you well. You know as much as I do. We have been together many years."

"I know," said Stone. "It's just we always depend on you to somehow always find a way. You know I will do you proud. You know that," he repeated.

The three left; now, the sun had fallen. "It will be dark out here soon, and there will be not much moonlight. You know we cannot light a torch."

"We will find something," said Tyron. They took turns to prop up Jubly to help her walk. They stayed close to the cover of the mountain, looking for the dragon's lair. Tyron thought he had an idea where they lived.

"I am feeling pain again for the baby," she said.

Asim was still unsure why. "Let's hope we can find the lair to work on the dragon's injury, and we leave before they know we were there."

"The mother and father won't mind."

Tyron gave a quick laugh, looking at Asim.

"I am hoping they spared us for a reason," she said, her head down.

"Let's hope it's not so we can burn to death on the mountain," Asim replied.

"You think this is futile, don't you?" she asked, looking at Asim.

"Let's just say we are with you no matter what happens."

Now Asim was deep in thought, not noticing in the dark a small tree root sticking up from the ground. Catching his toe, it tripped him. As he was still helping Jubly, both fell to the ground. Tyron could not stop himself from laughing while trying to help Jubly up, who was laughing too.

"You are an ordinary man," she said to him. "I have never seen you do anything silly that everybody else would do."

Asim laughed. "You know it can happen to anyone. Are you all right?"

"I needed to laugh, even though my ankle is painful again."

"Your landing still needs a lot of work," jested Tyron, still snickering.

"I guess we can't spend all our time looking in the air. You must look down now and again."

"Said the man who just fell!" Tyron snickered. "At least there are no signs of any dragons flying around. I'm hoping that's a good sign, but we still must try to find a way up this mountain before it becomes too dark and we cannot find anything."

"Could there be more dragons around than those we saw today?"

"Yes, I fear there are," said Tyron. "But they rarely stay too close together."

"Still can't believe we are doing this. I'm feeling fired up inside."

"You may well be when we arrive." Tyron smiled.

"It will be a merciful thing." Jubly was smiling at them both.

"I know it will," said Tyron, who now had his eyes fixed on a large crack in the side of the mountain. "It seems it could be our way. If it takes us to the top, we can have a better view of the lair from up there."

Tyron was checking the shaft as it went upward. He could see a small passageway. "I will climb up. It's too dark for me to see at this distance." He soon returned. "It seems we can go to the top. It's dark inside, so we should watch our step!" He looked at Asim and smiled. "It may be hard for Jubly, but we must try."

"Maybe we should tie a rope around her in case," Asim was thinking ahead.

"I don't mind. I will give it my best effort. You know I won't give up on you."

Tyron went up first, stopping every couple of steps to pull on Jubly's arm, as Asim was behind to give her a push at the same time. It was a small passage through where the rock had split, but over time, a path had formed. They stepped up before it turned once more. This time, he could see a rock to climb. They put a rope around Jubly. Tyron pulled on the rope while Asim pushed until they reached the top.

Jubly had to sit down and rest her sore ankle. They found her some cover under a large pile of rocks, just in case anything was flying over.

"We need to see if we are close to the lair," said Tyron. "We need to look out on the front of the mountain so we will have a better view." They approached the edge. "I will look over," he said. "I need you to hold my legs so I don't go too far." He bent down on his knees, lying flat with his head over the side. Asim had a good hold on his feet as he inched out further and further.

"I can see it," he said. "Well, I'm mostly sure I can, anyway. It will be closer to eight lengths farther along. Then we can look for a way into the lair from up here."

"We can leave Jubly where she is, for now. She needs to rest her ankle, anyway. At least until we find something." He walked back to tell her of the plan.

"Let's move up about eight lengths."

As they continued forward, Asim noticed the stars were bright, but the night was dark with a small amount of moonlight.

They were trying to figure out where the dragon's lair was again. "This should be about it. Hold my legs again. I will need to make sure." Leaning out over the edge again, he could see they were above the entrance. "I believe this is it," he said. "We are right over the top!" Asim helped him come back up.

"We will try to find an opening on top first and hope it takes us to the lair." Both men looked, having to use what light they had from the moon, trying not to catch their foot or fall into any small cracks or holes. "It seems too quiet up here," said Asim. "Nothing appears to be moving. There is not even a breeze. Do you think they are in their lair right now?"

"At a guess, I would say yes," said Tyron. "We should wait until we know for sure."

"That was the plan I was thinking. I would not be looking forward to a meal if we were the meal."

They both had been looking along the top for the longest time. Asim was about to tell Tyron they would have to lower themselves over the edge when Tyron gave a small yell. "I found something. I will lower myself down to see where it goes." He slowly dropped into the hole.

Asim waited above; it was more a crack in the rock that went across then down, only large enough for one person to climb down. "I need a rope. The bottom is like a large chute with about a two-length or more drop. I will go back again, but I'm sure it's the lair. It had a burning smell inside."

"That's good. Save your energy for when we need to be in there. Let's bring Jubly here so we will be ready at first light."

They walked back to where they left her.

"Jubly, how is your ankle holding?"

"I will make it. I have to!"

Tyron had camped himself close to the edge of the mountain to be sure to know when the dragons leave. In the distance, he was seeing the sun as it began rising as a crack in the sky over the distant mountains. There was a roar; the mountaintop trembled. He could see the smoke as he felt a rumble coming up from underneath him. The great beast took off, flying over the top of the next mountain. Not long behind, with another roar, the second dragon flew in the same direction.

This is our chance, he thought. "We must go now." He smiled as he grabbed the rope. "Tie this end around a rock, and we will hope it will be long enough." Back into the hole he went, followed by Jubly and then Asim.

Tyron was right. It was a long drop to the bottom, and unfortunately, the rope was over a length short of what they needed, but he dropped himself anyway. "I must try to catch you," he said to Jubly, who was struggling, dropping as far as she could lower herself, letting go. Tyron was underneath, grabbing her body. Her foot still hit the ground hard, sending pain shooting up through her ankle. She shrieked.

"Quiet!" shushed Asim, dropping himself to the ground.

"I'm sorry, that hurt!"

They both grabbed her so she would not have to put any weight on her ankle. They could tell she was fighting the pain, trying not to scream out again. They were in a small cavern area led out into a smaller cave and then into another one larger. The heat inside was searing, and all three were soaking wet with sweat. Looking out the entrance, they could see daylight creeping into the cave as the sun continued to rise.

"We have little time." Asim could see in the corner of the more extensive cave where they found the baby dragon on the ground, its tail curled up. It was still breathing. You could hear what was a small whimper of pain in its breath. They saw the arrow sticking out from its neck with a trail of dried-up blood had dripped from the wound down its scaly chest.

Asim and Tyron carried Jubly to the dragon, sitting her on the scales on its chest.

"We have to take the arrow out. Can you pull me up higher?" Tyron climbed up onto the dragon's chest, offering his hand to pull her up as Asim helped push. With everything that was happening, the baby dragon stayed still as if in a deep sleep. It was more complicated than they thought, trying not to slip on its scaly skin.

"We need a fire," she said.

"We don't have that much time!"

"I mean it!" She was busy with a water pouch, cleaning around the wound.

Tyron looked at Asim in disbelief. "Where do we make a fire in here?" They both wandered around the lair, scraping up any small sticks and dead brush they could find. "I'm not sure we have too much time left," shouted Tyron. "I'm sure they will be back with food real soon. We will have a big fire then! Can you hurry?"

"It takes time. I need help. Is the fire burning?"

"Yes."

Asim had climbed back up next to her on the dragon.

Taking out her dagger, she threw it down to Tyron. "Put this on the fire," she shouted. He laid the blade over the flames. "Help me pull the arrow out," she told Asim. They both grabbed the shaft; it was rigid. It took every ounce of strength from them both to pull it out. Blood came with it, along with some green-looking pus.

"I need the dagger now, Tyron, and a large piece of burning wood." She was still cleaning around the wound as Tyron climbed up the side of the dragon. Asim took the dagger from him, and she took it from Asim, using it to cut out the infected parts; the dragon moved with the pain. With their feet slipping, it almost tipped them all off. "The wood," she asked. Tyron moved up close enough to hand it to her; they heard a tremendous roar from outside the cave as she took it.

"They are coming back," he shouted.

"Hold on to me." Asim grabbed her.

She took the wood, blowing gently on it, and placed the now red-hot end on the wound. The dragon reared up, letting out a muffled noise, which had to be of pain. It twisted, and its eyes shot open, turning slightly. Jubly lost her footing. Asim tried to hold her tight, but he felt himself slipping. Tyron had already fallen to the ground.

"We must go. Time is up!" Tyron shouted back up to them as he looked out the entrance.

"Yes, I know. We are having trouble holding on. Let's go."

Jubly took a large strip of cloth ripped from her shirt to cover the wound.

"No time," he said.

"We need to go," shouted Tyron. There was a massive rumbling which seemed much closer. "They are coming back!"

"I will not leave. I'm still not finished."

"You must," Asim told her.

"I am not leaving you here!"

"We have to go, and you must go too. The dragons will be here, and you will not be able to leave."

"I cannot walk, and I will not be a burden to you. There is no time to put me back on the rope."

"I am not leaving without you. It will be sure death."

"For you, too. If you don't leave out of here. Please, this is my choice. Some things you can choose in your life. This is mine. It is my purpose. Now you must go!"

"How can I face Lanee if I leave you?"

"She knows my heart, and she will understand. Now go!" Tears rolled down her cheeks. "Please!" she pleaded with him.

As a robust, warm wind blew into the cave, Asim slid down the scales to the ground.

"You are a brave warrior," he shouted as he ran back to where they had entered.

There was a hard, loud thud. He knew the first dragon had landed back into the cave, knowing he had no time to look!

Tyron had already made it to the rope. "Use my back," Tyron shouted as he bent over.

Asim, in one movement, jumped, using his back to spring himself up to the rope, catching it with both hands and holding on tight.

"All right," Tyron jumped and latched onto Asim's legs to climb up over him. They heard another screech and another loud thud. They knew the second dragon had landed. There was a sharp glowing heat shot through the cave. They knew at least one of them had spewed fire. It was almost too hot as they clambered back up the rope through the hole again as fast as they could. The smoke was unbreathable, so they held their breath until they reached the top. Falling, gasping for air, they were both out now. A puff of smoke followed them out of the hole.

Tyron looked at him. "I don't understand," he solemnly said.

"I am at a loss, too." Both rested, trying to clean the sweat and smoke from themselves. It was a sad time for them both.

"We must move on," said Asim firmly. "We need to join back with the others. I'm sure by the time we make it back to the camp, they will have gone. Stone will have them running today."

"Well, we can use the mountaintop for now," said Tyron. "It will be easier than climbing back down."

"We will need to keep an eye out for serpents overhead."

"So we know they will look for a way inside the mountain. We can do the same from up here as we move closer to them."

They moved over the rocks on the mountaintop and kept a vigilant eye on the sky above them, having to dive and hide each time there was a close squawk or screech in the air. "Tell me again," asked Asim, "why we did this?"

Tyron was quiet as he looked at him. He was shaking his head, deep in thought.

Chapter 16

DWARF TROUBLE

Stone arose early this morning. The sun was rising high over the mountains, shining brightly. The glare had him shading his eyes in that direction as he scoured the camp for Asim, Tyron, or Jubly, to no avail. It saddened him a little. He had hoped they would be back.

"Everyone up," he shouted. "It's a beautiful day to find a way inside this mountain." Everyone was waking up and packing their things. Stone called together Zollo, Lube, Wilt, Tan, and Lanee to tell them Asim had not returned.

"Where is he?" asked Lanee, very concerned.

"It's a long story," he said. "I will tell you all later."

"So it will be up to all of us to carry out what we set out to do. We're not expecting a problem this day."

"Lube, you and Zollo go out ahead of us. Make sure you stay vigilant. Find a way inside this mountain." He thought for a moment. "Maybe you should take Duf with you in case?"

Duf looked at them, smiled, and walked forward.

"Then I should go," said Wilt.

"Fair enough," said Stone, deciding it could be better.

The four were ready to leave ahead of the others. Traveling close to the bottom of the mountain, hearing the early morning serpent activity, they listened to the loud screeches in the distance and some deafening squawks closer to them.

There was an unusual bird above, different from what they had seen; it looked something like an eagle. Only this one seemed like it was at least a hundred times larger as it flew over the mountaintop, soaring above them, casting a giant shadow over the top. They were thankful it kept flying, knowing it could be trouble if it spotted them.

"We will not have the cover of the trees while we look for a way into the mountain. So I will have Anson, Benson, Lanee, Toya, and Tan walk the mountain base. And I will need everyone else to follow us along in the forest. We're vulnerable, and there would be too many at the base of the mountain. Spread out in twos. One look high; the other look low. I want to stop at anything like a cave or a large crack in the wall."

"We will look at this mountain the same as the others ahead of us?" Tan was confused.

"Yes! We will, but a different pair of eyes may make the difference. I will stay at the back with Lanee, watching for anything above us. We can talk about Asim's departure," he said to her.

The four left and went on ahead were keeping a keen eye on the mountain and their surroundings.

"What is the chance I'm the one to find a way into the mountain today?" asked Zollo. "I will even make a small wager I do." He smiled.

Oh, a wager, thought Wilt. "I will take some of that. I will be the one to find a way in today."

"What about Duf?"

"I can ask. He doesn't speak! Do you want to wager?" Wilt asked him; the big man looked at him, smiled, and nodded. "We will search together."

"I'm on my own," said Lube. "I know I will find a way in first." Duf put his hand lightly on Lube's shoulder. "All right, big man. It will be fine when I take your coin."

"The bet is just for today only—this is my rule," said Wilt.

"Fair enough," said Zollo.

"What's this?" said Wilt. "Ha!" He laughed, already seeing a crack in the mountainside. "Help me up." Duf grabbed him and lifted him high in the air, pushing him hard against the rock.

"Hey, softer would be nice," he said, looking at Duf, who just smiled back at him. "It stops!" he shouted. "It only goes up a small way, then it ends."

"Can't make it in that way." Lube laughed.

There was a loud clank as an arrow struck the mountain wall right by Wilt's head! "Drop me!" he shouted. He fell out of Duf's hands, landing hard. "That hurt." He looked up at Duf, who smiled again as another arrow glanced off Duf's shoulder, this time tearing his jacket as he dropped with them.

"We are under attack," shouted Lube as another arrow whistled close to him. Everyone was flat on the ground now.

"It's coming from the woods," shouted Zollo.

"Are you all right?" Lube asked Duf." He looked at him and nodded. "Let's try to crawl to the next pile of rocks over there." Lube pointed ahead of them. "We will be shielded better." They crawled, trying to keep as low as possible. Arrows were still flying above them.

"Do you think this is dwarfs?" asked Zollo.

"Well," Wilt replied, "my best guess is dwarfs. If it were hunters, I don't believe they would have missed so many times."

"When you say 'dwarfs,' you mean dark dwarfs, right?"

"Yes," Wilt said again, "Anson and the others are good dwarfs."

"What we see here is a hunting party," Wilt said. "Not enough arrows for it to be too many." All four of them were down behind the rocks as the arrows were hitting a loud clank all around them.

"This will make for a long day," sighed Lube. "We need to do something."

Right before Zollo could say anything, Wilt said, "They will try to surround us from the right and left. The others will try to keep us down behind here. We will need to move to the next small rock pile up further."

Lube talked to Wilt, "Do you have a plan?"

"Yes." He picked up two of the dwarf's arrows from the ground. "We will leave Duf here. Duf, put your pouch under your shirt and lay out flat," he said. As Duf lay there, Wilt pushed the arrows into his shirt and the bag so they would stand out. "Does he look dead enough?" Wilt asked.

"No blood! But yes," said Lube. On the next volley of arrows aimed at them, he let out a loud shout like an arrow had struck someone.

"By the time they figure he's not dead, it will be too late! Play dead, big man," he said as they crawled to the next pile of rocks. Zollo shot a few arrows at the dwarfs so they could move quicker, aiming toward the forest. The dwarfs shot back at him as he ducked and followed the other two.

"They have a significant advantage," said Lube, continuing to crawl to the rocks. The dwarfs continued shooting arrows at them.

"They know we're moving."

"Zollo and Lube, you stop the dwarfs who will come in on this side. I will keep them busy for you to leave." He jumped up to shoot his bow in rapid succession. He then dropped down again as more arrows flew toward him as he stayed down behind the rocks.

Now, as Wilt had predicted, two of the dwarfs moved in from the left side, sneaking up close to the base of the mountain. As they inched closer to Duf's body, they could see the arrows sticking out of his chest.

One dwarf boasted to the other, "That's my arrow that felled the giant."

"No, it's mine," said the other.

"Maybe it's both of our arrows?"

"But mine would have been the one to kill him."

"Quiet," said the other dwarf.

"We need to grab those arrows and see before we kill the others."

Both at once grabbed the arrows from Duf's chest.

"It is mine," one whispered; both had their hands on the arrows when Duf seized both their heads with his massive hands, closing his large fingers, squeezing and crushing their skulls against each other. Both dwarfs fell lifeless to the ground.

Duf was on his knees, moving back in the same direction the dwarfs had come, slipping back into the forest to ease in behind the other dwarfs, who were now standing behind a large rock and shooting arrows at his friends. So caught up in their battle, they did not hear Duf, who grabbed a massive, long, thick tree branch he had found on the ground and was moving toward them, holding the branch as a club. Taking a mighty swing, he knocked two down with his first blow before swinging again for a second strike, taking down the other two.

All four dwarfs painfully squirmed on the ground. Duf threw the branch down. Grabbing the first one with his left hand, he struck him in the face with his right fist, making sure he would not be up anytime soon. He grabbed the second and did the same. Seeing the third was up to attack him with a sword, he stepped back to grab the branch. Again, Duf swung, knocking him back to the ground before dropping the branch as he saw the fourth dwarf standing. He scooped him up in the air with one hand, throwing him headfirst into a nearby tree. Only the one annoying dwarf, who was up for the second time, remained. Duf gripped the dwarf's neck tightly, smashing his head against the rock this time. He lifted him above his head, throwing him over the large rock toward Wilt and the others.

Zollo and Lube were hidden, waiting for the two dwarfs sneaking in from their side. The dwarfs became distracted by the sight of their friend thrown high in the air, out from the forest, making it easy for Lube and Zollo both to dispatch their arrows, striking deep into the dwarfs' chests. They dropped to the ground.

"All right," Wilt shouted, who was standing on the rock, knowing it was the last of the dwarfs. "That's how we do it." He smiled.

"We will need to collect up the bodies and hide them behind these rocks. We can use a rope to tie them and rip their clothes to make a gag for the ones still alive, that is!"

"These two are going nowhere," shouted Lube, grabbing and carrying them over to drop them with the others. Duf was carrying the dwarfs from the forest, dragging them as Wilt helped, wrapping the rope only around those who were still alive.

"I will go back and alert the others so they can move on past this area," Zollo shouted.

"Yes, all right, these dwarfs have a camp somewhere. I hope it's not too close."

"We will go on," shouted Lube. "Excellent job today, Wilt. You know your dwarfs." They laughed.

"We have had many run-ins with them. They are sneaky," said Wilt.

"Duf, you were a champion today," said Lube. Duf just smiled. They made sure the dwarfs were tied tight and gagged before they moved forward, keeping close to the mountain.

"Hope we find something soon," expressed Lube. "Now we know there are dwarfs in this area." They had only walked a short distance along the mountain when Wilt had spied another crack in the cliff face, asking Duf to lift him again. "Softer this time," he pleaded with Duf, putting one foot on Duf's shoulder and pulling himself up onto the crack.

"Can you see anything?" Lube shouted.

The crack twisted back toward the mountain, and Wilt noticed what he figured to be a small cave. It looked dark, and he could not see inside. He knew it was time to return to let them know what he had found.

"Now you must pay up," Wilt shouted to Lube, smiling, and although he was not raising a big smile back after the fight with the dwarfs, he was content in knowing they had found a way inside the mountain. "I'm staying up here while we wait for the others. We need a rope to tie off so everyone can climb." It was not too long before the others arrived.

"There is a small cave set back in the mountain," Wilt told them. "Everyone should be able to enter with no problem. We will need a torch, though."

"We saw the handiwork on the way," Lanee laughed. "They looked like they were tied tight, but I'm sure it will be a good thing for us to disappear."

"Once we are up here, they won't follow anyway," replied Wilt. "They don't go into the mountains, not in a cave anyway."

Everybody climbed up the rope, and for those who had trouble, Duf lifted them so they could reach. Duf was the last one up, pulling up the line behind him, making sure he left it in case they came back that way. Before entering the cave, Stone collected them all together, making sure everyone was there as they were lighting the torch. All now were ready for whatever stood ahead of them.

Chapter 17

FINDING A WAY

A sim and Tyron still moved ahead on top of the mountain, having to maneuver around rocks, and sometimes underneath, on their continuing journey to catch up with Stone. So far, they had to dodge two giant birds and a dragon or two. Hiding under the rock piles had been slowing them down, never knowing when to expect an attack from the sky, hiding from each screech, squawk, or roar from above. Asim still figured they would catch up with the others, knowing that finding an opening in this mountain could be a slow task.

"We should be close to where we left the camp last night."

"I think you are right," agreed Tyron. "I'm sure we have traveled at least that far along the top. We may have passed the camp?" Asim moved closer to the edge, trying to have a better view of the area below.

"I don't see too much. I know they will try hard to find a way as soon as they can. We will have to figure out soon where that could be on this mountain. If it's anything like the last one, there will be many caves inside to choose from. We could have a problem finding them."

"I can see a curve up ahead. We will have a better view." Tyron was now hurrying.

As he stepped closer to the edge, he had a broader view of the area below. "I don't see them, but I see where they may have been." He was looking into the distance. Asim was careful, stepping closer to the edge. Tyron was pointing to a spot further up. "That looks like dwarfs if I'm not mistaken."

"It does," said Asim. "They seem to be tied up. It looks like one is stirring. If it was Stone, we are not too far behind them."

"Let's keep going then and hope it was."

"What do you think dwarfs were doing out here?" Asim was wondering.

"Best guess would be a hunting party, which means there are a lot more of them camped somewhere and will soon look for their party that disappeared, so this could be good in two ways: One, the others have moved on. Two, we are up here." Asim had to smile.

"I know they would take the first entrance that would lead them into a cave, not taking any chance of running into more dwarfs. So let's keep going."

"Do you think it was our people that tied them?"

"Difficult to say from up here," said Tyron. "But I don't know who would do that otherwise? Hunters would have just killed them."

"True, I was thinking aloud." They had not traveled far when Tyron spied a large crack in the rock. It looked like it could go down into the mountain.

"Do you think they would have climbed up to the top?"

"It's possible, but I don't believe Stone would do that."

Tyron climbed down in the crack.

"Where are you going?"

"I'm checking." He came back up after a few seconds. "No, it doesn't go very far. They could not have used it." Just then, there was a deafening squawk that filled the air. Asim jumped into the crack along with Tyron. "Down," he shouted as the giant shadow of a bird flew right above them.

"That was too close."

"Well, I guess you can unhand me now." Tyron was trying to stand up.

"Sorry." Asim laughed.

"Just our luck." Looking up at the sky, he could see the clouds drawing in close; dark clouds were brewing. "It will make any flying bird look for cover," exclaimed Asim.

Tyron was thinking the same. "We will need cover, too," he shouted. Both men ran to find any rock cover. As a pitter-patter of rain hit the mountain, all Asim could see were black clouds. There was a lightning strike, and soon, a rumble in the distant sky, starting slow, then boomed louder; another giant streak of lightning lit up the sky.

"This could be bad," said Tyron. They could see a significant rock pile up ahead, and they both ran faster, sliding down under the rocks. The sky rumbled louder this time as a massive gush of rain poured down. A lightning bolt shot down as it danced on top of the mountain for a second before it disappeared, followed again by an enormous clap of thunder that seemed to shake the ground beneath their feet. They were both soaking wet as they tried to huddle under the rocks.

Tyron could see the gushing flooding water heading toward them. "I see we are on a downhill," he said, looking at Asim, who was now watching the water as it passed him. It seemed to go into a large drain hole.

"Will you look at that!" Asim turned to see where the water was going. They both stood up to look at the water swirling into the hole. "This could go down inside the mountain," he said.

"It's possible it's just a hole," said Tyron.

"Too much water. I will see how far it goes."

"You could drown!"

"I will not go too far." The next second, Asim disappeared down the hole. Tyron tried grabbing him; there was nothing in the water.

The rain was beating down on his head as he sat there waiting for Asim to return, but he never came back. Now feeling anxious about what he should do, he questioned himself, "Should I go down, or should I find cover until this rain stops? What if he is in trouble!" Thinking aloud again, he said, "What if he has drowned? What if I drown!"

It seemed the more he thought about it, the harder the rain came down. The thunder sounded louder, and the lightning struck closer. Sitting there, he slipped his feet into the hole, still pondering as the rain beat hard on his head and the thunder deafened his ear. As the water swirled around his legs, he continued to slip into the hole. Suddenly sliding fast, he tried to stop himself, but the water sucked him into a vortex. He continued to drop, twisting and turning all the way down. His lungs felt like they were bursting for air when he hit the ground with a soft landing; the water seemed to break his fall. He sat there, letting the water pour over his head. A hand came in and grasped his arm, pulling him out; it was Asim.

"What took you so long?"

He was wiping the excess water from his hair and face as he looked at him.

"It was hard to decide."

"Glad you made the right choice." Tyron looked around through the fading light and he could see they were in a large cave.

"Let's go."

"Do you mind if I catch my breath?" asked Tyron.

Asim laughed. "When you're ready." Both were soaked when they continued down the passageway in front.

"I am almost sure we are going the right way. What do you think?"

"I think my body twisted around too many times, and with all that water landing on my head."

He smiled. They seemed to move well despite not having a torch.

"It seems to be lighter ahead," said Tyron, trying to have a better view. The path they were on broke into two passageways; now, they faced another decision: one was larger, and the other a thin bridge-like pathway.

Asim looked at Tyron, who jumped on the first step of the bridge.

"I like your answer." They continued to follow the path over the bridge as it started downwards into a darker, larger cave. "Let's hope we chose the right one." It was dark. They managed by sliding their backs along the wall, hoping it would lighten soon.

"I believe that it is lighter ahead," Tyron thought aloud. "Unless my eyes are used to this dark."

"No, you are right, definitely lighter." Another passageway joined them, heading toward where they could see a small light!

"It could be a torch, I hope." As they came closer, they were sure they could hear voices, not loud, just sounds. Relief eased their minds as they knew they had found Stone and the others. Seeing Duf and Spen at the back of the pack, he shouted to them.

"My god!" said Spen, waiting for them. Duf turned to hug Tyron.

"Stop! You are squeezing the life out of me," Tyron huffed, and Duf smiled.

Asim grabbed Spen's neck. "Good to be back with you."

"We thought you were all dead! When we heard where you—"

"Not yet!" Cutting in, he laughed and slapped him on the back as the others all gathered around.

"I am so glad you're back!" said Stone with a look of relief on his face.

"We knew you all would have died!" He grabbed his shoulder.

Lanee came and joined them, wrapping her arms around them both.

"Never go off without telling me again," she scolded him.

"I know you would try to talk me out of leaving."

"You know I—wait! Where is Jubly?" she said in a panicky voice.

"She did not make it back with us." He saw a tear well up in her eye.

"I tried to talk her out of there, I did, but she would not leave. She told me you would understand and that you knew her heart."

"I do," Lanee said quietly as a tear rolled down her cheek.

Asim stopped it with his finger and held her tight. Radel and Toya came over to console each other over the loss of Jubly. He embraced them and then slowly stepped back.

Zollo grabbed him by the shoulder. "What happened?"

"Well, we achieved what we wanted to do with the baby dragon, but we lost another loved one. It was not a good day! I will explain it all later." Everyone had welcomed them both and was glad they had made it back, although the news of Jubly saddened them all.

"I'm glad you are back to take over," Stone told him.

"Me too," said a more ironic Zollo. Stone punched him hard on the arm.

"Ouch, just a joke," he said. Asim gave them both a smile.

"Stone, you did a good job leading everyone here."

As they all sat around a small fire, they made. Stone and the others told Asim and Tyron of all that happened while they were gone, as Asim told them of the journey to the dragon's lair.

"Well, it's time we moved on again." Their clothes were about dry now. The cave continued to look dark up ahead. As they continued to travel forward, Asim noticed what seemed to be another darkened area and was glad they had a lit torch this time. After they had walked in the cave for a while, there was a strong, musty smell now filling the air. He was sure he had never come across an odor quite like it. As they kept walking, it seemed to become stronger. The passageway slowly widened. It had been a long day for them. "I know this smell is a little strange, but we must stop for a while and recover some of our strength before going further. So we will rest here." He could see Lanee already turning her nose up at the stench.

Chapter 18

Meeting a Warlock

Having rested for a while and feeling their strength had returned, he hoped everyone would be ready to move on, not knowing what was up ahead. Again, they had to decide on two separate cave entrances. Asim could only shake his head.

"I'm not splitting up this time," he decided.

Tyron said. "I will take Duf, and we can see where the smelly cave takes us If you like."

"Very well, we will wait here. Do not stay long if you can help it! We may still have a long way to travel."

Tyron grabbed a torch as they both left down the tunnel.

"We will wait then?" asked Lanee.

"I think it best we do not split up right now. We only have an idea of where we are going. Are you all right?" He was looking at her.

"Yes, just a little sad about Jubly."

"How are the others?"

"They are doing better. No one could have known, but we all know what can happen."

"I tried to make that clear to everyone. It is a shock when it does. I want no more loss," Asim said with a sorrowful tone.

The passageway Tyron and Duf had taken seemed to be winding downward. They were looking around at what they could see in the dim light; they were in a vast cavern. In the distance, it appeared to be darker, and the odor a lot more pungent.

"Maybe we are on our way to something," he said to Duf. "Or maybe we're running into the wall."

Duf just shrugged his shoulders and kept on walking. Straining his eyes to see, he stretched his arm, pushing the flaming torch out as far as his arm could reach. He could make out what he thought to be another cave entrance. *A cave inside the cave*, he thought.

Soon, they approached the entranceway.

Tyron knew now the odor they smelled had to be coming from this cave. There was a high ceiling. It was still dark. When they traveled a short distance, it suddenly became more substantial. Now, he could make out the entrances of two more caves going to the left and right. "Just our luck; Asim was right about these caves. Never seen so many tunnels." He sat down to think if they should go on. "Maybe we should go back. We have been looking for a while and found nothing." He thought.

Waving the torch around, he noticed a bridge. *That's strange*, he thought; *I don't remember seeing that there before*. He was looking all around. The bridge went up and over as if it were over a small stream. He could see no water. "I wonder…" He pointed to the bridge. Duf nodded as if in approval. They both stood at the bottom before walking up the steps on the bridge. It seemed strangely steep going uphill. They were not able to see where it was leading until they reached the top.

Looking outward, he could see it was leading to another cave. "What else would it do?" At first, he saw past what he believed to be two statues. Both figures formed in the body of a lion. On approaching, he could see them move, ever so slowly turning their heads towards them.

Tyron's eyes were looking at what he thought to be a ghastly sight; the statue had the head of a man. *And not a very attractive one*, he thought. It had the body of a lion, though, right down to the furry mane, muscular front torso, and the tufted tail, weighing around two to three hundred pounds each.

"What kind of sorcery is this," he said to Duf, who looked at him with disbelief in his eyes as he shrugged his shoulders. They both stopped as the beasts lunged forward toward them. "Leave or die," growled one beast. "Nobody enters!"

They jumped back, taken entirely by surprise. Not only did an ugly statue move, but it also spoke! Tyron, although hesitant, had to ask the beast, "Where would we be entering?"

"You are not!" snapped the beast sharply.

"Duf," he said, "I believe these lion-men things are planning to stop us crossing the bridge."

Duf gave him a broad grin as he walked toward the first one, his large muscular body overshadowing the beast.

Duf grabbed its head with his giant hands, squeezing and digging his fingers into its skin. It squealed and squirmed. Its claws were slashing him, ripping his shirt sleeve and skin. Duf continued pressing harder. With his sword in hand, Tyron faced the second lion-man as it lunged itself toward him. His sword struck its body, slicing into its shoulder. It yelped loudly as its blood spurted. The creature, falling backward, rolled over back on its feet again. This time, Tyron was staring into the beast's eyes as it faced him, rearing back to lunge at him again. With a pivot of his body, Tyron made the creature miss him. He struck with his blade across its neck; blood spurted again as it fell flat and stopped rolling. Tyron gave another quick, sharp strike into its chest for good measure. Blood was squirting from the other beast's head as Duf continued pressure on his grip. Its arms had stopped flailing as he kept squeezing until he laid it limp on the ground.

"You know, I don't like it when they tell me I can't do something." He looked at Duf, who was smiling at him and wiping his bloody fingers in the mane of the beast. "Let's go see what we're not supposed to enter." They continued walking toward the cave entrance, leaving behind the blood-soaked beasts sprawled out on the ground.

Two more of the beasts suddenly appeared from out of nowhere, standing at the entrance.

"I know," Tyron said. "I suppose we cannot enter here either."

"You will die!" growled one of them.

Duf had his club out in one hand and his sword in the other.

"You know, you could be nicer to us. We don't come this way often," said Tyron.

"Don't come any closer." The beast was looking as if it was ready to attack them.

"Here we go again." Both beasts jumped, one at Duf, the other straight at him. Its arms had wrapped around him, and he could not swing his sword. It was using its head, trying to bite him; Tyron could see the sharp teeth in its gaping mouth. *I don't think so*, he thought, drawing his head back to butt the creature in the face, knocking its head backward. He immediately felt a sharp, overpowering pain in his head, knowing his head did not catch the beasts the way it should. Now, they both rolled in pain on the ground.

Duf's beast had grabbed his sword arm, painfully digging into his flesh with its large claws. As his club arm was still free, he brought the club down swiftly on the beast's head, knocking it to the ground. As it tried to spring back up, Duf struck it again, this time with a sickening crack; he knew he had broken bones in its skull.

Duf turned his attention to Tyron, seeing he had grabbed his dagger, and with the beast on top, its claws ripping into his chest, as they tangled. He drove his blade deep into the lion-man's chest with a howl. The blood was dripping from the beast's chest and his own as Duf grabbed the creature up from his body, throwing it hard against the stone bridge, crushing its face against the rock wall.

Duf helped Tyron back up to his feet again. "Thanks." He slapped him lightly on the back; Tyron was still rubbing his head.

Asim was pacing up and down where they had camped, still expecting their return. They were taking a long time, which was giving him an uneasy feeling. He looked around at the others; each person seemed to be resting quietly.

Lanee approached Asim. "Tyron and Duf have not returned yet?" she said anxiously.

"I'm worried myself," he replied. "I need to go look for them."

"Not without me, you're not."

"What about looking after the others?"

"What about looking after you?" she replied.

He looked at her anxious expression. "All right, grab one of the torches."

Walking over to Stone, he said, "We are going to see what's taking them so long."

At that same time, Spen slid down a rock, pouch in hand. "I'm all right," he slurred, looking at Asim, dazed. Asim could only watch and smile.

Asim and Lanee both left down the cave entrance, torch in hand. "I'm not sure I like this. I have a bad feeling. Tyron and Duf should have been back." It seemed to be a long walk through the cave, Asim thought, noticing how dark it was. He shrugged, looking at Lanee when they came to another cavern inside the one they were in. "Strange." He shook his head.

Approaching the entrance, Lanee turned her nose up. "This stinks. It's where this smell has been coming from, or we have been traveling too long?"

They had only traveled a short distance past the entrance when the cave opened into another, more massive cavern. *More caves are not good.* Asim could see two more caves going left and right, but no signs of Tyron or Duf.

"Can I scream?" she growled. "How many more caves?"

"I don't think they would have gone down these two. Tyron knows it would take too long to check them."

"Then where can they be?" she asked.

He was turning his body around with the torch when he noticed the bridge. "Was that there before?"

"I didn't see it," she said. "And that's strange; there is no water underneath. Should we follow it along?" she asked. "This could be the way they went."

"We can go a little way up, but if there are no signs of them, we will need to go back for the others so we can all search."

As they reached the top of the bridge, they could see in the distance the dead bodies of the slain lion-men.

"What in the stars is that!" asked Lanee, looking at the bodies as they approached. "They have a human head. Well, one did anyway; I'm not too sure about the other. That's just nasty," referring to their heads, "and the bodies of lions?"

"I'm not sure. I think sorcery has something to do with it. So I would say they came this way." They were looking at the next cave further up and two more slain bodies of what looked like more lion-men. "This does not look good at all." They both drew their swords. They continued forward, ready for anything.

Tyron and Duf had entered a small cave leading to another. The second one looked like it may have a door; he looked puzzled. They were, again, met by two lion-men arriving at the door.

"Stop!" growled one beast, which was already in an attack stance.

"I know, we can't enter here. This is becoming old. What is in this cave?" he firmly said.

"This is the cave of the warlock," growled the beast. "Go back or die."

Tyron had already made up his mind to step forward when both beasts lunged straight at him. One grabbed his outstretched arm, its claws cutting deep into his skin, causing him to drop his sword. Blood trickled down his arm. Turning to sidestep made the other one miss him. Duf turned, clubbing the creature on the way past! Tyron still had one holding on to him tight. Its claws dug deep as they wrestled to the ground. He was enduring the pain. Tyron used his free hand to grab his dagger, plunging it deep into the beast's side. It squealed and threw back its head. Its claws dug deep into his arms. Duf could see the creature's head thrown back; stepping forward, he clubbed the outstretched head, splitting and knocking it loose from Tyron. It screamed, splashing blood on the ground that splattered up the door.

Tyron could see both bodies of the beasts sprawled out dead on the ground. Duf, to make sure, stomped on the head of the first creature. Tyron, picking up his sword and checking his bloody arms, wrapped pieces of cloth he had torn from his shirt around the wounds.

"Why would they not tell us at the beginning? So do we knock or do we go in?" he asked. Duf kicked open the door.

"You have style."

It opened into a vast hallway that extended further than he could see. *Impressive*, he thought, for a split second, forgetting he was in a cave. He could see four more of the beasts dashing toward them.

"You know I love a fight, but maybe this is the time when we should go back." Duf was smiling as he started forward, swinging his club. As the creatures continued to run toward them, he knocked the first one back. It let out a terrible squeal, turning to a whimper as the club beat it to the ground. The second beast bit into his shoulder as it lunged at him. Its teeth locked on tight. Turning, he ran the creature into the wall, crushing it between the rocks and himself. Letting go as blood flowed from its mouth, it slid down the wall. He could see the blood gushing from his shoulder. With one hand, he checked to see how deep it was.

At this point, Tyron had wrestled a creature to the ground, using his foot to push it away. Lifting his sword, he reached forward, and a swift, forceful stab penetrated the lion-man's chest. Trying to pull back his sword, he found himself wrestling with another that had jumped on him, snapping at his face. Duf, on his way, saw out the corner of his eye more of the creatures moving toward them, shouting and squealing as they ran. It was going to be quite a melee now. On the other side, he could see even more were joining the action.

He grabbed his club tightly. He knew they were in for the fight of their lives. Two at once lunged at him; he struck one as the other jumped on top of him, followed by another, then a third one. Using all his strength, he fought them off, refusing to let them take him down to the ground. Tyron was still rolling with the creature. Throwing it off, he was quick to his feet, extracting his sword from the dead beast. He used it to kill the creature with two final thrusts of his blade, just in time, as two more were lunging at him. He sidestepped, pivoting as his sword blade cut deep. Blood splattered everywhere. Although some creatures were dead on the ground, they both continued to stab and club, trying to move through them to grab an inch of space while still trying to wrestle off more of the beasts that were overwhelming them.

Tyron was looking at a leaping beast in midair when an arrow struck the creature in the eye. Screaming, it fell to the ground. An arrow hit the head of another creature. Tyron looked back and saw Asim and Lanee shooting arrows into what seemed at this moment to be an endless number of creatures attacking them.

"You're just in time," shouted Tyron. "I wouldn't want you two to miss all the fun."

"We could see you had it under control." Asim laughed, shooting again. "Do these things ever stop," he shouted over the noise that was now intensifying. They could see more were moving toward them.

"We will run out of arrows at this rate," shouted Lanee, seeing the pile of beasts stacking up. There was blood and fur plastered everywhere around them.

"Keep going. We must push them back," shouted Asim. "Grab arrows from the dead if you need them."

Duf was continuing to wade through, crushing as many as he could, catching some with his bare hands, then using his club to beat them down.

Lanee helped Duf shoot arrows at the beasts close to him.

Asim, throwing his bow back over his broad shoulders, pulled out his sword, thrusting it into the chest of the first beast that lunged at him. Duf had two more, grabbing at his legs. Lanee had now put away her bow, exchanging with her sword to fight them, slashing a massive cut into one attached to Duf's leg as another lunged straight at her. She dropped swiftly to her knee, causing the lunging creature to fall on her outstretched blade. She stood up again as one jumped into the air, knocking her down and landing with its claws digging into her shoulders. Its mouth set to bite, but Duf cracked its skull with one swing of his club. He grabbed her arm and pulled her back up. She stabbed another hard as her blade tore through its skin. Blood seemed to cover the ground now.

Asim was still fighting on his feet even after a couple of close calls, his shirt slashed and blood dripping from his chest and arms. He took down another of the beasts with a slicing strike to its neck before turning to help Tyron, who had two of the creatures both clawing at him as he was trying to fend them off. Asim, with a hard downward stroke, took a slice from its head that sent it screaming to the corner. Looking up, he could see more heading their way.

"We are completely outnumbered!" Asim shouted. "We will have to make a run for it."

When every one of them stopped right where they were, everything went strangely quiet as slowly, one by one, they disappeared. Duf clubbed one more before they were all gone. He turned back to smile. There was still a buzzing in their ears, even though the noise around had stopped.

"Where are they going?" asked Lanee, now confused, as the bodies on the ground disappeared.

"This is more than strange," said Tyron. "As long as there is not something worse in store."

Asim was looking around in amazement. "Grab your arrows," was all he could say at that moment. All the arrows were lying on the ground where the dead beasts had been! Asim stared at Lanee, Tyron, and Duf. Each one of them had sweat and blood specks covering their faces, torn, bloodstained clothes, scratches, bite marks, and bruises all over their bodies, knowing he probably looked the same. "Now *that* was a battle!" he said, exhausted.

"I'm glad you came when you did," said Tyron. "I know now we should have come back, but as we went on, we couldn't stop."

"Should we go back and bring the others?" asked Lanee.

"I would say yes, but I'm curious. Why did they try to stop us like that and then disappear? It's as if the warlock, who I'm sure is behind all this, wants to meet us?"

"One of the things said this was where the warlock lives," said Tyron. "But after what I heard about him and what we have witnessed, do we want to meet him?"

"What if it's not true, and these things were defending him?" said Lanee. "He could help us."

"There is only one way to find out."

They all looked at Asim, knowing what he was thinking. As the four of them walked the long hallway, they could see a small light. It was a lit torch sitting above an old large oak door. "Will you do the honor?" Tyron looked at Duf. His large foot went to kick it open, but it suddenly opened on its own. Duf jumped back.

"I already do not like this," Lanee spoke out.

But as they looked inside, they could see it was not only large but strangely homely. There was ample space in front, close to where an old oak table and chairs were sitting. And it was now evident the smell was coming from a cauldron hanging over an open fire, way at the back of the cave. The steam puffed up, and the odor wafted toward them. The walls filled on one side with bottles of all sizes. Some containing strange things. Some bottles filled with powders and liquids. *Somewhat like Apora's home*, Asim thought. He noticed there were lit candles of various sizes throughout, giving light to the place.

He noticed a tall, skinny man standing at least six feet eight inches tall, wearing an old, long, multicolored coat that was a little frayed at the bottom. The arms seemed too long, with his long bony fingers poking out from underneath, appearing lost in the giant sleeves. His long silver hair cascaded over his shoulders. As he turned, they could see his piercing eyes deep in his sharpened features, having a long-pointed nose and silver beard wrapped around his wrinkled and aged-looking face. He stood with a slight hunch, but what mostly seemed out of place was the long-looking pointed shoes on his feet.

"Who are you?" asked Asim.

"I am Zabin," he snarled. "What is more important is who you are and what you want here! It must be of some importance that you stand up to my guards. You must go through me If you are here to harm the king. You will die before you reach him."

"Oh, really," sneered Tyron. "Again with 'you will die.'"

"Don't push me, you peasant, or I will make sure you die now! I am already growing bored. You all need to leave. You have no business here. Go to another land, or you will feel my wrath!"

"You bore very easily, but we cannot do that."

"You will regret you said that." Eight of his lion-men suddenly appeared right behind him. The creatures slowly moved forward as the warlock spoke.

"I wanted to see your faces before you die! What are your names?" he said and laughed.

Asim did not speak.

"I am not seeing the joke." Tyron was unimpressed, shaking his head.

They all pulled their swords back out again. The first one lunged through the air at Asim. Maneuvering skillfully, he turned with a slashing blow, cutting the head clean off the beast. The head was falling to the ground while its body just seemed to continue its flight. Suddenly, there was a fountain of blood from where the head used to be. Smiling, Duf then kicked the body to the ground and clubbed to death another that was lunging at him. He put a large gash on one more as another jumped at him. He pushed it away with his massive arms, knocking down candles and bottles close to the wall. Suddenly, smoke, then fire, with liquids falling off the shelf.

Lanee sidestepped and plunged her sword blade into a lunging beast with its mouth wide open, missing her face by a whisker. More of the creatures continued to appear before they could kill the first ones. Tyron was cutting into one as another tried to attack from behind him. Seeing what was happening, Asim reached across, stabbing the lion-man in its chest.

There was a fierce buzz of steel as blades flashed through the air. The fights continued as the creatures continued to attack the four of them. The ever-filling pools of blood were part of the battle, as the four warriors were determined to win this one. Heads were cracking under Duf's mighty club; blood spilled. The carnage was all over the ground. Still, the creatures attacked.

Asim was looking for a moment to see what happened to the warlock; he could see the look of anger on his face as he walked toward the wall. Without stopping, he walked right through, shouting, "You will all die here," and he laughed again.

Chapter 19

A TIME TO SAY GOODBYE?

Asim stood there looking mystified, staring at the wall in disbelief. He blinked in the hope it would make some difference. *What have I witnessed?* he thought. He readied himself to join the others, who were still fighting. *What person—no, what warlock does this and disappears?*

The moment was over! A lion-man latched onto his skin. The pain brought him back to the reality of the battle. He wrestled with the creature, its enormous claws ripping into his shoulders. He shouted out in pain. Just then, a sword blade struck the beast with a direct blow to its head. Falling, it screamed. Asim was now able to throw it off his body, looking up to see Tyron smiling.

Strange as it seemed, the creatures were thinning out. With a little bit of difficulty, he could now see the cave's back wall through the smoke and flames that had ignited from the fallen bottles, helping him feel somewhat better about this fight. *Giving a black eye to the warlock*, he thought, stopping to focus on the wall on the side where the warlock disappeared. His eyes strained through the haze, not sure if he was hallucinating.

The wall appeared to be moving, and through the movement, the head of a snake appeared, pushing its way through the wall, then another and another. The snakes were large-headed, about the size of a small cat; their bloated body dragged along behind, adding almost a length to their size. On reaching the ground, they slithered toward them. Asim was standing, ready to face this oncoming foe.

Duf was oblivious to the snakes. He was still cracking the skulls of the lion-men on the other side of the cave. Tyron was on his way over to help him take care of the few left. Lanee had seen the danger of the snakes moving closer toward Asim, still blinking his eyes in the sureness of what he was seeing. As the first one slithered toward him, it reared up its head. Asim was looking directly into the snake's large, round green, illuminated eyes, of the snake now staring him down. Its wide-open mouth and enormous six-inch fangs dripping with saliva, poison, or both, as its pointed tongue darted in and out. Having lifted his sword in defense, with one mighty swing of his blade in swift precision, he sliced the head from its body. Blood spurted out, its body motionless for a second before collapsing. Three more snakes were right behind the first one, writhing their way toward them. He took a quick step back; glancing around and seeing the danger to Lanee, he shouted as one had reared up behind her; turning to contort her body, she plunged her blade into its neck before it could strike.

"That was too close," she screamed. Asim had stabbed another of them, having to pivot his body as another slithered toward him.

Duf, with his whole arm and his entire club now covered with blood, continued to beat down every beast in range of him.

Two snakes now struck at the same time as Asim used his sword as a shield, diverting the attack by pushing them away. A third one crept in, but a powerful slice from Lanee's sword struck it down. More snakes continued slithering through the wall. Many more were on the ground, writhing on top of each other, moving toward them, with more sliding around the walls. Asim was stabbing one in front. Moving away, he turned to kill another with a sharp blow to the head, stepping forward again with a mighty swing cutting deep into the throat of another. A significant amount of the dead lion-men on Duf's side was stopping the fire from spreading toward them as the body count went higher. Flames had burnt into the bodies, giving off a smoky meat smell.

"This smell is much better than whatever is cooking in the cauldron," Tyron shouted as he sliced deep into one of the snake's heads. The ground was now covered with blood, guts, and snakes, both alive and dead.

"They are starting to overrun us again," shouted Lanee.

Tyron could see the vast amount of snakes as he disposed of another. Lanee was still wielding her sword with precision at any of them slithering close to her.

Duf was now finishing the last of the beasts. He turned his attention to face their new adversary. He clubbed one of the snakes that reared up close to him, smashing its head to the ground.

Each time the slithering snakes would stop, it was only to raise their ugly heads to strike. It took great patience and attention to the battle by the warriors, who had to watch the ground for these slithering beasts and look up for their strike.

Lanee was unaware that one of the snakes had slithered in from behind her between her feet. She could not stop it from twisting its body and pulling her off balance as it wrapped around her leg.

She shouted to Asim, who saw her dilemma; she was not able to keep her feet on the ground, and she fell back, striking the ground hard with her head. Asim maneuvered himself into a position to help. Suddenly, a snake reared up with its hard head, catching his hand and jamming his fingers hard against his sword handle. The sharpness of the pain caused him to drop his sword. With an immediate reflex, he ducked under the snake's giant head and twisted his body, grabbing his sword and turning to strike his blade across its slimy body. Rapidly turning back to Lanee, he saw her with a dagger in her hand, fighting with the snake latched on her leg. She struggled and wobbled back onto her feet. Asim could see she was dazed. He knew he would be there for her, but in a split second, he was suddenly frozen, horrified;

he saw a snake lunge at her with a hard strike to her body. The enormous saliva-covered fangs sank deep into her chest; it stuck there, not moving. Letting out a small scream as the breath seemed to leave her body, Lanee fell back under the weight of the snake, hitting the ground.

Asim's heart sank, seeing her lying on the ground, not moving. Filled with anger, he sliced the head of a snake close to her as he stabbed another, using his hand in one motion to grab and squeeze the neck of the snake, snatching it from her body and throwing it across the cave into the raging fire. He turned and plunged his sword deep into the snake that had rewrapped around her leg as more continued to rear up at him. Suddenly, Asim was consumed by rage, now swinging at every snake that moved around him. Slashing and twisting, he turned, sliced, and kicked as he went, leaving many headless snakes in his wake. Duf and Tyron could now see Lanee's motionless body on the ground. Both reacted with similar anger. They, too, swung sword and club at every snake around them.

Asim had reached the wall. Now, when the snakes appeared, he chopped their heads off nonstop. It was not long before the snakes stopped protruding their heads through the wall completely. Turning back to make his way to Tyron and Duf, he continued to use his sword. One slithered by his foot; he jumped on its neck and rammed his sword blade into its head, kicking back another. Slime, blood, and the oozing bodies of the snakes were everywhere. Tyron, stepping forward, slipped on a slick blood pool and was about to take a tumble when Asim grabbed his arm to stop his fall.

Duf, standing close, dealt with a snake that reared up to strike at them both, reminding Asim of the camaraderie they had forged. Duf, seizing another that came from behind him, turned it around as Asim sliced off its head! Over and over, the three slashed and smashed at the snakes that still attacked. Suddenly, there was a loud crack, and a big ball of smoke appeared. A large bottle of liquid had fallen, splashing onto a lot of the snakes. It instantly dissolved them, leaving only a few snakes slithering on the ground as Duf took after them with his club.

Asim put out the fire as it crept close to Lanee. Seeing a couple of small flames burning her shirt, he grabbed her up in his arms, holding her tight, smothering the flames against himself. Tyron threw everything off the oak table, leaving to help Duf put the fires out. Asim placed her body down on top, checking to see if she was still alive. All he could find was a weak heartbeat and slow, labored breaths. Duf and Tyron soon joined him at the table. Duf had found a blanket that they now laid over her body. All three, with solemn faces, were looking at Lanee.

They looked at each other and again and down at Lanee's body, not speaking a word. Asim slowly drew back her shirt, revealing the black and blue marks made by the snake's fangs on her chest.

Her skin had swollen, and the blood was now festering around the large, slimy bite marks. He could tell that the poison had spread throughout her body. He walked back to the fireplace, taking his dagger, and jammed it into the flames until the blade was red-hot. He pulled it out, looking again at Lanee's wound as he cut into her chest right below each bite mark to release any poison. Still, he could not tell if she was alive. She did not move as the blade sliced into her skin. Slicing through the swelling, he could see the slimy green pus seeping out. Tyron could see by the look of grief in Asim's eyes that he was willing the life back into her body. He could tell in his diligence there was a closeness and a tight bond that they shared together. They had known each other for a long time. Asim patiently wiped the pus away and used a different cloth to wipe her brow.

"I will go back and bring the others here," said Tyron. "I hope it will be safe here for a while, anyway. Duf will stay here with you." Asim nodded his head in agreement. Duf had found water that they could use to keep her wounds clean. Not seeing anything leaking from the incision, he covered up the wound the best he could, wiping her brow again, although there was nothing there.

Lanee was still and did not move. Tears welled up in his eyes when he thought back to the first day he had met her. How bold and so sure of herself she had been. They were both the same. Like iron striking iron, they fought that day and became friends. He remembered the black eye she gave him. That brought a quick smile. He recalled how they argued almost half the night, and a smile again came to his lips. All the adventures they had been on since that day. Duf put his hand on Asim's shoulder. Turning toward Duf, he could see the hurt on his face. He smiled back at him, still holding back a tear; he wiped her brow again. There was nothing but silence; he knew that Lanee had gone. He could feel no heartbeat or find breath in her body.

There was an old rock close by. He sat down and cried out with rage.

Tyron returned with the others. Toya and Radel went straight to Lanee.

"Is she dead?" Toya was frantic.

"She is not showing any life," Asim said. He stood up with them.

"How?" asked Radel.

He pulled back the blanket to show them the bite. Everyone else had crowded around now; each one was comforting the other. Radel loosened the makeshift bandage and was listening for anything that might show there was still life left. Toya was now crying while being consoled by Zollo and Stone.

Asim was trying to explain what had happened and the strange happenings with the snakes.

"Was it a magical snake?" asked Radel.

"I would say so," he said. "They came from out of the wall. I'm sure the warlock conjured them up somehow."

"Draining the poison was good, but magic killed her, and I believe the only thing that could bring her back is magic if it's not too late."

"What about this warlock? We must bring him back here!"

Asim shook his head. He went back and sat down again.

Tyron looked at Radel. "I think she has passed anything that we can do anymore. And without a doubt, the warlock would not lift a finger. He wanted to kill us all."

Asim sat there. His mind wandered back to Apora and what the witch had said to him when she had handed him the pebble. Sliding his hand back into the deep pocket, he reached down to find the small bag that contained the round pebble. Pulling it out of his pocket, he took the pebble out of the bag, twisting it around in his fingers before putting it back. Everyone in the cave was now just nonexistent to him.

He blocked everything around him. *"If you reach the point of life or death and there is no other possible human answer…"* He was deep in thought. *"It can bring life, or it can bring death." That is what she had said.* He pondered on those words. He had little time to think about the pebble after she gave it to him. When he received it, at first, he thought he would use it to ensure every one of his people and the children escape out of the castle. A decisive battle would be impossible to win; the soldiers and all those things raced back through his mind. *Can we defeat this warlock?* He thought! Then his mind slipped back to Lanee. *I cannot lose her either.* He sat back. It seemed the whole weight of the world was on his shoulders. His head was in his hands.

Tonas could see Asim was in deep thought. He could tell by him pulling on his hair, he was distraught. Placing his hand lightly on his shoulder, he asked him, "What is it that troubles you so much? It seems you are struggling with more than the loss of a friend."

"I am the one who has no problem making decisions, but I am at a loss right now." Asim looked at Tonas.

"I am not a great wise man," Tonas stated. "But if you will confide in someone like me, maybe I could slip up and say something that might just help." He put his arm on Tonas's shoulder and made room on the rock to sit next to him, trying to smile when he looked at him, thinking Tonas could be old enough to be his father, although he had never seen his own!

He told him of the pebble and Apora, what she said it had the power to do, and he had in his mind to bring the children back. The pebble would have a significant advantage in a battle, even with the warlock.

"She gave it to me to fight an impossible battle, and the more I think about it, the more I am not sure we have a chance without it. But I think—no, I know that I love that woman. I don't know another way to explain it! My best friend, I am sad right now."

Tonas stood up in front of him. He put his hands on his shoulders and looked him in the face. With what sounded to Asim like a fatherly voice, Tonas explained, "In the beginning, what I had was a rage. Yes, I wanted to kill that king and bring our children back. I showed no consequence or had any idea on how to handle a quest. And then the excitement that stirred in us when meeting you and all the warriors who were willing to give their lives to help us. It was more than we could ever ask for or even to hope or think! We suddenly had a direction. You even told us that none of us would come back alive! It did not matter. It was you. Yes, it was you, my friend. I hope I can call you that." He placed his hands on Asim's arms. "You are the one that has given everyone belief and hope that we will return the children."

"Nobody wanted to see any loss of life of our dear friends. But this was not to be. I am sure that no matter what happens here, we will always have a fighting chance with you leading us to the children. I know we don't have to lose Lanee, not to evil sorcery like this. Going forward, each one of us knows and understands the cost! No matter what may come against us."

Asim stood up from the rock as Tonas gave him a hand. When he was standing, he cupped Tonas's face with his hands, looking deep into his eyes. "Thank you, my friend." Tonas stood there, looking content. "I know the way now. You have helped me separate my thoughts." Letting him go, he walked back to the table. Reaching into the pouch in his hand, he pulled out the pebble.

"I must do this to bring Lanee back. This was a gift from Apora. She did not go into much detail. We will hope." Taking the bandage away, he once again saw the ugly wounds on her chest; he placed the pebble in the middle of the wounds. "I hope I'm doing this right." He said it once, "Apora," before saying it twice. The pebble sat there; nothing was happening.

A few seconds passed that seemed like an eternity. Everyone stood in awe, watching, when suddenly there was a sparkle of tiny bright lights; everyone had to shield their eyes. It appeared to be powering life back into Lanee's body. Her now purple lips were changing colors, and her pale face seemed to glow. The wounds on her chest healed themselves from the inside out. Air suddenly filled her body again. The wounds now had disappeared. Her color was back, and her eyes suddenly opened, looking around. With a deep breath, she sat up. Realizing her shirt was open, she grabbed and closed the front. At the same time, Radel pulled up the blanket. Lanee was embarrassed; a slight redness filled her cheeks.

"What happened?" she shouted. "What am I doing on this table, and why is my shirt open? Well?" she shouted again, looking straight at Asim.

"Ah-hmm," he cleared his throat to speak clearer. "I am afraid you died," he said. She looked at him with a bewildered look.

"I what?" she demanded.

Asim was quick to follow up with, "You died, but we brought you back to life again." She stepped down off the table, looking confused by what he said. She was trying to close her shirt and tuck it into her pants.

"I feel strange," she said, "but it's a peculiar feeling. I feel as strong as ever." She put her arms around Asim. Lanee encouraged Toya and Radel to join them. Then she shouted for all the others to join. It was a real moment as everyone cheered. Everyone was trying to touch her to show their love.

Lanee whispered to Asim, "Did everyone see my chest?"

He smiled. She reached back and hit him in his shoulder.

"It wasn't what you think," he said. "Well, maybe at the end. I will explain it all to you when we have more time. I'm just glad you're here." Toya and Radel jumped on her, holding her tight.

"It would be a good idea for you four to clean up before we leave," Radel said, talking to Lanee, Asim, Tyron, and Duf. She laughed.

Chapter 20

THROUGH THE MOUNTAIN

The happy party must end," Asim said. "We should move out of here. We cannot be sure if or when the warlock could return. I am sure he thinks we are all dead, well, four of us anyway. I'm sure he does not know how many we are or what our purpose is for being here. We will keep it that way."

They all moved out from the cave through the hall back down over the bridge, arriving on the ground of the cavern.

"What is our next step to the castle?" asked Lanee. She was so full of energy again.

"Well," he said, "all we have to do is find the castle from here. I feel we are not too far away. Oh, we also need to kill one warlock and the king, with his army, and save the children."

"Is that all?" she asked. "In that order?"

"Not necessarily in that order," he said, smiling.

At the bottom of the bridge, Asim realized there were two more caves. Spen burped loudly.

"Oh my." They laughed.

"All right!" Asim was shaking his head.

"Well said, my little drunk man." Tyron smiled.

"This is what we will do. Stone, you and Zollo go into the cave on the left. Wilt, you and Tan, go to the right. Take torches and go in armed in case. See where you feel it will lead and report back as soon as you can." *We don't want to be here long*, Asim thought.

"Everyone else, we will spend our time under the bridge until they return. We will have to be quiet, especially you, Spen." He smiled. They all waited. Stone and Zollo were the first to arrive back.

"We followed the passage. The more we traveled, it seemed to take us away from the direction we felt we needed to be going," said Stone.

"I wanted to go a little further to see if it changed. Someone didn't want to." Stone punched him on the arm. "We went far enough. We were going back towards the way we came."

"Thank you, both of you. Hopefully, we will have better news from Wilt and Tan, or we will have to decide our next move."

A little later, Wilt and Tan returned.

"Good news, I hope," he asked.

"Well, yes!" said Wilt. "The passage further up splits into two more caves, if you can imagine." He smiled. With two more directions, one that goes down, we followed, and eventually, it took us out of the mountain. Not only could we see the forest, but we could see the castle. And breathe fresh air," he said. "We are close. and believe me; the air was honey-sweet." He smiled again.

"We went back upward as we were curious as a cat now," said Tan. "We followed the other passageway in the opposite direction. It took us up to the top of the mountain. It was a long trek with a rough trail, and there are a lot of rocks to climb over, but everyone should be able to make it to the top if it's the way we choose. It took us out the side of the mountain, close to the top. But you can still see the castle in the distance."

"Hmm," said Asim. "We can go up above the castle. I imagine it's too high for any attack. I'm sure they planned it that way, but it may just give us the answers to the plan we need. We will all take the higher path so we can go to the top of the mountain."

They all moved out, ready for their next trek. When coming to the split, they took the higher pathway, climbing over the rocks, arriving at the hole in the mountain wall three lengths from the top on a small ledge. Asim was smiling, and he could see they were close to the castle. Looking around a short distance away, he could see a ridge close to them. He knew they would have to climb, figuring it would be easier to climb to the top to cross. They should have an unobstructed view of the castle. Then another hole in the mountain caught his eyes, like the one they were standing at, only closer to the ridge and the castle.

"We need to go to the top!" He looked at Zollo. "Find a place you can climb and drop a rope down."

Zollo came back. "The wall is too sheer. There is no way to climb with nothing to grab onto."

"So how will we climb to the top?" asked Tyron.

"How many people do you think Duf could hold?"

"Don't know. He is solid." They called Duf over.

"Do you think you could keep four men on your shoulders?" asked Asim.

Duf nodded.

"All right, he said. "Let's go with Stone, Tan, Zollo, and Anson. I need you four to climb on each other's shoulders to reach up to the top. Can you all do it?"

"Yes!" they all agreed, and Stone jumped up on Duf's shoulders first, facing the wall. Zollo was next. Tan jumped up, climbing on all three to reach and stand on Zollo's shoulders.

"I can't look," Radel squinted. "This is scary."

Asim smiled at her.

"You're the one," he said to Anson. "Make sure you have the rope." He pointed to his back. "Are you all right, Duf?"

He nodded. Anson climbed on each one, treading lightly. Tan helped him onto his shoulders, and he raised to the top. He pulled himself up onto the edge, finding a rock to tie the rope, throwing it back over the side to the others below. Everyone climbed down from each other. Asim thanked each one, especially Duf.

"Who will go with you?" Tyron asked.

"I'm not going to have everyone climb up there. Lanee, Tyron, Stone, Zollo, Toya, Lube, Tan, and Anson, stay where you are," he shouted. "We will go. Everyone else will stay here for now and stay safe in the cave."

"Radel, you are in charge. And Duf will look after you all," he said. Each person took their turn climbing the rope. Asim was the last person to go. He grabbed another rope to make sure they had one and threw it over his shoulder as he climbed. Everyone was waiting on the mountaintop.

"Let's keep our eyes open while we are walking," he said. "Check for cracks or holes along the top where we could drop into a cave without having to go over the side." They could find no hole large enough for them to fit into. Asim looked down over the edge; the sun was giving off a bright glint from the rocks below.

"This could help us. It will provide us with cover, making it difficult for the soldiers to see us from the ground." Finding a rock close to the hole below, he tied one end of the rope and threw the other end down.

"I will take Lanee and Tyron," he said. "This way, we can check the cave. I want to make this quick! Everyone else, keep looking for another way in and set up shelter from anything that could attack from above!"

"We will see where the cave will take us; maybe somewhere it can be useful." They climbed down the rope to the lip of the cave.

Lanee entered first. "It's light in here. We may see where we are going without the torch."

That's strange, thought Tyron, following close behind her.

"What are you seeing?" he asked.

"Nothing." Both Tyron and Asim laughed.

"Are you sure you don't need a torch?" asked Tyron.

"Well, rocks and a passage." She laughed, thinking about her first answer.

"Let's follow it then," Asim shouted. "And see where it takes us."

The path veered to the right, seemingly heading toward the castle. The passage widened, stopping only when the pathway split.

"Well, that's a change," Tyron said sarcastically.

"We will see where both ways will take us," Asim shrugged. "It may take a little longer, but we know we are close to the castle." They entered the passage leading the opposite way first to see if it would lead them out of the mountain, following it as it was winding downward.

"We are definitely going down the mountain," Lanee assured them. "But it still appears to be going nowhere!"

They turned one more bend as the pathway evened out. Looking down, Asim could see the ground leading them into another passage. In the distance was a small bright light that he hoped would lead them out of the mountain. They were close enough now to see a crack in the wall large enough for an average person to go in or out of; they could see the daylight pouring through from outside.

"I don't think Duf will fit through that hole," said Tyron, laughing. In front were a lot of rock piles to climb over to reach the opening.

Asim jumped across, determined to make sure they could reach the crack. Looking outside, he thought there seemed to be a length from the ground in a crevice in the mountain.

Returning to Lanee and Tyron, he told both that it could be useful later. Asim was feeling good; they had found another way out.

"That will give us two effective ways in or out of the mountain," said Lanee, smiling.

"Now, we need to check if the opposite way takes us to the castle." Heading back until the passageway split, they started down the opposite direction. Just as the first passageway they took, it went on a downward spiral, twisting and turning; the visibility was not good. But there was enough light for them to make out their surroundings without a torch. As they climbed over small rocks again, the pathway straightened out, and they could see a rock wall standing a length high. They would need to climb if they wanted to go further. They heard a strange growling sound from the other side as they approached the tall rock.

Lanee, being curious, had to find out as she climbed to the top of the rocks. Looking over, she saw four large, mangy creatures, what she thought could be dogs. She also saw an iron gate behind the animals that looked old and was probably locked.

Sliding back down, she told them what she saw. Although she was not sure if they were dogs, wolves, or a mixture, she only knew they were mangy and looked ferocious. Asim and Tyron scampered up the rock curios to see over the top. Asim could see they were bigger than a wolf, with a larger head and a scraggly, long-haired gray coat mixed with brown. They had large red eyes and teeth that looked more like fangs.

Returning, Asim shook his head. "They don't seem like any dog or wolf I have ever seen."

"Must agree there," said Tyron. "They are, for sure, ugly!"

"The warlock has a lot to do with this. I'm wagering on the other side of the gate; we will be at the castle."

"Not taking that one," said Tyron. "I'm sure you are right!"

"We have arrows," said Lanee. "Let's see what we can do to move them."

Agreeing, they climbed up the rock together; at the top, all three shot their bows, striking three of the beasts. Yelping, they fell with the force of the arrows. Staying at the top of the rock and loading again, they saw the three creatures stand back up on their feet, growling and snarling as their piercing eyes looked straight at them.

"I knew it!" Tyron shouted. "Here we go again." All three slid back down from the rock. The first one was ready to jump from the top. Although Tyron shot another arrow into its body, it was not enough to stop it from jumping. With a loud growl, it hit him full-on. They both fell to the ground. Tyron dropped his bow when its claws dug into his skin; it was struggling to bite him. Tyron, with his hands, gripped around its neck, trying to hold it off. Its large back feet and sharp nails painfully scratched at his body.

Lanee was at Tyron's aid, pulling her sword out to plunge into the beast; it roared, arched its back, and turned its head but did not stop. The distraction was enough for Tyron to throw it off him. Standing up, he seized his sword and thrust his blade into its snarling head. It roared again

and threw its head back; it did not stop. The other three beasts were jumping from the wall now.

Asim dispatched two more arrows into one; it was not enough to kill it. Nothing they were doing seemed to faze these things. One was lunging at him. Loading his bow, he was able to shoot another arrow, hitting the beast again. Still not stopping its forward motion, it landed on top of him. They both were rolling on the ground. Its claws dug deep into Asim's skin. He put his foot out to wedge underneath the beast, levering it off himself. He was back on his feet, clutching his sword tight. As the beast lunged at him again, with a skillful thrust, he struck it hard in the neck. It rolled over as Asim stabbed it again. This time, his blade penetrated through its heart. The beast rolled over on the ground with a tremendous roar, followed by a whimper. This time, it did not stand up again.

"The heart," he yelled. "Strike the heart. You must stop its heart."

Lanee was cornered by two of the snarling beasts. Both lunged forward at her, knocking her to the ground. Tyron was still wrestling with another close to the rocks, standing firm to resist while it continued to attack him. Asim now stood in front of the two beasts snarling over Lanee. Their mouths dripped with saliva. This time, he was ready. Asim plunged his sword deep into the neck of one. Its snarl turned into a roar, turning its dripping mouth toward him, giving him the chance to swing his sword, hitting the beast on the side of the head, causing it to roll over, allowing him time to plunge his sword blade deep into its heart. It did not move. Lanee was wrestling with the other beast, rolling over as it was trying to bite her, scratching her arms. She held on tight. Asim struck the creature on its head, knocking it off, giving Lanee time to grip her sword and stab the creature in its heart. Tyron continued to repel the beast with his sword. Twisting as he stepped back, he turned his sword in a final striking blow to its heart.

All four creatures were lying on the ground; all were dead. They looked at each other, scratched, bleeding, sweaty, and disheveled. "What a mess we are," said Asim.

"And Radel won't be smiling about the way we look." Tyron chuckled.

Asim Strolled over to one beast and, in two sharp hacks, cut its head off. Lanee and Tyron did the same, while Asim took care of the last one.

"Well, that was fun," said Tyron, dusting himself off.

"I don't trust these things," said Asim. "We will take their heads away from them." They threw them as far back in the tunnel as they could before dusting and straightening their clothes.

"Are you ready to see what that iron gate is about?" They climbed the rock again, looking at the iron gate. It had been there for a while; it was covered in a lot of rust. "It will be tough to open."

"We must be close to the castle," said Tyron. "There would be no need for a gate, otherwise, or the ugly demon beasts from hell!"

"We will find out when we go through. What do you think?" Lanee. "I believe we may have a way into the castle," she said, smiling. "Although there is an odor coming from somewhere." She turned her nose up. "We may need Duf to knock this gate open."

They laughed, deciding not to open the gate. On the way back, they took another look to make sure the beasts were still there. As they passed the four heads, Asim decided they should cover them with rocks." Then, they were on their way again.

Going back out to climb the rope, Asim realized it was dark again. "We will all camp on top."

When they reached the others, they told them of what happened below. Everyone, relieved, was laughing and talking now that they heard there was a way inside the castle.

Chapter 21

A PLAN IS HATCHED

Early the next morning, a light breeze was blowing; they were feeling the full effect of being on top of the mountain. The sun had risen high above them, shining through a vivid blue sky, mottled only by a few small drifting clouds. Asim was looking over the edge of the mountain; the sun was blinding as it glinted off the rocks. *Perfect,* he thought, shading his eyes to look down toward the castle. He noticed a crack in the foundation that had formed a ledge which looked to stretch the length of the castle as they climbed down the rope. It was a small jump to where the crack began.

"Let's try to be careful. The sun is helpful, but they may still see us." The lip was high enough they hoped they could not be visible looking up from ground level when they crouched down. Asim could see, although high up, it did indeed stretch the entire length of the castle.

"This is what we will do," said Asim. "I will warn you, it will be a long day.

"Lube, Toya, and Anson, you take the back part of the castle as we overlook it. We need to check for activity throughout the day.

Keep your eye out for guard changes or any times that areas look weak. How many will come and go from the towers, and what's the layout? Anything we can use to our advantage."

"Anson, look and see if you can see past the back wall to have a good view of the land around the outside.

"Stone, Zollo, and Tan, you take the middle section and do the same, especially the layout and how everything is set up inside, strength and weakness. Lanee and Tyron, we will watch the front. It is early morning. We should have a good idea of a day in the castle. Oh, and above all, keep an eye out for any of the children or where they may be keeping them. I need to know what we will face, so I hope we can plan or at least put together the layout right for when we go inside."

They all left; Asim continued to gaze over the castle. He could see the four corner towers. A gargoyle statue stood above the castle walls on the top of each tower. The outer walls were drab gray brick, and flags flew in the corners, with their crest that looked like a two-headed beast circled by two axes curling and fluttering in a light morning breeze. The massive castle gate sat below the battlements. Loopholes were built into the walls for their archers. Everything surrounding the courtyard seemed to be in two areas: a large one at the front and a smaller one at the back. He presumed the king's chambers and housing were sitting back from the end of the lower courtyard, as was the grand entranceway leading to the grand halls. He could see what he thought were stables close by smaller buildings. You might say the castle had a specific, strange, and stately look to it, but there was still something dark and evil shrouding it all. Asim knew it would still give an unnatural feel when they entered.

It had been a long, hot, tiring day of watching the castle activities. Asim gathered everyone back on the top of the mountain. He listened intently as each section of the castle was explained to him.

Asim started with Anson, asking about everything he could see behind the back wall and whether any activity occurred.

"Not right behind, but there is a track that stretches back. There are villages and farmlands back farther than I could see. Some of these people travel early to bring their goods in the morning. I'm sure they came to swap or barter. I could see a few ox and carts wheeling along. I saw water birds, so we must be close to the river."

"Where the castle draws its water from," said Asim. "They start early at first light, I would guess."

Lube explained, "Not a lot was happening at the back of the castle. They keep guards in one tower, and the back-corner tower appears to be empty. At least we saw no guard come or go. They changed in the morning, then changed again around the middle of the day, and later again before we left. It was strange; the guards marched to the front, unsure if they left anyone behind. It looked empty, and we could see no one before the new guards returned."

"No, that's right," said Toya. "After a while, new guards came back. But there only seemed to be, at the most, six at a time. There was a building at the back of the small courtyard area. It had one guard at the front, and the guards from the tower went in and out at odd times during the day. At guard change, they had a small amount of food delivered. It could be a second holding jail?"

"Could the children be there?" asked Asim.

"We saw no activity," she said. "None of the common folk stepped anywhere back there. However, there was housing for the king's workers closer to the back towards the mountain. We saw a small group of children, maybe five? Later in the day, they seemed to huddle together. I believe it was children who lived here, but they were playing, and not the amount we needed! They disappeared with the workers later."

Stone, Zollo, and Tan reported, "We saw a lot of activity towards the king's quarters. The king himself was surrounded only by his knights. Mostly, the guards were in and out. We saw maybe fifty during the day, mostly marching to the front and back again, yet we only saw the king one time. Workers seemed to come and go in the king's quarters and the stable, where they held the king's horses. The open stable was on the other side of the courtyard. The villagers set up large tables to put their goods on in the large courtyard, where most of the people gathered. We saw no one in the castle other than the king's guards who carried weapons. There was a tavern in the same area. We did see a couple of drunks wandering around."

"No sign of the children?"

"None," said Stone. "Later in the morning, there were many people crowded around, some jugglers and minstrels wandering around."

"Nobody from the outside had weapons?" Asim responded.

"None," said Stone, thinking about the people.

"Zollo and Tan, anything else?"

"The guards do not defend the market well, maybe only two guards all day," said Zollo. "We would have a good chance to blend in with the villagers."

"Little activity on the far wall," added Tan. "Only at guard change."

Asim said, "We know there are a lot of guards on the front wall. I think you are right; no one stays in the tower closest to the mountain wall. A lot of guards are along the battlements, mostly in the early part of the day, and decreases later."

"They stopped everyone coming in, and we saw no people just walking in, only with horses, carts, or barrows. As they entered, it did not look like they checked the goods well. They collect money, maybe jewelry, clothes, or livestock, something for a tax? Only seemed to change the guard once." Asim stopped. He sat and talked with Tyron and Lanee for a while.

"What if the children are not here?" She felt concerned.

"They could be locked up in the king's quarters or even the dungeon," he said. "I'm sure they will try to draw the very life from them. They can train them easier when their reasoning has gone!"

"They are demons," said Lanee.

"True, but us being outnumbered will be tough. I think we also need to have a better look at the building at the back." They all sat there quietly, looking at Asim.

"Under and into," Asim blurted out. "Under the castle and into the front gate."

Tyron scratched his head.

"Now I know what we need to do," said Asim. "I figured out a plan, but we must leave soon. It will be better to tell you when we are back with the others again. It's almost dark, and this must happen tonight." Leaving to go back, they were all soon together again.

Asim gathered everyone together. "This is what we will do. And it must happen tonight. We have a disadvantage in a straight fight, outnumbered by the guards. Let's try to stay away from one!

"We will enter the castle in groups so as not to draw attention to ourselves. That means we will split up, so if anyone finds the children, try to pass the news to everyone else. If that is not possible, try to sneak the children out of the castle with whom you have with you.

"I need Tan, Duf, Exim, Brantil, Toya, Radel, Mup, Dooly, Pooly, Tig, Sooly, Wooly, Benson, Jig, Boben, and Senso; you will break up into two groups. Go back down the passageway to the outside. Make your way across to the river. I want both groups to walk to the village. That's why you need to leave soon. We don't know how far they are away.

"Go to the closest outlying large farm, and each group will steal an ox and cart. Go quietly. Oh, do not fail!

"Tan, you will take one team: Toya, Brantil, Exim, Pooly, Dooly, Sooly, and Wooly.

"Radel, your team is Duf, Senso, Boben, Tig, Jig, Mup, and Benson."

"As you find the carts and ox, be ready to head back to the castle. The dwarfs will go inside the carts along with all the weapons. No one can enter with weapons. Make sure you cover them with enough wheat or something to go through the gate. You must make this happen tonight so that you will return to the castle in the morning.

"Once you arrive at the castle, act like everyone else—you are villagers! Put out a little wheat on the tables and have someone watch it like normal. Go to the outer wall and drop the carts. Put the ox in the stable and start your search for the children. You will need to leave Duf, Exim, Pooly, and Toya at the carts to watch for the guards on the front. Do you see any problems?"

"I'm sure there will be some," said Tan, "but we will overcome them. We will see you in the morning."

"I like the truth, and I love your outcome," Asim said. They all left through the passageway. "Everyone else, in case you are wondering, we are going back through the mountain. Stone and Wilt go with Tan and Radel to make sure they are all right, with no hold-ups. Once they are out of the mountain safe and start on their journey, come back to join us."

Chapter 22

LET'S FIND AN OX

As Tan and Radel left with their respective parties, they soon headed toward the forest, using the trees to keep their profile low. The moon was not bright. Only at a quarter of its fullness, giving them just enough light to prevent them from walking into a tree!

"Let's keep together," said Radel as they approached the river. "Keep close to the bank and try not to fall in!"

"We're all right." Toya smiled. "Spen is not with us." They laughed as they moved along the bank toward the village.

"Are you much into robbing people?" Tan asked Radel.

"We don't rob people. Now killing and castration, that's another story," she said.

Tan swallowed hard and stayed a little quiet after that. Soon, they were watching the dim lights from the castle in the distance. Knowing there were guards in the tower, they kept low, unsure if they could be seen from that distance or not. Once they were past the castle, the lights were just a flicker in the distance. Now, they moved onto the cart trail leading to the village. At least they felt safer not walking close to the river. The village was still a distance away. Later, when they approached the village, they noticed a few lights. It was a small village, which, for their purpose, made Radel smile.

Radel, conferring with Tan, figured they would split up for now. They would look for a remote farm to the right.

"We will go around to the left then. We will meet up soon on the other side of the village."

"Sounds like a plan." Radel smiled. "Make sure you are on the trail before morning light."

"We will be there. Look, if you have a problem or run into one, send someone, and I will help you."

"Have you ever stolen an ox?" she asked.

"Well, no," he was a little hesitant.

"Well, thank you for your offer, but we are both new at this," said Radel as they split up.

"I have stolen a horse!"

She heard him mumbling in the distance; she smiled to herself as they started across the field away from the village. The crop fields were large. Senso was the first one to see the light in the distance.

"Must be the farmhouse?" she hoped as they kept heading toward the light.

I hope no one is awake or has dogs, Radel thought. "We need to find out where they keep their carts and oxen." On their approach to the house, they could make out the stables were to the right side.

"We will find the ox. Tig, Jig, Mup, and Benson, see if you can find a cart anywhere."

As they all moved closer to the house, she felt a little relieved there was no dog. *Strange*, she thought, *way out here, but that's good.* There was a small light of a candle coming from the house. It was dark as they tried to find a door to open the stable. Soon, they found the large door, opening it as quietly as they could. They all stopped! There was enough light to make out a dog. It looked like a hunting dog asleep in the straw. She put her fingers to her lips, motioning for quiet. Each person stopped in their tracks. Boben looked at Radel, and she shrugged her shoulders.

What would Tan do in this situation? she thought, dismissing it. Senso took his bow from his shoulder. "No," she whispered as quietly as she could, shaking her head. Duf tiptoed past her. Slowly, he walked up to the dog, and she put her hands over her eyes. He could see it was an older dog lying on an old blanket. He smiled to himself. So far, the dog had not moved.

"Is it dead?" asked Senso quietly, again seeing the fingers to the lips from Radel. Duf dropped to one knee, grabbing the dog's mouth to keep it closed in his large hand. He picked the dog up as it squirmed, but Duf held it tighter to make it stop.

Radel, Senso, and Boben slipped quietly into the stable; they soon found where the oxen were. Untying the rope, Boben was ready to take one out. Senso found where they kept the yokes. Throwing it over the ox, they walked the large animal out of the stable.

This is going well, she thought. Then she looked at Duf as they passed. He was smiling. Boben reached back and grabbed a blanket from a shelf, and they were out in the yard. Looking back at Duf, they wondered what he was about to do with the dog and hoped Mup and the others found a cart.

Duf walked with the dog cupped in his arms. He checked inside his pouch to find an old piece of cheese he had taken from the warlock's cave, saving it for some time on the journey. He pulled it out of the pouch and slowly placed the dog down. Still, with his hand over its mouth, he let the dog smell the cheese, slowly taking his hand from its mouth while breaking a piece off to let the dog eat. The dog growled, then gobbled the cheese. He stepped back, only moving two steps; the dog looked and growled again. Crumbling the cheese he had left, he threw it down on the ground, away from the dog. It ran to eat each piece. Stepping swiftly, he had enough time to step out and close the barn door behind him. Smiling to himself, he caught up with Radel. He smiled at her.

"I know you did something good," she said and squeezed his arm. They were away from the house and on a path she thought would lead them to the cart track to the village. She sent Senso and Boben to find the dwarfs. Crossing the large field, they found them trying to push a large cart. Duf went to help push it the rest of the way, putting it up behind the ox and strapping up the yoke. The dwarfs jumped inside. Duf, Radel Senso, and Boben took their weapons, loading them in the cart with the dwarfs. Duf threw a blanket over them. Later, they pulled a significant amount of wheat from the fields to put over the top of the blanket. Radel and Senso climbed up on the top as Duf and Boben strolled by their side on their way to the outskirts of the village to meet Tan and the others.

"Well," Radel said to Senso, "that couldn't have gone any better. It was easier than I thought it was going to be, plus nobody woke up." They were both smiling.

Tan and the others continued to move around the left side of the village. Tan noticed a light in the distance. "At last," he said after they had been walking for a while, "that should be a farmhouse, so we will need to be quiet as we approach." Still on the pathway, as they neared the house, they came across a filled cart in a wheat field close to them.

Tan sent Brantil and Exim to empty the cart and bring it closer to the path while they went to the house. "We will meet you back here."

"Don't you think we should stay off this path?" asked Toya. Tan stared at her. "We are heading for the front of the house," she said. A dog barked loudly, this time. Toya stared at Tan, and they all stopped walking. ,

"The rest of you move across the field," Tan insisted. "We must try to find the stable."

"If we cannot keep the dog quiet, we won't need the stable," Toya quipped.

"I will handle the dog; you find the ox." He moved around to the front side of the house, where the dog was barking.

While picking up a large piece of wood on the way, he confronted the dog, who had stopped barking. It now turned to snarling and growling at him. Watching the saliva drip from the dog's mouth, he stood there, daring the dog to attack him. The dog growled one more time as it lunged at him. Tan held the wood in both hands; with the dog in mid-air, he hauled off, hitting it on the side of the head and knocking it to the ground. It yelped and whimpered as it rolled over. Swiftly, before it could stand up, he struck the dog square on the top of the head. Its limp body fell sprawled to the ground. He checked to see if it was still breathing. It was! That made him feel better. *I didn't want to kill it*, he thought. He heard a stirring coming from the house and saw a light moving around, now on its way to the front door. Tan dashed to the door before anyone could arrive there. The front door opened, and a man stepped out. He looked to be an older man, maybe in his late fifties.

"Anyone out there?" he shouted. "Patch, are you all right?" he shouted again.

Tan figured Patch was the dog's name. He struck the man on his head with the wood; he fell forward to his knees. Tan caught him before he hit the ground, checking if the man was still alive. He dragged him back into the house, not hearing anyone else stirring. The room was silent. He checked toward the bedroom; it appeared the older man lived alone. Finding rope, he tied the man to a chair, making sure it was not too tight but would take a good day to free himself; moving out of the house to pick up the dog, he put it with the older man. Now, he was ready to find the others, who had found the stable and moved the only ox out; they walked it towards the field.

"What did you do?" asked Toya. "Did you kill the dog?"

"No, I took care of it!" he snarled.

"I hope you didn't kill the dog."

"No, I did not!" he defended himself.

"Well, good!" she said. "I don't want to know what you did, but there is only one ox."

"We only need one."

"But they will miss it."

"I took care of it," he growled. "Did we find a yoke for the ox?" Everyone stood silent.

"We must have a yoke to pull the cart!" Pooly decided he would go back.

"Grab a blanket while you are there." Pooly soon caught back up to them with the blanket and yoke; they met with Brantil and Exim, who had the cart waiting.

"We left this pile of wheat to fill it," said Brantil.

"Good thinking," Tan was pleased.

The dwarfs were climbing in as they covered them with the blanket and put the wheat on top. Tan had attached the yoke to the ox and the cart; now they were ready to go. Toya and Brantil sat on the top while Tan and Exim strolled by their side. They were on their way to meet Radel and the others.

Radel was sitting, waiting for them. "Any trouble?" she asked sarcastically.

"Nothing at all." She noticed he did not sound as sure as he was.

"A problem with a dog?" quipped Toya.

"I took care of it!"

"You did not kill it, I hope," asked Radel.

"What's all this dog stuff? No! I did not kill it."

"Good!" she said. "Oh, and before we make it to the castle, you better put your weapons in the cart."

He nodded and muttered something that she did not understand and was not about to ask him; she smiled to herself.

They all put their weapons in the cart; it was a slow ride back towards the castle. Not much was spoken while they followed each other on the cart trail.

Toya was yawning while she sat in the leading cart. "Let's stop a little way out so we will be at the castle by sunrise."

Chapter 23

FINDING A WAY IN

Making sure they were away on their journey, Stone and Wilt came up through the passageway to join Asim and the others who were about to embark on their way to the first hole in the mountain wall.

"It will not be easy," he said. "I will give everyone a choice: climb up the wall and over the top or go back down and walk around the long way. How do you feel about climbing?" He looked at Tonas and Spen.

Spen continued to sip on his pouch. "I don't think I can climb a rope; I have a little too much weight!"

"Honest," said Asim. "All right, this is what we will do." He sent Stone and Zollo, along with Spen, Tonas, and Yuby back down the same passageway to where Radel and the others departed. He told Stone, "Keep to the side of the mountain. Move forward until you find the crack in the wall. I will be there to guide you."

Leaving down the pathway, they were soon outside the cave. Stone had everyone stay close to the mountain wall, treading carefully in the moonlight to meet back up with Asim.

I need to hurry, Asim thought, *to be there for them in this darkness outside.*

They all climbed the ropes to the mountaintop and across to the second cave. Lowering themselves to the cave below, they waited for Asim and the others.

His journey down the passageway, climbing over the rocks, seemed further than last time. Not taking too long, though, Asim made his way to the outer cave, slipping through into the fresh air in the crevice, where he sat and waited for Stone to reach the crack in the wall. He could make out their figures walking in the darkness and did not have to wait long.

"Here," he shouted to them. "Just a little step this time." He placed his arm down to help each of them. Soon, they were in the cave, heading upward on the pathway leading toward the castle, climbing over the rocks until they reached the top of the cave, meeting back up with the others.

"Now we go down again," he said, smiling. They went on their way to the gate they hoped would put them in the castle. On the way, Asim checked the corner of the tall rock wall. He made sure the beasts were still dead before proceeding. Now feeling a sense of relief, they climbed over. They were all now at the iron gate.

Tyron now worked tirelessly on the lock with his dagger. Stone and Wilt worked on the hinges. "It looks like this gate is rusty and has not been open for many years," declared Tyron.

"Maybe we should have brought Duf," jested Lanee, smiling.

"We can do this," said a determined Tyron, using his sword to lever the lock bolt. Zollo, Stone, and Wilt chipped away at the wooden hinge blocks of the gate around the metal hinges; now, all three helped Tyron try to jar the lock bolt free, using all their muscle. "I thought it gave way a little," grunted Tyron. "Keep going."

Asim and Lanee jumped in to help; with the six shaking the gate, it gave way. The lock cracked, and the bolt fell to the ground. They gave a small cheer! Now, with all six, they could slowly pull the gate open enough for them to slip through.

"That was one stubborn gate." They moved forward on the other side now, feeling a lot more dampness in the air.

I never noticed, thought Tyron. "This has to be why that gate was so rusty, being so close to water."

"Close to something," shouted Lanee, turning her nose up again. "It stinks right here." Continuing on, they soon came to the river, looking across; it was five lengths wide.

"Not sure where this river runs," Asim wondered. "There is no moat in front of the castle, so it must go underneath. Its direction is heading back towards the mountain."

"At least it's not boiling," quipped Lanee. "But it smells." She was turning her nose up again.

"We need to find where it flows and follow it. There must be a well in the castle for everyone's water supply."

"I believe I saw a well towards the back of the castle, close to the living quarters," said Zollo. Stone hit him on the arm. "What was that for."

"Why didn't you say so before?"

"I did now," he said, rubbing his arm.

"Let's follow the flow towards the mountain." As they continued their walk, the river opened wider. They came to a ridge looking across the expanse.

"Over there," Zollo pointed.

Asim was now seeing the opening in the rock wall where the water was flowing. Moving closer, they could see another gate they would have to open to enter.

In the distance over the ridge where they were to cross, he saw the river had widened. "More of a challenge now." He smiled as they had a distance to cross.

"Let's hope this river is good to us," said Lanee. "At least the smell seems to have gone."

Tyron and the others waded in first while Tonas, Spen, and Yuby stayed by the bank. They waded until they had to swim to the gate. They found they could stand up again in the water, which only came up to their chests, except for Anson, who was clinging to Stone's shoulders. Once again, they were ready to work on the gate. Anson moved forward, grabbing the gate. Taking his knife and twisting it a few times, he opened the gate with no problem.

"Where were you before?" asked Tyron.

"I was watching," he laughed. They grabbed the gate, pushing it open.

"This calls for a drink," shouted Spen, looking at them from the ridge. Asim sent Stone, Wilt, and Lube back to help the three swim across, using their bodies to help them float.

"We will need to remember to bring a rope if we come back this way," he said. Entering through the gate, the water stayed at chest-deep still, except for Anson, who was now holding on to Tyron to keep above the water line. They saw stonework ahead.

"Must be the castle?" He was sure. The water flowed off to the left, heading toward the mountain. One stream of water went straight through the wall and seemed to go under the castle. "To the well on the grounds, I am sure," exclaimed Asim.

"This is what we need to do. I will need some of us to follow the water up further. Stone, I will send Spen, Yuby, and Baylin with you to enter the castle through the well. Remember, when you find it, come up before sunrise. Make sure everywhere is clear. You should be able to bring Spen to the top by hoisting him up on the bucket. Once you are in, find the ox and carts to locate the others."

"Let's go." They followed the river that flowed up into the mountain. The water was deep, and they had to swim again.

"I hope we find something soon," Lanee said. "It will be strange with all of us coming out of the well," she laughed.

Everyone was steadily moving along when they found another gate.

"Yes!" He grinned. "I was hoping we would find something." They bought Anson up to take care of the lock. Once open, they moved forward, climbing a few rocks and coming to an opening with two separate pathways. Asim shook his head.

"Now there's a shocking surprise," shouted Tyron. "One headed straight, the other going upward."

"Tyron, Wilt, Tonas, and Anson take the upward passageway. Try to locate the others. We will take the other path."

"I like what you're thinking," said Tyron.

"We will meet you on the inside somewhere. If not, we may have to meet back here again," he laughed.

"Let's hope this cave will take us to the castle grounds," Tyron said to Wilt while the other two followed. They continued upward.

"Are we going the right way?" asked Anson.

"There is only one passage." He looked at Anson, mystified. The passage bent to the left, opening up to more rocks and rock mounds ahead. Climbing over, they continued their upward climb.

"I feel we will be at the top of the mountain if we keep going," Tyron laughed. The passage evened out and ran down through more rocks as it opened wider, moving around a bend and ending up at a large iron gate.

"I guess that means we could be somewhere. Where is the question?"

"Where's Anson?" he asked. "What do you think about this?"

"It is a little rusty." Anson was looking at the gate. "It may take a bit longer."

"How did you learn to pick these locks, anyway?" Tyron asked.

"Just a gift, that's all. Anytime I found a lock, I would play with it until I knew how it worked." Standing in front of the iron gate with its wood inserts, Anson went to work. They stayed back and watched; it took a little while, but Anson still opened it.

"You are a master," said Tyron. "Just not great on directions." He laughed.

"I try," he said, laughing with him, thinking back to what he had asked earlier.

To pull it open, they all had to tug on the gate. "You were right; this gate has not been opened for a while." It took all four to open it, enough for each one to pass through. Moving into the passageway past the gate, they hoped to see daylight but found themselves in another passage leading to a door in the distance. This one was made of wood.

"Why all the gates and doors?" asked Wilt. "What's the reasoning for putting up a gate and putting in a door?" Tyron could only look and shrug his shoulders, calling Anson again to work on the door. He soon had it unlocked. Tyron found he could slide the door back just enough as fresh air drifted into the cave. It was dark outside as Tyron stood just breathing in the air. "Amazing!"

Stone, Spen, Yuby, and Baylin had continued in the water down the tunnel, still up around their chest; Spen was mumbling all the way. First, it was "too wet," then "too cold," then it was "too long." He slurred, "I…am running low on mead."

"Shut up for a while," shouted Stone.

"Well," he mumbled, taking another sip from his pouch.

"I think I can see the light ahead," said Baylin. "It could be the well."

"Oh, great, I see another gate. Just what we need," said Stone. "I hope we can break this one open." It was a thin barred barrier with only small holes to keep animals, people, and other things out to keep their water clean. Stone took out his dagger to work on the lock with help from Baylin. It did not take them too long to pry the gate open.

"A-ha," said Stone, "that was easier than I thought it would be." He felt very pleased. The water had lowered to just over their waist as they continued until they found the hole for the well. Stone could see the rope hanging down; grabbing it, he pulled the bucket out of the water. He figured it was still early morning, looking up to see a darkened sky; although it was becoming lighter in the distance, the sun was only just poking its head up in the sky.

"We cannot wait," said Stone. "I feel we will have a better chance if it's not daylight." Grabbing at the rope, making sure it was as tight as it could be, he climbed.

"I will make sure it's clear up there. Spen, do you think you will make it? It's a long way up?"

"I will try!"

Poking his head over the side of the well, he looked around; he saw nothing, or at least no one. As Stone pulled himself out, it was dark and deserted. *That's good.* The well itself was in an accessible area, having a back built against a wall away from the pathway. He thought he could see the front gate in the distance, but maybe not. Going back to the well, he leaned over to quietly shout, "Clear."

Yuby was next up his climb. He was a little slow, but he made it. Both were looking around; it still seemed deserted. "All clear," he quietly shouted down again.

Baylin had Spen stand on the bucket. "Go," he quietly cried out as Stone and Yuby tried to pull him up, but it was very slow; he had only moved a few feet when they lowered Spen back down. Stone leaned over again.

"We need you up here, Baylin. Spen is too heavy." Climbing the rope up to the top, Baylin quietly shouted for Spen to be ready. Spen was still standing on the bucket as all three pulled now. It was still slow, but they brought him to the top. Stone grabbed him and pulled him over the lip of the well. All four were on the castle grounds. Stone felt pleased; they had made it at least that far.

"Will the tavern be open?" asked Stone. Spen nodded his approval. "We will need to keep hidden for a short while until the others arrive," said Stone. Walking around on the pathway, they kept their eyes out for any of the king's guards who might wander around. Not seeing anyone so far, they looked at all the buildings until they saw the tavern sign. There was a small light they saw under the door; as they entered, Stone looked around. *No guards. That's good*, he thought. Some of the people inside were asleep, and a few were talking on a bench. They moved to a table in the corner. Stone stopped at the bar as he ordered four ales. The man behind the bar looked at Stone; he thought him to be the tavern owner.

"You are wet," he observed.

"Fell in the well," mumbled Stone.

"Not a good day then?" said the man.

"No! But it will be better."

"I need you all to hide your weapons in the corner if you will," he asked, adding, "I saw nothing! Don't want no trouble in here."

"Will do. We don't want trouble either." He returned to the others, and they all removed their weapons and sat at the table to drink.

Chapter 24

EVEN THE BEST-LAID PLANS

Tyron peeked his head out of the door, taking a deep breath of fresh air. "My, this feels good," It was early, before sunrise, and he was straining his eyes in the darkness. He could see no one, and it seemed they were at the back of the castle.

"It is early," he said, turning to the others. "I'm sure the sun will come up soon. I will take Wilt and have a look around to see if we can find anyone else. We will come straight back for you."

Stepping out the door, they closed it behind them.

"We need to see if the others have entered. Let's try the tavern. We could be too early if we see no one entering the gate."

"Sounds good!" said Wilt, tagging along. "It will be a long walk from the back of the castle."

"We should have looked at the building back here. Oh well, on our way back. It feels good to be outside on the ground." They were walking toward the front, close to the houses where the king's workers lived.

"You know," he exclaimed, "the more I think about it, the more I feel we should go back to see what is in that building while it's dark." As they were about to turn, from around the corner came two formidable-looking guards walking toward them, clad in black, with red tunics, silver helmets, and high black boots. Both carried a spear and shield, with a sword and dagger tucked under their belts. Tyron tried to ignore them and walked past them.

"Halt!" yelled one guard. They both stopped.

"What's wrong?" asked Tyron, to give the impression they should be out walking.

"We can take these two," he whispered to Wilt.

"Where are you both going this time of the morning?" the guard asked.

"Just our early morning walk," Tyron said, smiling.

"Why do you have weapons on you?" That was when Tyron realized they had forgotten to leave them behind. His smile dropped.

"We are new to the village," he blurted out.

"You should have handed them in at the gate then," growled the guard.

"I don't believe they ever asked."

"You're not from here—" He stopped. "And why are both of you wet?"

"Nothing slides by you, does it?" said Tyron sarcastically. He was about to draw his sword when he saw six more guards marching up from around the same corner, dropping his hand until they passed. Now, the two guards took out their swords.

"You will have to come with us," the guard scowled.

"Good day for a fight." Tyron took his sword out.

"I think so." Wilt followed suit.

"Where were all these guards when we were looking?" He moaned.

"It's early; we must have missed them." They charged the two guards, overpowering them when six more guards now run back toward them. Suddenly, four more were running in from behind them.

"We would have to pick changing the guard time for a walk," shouted Tyron.

Wilt had no time to answer, swinging his sword at the first two as Tyron punched the first guard that came to him hard in the face. Their swords clashed early in the morning, with a shrill ring in the air.

Tyron overpowered another of the guards, kicking him to the ground while his blade clashed with two more. Wilt stood right behind him, and they were fighting back-to-back. Now, more guards surrounded them; Wilt slashed one to the ground. But a swift spear swung from a height and struck Wilt hard on his head; feeling the sharp pain instantly dulling his senses, he collapsed on the ground.

"I don't hear you," shouted Tyron, surrounded by five guards. Their swords aimed at his throat.

"Drop your sword, scum," snorted one guard.

"You appear to have me at a disadvantage," he smiled. "But I would watch your words; I will make you pay."

The guard laughed. "You will hand your sword over and come with us, scum," he snorted again.

Tyron dropped and swiftly punched the guard in the face, knocking him backward, stopping promptly to drop to one knee, offering his sword at once. A sharp, painful object struck his head a split second before he passed out.

The guards grabbed them both, and they were dragged down a flight of stone steps to the dungeons below. Upon arrival, the guard sitting at a table stood up and opened two thick wooden doors. The warriors were thrown into separate cells, both landing hard on the ground, comprised of rock with just a little scattered straw.

Regaining his consciousness, Wilt realized he was alone.

"Are you there?" Wilt shouted, rubbing his shoulder.

"I'm here," Tyron shouted back, rubbing the back of his head.

"Shut up, you two," shouted the guard.

"I think I'm pretty bruised up," Wilt shouted. "I must have landed badly in here, or out there, or both."

"Shut up," yelled the guard again.

"I guess this will mess things up for now."

"For now," shouted Tyron, who was still rubbing his head.

"Can you two just shut up in there? I'm here staying away from my wife with all her constant talking," shouted the guard again. "I don't need it here."

"We didn't ask to be here," Tyron shouted. It was quiet as they now reflected their time.

Now that the others had left on their separate ways, Asim, Lanee, Lube, and Zollo continued up their passageway of choice. They were all still wet but glad they were back on the dry ground again. The passage started upward, but it evened out; there were a lot of rocks to climb over. It kept straight, only veering right on a slope going down, where a large gate loomed in front of them.

"Oh my," Lanee sounded exhausted. "Another gate, and no, Anson." She sighed."

"I should have known," he said. "We won't finish with the gates until we are in the castle, which is my best guess."

Near the gate, there was a small rock formation they had to climb over. "It does not seem they use this gate at all," said Lube.

Zollo looked through the bars, seeing a door in the distance. "Another door," he moaned. "I hope this one will go into the castle."

"We must make it past this one first," said Asim. All four of them, taking their daggers in hand, chipped away at the bolt, taking time until it was exposed. With all of them pulling, it broke free, opening enough to let them all squeeze through. They moved on to the large, thick wooden door. Zollo had seen the tumblers; opening this door would need a little skill. Zollo stepped forward. "I happen to know a little about this type of lock," he declared, using the tip of his dagger to work on the tumblers inside the lock and slowly moving them until they aligned. The bolt pulled back, and they could open the door. He smiled.

"Woo, Impressive," admitted Lanee. "A skill you learned to break into maidens' bedrooms?" she said sarcastically. Zollo was flustered, but he smiled and said nothing. The door sat back on a small path with large rocks on either side leading to a walkway heading to the right or left.

Asim walked toward the left. But hearing voices coming his way, he made everyone move back behind the rocks.

An older woman and a guard passed by with a tray, talking as they passed them. Asim wanted a better look as he jumped up on the top of the rocks above them, heading in the same direction. The guard and woman walked down some stairs. Moving closer, he could see it was leading to the dungeons. Sliding across the rocks, he looked over the top. Two guards were sitting playing cards as the woman and the guard made it down to them.

"About time," said a guard sitting at the table.

"Think yourself lucky to have anything," she scoffed, handing them a wooden plate containing a large piece of cheese and two thickly cut slices of bread. The two guards ate from the plate.

"Anybody inside the doors?" she asked.

"Two earlier," said one guard.

"I will bring them something later today." She coughed, taking up the empty plate and leaving again with the guard.

Interesting, thought Asim. *But no children here*. Going back to the others, he told them what he overheard.

"Well, should we look to see who is locked in there?" asked Lanee.

"No," said Asim. "We will follow the walkway and believe it will take us inside the castle."

"Supposing they can fight?" said Zollo.

"Supposing they are drunk?" quipped Lube.

"We lost time in the cave. We need to be out on the castle grounds," said Asim.

Starting along the walkway once more, they had not traveled far this time before hearing loud footsteps coming their way. Running back to the rocks, they watched when four guards marched near them.

Strange, thought Asim. Telling the others to "Stay back behind the rocks," he kept low and followed the soldiers back far enough so they would not notice. Crouching at the top of the stairway, he overheard a guard say, "We are taking the prisoners to the king."

Oh, he thought, *they must be more important than drunks*. He was about to turn to join the others when he felt someone's hot breath at the back of his neck. His heart pounded in his chest. *Captured!* was his first thought. He turned, expecting to see a guard! Lanee at his back, along with Zollo and Lube, all crouched and smiling right behind him.

"Why are you all behind me?" he sternly whispered. All three continued smiling.

"Change of plan," he whispered again, putting his fingers to his lips. He walked down the stairway, almost at the bottom. He was looking at the guards, who were confused. They looked at him, taken by surprise. Asim jumped, kicking the closest guard hard against another, knocking them both to the ground. Using his fist, he punched one more of the guards, beating him to the ground as Lanee, Zollo, and Lube joined in from behind him to overpower the others. All six were lying on the ground now. Lanee and Lube had their swords aimed toward the guards' heads. One jumped up, trying to escape, but with a quick twist of her blade, Lanee sliced his cheek with the tip. He yelled in pain, holding his face to stop the blood.

"Next time, it will be your head! I slice off," she shouted. "Don't test me!" They all lay on the ground. Asim had Zollo grab the keys to the doors while Lanee and Lube made the guards take their weapons and throw them in the corner. He opened the first locked door, taking his sword out just in case. To his surprise, there, sitting on the ground, was Tyron.

"You will not believe this," he smiled. Zollo came to look, and a grin burst out; he gave the keys to Zollo to open the next locked door to find Wilt was sitting on the ground.

"What are you doing here?" Asim asked Tyron.

"Misfortune!" He said in a moronic tone. "Just misfortune."

Lanee laughed as she saw both men walk out of the cells.

"Put the guards in the cell! We will need their clothes."

"We will be the new king's guards." Asim smiled. They had the guards strip, and once they had their clothes removed, they used what could fit them. They locked the guards up inside.

"You won't be able to escape," shouted one of the guards.

"Oh, I believe we just did." Tyron smiled, now clothed like a guard.

"Try to look as much like a guard as you can. Lanee and Zollo, you are our new prisoners until we are outside. Grab the helmets, spears, and shields. We're walking out of here."

They left with Lanee and Zollo leading the four behind them. "Let's hope the others made it to the market square."

"Now tell me again how it was you ended up in here?" Asim asked Tyron, laughing.

Chapter 25

LOOK WHAT I FOUND

The old cart trail led back to the castle. Toya and Brantil were on the first cart, the oxen ready to plod along the track. They started toward the castle as it was close enough to sunrise.

"Too long sitting on these old seats," groaned Brantil, happy they were moving again.

"They are not comfortable, for sure." Toya smiled as they laughed. Tan and Exim were walking close to the ox.

Just behind them, Radel and Senso were sitting on the cart while Duf and Boben walked with the ox. A few villagers had caught up with them as a couple on horseback had passed them already.

Good! Radel thought. *We will be on time.* The castle loomed in front of them with its drab and desolate presence. Already, some of the villagers had entered, and they waited for their turn in line; as soon as it was Toya's turn, she watched as the guard walked around the cart, his sword in hand; he moved some of the wheat. The dwarfs were feeling vulnerable at this point and being as quiet as they could. It was difficult as he pushed some of the wheat. They were trying their best not to scratch or sneeze. Tan handed a small purse to one of the other guards, who waved them through. Now it was Radel's turn, and again, the guard went to the back of the cart. Boben handed one guard a small purse; he did not wave them through. He wanted to talk to Duf.

"You are not from here," he said. "Such a big man." He smiled, touching the muscle on his arm.

"He doesn't speak," Radel spoke up. "His mind is addled." She shook her head.

"Very well," said the guard, "but no trouble from your large man." He looked at Duf, who was nodding and grinning, playing the part.

The guard behind them had decided to check the wheat, raising his sword high, ready to plunge his blade deep into the cart. Radel looked back in panic. Suddenly, a horse reared behind them, catching the guard's attention. Lowering his sword back down, he watched the man bring his horse back under control as they eased on through the gate.

"My heart was in my throat," declared Radel to Senso.

"Mine too," came a little voice from under the wheat.

They were on their way to the center of the courtyard, the tables already set up with anticipation of the day. Duf looked at Radel and shook his head.

"Sorry! It was all I could think of that quick."

The sun was rising fast this day, soaring in the bluing sky as the darkness had disappeared. Pulling the cart up next to Tan, they unloaded a little wheat from both onto a table. Senso and Boben stayed to bind up the wheat into sheaves while the others took the carts to the outer wall so as not to draw any unwanted attention. Unhooking the yoke of the oxen, Duf and Tan walked both oxen to the stable.

"I wonder where they are. They have been gone too long," fretted Tonas as he spoke to Anson. "They would look for the others and come right back, is what Tyron had said. It's been too much time, I'm worried."

"Don't worry," Anson tried to calm him down. "I'm sure they know what they are doing. Let's have a quick look outside for peace of mind." Pulling the door back just enough for them both to look out, Tonas stuck his head out high, and Anson stuck his head out lower. The sun was rising, becoming daylight. They saw no one or anything, figuring they were somewhere on the back wall of the castle. Pulling their heads back in, they closed the door.

"Do you think we should go out there to look?" asked Tonas.

"I don't know." Anson thought for a second. "They should have been back. I am sure if we're not seen going out the door, we can find where the village people are."

"Do you think we can?" asked a now alert Tonas.

"We will go out into the courtyard, slip around the back. I saw no villagers this far back yesterday, so we should be careful. We don't want to be seen by the guards."

Tonas agreed.

"Well, straighten up and be prepared for anything. Let's go!" Pulling the door open. Still not seeing anyone, Tonas and Anson stepped out and closed the door.

Anson looked up at the tower; it appeared to be empty.

"That's strange; let's slip around the back of this building. Maybe we can work ourselves down along this wall."

"Whatever you think is best." Tonas sighed.

Suddenly, they heard voices along the wall. They moved back behind the building.

Anson grabbed Tonas, hiding them both at the back.

Peering around the corner, Anson could see six guards marching up the ramparts toward the tower.

"The guards are coming this way."

"Oh my, it's not our day, is it?" Tonas muttered in a nervous tone.

"Could be better! Let's move towards the front of the building." Tonas followed. As he looked around the corner, Anson saw a guard sitting on the steps of the building.

"There's a guard on the step," he whispered.

"Could this be any worse?" he whispered in a very panicked tone. "I'm not a great fighter," he nervously confided in Anson. "But I will do the best I can."

"We will only fight as a last resort," he whispered. "I never planned on it with just the two of us here."

This made Tonas feel a little better.

"We need to move around to the back again." He watched the guards go into the tower door.

"Let's go." They slipped around to the back. Then, both suddenly stopped, hearing a muffled scream inside the building.

"I know this sounds crazy, and they could catch us, but I must look," Anson whispered. "You must help me up to the window." Tonas bent over as Anson climbed on his back; as he straightened up, Anson was climbing onto his shoulders, his fingers grabbing Tonas, who was feeling the pain. He pulled himself up until his head was high enough to look in. He could see a vast number of children, some asleep, some playing, some were sitting down weeping.

Suddenly, the front door flew open, and the guard from the front step walked into the room. The children scattered, cowering, by the walls.

"Down quick!" he whispered. "We must go." He dropped onto his shoulders and slid down his back, causing Tonas to fall to the ground.

"Let's go." He grabbed Tonas by the shirt and pulled him to his feet. They were in a hurry to run to the wall. "We must move fast." Anson dragged him by his shirt to the wall, heading toward the market square.

"Hold on," Tonas whispered, trying to catch his breath. "You will pull me out of my shirt if we keep going."

"I saw many children, young boys," he was whispering to him. "Many of them." Out of breath, Tonas was trying to tuck in his shirt.

"The children?"

"Yes, that's where they are keeping them. We must find Asim."

"Was there a lot of children in there?" He stopped and tried to look back.

"No time." Anson grabbed his shirt and dragged him again.

"How did they not see us?" he asked.

"Don't know, don't care. Keep going." They were close to the stables now. As they were passing, they noticed Duf.

"Duf," Tonas shouted, "you are a sight for these old sore eyes." Duf came out and picked them both up for a hug.

"Shhh, quiet!" whispered Tan and put them down. No attention, remember?"

Duf nodded, dropping them. Tonas and Anson landed back hard on the ground again.

"Have you seen the others?" Tan asked. "And why is your shirt all wrapped around you?"

"We are only two," said Tonas quietly. "We were with Tyron and Wilt, but they left and did not return. I fear the worst. We were trying to run here as quick as we could."

"I'm sure they will be fine," muttered Tan.

"We have found the children." Tonas jumped and did a little jig. "Anson saw them in the building." He was twisting around.

"Which building? And stop dancing around."

"The one standing alone at the back." He was out of breath again.

"We will need to figure out how to break them out of there and break us out." He smiled.

"Let's go back to tell the others the good news!"

The others were standing behind the carts. The dwarfs had jumped out and were standing with them. Radel and Toya, seeing Tonas and Anson, gave them a quick hug. Tonas was still happy as he told them about the children. Everyone listened.

"That's wonderful news." Radel jumped up and down with Tonas as some of the others clapped.

"Stop!" shouted Tan. "No attention, remember."

"Now we will have to find the others," she said, "so we can break them out of here. Let's look around to see who we can find. We can split up into groups of two. There will be less chance of them stopping us for any reason. Tonas, put your shirt in, and we will go together. Anson goes with Senso, and Brantil can go with Toya. Tan, stay here in case anyone comes back. If there is any trouble, we will need you here with Duf.

"We will walk towards the living area. Toya takes the middle, and Senso try the tavern. I'm sure if Spen made it in, he could not resist the temptation." they laughed.

"We will check the well," said Tonas. "That's the way Stone was coming in. They may still be there."

"We can do that first," said Radel. "But we will need to leave our weapons here so that we won't be stopped by the guards."

The six of them walked to the market square and then split up from there.

"We must find the well." Radel pulled him toward the right side.

"I think it could be close to the living area," said Tonas. "Let's make our way back there," looking in each direction up and down for any sight of the others on the way.

When they arrived at the well, it was in use, as a woman was drawing water. They waited until she finished. Walking away carrying her bucket, she turned her head to stare at them before continuing her way.

"What was that about?"

"Maybe we look a little different! Or the fact we don't have a bucket?" Radel smiled as Tonas let out a quick laugh.

Tonas, still smiling, made sure no one was around before returning. Standing at the well, she bent her head over the top. "Stone!" she shouted. "Stone, are you down there?" No answer.

"Let me try," he said, leaning over the top. "Stone! Stone!" he yelled. Still, there was no reply.

Now, they both were shouting for Stone, but still, there was no answer. Hearing footsteps, Radel pulled her head up. Another woman approached from behind them, looking at Radel strangely. Tonas still had his head in the well. Grabbing his shirt, she pulled his head out.

"We lost our dog!" she exclaimed, grabbing his arm and they walked away, more embarrassed than anything, trying not to laugh.

"I'm sure they were not there," he said. He was busy tucking his shirt back into his pants.

"I think you are right."

"Come on, let's find that dog." He smiled, and then they both laughed, making their way toward the others.

Senso and Anson had stopped to talk to Exim and Boben on the way to the tavern to tell them about the children. And if, by chance, they had seen any of the others passing? But they had seen no one.

Anson noticed the tavern sign on the building in front as they walked toward the door. There was a lingering stench in the air.

"That's a foul smell," said Senso, holding his nose.

"Woo," said Anson, "it stinks even worse down here."

Senso looked down at him. "Try holding your breath until we are inside," he said. "I am sure it's coming from here, not the market."

As they opened the door, the smell wafted over them. There were a few people on the floor drunk. The tavern owner reclined on his elbows at the bar. Catching Senso's eye in the corner of the tavern, sitting at a table were Stone, Spen, Baylin, and Yuby, tankards in hand as they approached them.

"I see you have all settled in," quipped Anson.

"I swear we just arrived," said Stone, smiling.

"More ale!" shouted Spen.

"No!" said Stone. "That's enough."

"Come up here," shouted the owner. Spen shuffled to the bar, telling the owner, "Fill this pouch up with mead, my good man." He took his drink to the table where Anson and Stone had been talking.

"I need a drink," he slurred. "Just one more."

"We need you sober." Stone looked at him.

"I can assure you, I am fighting fit," he slurred.

"You may need to be ready." Stone leaned over and whispered about the children in his ear.

"Well, let's go then." He stood up, leaving his ale as they walked toward the door. Spen paid his money and grabbed his pouch as they stepped outside.

"My eyes!" he shouted, covering them with his pouch from the sunlight after walking out of the darkened tavern.

"Wait!" Stone stopped. "We have forgotten our weapons."

"Don't put them on," whispered Senso.

Going back with Baylin, they grabbed them all, wrapping them in their coats, trying to hide them as best they could for the walk across the courtyard.

On their way back, they grabbed Exim and Boben to ensure they were all together when they reached the carts.

Toya and Brantil had made it back. "I'm sure we saw Radel still out there."

"Stone!" Toya smiled. "I am glad we found you." She hugged him. "What should we do now?"

"Well, we will wait while keeping low," he said. "We will hold out for any news from Radel or the others. Together, we can come up with a plan to release the children. Let's use our time to think of anything that will help." He paced back and forth. *Where are you, Asim,* he thought to himself. The frustration was now building on his face.

Chapter 26

IT'S TIME TO GO

Now dressed like guards, Tyron, Lube, Wilt, and Asim marched up the great hall. Lanee and Zollo, their prisoners.

"Halt!" shouted Asim. They stopped for a moment before starting forward again.

"You said that with high authority." Tyron smiled.

"We would do ourselves an injustice not to look around these chambers for the children while we are here." Asim smiled.

"Lanee and Zollo, look outside but don't wander too far. Once you're out, you should blend in with the other villagers. Lube has your weapons if there is any trouble. They will walk you two out. We will meet you when we finish looking around in here."

"Let's go, Tyron." They marched back up the hallway, looking for any rooms or areas where they could keep the children. Marching through the halls, they passed other guards. "We have this salute down now as." A raised fist to the chest and out.

"You truly make the little guard," Tyron jested. Walking down a few steps, they found themselves in the kitchen.

"We need not to be in here—" Asim stopped in midsentence.

"What are you two doing in my kitchen?" boomed a voice behind them. They turned to see the cook; she was a small lady around five feet four inches tall, with a rounded body and a homely-looking face. She looked to be maybe fifty years old. "Guards are not allowed down here. You know the rules. Do you want me to fetch the king?" she said nastily.

"We are hungry," Asim was thinking fast.

"Yes," Tyron added, "we have not eaten in two days!"

"We wanted to see how beautiful you and your kitchen looked today and just to have a smell of your wonderful cooking." Asim was smiling at her.

"Well!" Changing her demeanor, she laughed, showing a smile with a few teeth missing.

"All right! I know that beastly old man doesn't feed you men, right? "She said, referring to the king, and she handed them both large chicken legs and a slice of bread each.

"Thank you," Asim said. "You are beautiful." They were trying to eat swiftly.

She looked at Asim. "My name is Kora. If you are even more hungry later tonight," she told him in her sexiest voice.

"I will keep that in mind." He smiled just as he closed his visor and turned to leave.

"It was all I could do not to choke." Tyron chuckled as they walked back up the stairs, still trying not to laugh. They continued their search for the children. They were walking down the hallway when a door flew open in front of them. It was the king himself, Brayon of Nordak. He was accompanied by two of his knights. He looked at them both with his irascible self.

"Move," he commanded with a flip of his fingers.

One knight turned to them. "Move out of here!" he blasted. "Move out now! Don't let me see you two again." He turned and continued to follow the king.

"I had to bite my tongue, but that was strange." Tyron shook his head. "We were in the hall. Did he order us to leave the hallway or the castle?"

"Or maybe both?"

"Let's keep looking. Maybe we should look in the other chambers."

"Hope we don't run into that nasty little man again, or I may have to hurt someone."

"Let's focus back on the children."

"You're right, but I would still like to hurt someone." Seeing Tyron angered, Asim shook his head. Busying themselves, they looked through the different chambers and hallways.

"It does not seem like they are here; we should go back outside."

"I believe that it could be this way," pointed Tyron, a little confused.

They walked down a long, winding hallway. Seeing a door ahead, they walked out and realized the hall had taken them to the opposite end of the king's court, close to the living quarters. Deciding to walk out anyway, they walked down the steps, noticing all the people busy on their way to and from the market or on their way to work at the king's court. As they reached the bottom of the steps, he noticed Radel walking close; he nudged Tyron. "It's Radel and Tonas."

"Radel," he shouted. She stopped, turning around to see who called out. Other than people scurrying by them, there were two guards on the steps; she could see no one else. Nobody had stopped.

"Radel," Asim shouted again and again she looked around.

"That sounds like Asim's voice," she whispered to Tonas. Asim and Tyron had moved closer now as they approached them. Tonas grabbed Radel's arm. "Let's go!"

Asim lifted the visor on his helmet. "Radel, it's me." Looking back this time, she saw his face.

"That's a relief," she sighed. "A good disguise. Is that Tyron?"

"It's me." He lifted his visor.

"Are there just two of you?" she asked.

"The others are close," he replied. "I was about to ask you the same thing; I'm happy to see you both. Are the others all here?"

"Most! Everyone that came through the gate," she said. Tonas was now talking to Tyron.

"What happened?" he asked.

"It's a long story. I will tell you when we have more time."

"Well!" Radel said. "You will be happy to know Tonas and Anson found where they are holding the children."

Asim put his hand firmly on Tonas's shoulder. "That is more than good news. Where are they?"

Tonas explained they were in the building at the back courtyard, with a guard on them.

"So you have not seen Stone and the others?" he asked.

"No, we have not seen him. We thought they might be with you. We sent others out to look for them."

Asim's mind was working.

"This is what we will do," he said. "I want you two to go back. If Stone is there, that's good. Then it will be Stone, Duf, Tonas, and you. If he is not back, take Toya with you.

"You will sneak the children out of the building. But you must be precise in your timing. You will wait until the guard changes, then move to the back courtyard and take care of any guards in front of that building.

"Take the children through the door in the wall, the one you came out of earlier, and Tonas, you lead them all back through to the entrance in the mountain. When you arrive, stay in the cave and wait a reasonable time. I will try to send someone. If no one arrives, leave with the children."

"What will you do?" she asked.

"We will go back, find Lanee and the others, and look for Stone. Have everyone stay safe and be ready. I am hoping we can save the children and find our way out of here without a fight. Well done," he told Tonas again.

"I will take the message back for the children, and if Stone is there, we will carry out the plan together," said Radel.

Radel and Tonas then crossed the courtyard, past the market square, on their way back, keeping an eye out for Stone. When they arrived back, Radel was all smiles, seeing Stone was there. After she had greeted him, she told him of her meeting and the plan that Asim needed them to carry out.

"It sounds like this plan will work." He walked over and talked to Duf, then called Tan and Toya over and told them what was about to happen. "You two will be in charge. Keep down and keep quiet. Wait for Asim's return. And hope we can slip out of here without a fight."

Stone, Radel, Tonas, and Duf tightened their weapons before they left. Moving along the wall to the stable, they waited under cover until they could hear the guards marching to change shifts. It was not long before the guards started across the ramparts.

"As soon as we hear them pass, we will run to the other end."

"I will do my best. Please don't pull my shirt," asked Tonas.

"Keep up as best you can." Stone was confused at what he was asking, looking at him strangely. "The tower should be empty for a short time."

As the guards passed over, the four of them took off running toward the back wall. Tonas was lagging a little behind them. No one had dragged him. He was smiling as they kept close to the wall.

"We don't have a lot of time," Stone said to Duf, looking at the door of the building and the guard who was sitting on the step outside. Stone was aghast when he saw Duf approach him, and the guard stood up.

"Halt!" shouted the guard, and that was the last thing spoken when Duf punched him hard. He landed up against the door. Turning his head, Duf smiled, grabbed the guard, and threw him back on the step as Stone ran to him and pushed open the locked door. The children were startled; some screamed. Tonas, who most of the children had seen before, along with Radel, were able to quiet them, bringing them under control and having them all follow them when they were leaving the building.

"Where's the door?" asked Stone. Tonas pointed to the back wall. Stone was helping them move out.

"Tonas, go in front. Duf, open the door." Duff walked ahead and pushed it open. Radel and some of the children ran; they were all trying to keep up. Stone hurriedly closed the door to the now-empty building, propping the guard up as best he could on the step.

Stone still had his eye on the guards, even at the other end of the castle. It looked like they had stopped there. *Why are they not coming back?* he wondered, swiftly picking up two of the children to help keep up with the others. Now all the children were in the cave, Duf closed the door behind them.

We should be safe for now, thought Stone. *The guards were a long way off, and they had not come back, so I believe no one saw us move the children.* Stone instructed them all to go back through the other door and gathered everyone together back further into the cave.

"That means every one of you must be quiet. No one will know we are here, and we will take you home." That started little murmurs. "Quiet, remember." They went silent again as Stone put his fingers up to his lips. Some children still clung to Tonas and Radel; two small children were hanging on tight to Duf's legs. He was happy to give them a ride.

"Tonas and Radel," Stone beckoned them over, "I need you to watch the children. I must go back to find out why the guards stopped so long at the front. Something seems wrong. Everything is going too well. I am hoping it has nothing to do with the others. But I need to know. I will take Duf. If we are not back, or anyone is not back, in a reasonable time, take the children back through the mountain as planned. Tonas, do you remember the way you came here?" He nodded. "I don't think it will do any harm to move back further into the cave while you wait."

"Let's go, Duf." When they were at the door, Duf pulled it back enough for Stone to put his head out. Looking around, he could not see any guards in the tower.

This is strange, he thought. "Let's walk back the opposite way. Maybe we will have a good view from the other side." Duf nodded and closed the door once they were out. They moved toward the living quarters, hoping for a better view. They eased their way toward the market square. They heard a commotion on the other side of the castle on the far wall. Six of the guards were looking down from the rampart, although two were heading back to the tower at the back of the castle. Stone and Duf walked across close to the market square, heading toward the carts. Seeing there was a substantial argument going on, some of the villagers seemed to be shouting at Tan. And he could hear Tan yelling back. Not sure of what they said between them all, he watched as three guards from the front were on their way to join the newly formed crowd.

Chapter 27

NOT WITH MY OX YOU DON'T

Earlier, after Stone, Duf, Radel, and Tonas had left, an older man in his late fifties came to the carts where Tan and the others were, claiming his cart had been stolen away in the night. Someone had tied him up in his house and tried to kill his dog.

"That is not so," shouted Tan. "You have no proof that that is your cart."

"I do," the older man shouted while some of the villagers had gathered around. The guards on the rampart stopped to see what all the fuss was.

The older man explained that he had put a cross on the cart. Tan replied that anybody could say that! "How do I know? You could have painted a cross earlier."

The older man yelled, "You are a thief!" The guards on the rampart looked down. Now, one had walked to the front tower to summon help as three guards were strolling from the front. It was about that time Stone and Duf made it back. Stone could hear the villager's shouts.

"That's not right. They are thieves." one shouted. "They are not even from around here!" One of the three guards looked at the older man and then at Tan. "What is the problem?"

The older man told the guard that they stole his ox and cart and tied him up in his house.

"That is a lie!" shouted Tan.

"That's a serious charge," said the guard. "Do you have any proof of this?"

"There is a cross burnt in on the bottom side of my cart. He didn't even know it was there. He accused me of painting the cross on the cart?" The other villagers agreed. When the guards looked, they found the cross burnt into the wood. "There is also a cross burnt on my ox," he added.

"Maybe the carts are mixed up," shouted Tan in his defense.

"Let's look in the stable," asserted the guard. As they walked, a small crowd of villagers continued to gather and followed them to the stables, as two of the six guards on the rampart now headed to the back tower.

The older man went over to the ox and showed the guards the cross burnt on the ox's lower side.

"Well, that's not my ox!" shouted Tan. "Mine is over there," he pointed to another one.

"That's mine!" a voice shouted from back in the now-gathered crowd.

"The older man is right. They are thieves!"

"Not even from here!" someone else cried out.

"It's turning into a hostile crowd," shouted Tan. "You know this is a mistake."

"Well," the guard paused, "you will have to come with us. We have a serious matter here. You must answer to the king."

"I don't think I will do that." Tan stood tall.

The three guards pulled out their swords. Tan stomped with all his weight on the first guard's foot and punched him hard, knocking him to the ground. Stone stepped in to plunge his sword into one of the others, who had stepped backward when four arrows zipped through the air and swiftly struck the four guards on the rampart above them. They all toppled over on top of the stable roof, and part of it gave away; their bodies then fell to the ground. Duf grabbed the last one standing, holding him high in the air; he punched him hard. He landed in front of the crowd of people, who had now started running away screaming, running in all directions to move away. The older man scampered from the stable, heading toward the market square.

"You can keep the ox," the older man shouted back, "And the cart, too, if it means so much to you." The crowd dispersed fast as most had run for safety.

"Well," Stone smiled at Tan, "Looks like we have a problem now."

"I knew I should have killed that older man," Tan snarled to himself. "He has made a mess for us all. Let's go back and join the others."

"Duf." He pointed to the two unconscious guards on the ground. Duf entered the stable, grabbing enough rope to tie them both up together before moving them back to the stable, dragging the dead bodies of the guards back there as well.

Stone was telling everyone to put on their weapons. "I'm sure we are not leaving here without a fight."

They lowered the front gate while he watched. "There it goes." Stone shook his head. "Every one of you," now talking to the dwarfs, "thank you for the guards earlier. Now concentrate on those at the front of the castle. Keep your sights on the front tower so they won't pick us off."

"Duf, can you stick the carts in the ground handles first?" Duf smiled, lifting each large carts and rammed the handles into the ground.

"There." Stone smiled. "This should give us a little more coverage. Everyone stays behind the carts the best that you can."

"I'm wondering where Asim is now that the fun is about to start. I hope that he makes it back soon."

Chapter 28

AND SO IT BEGINS

Lube and Wilt had now moved with Lanee and Zollo out into the courtyard below the steps to the king's court. They both figured they were doing well and had mastered the greeting when passing the other guards.

"We need to look for the children in and around the stable areas," Wilt insisted.

Lanee agreed but decided to mingle and look further down. As they went to check the buildings closer to the market square, Lube and Wilt walked toward the stables.

"This is nice." Lanee inhaled the fresh air as she walked with Zollo. "We can walk around and not worry."

They walked into the first building to look. "Too small," she mused. Coming out, they encountered the king's guards marching in a hurry toward the market square and had to jump back out of the way.

"They are in a hurry." She was curious.

"What?" Zollo looked at her, puzzled. "I have trouble hearing due to the noise. Should we follow them?" he shouted.

"I don't know. Maybe we should find Lube and Wilt to see if they know what is happening?"

"Maybe we should find Lube and Wilt," he shouted, holding his hand to his ear.

She pushed him hard as they started running back toward the stable.

"What do you think?" yelled Zollo. She held her hand to her ears, mocking him and laughing.

"They look like they are going into battle," she shouted.

"I could not hear," he defended himself as they were entering the door. They soon found Lube and Wilt at the end of the stables.

Lube was concerned, seeing Lanee and Zollo breathing heavily from running. "What's going on with you two?"

"We don't know," she gasped. "All the guards are running towards the front of the castle."

"Well, that can't be good. Do you think the others are in trouble?"

"We don't know if they are even here yet." Her breath was slowing. "And we have seen no sign of Asim and Tyron. I hope they are not the ones in trouble!"

"They are in the king's court somewhere," Wilt added. "So they should be all right; whatever is happening is at the front. Although they have been gone a long time."

"Maybe we should look for them."

"They should have followed when all these guards marched out," Lube remarked.

"Should we all go to the great hall to see if we can find them," she asked.

"What about the others?" Lube was worried.

"What if they are in trouble?" said Wilt. "We need to follow the guards to find out what is happening at the front."

"You could be right. It would be best," Zollo thought out loud.

"Let's do this," Lanee posed, "go see what is happening at the front and then decide from there what we should do?"

"I agree." Wilt nodded. "They can look after themselves." Coming out of the stable, a few more guards marched past; they turned and followed behind them.

"It looks as if we are going to the market square. The guards have stopped there." Zollo was wondering why.

"Can you see anything, Wilt?" Lanee shouted. She was right behind him. Even being the tallest, he was still straining his neck to see over the top of the guards.

"Not so far," he replied. "I need to move in closer. It seems something might be on the outer wall, or perhaps it is toward the front gate. I see arrows flying in both directions." He pushed his way through for a better view.

As the first guards arrived in the square, they found cover, upturning tables to hide behind, waiting for more troops to run to the square. Villagers and merchants screamed and pleaded, trying to move out of the guard's way while they knocked down and trod on many, even kicking some to the ground. The guards turned over more tables while they pushed forward.

Stone and the others were back behind the carts when a barrage of arrows whistled in toward them from the front tower; most struck the wooden carts with a loud thud and some with a clanging chink, hitting off the castle wall.

Too far out from the cover of the cart, an arrow hit Mup, who screamed at the extremely painful strike to his arm. It knocked him back against the cart, pinning him to the wood as the blood oozed from the wound. Duf grabbed him, pulling Mup and the arrow out of the wooden cart.

"A flesh wound," he exclaimed. Pooly stuffed a piece of cloth in his shirt to stop the bleeding.

"You sure you're all right?" Stone asked.

"Not too painful. Ripped my coat up, though."

"Sit back and rest. It might be your only chance. Dwarfs, Toya, and Boben, aim your arrows at the front wall. Let's try to keep them quiet if we can. Everyone else, set your sights on any oncoming guards entering the square. Everyone shoots at will," shouted Stone. The noise was increasing as the battle raged on, ducking another barrage of arrows from the front of the castle. Just hearing the zing in the air, they knew to stay low as the arrows struck close around them. Now, they could retaliate before most of the guards could reload again.

"Good aim," shouted Stone. Seeing several arrows strike the guards, he watched them fall to the ground.

"Keep it up," he shouted to the rest as they stood firm, continuing to shoot at the guards at the market square.

"No need to aim. Shoot into the crowd." Several more guards fell. The arrows were hitting their mark despite any resistance with their shields.

Spen was now clutching his pouch more than his bow.

"You need you to use that bow." Stone stared at him.

"I will," Spen replied, taking a quick sip of courage.

Stone could see the guards moving again towards them from the square. "We must load faster. We don't want them closing in on us." Again, they dispatched arrows in quick succession; this seemed to slow the guards down, stopping them from gaining any ground.

"Yes, excellent work, everyone." Now, the guards were pushing and shoving everyone back behind the tables again.

"We're holding them again," shouted Tan. Much of the screaming had stopped while most of the villagers had ducked down, finding places to hide in the front of the buildings, or between the guards, and behind the tables.

The arrows from the front tower still had Stone and the rest of them trapped behind the carts, despite Toya and the Dwarfs continued battling with the front tower. *A tiresome battle so far*, Stone thought; they still held their own against the king's guard at the market. Stone knew they could keep the guards back until their arrows ran out! But he was not sure how long it would take until they did.

An arrow struck Boben, glancing off his leg. "Not much blood with that one," he boasted, hiding the pain. Another arrow caught Duf right above the shoulder, ripping his shirt and leaving a bloody gash.

"Their arrows are too close," yelled Stone. "Tan! I need your help." They both ran toward the stables as arrows flew all around them. They grabbed up the shields and spears on the ground; an arrow whistled through the air, painfully catching the back of Stone's head, ripping out some of his hair and a layer of skin. He grabbed his head, feeling the blood on his fingers, putting up a shield for cover. Radel and the others continued shooting arrows at the guards in the market square, dug in behind the tables.

"That was almost my head!" he shouted. On their return, Radel wrapped Stone's head with a piece of cloth to stop the bleeding. Knowing that three shields would not make a lot of difference, but it had to help.

Anson could see the guards at the front had now formed together and were advancing toward them on foot. "Problem!" he shouted. "They are marching this way." Standing, the dwarfs were shooting arrows in that direction. They struck a few of the guards, delaying them for a moment, but they continued to march again. They shot once more, but they only slowed them again. They continued to advance.

Duf, sensing the problem, grabbed one of the spears. Swinging his arm, the high velocity with which he threw it struck one of the guards, splitting his head. Blood spurted in every direction. The spear continued into the next guard marching behind him; both fell to the ground. Duf, grabbing another, threw again, this time penetrating straight through a shield. It struck, killing the guard behind, plunging into his chest, and he fell back against another. Panic gripped the faces of the guards behind them. Seeing Duf holding another spear, they turned and ran back toward the tower.

The dwarfs cheered, but then an arrow hit Duf, a painful blow in the shoulder. Radel was quick to pull it out. Duf smiled at her as she patched him. Again, the arrows flew in toward them. "Dig in," shouted Stone. "This could be a long one!"

Chapter 29

IN THE HEAT OF THE BATTLE

Asim and Tyron had changed their minds on their way back through the door they had just come out. Now, both were feeling good that they had located the children and had an excellent chance for everyone to slip out of the castle without a fight.

"We should have gone back the other way," Tyron murmured. "Don't know why we are going this way. We need to find Lube in the front area." There was no time to answer as they heard the thunderous steps of the guards running through the great halls. They hid behind a wall.

"What on earth?" whispered Asim. "I hope it's not what I am thinking."

Oh, Lord, Tyron thought. He gulped. "Why are we hiding when we have on their uniforms?"

"A force of habit. Let's go back out."

"With all that's going on, this might be a valuable time for us to look for gold." Tyron grinned.

Asim gave him a blank stare, raising his eyebrows.

"I guess you are right," said Tyron as they walked forward. "What about—" retorted Tyron but stopped and nodded.

"Wait," Asim blurted out.

"You've changed your mind?" This surprised Tyron.

"No! More guards are coming this way." They ducked back behind the wall again, looking at each other, and laughed. They let the rest of the guards run past them.

"We must go out," he said as they followed behind the guards, closing their visors not to be recognized as they came rushing out of the great hall.

Asim looked around, trying to see Lanee. Her long, flowing black hair caught his eye. She was heading toward the market square behind a mass of guards.

"When do we fight?" An eager Tyron was looking over Asim's shoulder.

"Well, we don't know who they are fighting, so we better find that out first!"

"I guess you are right." He shrugged.

As they walked down the steps, Asim could hear the king, surrounded by several knights, coming out from the hall behind them.

"What is happening?" the king shouted.

"We have intruders in the castle, my lord," one of the guards close to them shouted back.

"How many?" the king cried out. "And how did they break in here?"

"A lot of them, I believe, my lord. And we're not sure?"

The now red-faced king was at the top of the steps. "Fetch Zabin," he demanded. He was livid.

"Yes, my lord," screeched one of the knights.

"Bring him here now!" he shouted. As the knight left, the king stood there looking over the area with a disgusted look on his face.

"We must find the others." Asim grabbed Tyron and whispered, "I am sure we are the ones that are in trouble. I don't know what went wrong." They moved toward the square.

Wilt had moved close enough now to see what was happening. An arrow whistled within a whisker of his head. He could see people hunched down behind two upside-down carts. He was quick to recognize Duf and Stone. *Better go back*, he thought. He joined with Lanee, Lube, and Zollo. "It's our party," he shouted. "They have them pinned down behind two carts at the outer wall. What are we going to do?"

"We must stop these archers from shooting arrows at them." Lanee seemed determined.

"I think we might be a little outnumbered." Lube sighed.

"Well, we must try anyway!"

"You're right." Perking up, Lube threw his helmet off. Wilt did the same. "I can't breathe in these things." Taking his spear, he threw it into the back of a knight standing at the back of the crowd. The knight fell forward into the guards close to him. Wilt threw his spear, striking another guard when they turned to see what was happening. The guards did not know which way to turn as confusion broke out!

Asim and Tyron moved fast off the steps, heading to the market square, pulling off their helmets and taking hold of their spears to throw them at the guards standing at the back, hitting with a force that knocked them forward. Asim and Tyron continued running ahead, using their shields as a ram. With strength, they ran and pushed forward many of the guards until they both stopped, grabbing their swords; now, their battle had begun.

"Now you have your fight!" he shouted to Tyron as they wielded their swords against the guards, fighting now in the crowded market square. Lanee's long black hair caught his eye, turning his way.

"We were wondering where you were," she yelled.

"Good, I'm glad you had the same idea!" he yelled. "We are a bit outnumbered now, but have them confused." They were fighting 'tooth and nail with the guards at the rear.

Stone and the others continued to shoot at their front line. Now, the noise level had increased. All the shouting and screaming had disrupted villagers hiding under the tables. Anyone who moved too close to the battle was kicked and trampled. They ran, leaving them open to any stray arrow.

Still behind the carts, Stone stood up, looking perplexed. Not believing his eyes, he watched as the guards behind the tables stopped their barrage of arrows aimed toward them to turn their attention to something big happening behind them. He told the others to "stand and shoot." Now having easy targets, they took full advantage.

"Take your time," shouted Stone. "Hit your target." Tables and bodies were being pushed forward and strained while they were being stretched. Some were falling over each other, and they spilled out into the courtyard. Stone was sure it was not by choice. Something or someone forced the guards forward. Those at the front were turning to retaliate, trying to pull tables close to cover them from the arrows hurtling toward them.

"Looks like a fight has flared from the rear of the guards," Stone shouted. "I believe Asim is behind this. Draw your swords. We are going into battle to meet them! Toya and Anson, keep the guards from shooting us from the front tower." Stone looked out again; he could see the battle was about to rage, waiting for them to join in the fray.

Lanee, Lube, and Zollo continued to push forward, kicking, punching, and swinging their swords from the right side, striking down as many as they could. The battle was heating up. Tyron was sweating and bleeding, pushing up to close the gap along with Lanee to prevent the guards from circling back behind them. The clashing of steel was thunderous. Lube was backing up as a guard knocked Wilt down. A painfully sharp blade ripped his shoulder. He was glad he still had on the hard uniform top. Still pushing from the left, Asim was wielding his sword, feeling the steel of a spear that sliced his arm while pain seared his brain. Blood oozed through his now torn shirt. He turned, striking down one of the knights with a decisive sword stroke. Another blade whistled past his head; there was no time to stop. Wiping the sweat away, he sucked up the pain and continued to battle more of the guards.

Stone and the others had arrived, battling in the front courtyard. Steel crashed and flashed in the bright sunlight. Duf was now taking pride in clubbing the guards. With a vicious streak, he beat one down with a sickening thud of his bloody club. He was ready to smash the next one as he muscled his way through them, not stopping as a spear struck his chest. Blood dripped as he pulled it out to continue battling.

They knew they were not coming out of this one unscathed; the pain, lumps, cuts, the oozing, and dripping blood were all part of what their bodies had to absorb. Stone and the others were battling fiercely, intending to beat everyone they fought. They had waded well into the guards now.

Stone could see Asim, and he felt a smile come to his lips, with the aim to surround them. Brantil was handling his sword well, trying to keep them back. Baylin, with a black eye, and Exim, who had received a massive cut on his now bloody face, were working tirelessly together, as were the other villagers. The slimy mix of blood and sweat mingled with all their cuts and bruises as they were trying hard to battle at every moment, standing back on their feet when knocked to the ground. They continued to stand firm. The guards were also holding their ground and pushing back. Tonas, Senso, and Tig were overpowered and knocked to the ground. Tig screamed as a spear struck his side. They tried to rise. Then, a sudden swoosh of arrows came into the air, and guards fell. Shouts and yells rang out as more arrows struck. Merchants and villagers were screaming, trying to flee. A surprised Stone looked to see Toya, Anson, and Benson. All three were shooting their bows right behind them now.

"I thought you could use a little help," she shouted. "We saw you were in trouble, and it had slowed up at the front. I left enough of the dwarfs to hold them off."

Asim had come face-to-face with a spear forced in his direction. With just enough agility, he blocked and deflected with his sword, turning swiftly to plunge his blade deep into the guard still on the other end. The warriors kept locked in battle, fighting with pride for every inch of ground. Their struggle was real: the slashing, ripping, gashing, and hacking. Even when stabbed, kicked, or knocked to the ground, they kept fighting with the intent to overcome and beat these guards. Blood seemed to stain everywhere. The shouts of pain echoed loud. Each of them had fought as two people today. Asim was extremely proud of the way the villagers put their training to use. Lacerated, bloody, and bruised, they still continued trying to push back the guards.

Suddenly, there was an ear-piercing sound from a large horn at the king's court. They had to cover their ears; he could see the king back on the step. He had the warlock Zabin with him; the guards now backed up to the side, allowing a gap through the middle where they had been fighting.

They took advantage as Asim signaled everyone to gather. They were feeling tired but good about the battle so far, and now they were back together again, even though it was a hard-fought fight.

Again, he looked to see what plan they could be hatching. Asim knew the king still had his bad temper. They watched him shouting at everyone close to him, including the warlock. Asim saw that Zabin had a large pouch wrapped around himself. He saw his bony fingers reaching into the bag, picking out two big bottles. Putting one bottle in each hand, he poured the contents of one into the other, and he shook it well, placing the empty bottle back in his pouch. He could see both bottles had contained a dark liquid or powder. He could not determine what he was saying but was sure it was a spell or incantation. Zabin took the mixture and poured it in a line in front of him a length long.

Suddenly, from the ground, Asim could see smoke. A white cloud filled the air, turning darker and darker. It kept wafting up in the air, so thick they could no longer see Zabin or the king through the smoke.

Even in this fleeting time, each person had stopped to see what was happening.

Suddenly, there was a movement. Out of the smoke, there appeared a line of soldiers.

Standing around six feet tall, these were not regular soldiers. Not human looking but pale like chalk, as if dead; their eyes looked bright blood red. They wore tattered-looking clothes over a body of bones covered tightly with old skin that looked like it didn't fit anymore. They had lined up six abreast, but he could see more gathering behind them. Slowly, they marched forward. A slight glint of the sun bounced off their dirty silver helmets on their skulls, with their swords and shields clutched in their hands.

"We need to move back to the carts to regroup." Asim knew of the strange things the warlock could conjure. *Soldiers of the dead*, he thought as they were moving in a slow, methodical march toward them.

"What are these things?" shouted Tan, now catching up with the others.

"Something from Hades, I fear," shouted Spen as he kept taking large sips from his pouch.

"We need to regroup," shouted Asim. He could see Boben and the other dwarfs still shooting arrows at the front tower, keeping the guards at bay.

Chapter 30

QUEST FOR THE CHILDREN

S tone! The children? Where are they? What happened? Are they safe?" Asim said, concerned.

"All are safe," he replied. "They are in the cave. Radel and Tonas are with them. I even had them move down the passage so they would not be close to the door."

"That's all good! But I need you to take the children to safety!"

"I need to stay here and fight with you," Stone pleaded.

Asim put his arms around his shoulders. "You are the best man," he said to him. "I put my trust in you. This quest has been for us to recover the children and take them home. I know you want to continue to fight by my side, but you are the one I need. I know they will make it home with you.

"There is a real possibility we all may not make it out of here alive. If we do, we will meet you at the first cave entrance. If we are not there in a day, I want you to take the children, leave on the journey home, and complete our quest."

"I will take them back." Stone smiled.

"I also will need you to take Brantil and Spen with you. The last thing I need is to watch them die here. We have been lucky so far, a few cuts and bruises." Asim went over to Brantil and Spen, explaining what he wanted them to do.

Spen, taking a sip from his pouch, stepped forward. "I'm ready." Now standing, the three of them took one last look at the approaching soldiers of the dead; they had now reached the market square.

Stone made sure they moved briskly along the wall; reaching the stable, he could see the bound guards were waking. Taking the butt of his sword to their heads, he made sure they stayed out for a while longer. "Let's keep going." He took one last look at his friends.

He could see them running into battle, making him feel lost for a moment. Then, realizing the task ahead, he moved them along the wall, aware of the guards that could be at the building or in the tower. Stepping closer, Stone could see no one in the building.

They must have found the children missing, he thought. *That's not good*. But deep down, he knew it would happen sooner or later, though he would have rather it happened later! Looking at the tower, he noticed two guards talking together, staring outside the wall. They did not seem aware of what was happening inside the castle. Maybe they were thinking about another attack from outside and making it easy for the three to move to the front of the building unseen.

"We can take them," whispered Spen, taking a quick sip.

"That's the spirit," whispered Brantil.

"Let's hope your spirit is not all in that pouch," whispered Stone.

"We made it through without being seen." Sliding his head around the corner, he saw the guards still on the wall.

"Are we going to slip by them?" Brantil squeezed his shoulder.

"We don't have enough time to run to the door, even though they are looking the wrong way. We have been lucky so far. Spen is right. We need to take them down and hope it's only two."

"I'm ready," Spen quietly blubbered, with a little slur in his voice.

"How good with a bow are either of you two?"

"I do all right," Brantil whispered. "I still hunt, and I have shot a few today."

"We need to take these two out and pray there is no more inside the tower."

"I have your back," Spen slurred again.

"As we step out from this building, we need to aim and shoot." Stone took one more look. He could see they had turned around and facing them now. One was pointing toward the building.

"I'm not too good with a bow," slurred Spen again, putting his fingers to his lips.

"I already figured that. Just stay back and stop drinking. We need you sober." Spen let out a laugh, then put his hand over his mouth.

Shaking his head, Stone counted, "On three,"

They both ran from the side of the building. Stone could see both guards were moving. He shot his bow when his arrow struck the first guard high in the chest, knocking him down. Brantil's arrow hit the second guard in the arm, who had sensed the danger as he dispatched his spear straight at them. Stone was rolling his body, landing back up on his feet. *That spear was not close*, Stone thought, loading his arrow again. This time, it struck the guard in the head; the first guard stood again. Stone loaded his shot and pierced into his neck, knowing for sure he wouldn't stand up again.

"Glad that's over." He dusted himself. "I see no more. What—" Stopping, he looked back and saw Brantil down. The spear had struck him on the left side below his rib cage, and he lay on the ground. Spen had rushed out to help him.

"We will pull out the spear," ordered Spen, telling Stone to look in the building to find anything to bandage him. Stone rushed back with some cloth he found, now amazed at how Spen was taking care of the wound, giving Brantil his dagger to bite.

He told Stone to pull the spear fast. As he did, the blade dropped from Brantil's mouth, and he screamed in pain. Spen took his pouch, pouring mead into the slit and bandaging the wound tight as Brantil somehow seemed to look stronger.

"Remarkable," expressed Stone. "How do you feel? Can you stand?"

"I think so." Spen gave him the pouch, and Brantil took a drink. They both helped him to his feet. "It's painful, but I will be all right."

"Good." Spen took his pouch back.

"Ah, let's have one more drink." Spen offered the pouch to Brantil.

"Not this time."

"All right! I will have a drink for you." He then put his pouch back on his shoulder.

"Are you sure you will be strong enough to walk," asked Stone.

"I am," he said, "I'm not going to let you down." There were no more guards as Stone helped him walk to the door. Stone pushed it open enough for them to enter. Letting Brantil and Spen sit down, he picked up enormous rocks that he could find and stacked them at the door.

"A surprise for anyone opening it." He was sweating by the time he finished up. "Let's go find Tonas and Radel." They moved past the next gate and down the passageway. They heard voices when they walked past the small and larger rocks to the bend in the pathway.

"That doesn't sound like children," whispered Brantil with a cough.

"Let's be quiet and move slow," Stone whispered. Keeping close to the wall, they moved toward the voices, which were becoming louder.

"They are coming this way." Stone moved to the other wall to have a better view. He motioned for Brantil and Spen to keep back. "It looks like four guards," he told them.

"They have Tonas, Radel, and the children prisoners. Draw your swords. We will surprise them, but we will need to be careful around the children."

Spen moved back to the large rocks. "Stay behind them. You are our backup plan."

Spen took a sip. "I will be ready."

"Can you handle your sword?" he asked Brantil.

"I can, I'm all right."

They moved forward to meet them around the corner. Both the front two guards had torches, although it was not dark in the cave, two in the back with their swords out aimed at Tonas and Radel. And the children were in line between them. The guards now approached the corner.

Stepping out in front of them both, Stone and Brantil wielded their swords, not waiting for words as they plunged their swords deep into each of the guard's chests. One fell backward, while the other dropped forward, grabbing Brantil's arm to punch him hard in his stomach.

Stone, with one swing of his sword, sliced the guard's neck. Still holding on to Brantil's arm, he dragged them both toward the ground. Brantil, his body painful, he was trying to keep standing. "I'm all right," he rasped, coughing as he removed the guard's hand, working to steady himself. His legs weakened right before he fell. Stone reached and grabbed his arm, pulling him back up to his feet.

The guard dropped to the ground. Blood from his neck was spurting out, scaring the children. They ran, shouting, screaming, and causing panic, running into each other as they moved closer toward the other two guards.

One shouted, "Stop and shut up!" The children stopped. Most lay flat on the ground, and some whimpered and cried out. He bellowed again for them to shut up.

"What's going on up there," yelled the other guard. As Stone moved closer to them, Brantil was slow, walking on his own again, holding his stomach tight.

"I suggest you drop your swords," shouted Stone.

Brantil was behind him, trying to ease the children's fears, telling them everything would be all right, but most were crying and anxious at this point.

"I believe it's the other way around," shouted the guard with his sword blade against Radel's neck. "I will cut her head off if you move closer to us." The other guard had his sword blade tight against Tonas's neck. Stone could see a slight trickle of blood seeping from its point already.

"We will kill these two and most of the children before you can make your way back here," he shouted.

"So you two drop your swords, turn around, and walk in front of the children. Pick up those torches and lead us out of here. Try anything foolish, and I will cut her head off."

"I did not plan for that one," Stone scowled. They dropped their swords and turned back to pick up the torches. He gave one to Brantil, who was still holding his stomach tight. Stone could see new blood leaking out on his shirt.

"Are you going to be all right?" he asked.

"I will be fine," he coughed again. Stone could tell as he was talking he was holding back the pain.

"We will do as they say for now!" said Stone. Some children still whimpered, being told to stand and follow the torches.

"Move," the guard bellowed in no uncertain terms to the children, kicking them to move them quicker.

As they walked back up the passageway toward the door, the guards picked up their swords as they came to them. They had only walked but a short distance when Stone heard what sounded like a skirmish behind them, followed by loud shouts and a scream. The children were crying and screaming again. Turning, he looked back, at first not seeing the guards but then seeing Tonas and Radel hugging Spen. As he moved forward through the children, he soon saw the two guards lying on the ground.

"Spen!" Stone stood, astounded. "You have overpowered two guards, and no one was hurt! You amaze me."

"I amaze myself sometimes," slurred Spen as he nonchalantly took a swig from his pouch. "I believe I had a little luck." He was smiling. "I'm sure that surprised by me, the one guard tripped on a rock and fell into the other's sword, then as that guard ran at me, he tripped on a child, and falling forward, he fell onto my sword, I really don't know," he slurred. Stone hugged him.

Tonas and Radel worked to console the children.

"Grandfather! Grandfather!" Stone heard one child shouting. He ran toward Brantil, who had settled down on a rock, still holding his stomach tight. Stone figured it had to be his grandson Leham; he wrapped his arms around Brantil.

"Grandfather!" He kissed his cheek.

"I thought I would never see you again," Brantil said, trying to smile through the pain.

"Where is Father? Is he with you?"

"Yes." Brantil groaned with the pain, trying to lay back against the rock.

"He is close. We are here to take you home." The child smiled and hugged Brantil again. Stone approached them. He could see Brantil slipping back down the rock.

Hastily making his way to them, he put his arm around Brantil for support. Then he helped him sit on the ground to use the rock for back support. The pain was showing on his face.

"Are you hurt?" asked Leham. "Grandfather, you're hurt." Tears were running from Brantil's eyes as he held Leham tightly.

"Brantil," said Stone, "Brantil." He shook him lightly. There was no response. He had his eyes closed as the last teardrop rolled down over his cheek.

"Grandfather," said Leham as he moved back to look at his face.

Stone put his arms around the boy, easing him away from his grandfather.

"No, no," the boy yelled and struggled with him; Stone held him tight. Looking down, Stone could now see Brantil had died. Tears flooded Leham's eyes as he realized what had happened.

He was screaming for his grandfather as Stone continued to hold him. Tonas and Radel had made their way to them now, and tears already were in Radel's eyes as she saw Brantil and Leham. The other children also cried with everything that had happened. It was a solemn moment; looking at Leham, Stone released his grip and lightly moved him to where Radel could now wrap her arms around him, holding him as tight as she could.

"It's not fair," he sobbed in a sympathetic voice; tears were in his eyes.

"Sometimes life is not fair," she told him in a soft voice so he would feel secure in this emotional time.

Stone and Tonas moved Brantil's body behind one of the large rocks, making sure they placed it out of sight of the children, who were now slowly realizing what had happened. With nervous and agitated looks about them, they were trying to come to grips with everything that just unfolded. They had witnessed multiple deaths of the guards and now Brantil's.

"We need to cover his body." Stone looked at them. They looked for rocks. Stone dragged the bodies of the guards behind some large rocks, including the first two, so the children would not have to look at them. They covered Brantil's body with the rocks.

Stone approached the children, gathering them around. "With everything you have been through," he said, "I need you all to stand tall."

"This is a sad time. And you can cry." Spen and Tonas held their arms out for any of the children in need of a hug. Radel was still holding Leham tight, knowing he was still grieving; Stone had children clinging to him. "We want to help you all out of this mountain and home to your villages and your loved ones—your mothers, fathers, and friends."

Stone's words helped them feel better, assuring them they would be going home to see friends and family again after everything that had happened.

Chapter 31

THE BATTLE BEGINS AGAIN

Staying sheltered behind the carts, Asim poked his head up, peering over the rail of the cart and looking out at all the soldiers that the warlock, in his evil mind, had conjured up to march steadily toward them.

"It will be to our advantage to fight them out there," shouted Asim. "I don't want to be backed up against this wall, not now anyway. In our first attack, we will use bows. This way, we can hold their advance. They only have a sword, so we will reload as we go. It will give us time until we battle them sword to sword. Take up your bows and be ready.

"Anson, I will need you and the rest of the dwarfs to have our backs, defending us from the guards at the front wall. On my shout, we will start. Be ready for anything that could happen. Let's go!"

They moved, boldly dispatching arrows toward the advancing soldiers, most hitting their mark. Several of the soldiers dropped to the ground as the arrows hit. Asim and his men reloaded their bows on the run, shooting a second time with almost the same result. The arrows struck down more of the soldiers. Again, they slumped to the ground. Asim looked with disbelief as the soldiers that fell were back up on their feet again, not even stopping to pull out the arrows as they continued to march with the others.

"I don't believe this," yelled Tyron, rubbing his eyes.

"I'm not seeing any blood this time," Lanee shouted. "We could be in trouble!"

"Remember the dogs," Asim yelled. "Everyone! Their hearts, aim for their hearts."

"If they have one," Tyron yelled back, shooting again. This time, the arrows hit the heart, but still, they stood back up again.

"They are soldiers of the dead and alive!" Wilt shouted, confused about what he was seeing.

"Let's see if our swords will stop them," Asim yelled as they ran toward the advancing soldiers.

The fighting at the front towers had slowed down. Anson took a few of the dwarfs to battle with the soldiers. "Everyone else concentrates on the front," he told them. Putting their bows away and taking out their swords, they stood ready to join the others.

"Taragoo," shouted Zollo out of nowhere.

"What was that for?" Lube shouted.

"I felt like we needed to shout something going into battle. Well? What do you think?"

Lube shook his head, not knowing what to say momentarily.

"I think if it makes you happy, Taragoo," Lube shouted, laughing.

Now running toward the advancing soldiers, Asim noticed that although the soldiers had swords, they were slower and methodical in their movement. Now, they were spreading out.

"Keep attacking!" Asim yelled as he and Tyron were the first to confront them and to strike a blow against these strange soldiers.

Asim's aim was skillful in plunging his blade where the heart should be. The soldier fell to the ground. Using his foot, Asim pulled his sword from its chest, noticing what Lanee had said about no blood. Still standing on the body, he continued to swing a skillful blade, striking down another, then another.

As the battle launched to full force, he could see the soldiers continuing to stand back up on their feet despite being run through with a sword or an arrow. Beneath his feet now, the soldier was struggling to stand. He almost lost his footing. He jumped, plunging his sword back into the head of the soldier, stopping its movement. As before, it hastily returned to its feet. Loudly, the steel clanked as it sparkled in the sunlight. The battle stayed fierce.

Asim's blade, this time, struck the arm of a soldier, severing it from its body. It fell to the ground; with its sword still in hand, he kicked it away.

"Strike their arms," he shouted.

Tyron reacted, slicing the hand off another soldier. As its sword and hand fell to the ground, the soldier turned to pick it up, joining it back to its severed wrist, the sword still in hand. It continued to fight.

"We are making no headway," Lanee shouted, sounding exasperated. "They are coming back up and fighting again. We can't kill these things!"

"Taragoo," cried Zollo, striking another soldier to the ground.

"What's that shout?" yelled Tyron.

"It's my new battle cry," Zollo yelled with a loud laugh. Tyron smiled, shaking his head and continuing to fight.

There were several waves of the soldiers continuing to march toward them now, and it looked like more would join them. Reality started to set in. Asim knew they would lose this battle if they could not find a way to stop them. Even with their continued striking down, the soldiers relentlessly kept standing up.

"Ahhh!" Toya screamed in frustration again. "There is no stopping these things. All we are doing is slowing them down until they stand up again."

"I'm exhausted," Boben shrieked. "These things are wearing me out. How can we stop them?"

"We must keep battling," shouted Asim. "We cannot give up the battle. Draw from all the strength you have. Remember, we are doing this for the children to give them all the time we can, for them to go back home."

Asim struck another soldier with a blow to the chest. It fell to its knees. On the backswing of his sword, he sliced the soldier's head clean off at the neck; the head hit the ground, spinning. As he battled on, Asim glanced back to see the head that spun away, still seeing the eyes shining red directly his way, although he did not see a body trying to attach itself. Abruptly, the eyes dimmed. Asim blinked, then stared again. The eyes were dimming. He looked to see the soldier's body where it fell; it was still on the ground, not trying to stand up again. It stayed there, motionless. Staring back at the head, he could see, this time, the eyes were blank. "Yes!" he screamed, shocked and enthused at the same time, hoping he had found a way to defeat the soldiers, almost walking into a swinging blade.

"The heads!" he cried out. "Cut their heads off!" He yelled as loud as he could, "They cannot keep going without them." Turning to fight off the soldier when his blade parried another blow, twisting and striking it hard. As it fell, a powerful swing of his sword sliced its head off. It lay there stagnant.

This news had heartened each one of Asim's band of fighters who were dragging with exhaustion. Now, suddenly, they seemed to find inner strength, having something to aim at in this battle.

Locked in battle, the villagers fought desperately, trying to cut the heads off the soldiers, a feat that was not easy. It took a lot of skill and strength to perform the task. They found it more straightforward to knock the soldiers to the ground and then hack off their heads. Each time, they were kicking the head away to make sure. The soldiers continued to put up a fight, striking back hard; the villagers were not used to the battle, finding the fighting more difficult for them and trying not to die. Duf stepped in to help, using all his brute strength to knock the soldiers down, allowing the villagers to cut their heads off. At times, he stopped to use his bare hands to wrap around the soldier's neck, twisting the head until it tore off from its shoulders.

"You know that is disgusting," shrieked Toya while looking at him, repulsed. Duf just smiled as he grabbed another by the throat. Senso had also stopped for a second, watching Duf's incredible strength in awe.

He did not notice a soldier stand back to its feet, sword in its hand, running it through Senso's back. The blade protruded from his chest; the blood spurted from his body. Senso, distracted, did not know anything until the roaring pain surged through his body like an out-of-control grease fire. He grabbed the blade sticking out; the blood now oozed between his fingers. His brain was now in a state of limbo as he was not connecting with what had happened. His legs buckled beneath him as he collapsed to the ground.

Toya saw the horror of Senso's plight from the corner of her eye. He stood there for a moment with the sword plunged into his body. She turned, and with a lunging strike to the soldier, she knocked it to its knees. On her return stroke, she took immense pleasure in a slicing blow that decapitated its head from its shoulders. Now, with more rage inside, she kicked the head so hard that it struck Tyron.

Looking around to see Toya, he yelled, "One way to kick on ahead." Smiling at first, then seeing Senso drop to the ground, he was saddened, knowing he had died.

Duf also had seen Senso fall, which did nothing but infuriate not just Duf but all the warriors. They were even more determined to fight and destroy these things.

Duf and Toya were battling a wall of soldiers coming at them; she was wielding her sword like the warrior she was. Duf had returned to his club and his sword to make sure he cut all the heads off. Two soldiers sliced welts into Duf's shoulders while he waged deep into this battle. He shrugged it off even though the blood was rolling down his muscular arms. Gashes like this never stopped the big man from fulfilling his purpose; he continued to strike down and decapitate these soldiers. With a quick look at the carnage lying around at their feet, Asim felt better now that they could put these things down for good; having found the way to destroy them gave him a feeling of conclusion.

Across the courtyard, in the distance, Zabin caught his eye again. Making sure there was no one around him, he turned to watch, standing at the bottom of the steps with the king. Even from that distance, he could see the contempt on their faces change. Panic seemed to have taken over the king as he looked at the battle, seeing many of the soldiers Zabin had conjured become a pile of headless bodies on the ground. Asim and his fellow warriors were taking the upper hand in this battle. He turned to the warlock in total rage.

Once again, Zabin reached into the pouch wrapped around his shoulder. Pushing his long, bony fingers deeper inside, he sorted through and took out two more bottles. One contained a green-looking liquid, and the other looked black. Mixing them and shaking the one bottle, he tossed the other back into his pouch. Again, smoke billowed from the bottle, drifting high in the air. This time, Zabin did not pour it on the ground. He uttered something and looked up into the sky.

Suddenly, a soldier approaching caught Asim's eye. He pivoted, having to fight with the soldier, his sword blocking its strike. Punching and kicking it swiftly, he knocked the soldier down to the ground; taking his sword, he was quick to cut off its head.

Asim was looking at the sky again, now seeing the smoke gathering and forming a rather large black and ominous-looking cloud. *Rain?* was his first puzzling thought. His senses told him again as a sword swung close to his head, having to fight to defend himself. But during this fight, he found his mind wandering, curious to what Zabin had conjured up this time.

A slicing blade struck his forearm, bringing him instantly back to reality with a sharp pain. As he turned, dropping to the ground, he swept the legs from beneath the soldier with his leg. As its body fell to the ground, Asim stood up, swinging his sword precisely and slicing off its head.

"What is going on?" shouted Lanee. "What is that giant black cloud in the sky?"

"I think we can expect rain!" yelled Tyron sarcastically. "I have a bad feeling about this."

There was a movement in the cloud, and what looked like a giant bat appeared out of the darkness.

"What in the stars," Toya screamed, looking up to see a bat-like creature with wings that stretched a good twenty-four inches on either side of its black-skinned body, its massive head, small pointed ears, and enormous mouth with many sharp-looking teeth—or fangs, you might say. These bats had large feet with huge claws protruding from the ends and the large, bright yellow eyes that stared scarily at the warriors while they swooped towards them.

They have to be from the devil himself, Baylin thought in shock. The beasts headed straight at him. He dove to the ground, just escaping any injury. Everyone was still fighting off the soldiers, and now they had a new threat from the sky. They had to double their awareness of having to fend off these bat creatures.

"How do these beasts seem to know only to attack us, not the soldiers?" shouted Lanee, trying to swat one away with her sword.

"I think it must be the blood," Asim yelled. "These creatures want blood. Unfortunately, we are the only ones that seem to have any in this battle."

He could tell that Zabin, with more conjuring, was sending more soldiers of the dead to the fight. It had reshaped the battle back in their favor again. Once more, they were battling hard, fighting the soldiers from the ground and creatures from the air. The king's guard was keeping back toward the front of the castle for now.

"I don't know how long we can keep going." Tyron sounded exhausted.

"Everyone," Asim yelled for their attention, "fight in twos, one to fight the soldiers and one to fight the creatures. This way, we are not trying to do both. Fight them this way." It seemed to work as they defended themselves in both directions, although he could see more creatures on the way.

"What chance do we have of coming out of here alive?" shrieked Lanee, who had partnered with Asim.

"It could look better," he shouted, "We cannot seem to win this battle in the square. We're too open. We need to go back to the carts. At least we have the wall to help with these flying creatures. Then we can regroup. I can't believe this is happening!"

"We will have to stop Zabin. I don't know how yet, but we must kill him, or we will lose everyone. Move back towards the carts," he shouted. They continued fighting as they headed back.

Suddenly, screams rang out. Asim looked to see one of the bat creatures had dug its claws into Dooly's head. The flying beast lifted him up from the ground; while in the air, it used its massive claws to twist his head so it could sink its fangs into his neck. Dooly let out an enormous scream. Mercifully, he blacked out. Blood spurted like a fountain from the sky, covering both Dooly, the creature, and everyone close to them. A second later, in silence, it released Dooly's body from the grip on his head. His body dropped lifelessly to the ground in a bloody mess. Pooly, who had partnered with Dooly, was too small to reach the creature and had been swinging his sword wildly, but to no avail. He was not stopping, screaming at the beast and wildly slashing the air. Wooly, who was close to him, delicately grabbed Pooly's arm, pulling him away.

"It's over!" he shouted.

"I can't let it go away," Pooly screamed.

"Just this once!" he reasoned with him. "Let's go kill something else." Wooly was dragging him away now with the help of Sooly, who could see the rage in Pooly's face. They were all feeling the sadness of losing their brother as they continued to fight, moving back toward the carts.

Exim and Baylin teamed together; both were struggling to fight off the bat creatures. Exim, with his head in the air, had not noticed a soldier had moved behind him until it plunged its sword blade into his back. A crimson ring appeared as the blood dripped. Suddenly, feeling the pain that surged through his body, Exim dropped to his knees; a bat creature swooped in, digging its talons into his head. The day went strangely bright as the air in his body left; he sank to the ground. Baylin was defeating a creature when he realized what had happened to his friend, turning to slash down his sword and slicing into the beast's back. Turning his sword on the soldier, he hacked into its chest, knocking it to the ground. He chopped until its head came off.

Baylin saw Exim's dead body sprawled in a pool of blood, knowing he had no time even to say goodbye as more soldiers marched toward him. Deciding to move away, he continued his fight all the way back, wiping a quick tear from his eye for his friend as he headed toward the carts to join the others.

"Keep falling back," Asim yelled at everyone and continued heading toward the wooden carts. They had created a space between them and the soldiers, although the bat creatures continually attacked from above. Turning in midair and circling back to strike again, Asim was thankful for the dwarfs that had set their attention from the front to shoot down these creatures in the air. Their arrows penetrated, and bodies fell dead to the ground, giving everyone time to reach the carts and move in behind them. Asim looked at each one, with the cuts and scratches, as blood spattered and oozed from cuts and welts on their bodies. Their clothes were torn and disheveled, and the bruises and lumps throbbed from what seemed a never-ending battle. Asim himself was exhausted, knowing they were too. He stood there, his head held high, and spoke to them.

"Catch your breath," as he was trying to find his own. "I would like to stand here and tell you it's over. You are tired, and I know you are giving your all. I want you to know I am proud of every single one of you, but we still have to battle one more time to take the gate, and we must do this together!" Asim's mind was whirling for the answer, knowing they would not walk out of here alive if he could not find the solution he desperately needed, not knowing what Zabin had in store for them.

He gestured for Lanee and Tyron to come close to him, looking at both with a sense of urgency. "This is what we will do." He looked into their eyes. "You must make a break and take as many as you can with you through that gate. It will be tough. I know you can!"

"What about you?"

"I must stop the warlock somehow, or we will never leave here alive if he keeps conjuring these spells. The children should be safe. But we need to make sure they have the time to go home. I would rather not lose any more of us today!"

"Let us come with you," Tyron said again.

"No, they will need you and Lanee's direction. Nothing is in our favor right now."

The creatures attacked again. This time, Mup, Benson, Jig, and Tig, with a flurry of arrows, shot to kill these creatures.

"There is not too much resistance at the front tower," Asim observed. "The guards are keeping down, knowing we pick them off as they make themselves visible. This will change when you charge the front. Keep some of our bows on them." Looking across the courtyard, he could see the bulk of the soldiers had split up. One section was marching toward them, and the other was marching toward the gate, now followed by the king's guards.

"They are trying to cut us off to keep us in here. We must find a way to make it out through the gate, or we will be trapped and killed! The creatures in the sky are swarming to take our attention away from the soldiers." Asim grabbed Tyron and Lanee's arms, pulling them to him again.

"I know everyone's exhausted! But one more time, we have to give it everything!"

"You told us in the beginning," said Lanee, "there was no guarantee that we will come back alive. We are ready for this journey." Breaking away, Asim whispered something in Duf's ear. And then Pooly's. Duf looked at him and smiled as he picked up a cart from the ground. Placing it back on its wheels again, he pushed it forward, slowly at first. Pooly jumped inside with his bow.

"Let's go," shouted Asim. "Everyone, follow Duf's lead." They all ran after him as he was picking up speed. Asim stayed back as they left. His parting words to Lanee were, "If I don't make it and you do, take the children home." Duf was now running at a reasonable speed. Pooly was shooting arrows at the creatures as they charged toward the soldiers, plowing the cart into them and knocking over as many as he could. Pushing hard, he penetrated past the first wave of soldiers, heading for the second, marching toward the gate. With Duf's strong running, the cart was rammed into them. Stopping abruptly, he fell forward into the cart, which broke, and then to the ground, Pooly ending up in his lap. He laughed, and both stood and joined the battle.

In the wake of soldiers, they had run down, making it easier for the others following to cut off their heads while still on the ground. Now, having confused the creatures, they had a break before they swarmed again. Looking into the sky, Anson, Benson, and Tig continued shooting arrows to strike and knock them out of the air; Toya now joined them with her bow.

Duf, Tyron, and Lanee still fought the soldiers; the fierce battle was now in all directions. And it was showing no signs of slowing down.

"We still need to be first out the gate!" Tyron yelled to Wilt. "We need to make sure nothing stands in our way. Do not let them cut us off! Toya, shoot at the front," he yelled. She turned in that direction. Jig and Pooly came over to join her, turning their attention to the tower. The creatures were not easing up at all, still swarming above them with their infernal swooping, trying to pick off anyone with their extended claws.

The guards in the tower had moved outside and were shooting at the dwarfs again.

"Anson, I need help!" Toya shrieked; arrows were flying close around them. "Push them back," she yelled.

"Running out of arrows!" bellowed Anson.

"I'm sure we grabbed all we could," yelled Jig, looking all around.

"Do your best then." Toya wiped the sweat from her brow. "We must keep moving to the gate." Tyron could see that some soldiers had now moved in front toward the gate, but looking ahead, he could see Wilt, Zollo, Tan, and Lube had now moved away from the others and were fighting hard to keep in front, taking the battle right to the soldiers. It seemed to Tyron the whole group had broken into pockets of resistance. Everyone was trying to push forward to stay ahead and reach the gate before the soldiers.

"I can see the gate," shouted Tan to Zollo as they continued to battle forward.

It rooted Duf in the fight using his sword and his club, knocking the creatures out of the sky. However, this seemed like an endless task as another black cloud formed in the air, meaning even more creatures would soon be on their way.

Asim watched as they all took off into battle before he moved along the wall toward the stable. Looking down at the guards who appeared to be waking from the earlier beating, Asim took the handle of his sword, crashing it down on their heads to make sure they would not be standing up soon. He thought to himself. He needed to go much further past the stable, making sure he blended into the background before he crossed the courtyard.

Looking around, he could see the battles had branched out more now; he figured he could move up the side of the king's chambers, still wanting to move closer to the steps where he had last seen Zabin and the king without too much attention paid to him. This way, he could slip in behind them. He was now on the other side of the courtyard, easing along the front area where the king's servants lived. It was empty there. He moved toward the steps when two of the king's knights stepped out of the shadows.

"Stop," shouted one of the knights.

I don't have time for this, he thought.

"Put your sword down and come with us," the knight growled.

"No." He looked them both in the face as they drew their swords. Shaking his head and lunging forward, Asim engaged the first knight with a swift back-kick to the stomach of the second knight, trying to move behind him.

It amazed Asim how the sword in his hand felt light as he twisted the blade with strength, causing the knight to lose his grip as his sword fell. Asim thrust his sword up into his neck; as the blood oozed, he fell to the ground, still trying to stand up from his kick. Feeling his presence, Asim slashed his blade across the knight's face, cutting into it deep. He screamed. He left their bodies bloody and sprawled out on the ground.

Looking around, he stood alone again; no more knights were in sight. The two dead bodies were on the ground. *Good*, he thought as he continued moving in the shadow of the sun toward the steps. Two guards appeared from nowhere to confront him. *Why are these people not fighting at the front of the castle?* He thought. *It should be easier than this!*

Both guards, with spears, aimed at him. Asim, sidestepped the first guard and was quick enough to make the first spear miss, but the second caught his sword arm. He winced as the acute pain shot right through him, causing him to drop his sword, seeing the blood from the gash on his arm. Asim tried to grab his sword, but the guard pivoted and, with a hard strike, knocked him to the ground. Asim rolled over as the guard tried to pierce him. Hitting the ground hard jerked the spear, allowing Asim time to grab the shaft. Seizing it with strength, he twisted it with enough force, causing the guard to collide with the other, dropping the spear. The power of the impact caused both guards to topple over.

Spear in hand, Asim rose to his feet. Turning, he plunged the spear through one guard's chest, impaling him to the ground. The second was still trying to stand. A side-kick knocked him backward. Then, picking up his sword, Asim plunged the blade deep into his chest. Looking once again, he could see no one. The blood was dripping down his arm. He grabbed a sash from one of the dead guards and he wrapped it tight to stop the bleeding. *I hope this was the last fight until I find Zabin*, he thought.

Chapter 32

A FIGHT FOR THE GATE

Now pushing with all the underlying strength they had inside of them, they tried to move toward the gate in a ferocious battle with both the soldiers and the flying creatures, all seeking to obstruct their pathway; Lube, Zollo, Wilt, and Tan were battling ahead, knowing someone had to open the gate. Tyrone, Lanee, and Duf were the closest to them in a desperate fight to push the soldiers back. The dwarfs, out from behind the carts, were battling forward toward the tower, continuing to shoot arrows at the front.

"We must make a way to the gate!" shouted Wilt, who now found out the king's guard had joined back into the battle. Zollo knew they were close; he needed any weak spot to reach the gate release.

Anson and Toya were moving forward from the sides, working their way close behind the others. Picking arrows from the dead bodies as they traveled, allowing them to continue shooting the guards in the towers. Along with help from the dwarfs, Zollo found his chance to reach the gate.

Lube was still battling the creatures who continued to plague him, having to fight off three of the king's guards. He was now rescued by

Wilt, who was quick to step in to help. Tan locked in battle with a guard; he continued holding off the creatures swooping with their ominous aerial attacks. Wilt and Lube now battled together.

This is my chance, thought Zollo, seeing an opening in front of him. Putting his sword away, he ran past one guard, side-kicking him as he ran to the gate, rushing toward the lever that kept it locked, sitting just behind a large square rock. Jumping on the rock and down the other side, he reached the bar, grasping it hard with a downward pull until it stopped, unlocking the giant gate that was now ready to open. He looked to see the large wheel next to him, which rolled the gate up and down. He grabbed and pulled with all his strength, but it was barely moving. Looking up, Zollo could see a rope cut that opened the gate. He knew its heaviness was too much for one person struggling to make it turn. Looking back for help, he saw Tan was in trouble, fighting with two creatures above him and a soldier in front, with another moving in from behind him! He could see Wilt and Lube engaged in their battles with the soldiers and the guards.

Zollo yelled at Tan to warn him of the danger, knowing he was the only one close enough to help. A guard from the tower confronted Zollo as he moved forward to help, pulling his sword out to engage as the guard lunged toward him. Zollo promptly sidestepped, pushing him against the massive rock, and struck him hard with his sword handle, knocking him to the ground. And with a tremendous kick to his helmet, he snapped the guard's neck. Knowing it slowed him down, he jumped back across the rock. He could see Tan immersed in the battle in front of him as a creature attacked from above.

"Look out," Zollo cried out when a soldier worked its way behind Tan, knowing he had not seen it.

"No!" he cried in anguish, seeing he was too late. The sword had penetrated Tan's skin. He yelled out as the sharp pain ripped from his brain into his blood-soaked back. The blade had punctured him deeply as he fell, but Tan continued to fight from his knees, swinging his sword, trying to fend off the creatures above him as one large claw dug into his head. Zollo had reached the soldier. Grabbing its head, he pulled it back violently, dragging it to the ground, using his sword to chop off its head. He drew his dagger and threw it when the creature had its massive claws deep into Tan's neck. It seemed to swish in the air as it struck the beast between the eyes and it fell to the ground with a thud.

Zollo's sword, in a skillful swing, engaged another of the soldiers as he stood by Tan's side.

The hard blow struck it to the ground, then sliced its head clean off. Not seeing anyone around, he dropped to his knees, grabbing Tan, who still was desperately trying to fight off imaginary creatures on his knees despite his pain and a significant amount of blood loss. Zollo held him close to himself to comfort him. Wilt had arrived, fending off a creature attacking from above them while he decapitated another soldier. He looked at the blood-soaked body of Tan in Zollo's arms as the blood pooled around them. Wilt kneeled, taking over from Zollo and holding his friend's body close. His head laid back in his arms; there was a deep hole in his back, still oozing blood, where the sword had pierced an artery. He weakly opened his eyes to look at Wilt holding him, and he tried to speak. Wilt Leaned his ear closer to his mouth as Zollo stood guard over them both.

"Is the gate open?" he asked. Barely rasping out his words, but before Wilt could answer, his head dropped back in his arms. He knew he had died.

"Behind you," came Lube's voice. Zollo turned to see a soldier with a sword coming straight at him; Lube parried the blow just in time. Zollo thrust his sword through its chest. As it was falling in one swing, Lube struck its head off from its neck.

"Can we open this gate?" a now frustrated and angry Wilt shouted. Having now laid Tan's body down, he was back on his feet, covered with blood when a creature attacked; Wilt struck it, knocking it down to the ground with his sword, where he slashed it a dozen more times.

Zollo let Wilt release his anger before he spoke. "Maybe with two or three of us? It's too heavy for one, and they cut the ropes!" They now moved off toward the gate.

"All three of us if we can," snarled Wilt. "If we have enough time." They all jumped up on the rock in front of the wheel, now overrun with creatures. They stood their ground to fight them off.

"Go ahead," yelled Lube, "I will hold them back." Zollo and Wilt jumped down to grasp the wheel together. Lube could now see more soldiers moving toward him; even with both their strength together, pulling as hard as they could, the gate was hardly moving. Three more of the creatures had swooped down towards them. Lube was battling hard to hold them off while he was trying to give Zollo and Wilt more time. Zollo knew it was going to take more than two, knowing more were on the way. Zollo drew Wilt's dagger from his belt; it swished as he threw it, striking the creature's head. Screeching, it fell to the ground.

"We need your help," yelled Zollo to Lube. "It's too hard for us two, and more soldiers are heading this way."

"Keep trying; you can do it," Lube shouted. Zollo went back to help Wilt again, grabbing the wheel one more time; it was hard, and they were both using all the strength they had.

"I wish I had Lube's outlook," he gasped. "This wheel is just not moving quick enough, even without the cut rope. They made this gate heavy." The wheel moved the gate up about half a length as Lube continued to fight off the creatures, and the soldiers closed in on them. Still busy trying to turn the wheel, they both did not notice guards sneaking down from the tower, both still spending all their energy on the wheel. The guards moved in close around the rock behind Zollo.

Wilt caught the movement out of the corner of his eye. Suddenly, all the energy left Zollo's body, and an acute pain seared through his torso. In the realization of being stabbed, he twisted his body to see his attacker was too much for him. His mind drifted as his hand slipped from the wheel. Slowly, he fell to the ground. Wilt let go of the wheel. Grabbing his sword, he lunged at the guard, plunging the blade deep into his chest, taking no time in striking another of them with one quick thrust to his neck, steel clashing with steel as he continued to wade into the oncoming guards. Blood spurted, and one wild sword swing slashed a gash in Wilt's arm. Twisting, he turned and kicked the guard with force, pushing him into another. Lube was now seeing the clash, jumping from the rock to help Wilt. Both were battling hard against the opposing guards when a giant hand came down from above the rock, grabbing a guard by the head, lifting him from the ground, and crushing his neck on the high rock. Lube looked up to see Duf as he caught hold of another, pulling him up to his chest as he threw him toward more guards attacking from the tower, knocking two more to the ground and stunning another with the force the body struck them, causing a hasty retreat back to the tower. Wilt and Lube went to work on the three guards left sprawled on the ground, using their swords to dispose of them.

Lube ran back to Zollo, who was now covered in blood from the dagger sticking from his back. His eyes were closed. Lube looked at the impaled blade. He lifted him up close.

"He is still alive," he shouted, seeing breath struggling from his lips. "I need to pull out this blade from your back." Placing him and turning him, he clasped the dagger by the handle. "I'm pulling it out," he whispered. "Hold on, my friend," not knowing if he could hear. With one swift pull, the blade slid out. Zollo's body arched, then fell limp. He was still alive but barely breathing. Seeing a guard on the ground close by, Lube grabbed his tunic, ripping it from his dead body to make a bandage to cover Zollo's back.

"We must pull this gate open," Wilt shouted to Duf, who was destroying one of the creatures, pounding it with his club. He jumped from the rock, going over to the wheel. On the way, he put his large hand on Lube's shoulder and smiled; he then grabbed the wheel with both hands. Duf slowly turned the wheel, arching his back and tightening his grip again. His muscles were bulging as he turned it again, then once more. The gate was rising; Duf kept turning the wheel until the entrance was all the way open. The few soldiers close to the gate were heading out. The tower guards were sneaking back again as Wilt intercepted them.

"What are you all doing down there?" a voice came from the top of the rock. It was Tyron and Lanee. They both jumped down to help

Wilt with the guards. Once again, fighting them back toward the tower door they closed and hid behind, Lanee went back to Lube.

"How is he?"

"Barely alive," said Lube. "We need to take him out of here."

"We all need to leave here," shouted Tyron. "We will have a tough fight on our way out of the gate."

Duf carried Zollo as they moved forward.

Chapter 33

A GIANT MASS EXODUS

Asim's heart was still pounding as he tried catching his breath from the two run-ins with the knights and guards, and he moved toward the great hall. In the distance, he could make out Zabin and the king standing close to the bottom level of steps. He could tell the king was still unhappy, waving his arms and having words with the warlock. He could not make out why the king was shouting at Zabin.

He averted his eyes from them both for a second, looking toward the front of the castle. He could see the gate raised; this made him smile. Looking back again at the steps, he saw the king had moved away from Zabin and was walking back up toward the great hall. Zabin was searching through his pouch, reaching deep, and picking out one large bottle with a blue liquid or powder and a smaller container with a green liquid. Zabin was looking at the fronts of the bottles, uncorking them, and taking the small bottle to mix into the larger container. With one hand, he shook it up and down, putting the small bottle back in his pouch again. Now making a sign with his free hand, he murmured something while shaking.

Asim stood mesmerized at that moment, watching all this taking place, knowing he was not yet close enough to stop him. Taking the bottle, Zabin walked down the step onto the courtyard before uncorking it and pouring the liquid into four separate spots not too close to each other; he left two to three lengths between each place. When finished, he stood there looking and staring intently, as did Asim, although he had moved closer, trying to be as inconspicuous as he could while watching that no guards were sneaking up on him.

He could tell something was happening at each spot where Zabin had poured the liquid; it looked like a little person. Yes, he was sure little men had sprouted. They started small and were becoming larger, now taller than the warlock. Their bodies were filling out as they developed. To his amazement, they continued to grow. All four had grown to five lengths in height. These were massive giants, and their bodies matched their size. Zabin had them all bend down, whispering something in their large ears. It looked to him as if he were giving them instructions. They all stood up and, with their long legs, walked, picking up speed to a trot toward the front gate.

Still standing back in the shadows, Asim had to blink a few times to collect his thoughts on what he had just witnessed. He tried to focus on the job he came to do, knowing he was not close enough to stop the spell, but he needed to make sure Zabin made no more. Creeping forward, he was ready in his mind to intercept Zabin; he planned to grab him before he had made it back to the steps again.

At the front were a significant number of the soldiers and a few of the king's guards who had slipped around the back through the other tower now, trying to make their way through to the now open gate. Tyron gazed at the opening, seeing more soldiers going through the gate and knowing in his mind they had not made it quick enough for them to break free first through the gate.

Even if they could fight their way out, they would still be cut off from freedom.

"What do you want to do?" asked Lanee to Tyron. She was battling one creature, sticking her sword into it neatly in flight and dragging it to the ground. She plunged her sword deep to kill the beast. Tyron was quietly fuming.

"Do you think we have any chance?" asked Anson, having caught up with them. Tyron was staring toward the gate again, and the soldiers were preventing them from making it out.

"We must fight through," Tyron angrily blurted. "We cannot stop! I refuse to die in this castle."

"All the others will be with us soon," asserted Anson, and Tyron nodded. Anson looked at Zollo as he could see his bloodstained body resting in Duf's arms. Duf also had blood running from large, deep gashes on his upper arms. "Are you both going to be all right?"

Duf nodded.

"He is still alive," Lube insisted, "but is only hanging on by a thread."

"He is young and active." Lanee smiled. "We have hope he will recover. We need to clean the wound and apply a proper bandage and for Duf as well if we can escape from here."

Tyron was angry. "They are setting a trap outside the gate like they tried to do in here, so let's kill us some soldiers this day. Duf, do your best to hold on to Zollo. We all will help as much as we can." They moved towards the gate, and Duf still had his club in his hand, along with Zollo in one arm.

Suddenly, the earth seemed to tremble under their feet as a thunderous rumbling came from the courtyard. Tyron looked back and, to his astonishment, saw the four giants at a good trot heading toward them.

"My god," shouted Lube, now seeing them too. Their large shadows were darkening everything they passed.

"What on earth is this?" yelled Lanee. "And where is Asim?" Moving forward for a better look, she could still see the others locked in battle with the soldiers further back in the courtyard.

"We must fight our way out of here," stressed Lube. "I hope the others can, too." Looking up, Tyron could see that even the clouds that had before contained more of the creatures moving past the gate to outside the castle.

"Taragoo," shouted Tyron, and he was laughing while he ran forward into the soldiers, wielding his sword.

"Taragoo," shouted Lube, laughing, running forward into the fight right behind him.

Only a few of the creatures left now to attack them. "Taragoo," shouted Lanee, who was wielding her sword as she cut them down. Wilt and Anson were mounting their attack as they moved forward. Duf was guarding Zollo, who remained cradled in his enormous arm, as they, too, headed for the gate. He was using his club to knock anyone out of the way coming close.

"Fight hard," yelled Tyron, stabbing a guard with his sword.

Back at the market, the giants had reached the tables where the battle had started, although the fight had now moved a lot closer to the front gate. Breaking away from the others, Toya, Benson, Boben, Tig, and Mup had fought their way closer to the open gate and were trying to help Tyron and the others battle to push on through to the other side. Further back in the courtyard, engulfed in the surrounding fight, unaware of the proximity of the giants that approached, Pooly, Wooly, Sooly, Yuby, and Baylin struggled. They continued fighting the soldiers, but unfortunately, they were standing in the pathway as the giants were running at them. It was not until the giants' enormous feet were upon them that they even realized the giants were about to tread on them. They were desperate to move out of the way.

An enormous hand grabbed Sooly by his head, lifting him high in the air. Sooly was shouting and swinging his sword wildly as the pain was rushing through his body when his swinging blade caught the giant's knuckle, which made a gash in the skin. The giant, angered, squeezed his fingers around Sooly's head tighter. Sooly was shouting and screaming louder with the increased agonizing pain. Raising his arm high, the giant threw his body down with force. The sound of

Sooly's body hitting the ground was sickening. His lifeless body sprawled out in blood that oozed from his mouth. Still not content, the giant brought his foot down on Sooly's head, crushing his skull. The giant laughed loudly.

Baylin, close by, saw the extreme violence in taking Sooly's life and was so sickened that he had to bend over and vomit. An enormous giant's hand passed over his head just at that moment. Standing back upright, he was now enraged by the giant's actions; taking out his sword and jumping high, he struck the giant at the back of his knee, causing enough pain to make the giant hop and lose his balance, falling with his massive arms flailing to the ground. Twisting his body, he fell, grabbing out at Baylin. Though he missed with one hand, his other hand caught Baylin with a hard slap to his body, causing Baylin to tumble head over heels about three to four lengths toward the front gate. He stopped, rolling close to the feet of Benson, who grabbed him, helping him back to his feet, and dusting him down.

"That will give you a bruise," Benson quipped, making sure he was all right. Baylin was utterly dazed and in pain, and Benson held on to him.

The giant was back on his feet, following the other three to the gate. They all kneeled, pushing everyone out of the way with their broad hands so they could squirm through, pushing the few soldiers still at the gate to the ground in their hurry to break out. Tyron and the others were quick to seize the opportunity to cut their heads off while they were down. Now, they could go through the gate themselves.

Tyron was looking around as he moved outside the castle gate, looking at what was in front of him for a trap he had hoped would not be there. Standing outside the castle in an arc straight ahead were soldiers. There seemed to be a hundred of them, ready again for battle, as the king's guard, standing thirty on each side of the soldiers, had their swords and shields preparing to close the arc. The giants were in the middle, and the creatures were forming in the clouds above them again, preparing their attack. Duf laid Zollo gently down on the ground, away from where they were standing.

Pooly, Mup, Jig, and Yuby were still fighting, and they ran in late through the gate. Yuby and Jig had continued their fight with the guards past the entrance, stopping close to the giants, thinking they could run back to the others before they realized. Suddenly, one giant grabbed Yuby and, laughing loudly, ran his body through his hands. Yuby was squirming, feeling the pain as his bones broke; screaming, he tried to break free. Being grabbed and lifted in the air had caused him to drop his sword. Then, in an instant, the giant grew tired of him and threw Yuby, who had blacked out, hard on the ground in front of the soldiers. And even though his body was sprawled out on the ground, the soldiers ran their swords through him; blood streamed from the wounds on his lifeless body. Jig, seeing Yuby grabbed up by the giant, was using his sword to attack, hoping he would let Yuby go, but as he sought to stab him, a creature, swooping down, struck his head with its talons.

Jig was fighting the creature with one hand while holding his head to stop the blood with the other. Not looking in front of himself, his foot twisted as he hit his boot on the giant's massive toe. He toppled forward and fell to the ground, desperately trying to stand. Seizing their chance, the soldiers pierced his body; pain shot through him as blood escaped from every wound. It was all too much. His body numbed, and life drifted from him. Blood pooled around his body. It all happened fast.

Tyron, almost mesmerized, had little time to react to seeing what had happened. They both lay covered in blood. Grabbing his sword, he started toward the giants, but Lanee grabbed him by the shoulder.

"Come back here," she shouted, pulling him back to where they were all huddled around Zollo's body. Looking back over her shoulder, she could see a line of the king's guards had now formed along the open gate area, closing the arc, stopping any return to the castle. On one side, Lanee, Tyron, Wilt, Boben, and Toya were on the ground. She was holding Zollo close to her chest as tears ran down her cheek.

"Please stay alive," she was whispering to him. "Please live." Lube, Duf, Baylin, Tig, Anson, Mup, Benson, Pooly, and Wooly gathered to make a circle around Zollo's body. Each one of them was looking disheveled; they had taken a massive beating. They all looked at each other for an answer. Now, the guards beat slowly on their shields with their swords, and the giants bellowed, along with the blood-curdling screeches coming from the creatures as they were swarming around the clouds, ready to strike. The dead-like soldiers were just standing, dead in their tracks.

"This is it; they have us surrounded," said Lanee. "I see no way out of this but to fight again. Let's stand strong and brace ourselves."

"One final fight," said Tyron. Looking around at them, he could see and feel the exhaustion in each one as they stood there. He was looking at the bloodstained clothes, the sweat and dirt, the bloody lacerations, lumps, bruises, and gashes on their blood-speckled face and bodies.

Now, all of a sudden, they saw dragons in the distance.

"This day seems to worsen." Tyron shook his head. "I know we are all weary and completely outnumbered. Straighten your clothes and feel good about yourselves. We came here to save the children, which is what we did. Feel proud, feel very proud," Tyron yelled, as the noise was almost deafening. "Are you ready?" he yelled. They all turned to form one line. "Raise your swords," yelled Tyron. "And hold them high." Zollo lay on the ground behind them. "This is for Zollo and all that have given their lives already and the children."

"To the children," Lanee yelled. They could see the dragons nearing and the creatures swarming. The soldiers, guards, and giants all took a step toward them. Looking out at what they were facing, it seemed an inevitable death. It was a strange moment. It was like time was standing still, motionless, feeling like an eternity in slow motion.

Chapter 34

WARLOCKS AND DRAGONS

Asim moved within a few steps of Zabin, the warlock, who was too caught up in himself to notice him at that moment. Before Zabin could step up on the first step, Asim stood directly in front of him. Startled, Zabin jerked his head back and gazed directly at him.

"You!" rasped Zabin, lifting his head to see Asim standing there.

"Yes." Asim was nodding his head.

"This is the second time we have met," snarled Zabin. "Last time, it seems I underestimated you. I will not make that mistake. This time, I will kill you myself, and then I will make sure all your worthless friends all die along with you," He snickered. "You have made the biggest mistake of your life coming to this castle, and for what? So that you can die?" he sneered. "Do you even have a name, warrior?"

"I don't expect you to understand. Maybe even I don't," Asim uttered.

"You talk in riddles," Zabin grumbled. "Think you can come against me?" He sneered again. "I am invincible. I may make your death quick, or I may make it slow and painful. Your friends are about to find out." He laughed loud this time. "However, when I do, I will make you wish you were never born." He laughed again. Asim looked at Zabin, shrugged his shoulders, and smiled at him, which seemed to infuriate him.

"I will make you suffer for that."

Asim took his sword back out and stepped toward him, wielding his blade skillfully. Zabin laughed. "You think that swordplay is any match for me?" With a flip of Zabin's wrist and the word, "Butoah," suddenly it felt like his sword weighed three hundred pounds. Asim could not hold it in the air, and immediately, he dropped it to the ground, almost toppling to the ground with it as the warlock continued to laugh. Asim tried picking the sword back up with both hands. He could barely lift it off the ground. Zabin gave another sarcastic laugh, mocking him. Asim let go of the sword to rush him. A twisting kick caught Zabin by surprise, knocking him to the ground. He was about to attack again when the warlock opened his hand and pushed it toward him, saying, "Latua ma be." Asim felt like a tree hit him in the face. The force caused him to slide backward, falling on the ground in excruciating pain. Reaching his hand to his face, he wiped the blood running from his nose; his face was numb. Feeling dazed and unclear, he shook his head, trying to bring his senses back into focus. Zabin continued laughing.

"You are nothing!" He sneered. "Where is the big brave warrior who came to kill me? Is he a man who will now beg me not to? And beg for his mercy?" Asim was trying hard to scramble 0 to his feet, not listening to what Zabin was saying. As he stood back up, Zabin again pushed his hand forward, saying, "Latua ma be."

Asim felt like the same tree hit him again with force. He slid backward on the ground. The pain had doubled, seeming to smolder in his head. He lay there, not able to feel his bloody, beaten face, dazed and confused, with every ache magnified in his body, feeling he had no strength to stand up this time. He was struggling in his mind, knowing he had to climb back to his feet, or it would all be lost, but he was unsure he could take anymore. He was wondering if he had not made a big mistake to take on Zabin alone.

"I am tired of playing this game. I told you that you are nothing. I am invincible! You dared to stand with me?" He walked over to him, standing with his legs straddled over Asim's body. He looked into his bruised and bleeding face with a big sneer on his own. "Warrior with no name." He was laughing.

"First, you will die, then I will kill your friends," he repeated. "First you, then your friends, this time," he laughed again as he motioned with his hand and spoke, "Baris Lupa," and from nowhere, a lion-man suddenly appeared at Asim's head. Then again, the same hand motion and saying. "Baris Lupa," and another lion-man suddenly appeared. Now, there was one on the right side and one on the left side of his head. Asim's senses had returned. He could make out the two creatures at his skull and Zabin over his face.

"Don't worry about them. I will be the one to kill you. I want them to eat your flesh after I do." The warlock let out his largest laugh.

Suddenly, the sky went dark for a split second, as if a giant cloud had passed. Zabin had not noticed, having closed his eyes for that same exact split second; he lifted his hands to cast a spell that Asim was sure would be the one to kill him, but at that moment, a flame from afar had drifted the distance through the air. The heat momentarily singed the side of Zabin's skin by his beard. Startled, as it stung, he jerked his head back to see what had happened. Asim seized his one chance, grabbing his dagger from his belt. With all the energy and strength he could gather, he grabbed Zabin's coat with one hand, pulling in one motion and rising up in a flash. He plunged the blade deep into Zabin's throat before the warlock had time to flinch or even blink. The sharp edge sliced through his throat, brain, and out the back of his skull with such force; his eyes rolled back as he was falling. His now bloody hat tumbled to the ground, and his body slumped.

"*Asim* is my name," he shouted, standing, looking into the warlock's face. "*Asim.*" He pulled out the dagger, plunged, and twisted it into the vicinity of his heart. *If there was one there*, he thought. "That was just for good measure." The blood pooled around his head.

Asim's actions had startled the two lion-men. He retrieved his sword, which had returned to its normal weight, feeling right in his hand again. Glancing at Zabin, he swiftly, in two quick strokes, sliced both his hands off. Blood poured from the stumps. The two lion-men stood like statues, dead, not moving at all. He cut their heads off for good measure. Now, looking back down at Zabin and taking no chances, he cut off his head, grabbing it and throwing it up the steps toward the great hall. *A present for the king*, smiling as best he could. More blood poured from Zabin's neck. Asim then grabbed the handle of his dagger, pulled it out of his chest, and wiped the blood off on Zabin's coat. *So much for invincible*. He nodded to himself. Now he felt more satisfied than ever seeing Zabin's body surrounded by blood, knowing he had thwarted the king's evil plan to enslave the children.

They won't grow up to be the king's personal guards, he thought.

He suddenly stopped. As the adrenaline left, the pain flooded back to him again; he had to sit down fast on the step before he fell. His head was pounding.

Looking up into the sky, Asim could see two giant dragons now circling the front of the castle, continuing to dive toward the front gate. A hot flash of panic struck his stomach. He realized there had to be a dragon attack on top of everything else they were facing. One dragon swooped down. He saw the flames spewing from its mouth.

I must rush to the front. Then, another quick thought of killing the king flashed through his mind. *I know that we will have to wait for some other time*. He found himself running as best he could through the courtyard toward the front gate. The pain in his body had left again as the adrenaline had kicked back in with the desperation to reach his friends. He looked around. He could see a few of the king's guards, along with the people from the village still hiding out wherever they could find cover from the dragons.

Don't think I will have anyone stopping me along the way," he thought, keeping his sword out just in case since he was not sure which way the dragons would head. He could see the giant's heads as he looked over the castle wall. He did a double-take on what he saw. Giants were wandering around as if they were drunk; they seemed to have no direction. He saw the clouds burning in the sky and what he thought to be creatures falling in small flames, not feeling sure about what was going on at this moment.

He was continuing to run toward the gate when, out of the corner of his eye, he spied a horse that had come from the stable, already saddled as if someone was planning to ride out. Veering from his course, he grabbed the reins of the horse and jumped up onto the saddle, heading for the gate and riding fast; it was a little wobbly at first; it had been a while since he had ridden a horse. He had heard you never forget, though, so he grabbed the reins tighter and squeezed his thighs tight around the horse so as not to fall off. He saw guards running back in from outside the gate.

Cannot stop now, he thought, putting his sword away so he could use both hands to hold on tight to the reins. He was through the gate! Seeing the speed of the horse coming at them, most of the guards tried to jump out of the way. Knocking over a few, he rode to the other side, stopping as soon as he could. Asim, still on the horse, looked around and was in awe of what had happened. He dismounted close to where Tyron and the others were standing.

"Zabin is dead!" he announced. Lanee was first to run and throw her arms around him, and hug him tightly. Tyron slapped him on the back, wrapping his arms around him, followed by each of the others as they all were trying to hug him. There seemed to be a happiness spreading over them.

"We knew you would come through." Lanee smiled.

"We are glad you are back," Tyron said as the others agreed.

"I am also glad to find you all here alive! What happened?"

"We are not sure?" answered Tyron. "But we're still here talking, so it must be good. The dragons have been on our side. We're not sure why they did not attack us."

"Maybe we should find a little cover," Asim whispered. "In case they change their mind," He was loosening everyone's grip so they could walk together over to Zollo, where Toya and Lube were caring for him.

"How is he?" Asim asked. They both stood up, smiled, and hugged him.

"He is still barely alive," Toya sobbed. "But was not sure how much damage there is inside his body."

"What happened? Has he opened his eyes yet?"

"Stabbed in the back with a dagger, and he has not opened his eyes so far. We are happy he is alive still." She forced a smile. Asim could see the redness from tears in her eyes.

There was a massive thud as a giant fell and hit the ground. Another one stood there as a dragon hit his head full-on with the fire he was spitting at him. The skin was bubbling on his face as it fell; two were already on the ground. The dragon was flying back around, spewing fire on all four lying on the ground; they did not move. The other dragon was busy circling the soldiers, burning rows of them each time it passed over. The burning bodies were slumping to the ground. A few of the guards still left had made it back to the castle, except for a few that had not escaped the flames.

Lube, caring for Zollo, looked at Asim.

"I thought we were all going to die!" he said as every one of them gathered around. "We were ready and about to battle when the dragons arrived from nowhere. Flying over, they spewed flames toward and up through the castle. As they circled, suddenly, the noise stopped! Creatures fell from the sky like rain. Soldiers, at the same time, froze like statues. And the giants, all at the same moment, had no direction—walking into each other. As the dragons' flames hit the clouds, every one of them was burning. At that point, we thought we would be next or something else would come to kill us. It did not. We could not believe what was happening."

"Well, the warlock is dead," Asim announced.

"Thank god for that!" Lube shouted. "That must be the reason everything froze."

The dragons flew in a circle above them, then flew at the castle, sending flames at the towers at the front wall. The guards, so as not to be burnt, dropped behind the wall. Asim could see the gate lowered as the dragons circled one more time. Then they flew a short distance from them and landed on the ground. Asim was looking in the distance at what looked like another dragon; although it seemed to be smaller, but it was still far off.

"Let's hope it's not a cockatrice," Lanee said, squinting, looking into the distance. She turned her head back to see the guards had shut the castle gate.

"Hope you left nothing behind." Tyron smiled. "I don't think we are welcome back."

"No problem there." Lanee laughed.

"What is that?" Anson asked, referring to the dragon.

"It's a way off. I hope it's as nice as the other two," said Baylin.

"Let's hope we can slip out of here, dragons willing." Asim smiled. "Let's put some of these shields together. We need to make a bed for Zollo and attach it to the horse. We need to leave here so we can go to the cavern to meet up with the children." Now they were seeing it was a dragon, and it was a lot closer to them.

"Looks like it could be a person on top of the dragon," shouted Lanee.

"True!" Asim's mind was wandering about what had happened as he looked around.

This new dragon was flying toward the other two dragons and landing next to them. They saw a figure slide off the dragon's neck.

"Could that be Jubly?" shouted Lanee, ecstatic, as she ran toward her.

"What!" Asim shouted, his mind racing back to reality again.

Tyron was looking amazed. "She…ahh…was dead!" he spluttered out. They were both looking at each other as they walked toward her. Jubly still had a slight limp from her ankle injury. Lanee was now running; they both met and hugged.

"I thought you were dead!" professed Lanee.

"No! I thought I would be too." She smiled. "It's amazing."

"H-how did you…" Asim asked as they had caught up with the two of them.

"It was Baby, well, that's what I call him. I nursed him back to health, and all his sickness cleared up, and somehow, strange as it seems, I can communicate with the dragons. They appear to understand what I say, and I know what they are thinking."

"That's amazing." A blank-faced Tyron was shaking his head. "Although I don't think I know what you said."

She laughed. "The dragons were happy that their son was well. I told them I wanted to join you and that you could be in a large battle. They flew ahead to help."

"You mean they knew us?"

"Yes, back from the time we were crossing from forest to forest."

"I thought they didn't like us?" Lanee questioned with a big smile. "Their timing could not have been more perfect."

"Any later, and you would not be holding Lanee," Tyron smirked.

"You fool," said Lanee, turning and punching him hard in the arm.

"I am happy to see you alive." Tyron smiled at her as they hugged.

"They are friendly!" Jubly was looking back at the dragons, which had small puffs of smoke coming from both of their nostrils. "Do you want to see them?"

"Can I take your word they are friendly?" Tyron had a smile on his face.

"You look so well." Lanee was smiling.

"I feel well. I feel great. Just this little twinge in my ankle, but it's doing better. Look at you, even after going through a battle?" They laughed together. "We will have nothing to fear from the dragons now. They know you are my friends."

"This is unbelievable." Lanee was smiling inside and out. "I'm happy you are back with us. A weight has lifted from my heart."

They walked over to where the others were, and everyone was so pleased to see her. Concerned about Zollo, she showed great empathy with Toya, who hugged her, and Lube, who was still caring for him.

"Let's say goodbye to the dragons, though they will stay if you want them to."

"We should be all right. I don't think we will have any repercussions from the king or his army, now, he has no warlock to depend on, and half his army has gone. I feel we will be safe," exclaimed Asim.

She reached for his hands, holding both in hers. "I did not want to be alone in the dragon's lair. It scared me, but I knew I could not travel, even knowing it hurt your heart to see me stay." She tightened her grip on his hands.

Asim looked deep into her eyes. "I thought you would die if I left you there. I could not be more pleased to see you alive and well." He hugged and kissed her lightly on the cheek.

They walked back close to where Lanee and Tyron were standing. Jubly continued to walk over to the dragons and put her arms around them. They all bent their heads as she whispered to them.

"I have not seen anything like that." Asim stood amazed, almost unable to believe what he was seeing.

After the mother and father, Jubly went to the baby. This time, they could see she was shedding tears. Holding on to his neck, she whispered and kissed the side of his head. She moved back as they reared back up on their feet. With a high gust of wind, they flew up in the air. They made one circle over the castle. Asim could see the few guards left still watching from the tower. Upon seeing the dragons, they dived behind the wall. Asim smiled as the dragons flew off toward the mountain from where they came.

Asim looked around at everyone and the devastation. *This had been a battle*, he thought to himself.

Chapter 35

FINDING THE CHILDREN AGAIN

It was close to dusk, and everyone lay around, tired and exhausted after the day that they had had. Some wanted to wash in the river nearby. Everyone was ready to rest, and even though the caves were close to them, most just wanted the fresh air and a night under the stars. But they knew they should move deeper into the forest before they would feel comfortable to make camp.

"Let's pack everything we have. I know it's not much!" shouted Tyron.

"Is Zollo attached to the horse yet?" Asim asked.

"Yes," said Toya, who had not left his side.

"I want you, Lube, and Duf to stay with him as we travel. Maybe the water from the river will help him." They moved out and later found a place to camp.

"Tyron and I will take the first watch," Asim said. "I want everyone to rest."

"You think we will need a guard tonight?" asked Baylin.

"Oh yes," he retorted. "Oh yes," he repeated under his breath. "Make Zollo as comfortable as you can." He was looking at Toya. Asim could still see blood seeping from Zollo's gash. Toya, Jubly, and Lanee were trying to rebandage with what they had.

"Need more water!" Toya shouted from the other side of the camp.

"I will send Duf back to the river to bring some," Stone shouted. "I will send him on the horse."

"We only have the one water pouch?" Toya went hunting for another. Duf climbed on the horse. He looked strange; he was most definitely too large.

"Will the horse hold you?" Stone yelled. Duf turned his head and smiled; the horse had moved off slowly under his weight.

"They look a little strange together. I think it would look better if Duf carried the horse." They both laughed at that thought. Later, when Duf returned. Toya rewashed Zollo's wound and bandaged him again, keeping him close to a small fire, but even through the dim light, Toya could see Zollo's body sweating.

"He has a fever," bemoaned Lanee. Taking off the bandages, she could see the infection. "This is causing his sickness." She sighed.

On returning, Asim and Tyron went to see Zollo's condition while Wilt and Lube took their place.

Looking at the wound, Asim knew it needed cleaning and closing. Taking his dagger from the inside of his belt, he placed the tip in the fire, leaving it there until about three inches of blade turned red with heat. Tyron, Lanee, Duf, and Toya held Zollo's body tight. "This will hurt."

"Ouch!" Tyron shouted out loud.

Giving him a strange look, Asim shook his head. He placed the tip of the red-hot blade just inside the wound as he twisted it a quick turn. Zollo's body arched, but he made no sound. A significant amount of pus seeped out, rolling down his back, wiped up by Lanee.

"Hold him tight," he shouted again, pulling the blade out and wiping the wound off. This time, he placed the knife blade flat side down over the injury, hearing the sizzle of skin. Zollo arched his body again, still saying nothing; his whole body went limp as the dagger burnt into his flesh. Asim could see the wound had closed.

"Leave it open now. We will bandage the wound again in the morning." He will need his sleep, just like the rest of you."

"Will he be all right?" a hopeful Toya asked.

"We will know more in the morning." Asim joined the others.

Toya, Jubly, and Lanee stayed close to Zollo.

Around the fire, each one was reflecting the day. They all were happy to be still alive.

"I am proud of all of you," said Asim as he sat down with them. "I wasn't sure we would be here this night. Reflecting on our journey, which has been an extraordinary one, for sure. Spen is not here. We will have to toast with the water we have, a toast to those here and not here and the children." They passed the water pouch to each other.

The morning seemed to come fast as the bright sun was rising toward the mountains.

Wonder what this day will bring, Asim thought.

The little sleep they had seemed to refresh most for the day ahead. And even though a few bones ached, they made ready for their trek to the cave. Asim walked over to Zollo, knowing Toya had been watching him all night. Lanee was about to bandage his back.

"He is still breathing," she said. "You can tell he is fighting pain. He still has not opened his eyes."

"We will need to put him back on the bed of shields we made to travel."

A single tear from Toya's eye trickled down the right side of her cheek. Lanee reached over with her fingers, wiping the tear away. "He is strong," she encouraged her.

They all left to meet up with the children a short time later. Tyron and Wilt had gone on ahead to make sure everything was clear. It was a short distance to the cave entrance. Tyron and Wilt were waiting, sitting on the rocks.

"No one is here," said Tyron. He looked back toward the cave. "When we entered, we did not see or hear anything, although we did not travel far!" Asim's face dropped a little in dismay upon hearing that news. "I was sure they would have made it this far by now."

"Any chance they could have been here and left already?" asked Wilt.

"I don't believe so." Asim seemed a little down. "We need to search for them in the cave. Lanee, I need you to take Zollo, Jubly, and Toya. Follow the mountain to the crack at the first entrance we found, leading you to the warlock's cave. You could find something that will help him, at least something clean to put on his wound. Oh, and you should take Duf, Wilt, and Lube with you, just in case. I know the warlock is dead, but I don't want you to run into anything strange you may have to handle."

They set out, heading close to the mountain. Duf was in front of the horse. Wilt was in the rear.

"Tyron, we need to find the children and the rest of our party," he said. "Baylin and Anson, you come with us. Everyone else can camp out here until we come back. If we are not back by dusk, send someone back for Lanee. So together, you can try to find where we went? Keep your eyes open. You never know in this forest. Remember the dwarfs!"

Asim, with Tyron, Baylin, and Anson, reached the cave entrance. Entering, they climbed and jumped across the rocks on their way up to the passage.

"Don't seem to remember all these rocks?" he said, a little irritated.

"I'm sure they were here." Tyron laughed as they continued upward, then down on the other side.

"It's smelling a little foul in here." Baylin was holding his nose.

"I think I know why," Tyron replied. "A little run-in we had last time we were here." They kept moving down the passage, ready to climb the rock to the first gate. Asim could see the bodies of the beasts still lying dead on the ground.

"Here's part of your smell." He laughed, holding his nose.

"What happened to their heads?" asked Baylin.

"Precaution." He smiled. Climbing the rock, they moved through the still open gate, and they kept to the pathway with just a few rocks to maneuver around.

"We should be at the river soon."

As they continued, they could hear voices in the distance. They were low at first, then some shouts and faint screams.

"Draw your swords," whispered Asim. "Let's be cautious as we approach." They maneuvered around one more turn in the pathway.

"This should lead us to the river." They eased closer for a better view as the pathway straightened. Asim could see Stone standing on the ridge overlooking the river. They still approached with caution; he could see he had several children close to where he was standing. One of the children saw them approaching and grabbed Stone. Turning around, he was more than grateful to see the smiling face of Asim looking back at him.

"Asim," he yelled. The children seemed relieved. Now, they had found them; he was smiling large when he approached them.

"Stone, I am happy to see you and all these children." Asim smiled, watching them crowd around.

Baylin's heart dropped, a lump in his throat. He could see his boy, Leham, standing with the others around Stone. Now Leham realized that his father was not more than a length away from him. His eyes began to water and the tears slowly rolled down his cheeks.

"Father," he yelled, running toward Baylin.

"Leham," cried Baylin as his eyes started to tear up; they hugged each other tightly.

Asim knew at that moment the reason for this journey!

"I thought I would never see you again," Baylin said, looking at Leham's face and touching his cheek lightly with his fingers. "I am so happy. I thought I had lost you forever."

"Me too," said an exuberant Leham, staring hard at his father's face. "Are you hurt?" he asked, noticing the black eye and many cuts and bruises on his face.

"I am all right now!" he said, looking at Leham's face.

"I saw Grandfather."

"You did. Where is he?"

"He is not with us now."

"What do you mean?" he asked Leham with a puzzled look.

"Grandfather died," Leham said, trying to be strong. Then he cried. He pushed his head into Baylin's shoulder as he held him tight.

"It will be all right," Baylin told him. "It will be all right." He held him tight.

Asim was reaching over to Stone and grabbed his arm, pulling him closer to him.

"I am glad we found you. It worried me when you were not at the entrance."

"I am glad that you all made it out of the castle. I was not sure, by the way it looked, that you would. But deep down, I somehow knew you would find a way." He was smiling.

"We almost didn't," replied Tyron. "It was a close one." He slapped Stone on the back.

"I am glad to see you all."

"Me too." Anson grabbed onto Stone.

Stone looked at Asim. "You will have to tell me all about it, and I will tell you about Brantil and Spen. Unfortunately, we were not at the entrance because we have a problem swimming with them in the river. As you can see." Asim looked across the river.

"I put a rope around them, but some children are still too afraid." He could see Radel in the middle of the river. Tonas and Spen were on the other side with the children.

"Let's go join them." Asim smiled when they jumped in the water, leaving Baylin with the children at the top of the bank. They all swam to the other side, briefly stopping to say hello to Radel. Reaching the other bank, even the children seemed happy to see them. Asim grabbed Tonas and Spen, pulling them both close.

"I knew if anyone could come through at all, it would be you. You are magnificent!" shouted Spen.

"And you," Asim replied. "You even sound sober." He looked puzzled. "Is your pouch empty?" He laughed.

"You see before you the new Spen. I have the mead in my pouch, but I am remaining this way." Asim laughed.

"But you know what?" He was thinking. "As you are here, maybe just a little sip would not hurt—for congratulations, of course." Asim laughed again and slapped him on the back.

Tonas was looking at Asim. "I still don't believe we are here together again with the children."

"It was close. I will tell you later. We must take the children to the other side. We will move out into the river." He figured. "Stretch out so we can be close to the children as they cross. Spen, you stay here and make sure all the children start out on the rope."

He handed each child off, swimming just a little as they moved along the line. It was taking them a while, but soon, all the children were across on the other side. Stone swam with Spen holding him until they reached the bank.

"We are all wet!" He smiled. "But we will be all right. We have a small journey through the cave, and then we will be back out of the mountain and on our way to the villages." Some children were shouting and playing; everyone seemed a lot happier.

"Have we checked yet to make sure everyone is here?" Asim asked.

Radel counted. "Fifty-two strapping boys," she announced. "Eighteen for Marmelos and thirty-four for Tress, all accounted for and checked. I hope that was the number. That's every one of them going back." She smiled.

They continued through the passageway. "Hold your noses," shouted Tyron as they passed through the gate, going over and around all the rocks until soon they were back at the cavern entrance. Looking out, Asim saw Benson, Tig, Mup, Pooly, Wooly, and Boben had set up a small camp while they were waiting for them to return.

"Nothing to report here," said Pooly. "It's been peaceful. We have sent out scouts, but it's all clear."

The children came out of the cavern one by one. Boben had been waiting patiently. Then his eyes caught sight of his brother coming out. They ran and hugged together.

"This is good!" shouted Baylin, looking at everyone around him.

"Can I have everyone together," asked Asim. Looking up at the sky, it was almost dusk. "I want to make it to the other entrance before dark. Can we do this in twos? Line up one child next to the other. And we can keep a more watchful eye on them."

Being a short trek, it was not long before they saw the horse standing close to the forest.

"I think we must be here," said Tyron, looking at the mountain wall and finding the crack that led to the cavern. The sun had set; it was becoming dark.

"I'm sure everyone's tired. We will have to stay the night here." They traveled up through the passageway and over the bridge. They soon came to the warlock's cave. Asim had decided all the children would remain in the large hallway this night. "This will be a good place for all of you to sleep," he said as he went up to the cave with Tyron and Radel. Lanee was relieved now to see them.

"You found them all?" Lanee asked with a smile that would light up a room.

"Everyone but Brantil." Asim's head was down. "We have lost another friend."

Radel rushed over to hug Jubly. "You are alive!" she cried. Tears were in her eyes as they embraced.

Asim was on his way over to see Zollo, and to his surprise, Zollo had his eyes open and was talking. He was feeling a little impeded by the pain, but he was speaking.

"I found a few things to help him," Lanee said, smiling.

"Quite the wizard, or is it warlock?" quipped Tyron. She kept smiling.

Zollo looked at Asim. "You killed the warlock?"

"It's all taken care of." He put his hand on his shoulder.

"You're looking good," said Stone, who had walked over. "I heard about you, and it's good to see you alive." He grabbed him the best he could without hurting him.

"I don't know what happened." Zollo shook his head. "All I recall is that I woke up here. My back feels like the castle gate fell on it, yet I feel good. Well, almost good. I feel all right!" he said. Asim smiled.

"One guard ran you through with his dagger, so I hear," said Stone.

"I seem to remember something now."

"Talk again tomorrow," Asim said. "You need to rest. It is night, and we will leave in the morning." Stone pretended to punch him in the arm as they smiled.

"We have the children, and we will head to the first village early," said Asim.

Zollo gave a smile for an approval.

"The children are settling down in the hall, so we should all sleep well tonight."

Chapter 36

THE REUNION

Waking up early the next morning, they packed, taking everything they found helpful in the warlock's cave.

Asim was checking on Zollo. "How are you feeling?"

"Better than last night. I'm sure I can walk!"

"Don't overdo it. We have a horse. At least we had one last night. If not, stay with Duf. He will help you."

"I need to rebandage before we leave," Lanee shouted.

"I need to walk with you," Zollo told Duf, who smiled.

Zollo stood back on his feet as Stone came over. "I see you are on your feet. Are you going to make it?" Zollo punched him on the arm, and they both laughed. Duf gave a broad smile as he put his large hand on Zollo's shoulder.

"We are on our way to Marmelos," shouted Asim.

As they continued their trek, the early morning sun was making its way out, shining through the leaves in thin, sparkling stripes that bounced off the ground like a rubber ball. They were using their hands to shade their eyes from the brightness as they left the cave; looking around, he could see the horse was missing.

"It could have just wandered away?" Tyron smiled. "Maybe we will come across it again." They started their trek through the forest.

"We are a large party," Asim said, looking at them all. "Lube and Stone, go ahead of us, Anson, Benson, check the right. Wilt and Toya, you go left. I want to arrive there with *no* trouble."

The trek through the trees in the forest was a long, hot, and uneventful one. They were keeping everyone together as they walked. Zollo, despite having to rely on Duf a few times, was keeping up with everyone while he fought through the pain showing on his face. Still, there was no sign of the horse.

A curious pack of wolves crept close and were trying to surround the group. As one wolf moved in closer, some of the boys could see its sizeable snarling mouth and saliva-dripping teeth. One of the smaller boys screamed as it was aggressively trying to snatch him. Jubly, thinking fast, grabbed her bow; her arrow hit the wolf in the head, killing it as it rolled over on its back.

"Were you aiming for the head this time?" Asim asked, smiling with a hint of sarcasm as Jubly smiled back.

They calmed the children; the wolf's death had caused a panic, knocking a few of them to the ground in the scuffle. Picking them up, Radel put them back on their feet again, helping to keep them together.

The wolves, sensing the dead body, waited for everyone to pass. Then they attacked the dead wolf. They were tearing it to pieces and running off into the forest. It's not a sight for the younger children to see. Afraid that it might upset them, Baylin, Tonas, and Jubly had a time trying to stop them from looking back. Each time they turned a boy's head around, it turned back again!

Asim was walking out in front, just thinking to himself, *A minor skirmish, nothing worrying.*

Then, there was a slap on the back. "What are you thinking about?" asked Tyron.

"Well!" He thought for a second. "I am glad we can rest from all the action we have seen recently. Wolves we can handle with no problem, but I'm wondering if it's not too quiet."

"You know, you always seem to invite a lot of action," Tyron quipped.

"Me! you say?" In his defense, he stared straight at him. Tyron just smiled.

"You see!" Lanee was breaking in. "I told you."

Asim shook his head.

"We will soon approach the river, and you know what happened on the way here," declared Tyron.

"You must admit, we have had no luck with rivers." Lanee groaned.

"Well." Asim smiled. "I guess I will have to agree on our luck so far with the rivers, but maybe it's time for a change? Or maybe we can take one of Tyron's great shortcuts?"

"Hey, now, you're trying to offend me?" Tyron laughed. "It was not my fault! It was not far across. How was I supposed to know there was an eel in the middle!" Both Asim and Lanee laughed.

"We have a lot of children this time, so I will give you a chance to redeem yourself at the right place to cross this time." He gave another quick laugh. Tyron slapped him on the back.

"I will do my best for my friend," he said. Soon, they found their selves close to the river. Stone and Lube were waiting as the other four scouts joined them. *Strangely, it did not seem too far from where we crossed on our journey last time*, Asim thought, although he knew it could not be too close.

He looked across the river. "It seems closer from this bank to the other. What do you think?" Asim asked Tyron.

"Could be?" He shrugged. "I will swim across first. If a fish eats me, then I suggest you find a different place to cross."

"That sounds only fair," Asim said sarcastically as they both smiled. Jumping straight in, Tyron swam unscathed to the other side. Now picking up a rope, Stone had knotted together with another for length. He swam to the other side with one end to join Tyron.

"All right, this is what we will do," said Asim. "I need the weak swimmers and children who cannot swim. We are here to help you." Asim signaled to Stone to come back closer. "We only need the rope where it is deep," he shouted. Stone moved back in closer. "Duf can hold the rope tight this end. Lube and Wilt go to the other side with Stone to keep that end tight. Don't let him pull you under." You could see by the look on Duf's face he had thought that was funny. "Everyone else that can swim take up an area of the rope so you're spaced out all the way across as we move the children. Tyron," he shouted, "you grab them as they come off the rope. Put them on the bank. We have a lot of children to help across."

Lanee swam out toward the middle of the river, turning to face Asim as she shouted, "The river is not moving fast, but when you reach me, there is a powerful undertow. We will need to be careful."

We will, he thought, nodding his agreement to her.

Now, the others were swimming out to join on the rope. Everything started out smooth; Asim decided to let the younger children cross first, lining them up one by one and being helped by each one manning the rope. Baylin and Spen were at the front, helping the children onto the rope, standing next to Duf. Asim stayed close by, making sure everyone's crossing was safe. *This is the way it should be*, he was thinking to himself. He was shocked back to reality by a scream as one of the children, a smaller boy, slipped off the rope in the middle, eluding the hands of Tonas. The strong undertow pulled him under the water, dragging him downstream.

Now, seeing the catastrophe as Tonas went under, also drawn into the undertow. Asim dived in, swimming downstream, trying to catch up with the child in the swift-moving water, hoping someone would help Tonas.

Lanee also sensed the trouble and swam after the child; Lube dived under to help Tonas. Asim, now seeing the boy's head bobbing up and down in the distance, swam strongly. He hoped he was moving closer and the child had not swallowed too much water, but he saw another danger in the distance. Ahead, the water was twisting and swirling. The boy was being sucked slowly into an enormous whirlpool. Swimming strong, stroke after stroke, Asim seemed to gain, wishing he did not have all his weapons on.

They both had traveled a distance. Asim, seeing he was close, hoped to grab the boy before he drowned in the swirling water, giving him the inner strength to swim harder. Moving closer, his mind was thinking. With one quick stroke, he reached out to grab the child; at first, he had a handful of the boy's shirt, and the waters swirled around them both. The boy's head bobbed under in the water. Pulling as hard, he dragged him closer, hoping his shirt would hold up, holding his breath when he saw the material tearing.

Swiftly, he wrapped his arm around the boy's shoulders, placing his head on his chest and trying to keep his head above the water. Asim pulled hard to break free from the churning water, pulling his legs from under him and swimming backward, knowing he was being drawn steadily toward the middle of the whirlpool. Asim was relying on his powerful body strength to sustain them; he was continuing to kick hard to free them both while keeping the boy's head above water. Exhausted in this battle, with one last powerful stroke, he broke free of the water's pull on him. With large one-armed strokes, he was heading toward the riverbank, the boy resting on his chest, clutched tightly against him.

Asim swam to the far bank, seeing Lanee, who had swum vigorously behind them, veering away to intercept them both. She helped Asim carry the child up to the side of the river, placing him in a dry area; they could see the boy's lips were changing color. They both worked diligently on him. Lanee was pushing hard on his chest as Asim was pushing his knees slowly into his stomach. Suddenly, the boy coughed out streams of water from his mouth and nose. Asim sat him up, gently patting his back, helping the child release the water he was coughing out.

"You are safe." Lanee held the child, looking at his small face. He was trying to talk, but he could only cough.

"It is all right. Don't speak. Keep coughing that water out."

"Well," said Asim, "there is one good thing. You made it onto the other side of the river." The boy tried to smile as he coughed again. "No more river. I'm sure you feel you have swallowed enough today, anyway." He picked up the child in his arms and held him against his shoulder as they had to travel a distance back to the others.

"Are you all right to stand on your feet?" asked Lanee as they were drawing close.

He nodded as a "yes" croaked out! Between the two, they walked with him to join the others. All the children had made it to the bank now as they gathered around him. Only adult nonswimmers were left to cross. Spen was last, as usual. Stone swam with him to ensure he crossed as they pulled the rope back.

"That was more excitement than what we needed," said Stone, looking tiredly.

"A lot more than we needed." Asim yawned. He lay flat and rested.

"But no eels this time!" Tyron was laughing. In a short time, Asim was back up again.

"We have to keep going," he said. "Stone and Lube, go ahead. Anson and Benson go right, and Wilt and Toya go left. We will follow." They traveled through the forest on their way to the village. Asim was hoping the rest of the journey would be more peaceful as he took a deep breath, looking up at the tall trees with the yellowish green leaves blowing gently in the light breeze; he was absorbing the beauty, knowing most times he took this for granted. The majestic height of the many oak trees making up this forest. Chirping birds on the branches, after everything they had been through, this was a time to breathe. He was thinking, looking back at the children, ready to go home. His mind drifted back, remembering his time as a youth. A smile came to his face right before a big slap on the back.

"What are you thinking?" asked Tyron.

"I was thinking. I believe there is a band of dangerous robbers in this area. I heard the leader is a real ugly man who must wear a mask and moves around with a giant."

Tyron then realized what he was saying.

"Ugly, that's what you think? Why, I should rob you now." He laughed.

"What would you take?" Asim laughed.

"Why, all your smugness." He laughed again. Asim laughed with him, grabbing each other's arms.

"You two seem happy," said Lanee, linking up to them both.

"Way too long in coming." Lanee was holding them close.

"We should be in the village soon," said Tyron.

"Tell me," she asked Asim, "did you think we would ever deliver the children home?"

"I was not sure how we could complete this journey when we started, to be honest. I did not know then that I would have such brave warriors surround me."

She smiled.

Later that day, the village came into sight. Asim could see the smokestacks wafting up as they slowly disappeared into the air. A few dogs barked as they approached. Some of the villagers had come out to see what was happening. As soon as they saw the children, they ran to hug them; one ran back to the village square to ring the bell, alerting everyone in their houses, taverns, and any other place they were. The villagers were soon dancing and shouting.

"The children are home." Every mother rejoiced when Asim and the band walked into the village with their eighteen missing children. They were laughing, jumping, screaming with joy. They never thought they would ever see their children again. The whole village was filled with laughter and tears. Everyone was thankful to the band of warriors that had brought their children back home. The elders of the village were sorry they had lost two villagers but thrilled the children were back. They were more than thankful to Baylin, Asim, and the other warriors.

"Anything you need," the elder said. "We will try to accommodate you. Anything you ask, though we are not a rich village…" he babbled on.

"We don't want your money," Asim cut him off. "What I need is a bath, clean clothes, a large ale, followed by some food. Don't know about the rest of them." He left with one of the elders. Turning, he shouted, "Meet you all in the tavern later."

"Taragoo," shouted Zollo; Asim looked and laughed.

"Meeting at my favorite place," Spen said with a broad smile on his face.

Later that evening was a night of merriment for Asim and the others. The villagers had taken all the children from the village of Tress in for the night. There was a large calf roasting in the village square, a smorgasbord of food laid out for them. Later, in the tavern, they were all drinking, talking, and having fun. There were all the stories to tell each other and anyone else who wanted to listen to all the exploits and all the strange and extraordinary things they had seen and done. They welcomed even the dwarfs and the robbers in the village that night despite their dubious past.

A conversation started between Asim and Tyron. "You know, we will leave in the morning to help the rest of the children back to the village of Tress. I will never forget your bravery. You have been a loyal friend on this journey, and I could not have asked for more. Duf, Wilt, and Tan were magnificent, and I am so sorry we lost Tan. He was brave and important. I'm also sorry you came away with no gold! Only the lumps on your body and bumps on your head." He smiled.

"It has been a journey," Tyron retorted. "Never to forget! It has changed my life. I know it has changed the lives of my men. You, too, have been a real friend. Even gold has been far from my mind. Of course, you know, I would never turn it down when offered!" They both laughed.

"Will it be goodbye in the morning?" he asked. "I hear some strange things are happening in the west that I must search out."

"You know," said Tyron, "despite being almost killed one hundred times in the last few days, it has been fun, a real adventure, even with your smugness." He laughed. "If you don't mind us hanging around with you a little longer…"

"It would be our pleasure," he said and raised his tankard. "To friends." They all took a drink. Zollo was still using Duf as a crutch.

"To friends," he said to Duf, smiling, lifting his tankard, Duf laughed and hit Zollo's mug. Ale spurted up in Zollo's face, and he could not stop laughing as he wiped it off. Spen stood up, then fell again. "I'm all right!" he slurred. The large barmaid helped him up to his feet and kissed him on the cheek, causing a loud roar of laughter.

"Now that's the Spen we know," said Asim to Tyron and Lanee. They were all laughing. Wilt, Lube, Toya, and Stone had all their arms linked and were singing; it was a good night they all had earned.

Chapter 37

ANOTHER FISH STORY

It was the dawn of a new day, the final leg to return the children home. The bright, shining sun and deep blue sky were out as if they were saying, "You all did well!" Waking up this morning was difficult. It took a while for Asim to locate where everyone slept, making sure they were all ready to leave; it had been a long night of celebration.

All the thirty-four children who spent the night with the village families were up early and ready to leave. One by one, the others joined them while they all gathered in the village square, along with the people of the village.

"Thank you. We are grateful to you and the whole village," said Asim.

"No!" Elder Lotan spoke out. "We are the ones grateful to you, all of you, and you are all welcome back to our village." Asim was ready to leave out for one more journey for the children. Baylin and Leham were both waiting on the path leading out of the village.

"We cannot thank you all enough," Baylin said, "for my son."

Asim grabbed his arm. "You showed your bravery in a time of battle. I'm proud of what you, your Father Brantil, and your friend Exim achieved to retrieve your boy, and I'm sorry we lost them, I am glad, you have your son. Look after him."

They were ready to trek through the forest. "Mup, Pooly, and Wooly, I want you three to make a scouting trip ahead for a while. I am amazed at how easy it has been for us to travel from the castle all the way here with little trouble," Asim said. "Well, not the excitement at the river. But all in all, good."

"And this is a problem; why?" asked Tyron.

"I was thinking aloud. Maybe our luck has changed."

They continued their long trek through the forest. "Yes, one more river, and we will be on our way to the next village."

"Oh my! I forgot about that one," Lanee sighed.

"I don't like it. This is where we ran into the cockatrice things," Toya moaned.

"It seems there are a lot more beasts in this area." Radel joined them.

"Another river?" Lanee sighed again. Her head was down as she turned her nose up at the thought.

"Asim will tell us not to fear the river," Toya quipped.

"It is not so much fear. That's all just in your mind," Lanee scoffed. "It's that we have no luck with any of them. Something always seems to happen."

"Well, just think, we will soon have all these children back in their homes," said Radel.

Mup returned later, stopping to talk to Asim. "They were close to the river. But it seemed a lot deeper at this point. And the current looked much stronger."

"Not the news I wanted to hear. Let's go to the river and make camp. We will see if there is a better crossing from there." They heard loud screeching in the far distance. "Glad we are this side of the mountain." Standing on the river bank, Asim confirmed what Mup had told him; it looked much broader and a lot more profound.

Tonas had walked up beside Asim. "I don't know how the Nordaks crossed these rivers with the horses and wagon. They had to cross on the way to the village and cross on their way back again unless they found a way around it somehow. Although I don't see a way around this one?"

He could see that Tonas was thinking hard! "As if by magic!" Asim smiled with a wink, looking at him and watching like a light switched on in his head.

"Oh!" Tonas realized, a little red-faced as he nodded his head.

Tyron joined them now. "We could have a problem here," he said, smiling.

"You could not be more right. We will try to find something better if we can." Everyone was settling down. Radel had the children under control.

"Stone, I will need you, Lube, and Duf to go upriver." He pointed in that direction. "Don't go too far. See if there could be a better place to cross. If you find somewhere, send one of you back. Tyron and Wilt, we will be going in the opposite direction to see if we can find anything. Lanee, keep the children settled until we return. Keep them occupied." He smiled as she stuck her tongue out at him.

"We have not seen you today? How have you been feeling?" Asim asked Zollo.

"Been back with the children helping Toya. I am feeling good." He was nodding his head. You better watch yourself. I will be ready to take you down."

"That's my boy!" said Asim, "We will have to see about that, though!" He laughed.

When they left, Stone, Lube, and Duf were already on their journey upstream.

Asim, Tyron, and Wilt set out downstream. After walking along the bank for a while, they did not see a better place to cross. Wilt was close to turning back when he noticed the river was meandering in the distance. He pointed it out to Asim.

"All right, we will follow it around that bend." They were now seeing a land mass jutting out from the mountain into the river, noticing there were more rock formations spread into the water.

"This looks like it could be better for us to cross," Tyron said, surprised. "And we even have rocks to help us."

The current looked brisk, but that would not matter to them if it were a better place.

"Let me try to swim over," asked Wilt willingly as he slowly waded out into the water. "It's deep." He found he could hold on to the rocks to climb over to the open river. "The water is strong," he shouted, looking back at them. "It is good so far; there's just a long way to go."

"Will the children be able to cross here?" shouted Asim.

"Yes," he shouted, "they should be all right with a little help." Wilt could not tell the depth.

He figured it would be deeper as he left the rocks to swim toward the middle. The current seemed to have calmed down, and he moved away from the rocks, swimming slowly toward the other side. Asim, shading his eyes, could see bubbles coming up not too far from Wilt.

"What is that?" he shouted. Wilt stopped as he turned to look back at them, puzzled.

"Over there," he shouted, pointing downstream. Wilt looked to where the bubbles were. With no warning, out of the water protruded the giant elongated head of a fish. But all Wilt could see were giant razor-like teeth in the creature's oversized mouth, large enough to swallow him whole. The enormous dragon-sized creature jumped straight up and out of the water in one motion as it dived deep! Its black-skinned body was stark against the water.

"It's a buru," shouted Tyron. "That's a dangerous fish! Wilt, come back here quick."

"What is it with these rivers on this side of the mountain?" shouted Asim. "We must help him." They both jumped into the water.

"It's a long way. We will have to swim fast," shouted Tyron. "This thing can move fast." It had gone deep under the water, which gave them both some time to swim toward Wilt, who at that moment was motionless in the middle, treading water.

"Swim towards us," Tyron shouted. "It is heading straight for you."

Wilt swam toward them, reaching for his sword. He was glad now he had forgotten to take off. The creature came straight up out of the water high in the air and it landed with a loud splash close to where Wilt had been. Waves from the fish's landing pushed all three backward, bringing them closer together. It dived under again. This time, it returned, moving to the top of the water as it maneuvered itself toward all three. Wilt was still the closest. They had their swords out ready. As the creature closed the distance, they were prepared to strike for its head. As it swam toward them, Asim swung fast. His blade caught the beast, causing a deep slit in its head. Catching Wilt off guard, its giant head flinched, knocking him back with such force, he lost consciousness. With a deep, resounding splash, he ended up two to three lengths away. His limp body was floating on top of the water.

"Would you look at that! He's three lengths away," shouted Tyron, now maneuvering himself around to help him as Asim thrust his sword hard toward the creature's head. Tyron, now swimming close, pulled Wilt's head up out of the water. Asim's continual thrusts toward its large head caused it to turn away for now. Asim slowly swam back to Tyron and Wilt. The beast was turning again, following them. Wilt was slowly waking when Asim turned to strike at the creature again. This time, Tyron followed suit, and a quick blow from his sword put a thick slice in its skin, causing it to dive deep, rising again, all three pulled up high by its swift ascent, then falling faster, they all dropped firmly back into the water, landing in opposite directions a few lengths from the creature, which dived under again. Looking around, they regained their composure; now, all three were ready to wield their blades as it continued to swim back close to them. Asim, this time, caught the beast with another hard-cutting blow, knowing that he hurt the creature; it dived back under. A few seconds had passed. It still had not emerged, then Asim thought he saw bubbles downstream heading away from them.

"Yes," Tyron insisted. "We beat the buru."

"Well, for now," replied Asim. "I don't believe that we will cross here."

"Wise idea," said Wilt, who was back awake and aware now.

They all swam back to where they could climb the rocks to the bank again. Once on top of the rock, they looked around the river as far as they could see. But no signs of the creature. "Don't tell me," Asim exclaimed. "we were lucky it was a baby!"

Tyron laughed. "If it was, I don't want to meet mother or father, that's for sure."

"Let's hope Stone found something better," said Tyron.

"We have taken too much time now." Asim was looking at the river in some disbelief.

"We don't want that creature to come back," said Wilt, he looked at the river.

They started their walk back as Tyron still bragged about beating the buru. Asim and Wilt were having fun with his bragging. They stayed on the bank until they reached the others. On their arrival back, he could see that Stone, Lube, and Duf were already back sitting by the fire.

"How was your way?" he asked, looking at Stone.

"I slipped and hurt my knee. Other than that, no different to here. How about you?"

"Uneventful, other than a slight fishing trip. So we will have to cross here."

"Fishing?" Stone stared at him, looking confused.

"We had a run-in with a fishlike creature," groaned Wilt.

"But we ran it off," bragged Tyron. "We beat the buru." Wilt threw a stick at him.

"Sure, glad to hear that," said Lanee, punching Asim on the arm. "It's been uneventful here too."

"What was that for?"

"Leaving me here to babysit."

Asim laughed.

"We will need to make this easy," Asim started thinking. "Duf and Lube, see if you can find a hollowed-out tree trunk or something that we can float. Check around the forest area. We will not have enough rope, so we will have to make do if you find one."

It was a little later that Lube and Duf came back with a thick, extremely large tree trunk carried on his shoulder with help from Lube, dropping it close to the water.

"Just what I was looking for," he said. "Great job, you two. We need to attach a rope to both ends so we can pull both ways. All right, Tyron, take Tonas, Toya, and Radel and swim to the other side. Unload the children as they jump off the log. I want Duf, Lube, and Stone to attach the first rope on to the front of the log. You three will be my pullers to bring everyone on the log over. Wilt, Lanee, and Jubly will attach the rope and be my pullers on the back end. You will pull the empty tree log back. Zollo, Spen, and Boben stay at this end to help the children to climb on the log. We should try to put five children on at a time. I want all my dwarfs to keep the children seated on the log to stop it from tipping in the swift current. We will take everyone to the other side without dangling feet in the water on a rope."

Asim continued looking up and down the river as everyone took their places. He did not see any movement in the water. Tyron, Tonas, Radel, and Toya were on the opposite bank, waiting for the first of the children to cross.

"Do you think this will work?" Zollo asked him.

"We will soon find out. Let's load up the first children on the log." They found four would be a better fit and a little safer. Taking the rope, Duf, Lube, and Stone pulled as they swam to the other side. The dwarfs were three on each side of the log, with Wilt Lanee and Jubly at the back, helping to steady the wood as it crossed. It was working smoothly, plus the young boys seemed to have a fun time.

Everything was working out. Most were on the other side now. Asim had worked Spen and Boben in with the trips across so that he and Zollo would be the only ones left. They were waiting to put the last four boys on the log. Asim could see Tyron and Toya playing with the children on the other bank. Radel and Tonas had things in control; everyone seemed happy. It was a beautiful day, and the sun was shining. Zollo was now ushering the last of the children on the log as it arrived.

"We can go." He stood, looking to see all the children had gone. "Let's go." He waded into the water behind the log, which had already started across. Lanee was waiting for Asim to catch up with them. She was smiling.

"What?" He smiled.

"Finally, a river!" They laughed. Zollo was playing with Anson, Benson, and the children on the log. No one had seen the giant buru had returned upstream. The beast was heading toward the children on the tree trunk. It rose fast before diving under the water. Asim could see the young boys in a panic. Anson and Benson were trying to pull them from the log while Wooly and Pooly were helping to grab them and swim with them away from where the creature was heading. Asim could see Tyron dive in from the other side. The giant creature had opened its large mouth as it headed for the old trunk. The children were screaming; everyone was shouting directions in this chaotic moment. Asim and Lanee were close but could only watch as this disaster unfolded. Zollo, Wilt, and Jubly desperately swam away from the trunk as the creature dove under again. Zollo held on to a child. The creature was coming back up, rearing its head high out of the water. With its mouth open this time, it came down hard with a crushing force on the tree trunk, causing splinters and waves as the water shot out from either side of its enormous head. The force of the waves was pushing the dwarfs and the children a distance away. Fragments shattered everywhere, flying from the creature's mouth as it bit hard down on the trunk; crushed pieces hit Wilt and Boben. A sizeable bloody gash appeared on Boben's head, and Wilt's nose was now trickling blood. They were shaking off the pain.

"Do we have all the children?" Asim yelled. There was a lot of devastation from the wood the creature had caused; the noise was loud, and the waves were high. He could see Anson and Mup were heading toward the other side. Now Zollo somehow was closer to him, still clutching the child.

"Swim back this way," Asim shouted to him. Zollo swam to the bank.

Asim and Lanee had their swords out; Wilt grabbed for his as Duf and Lube, being pulled under the water, were both back and ready to face the beast. Asim could not be sure everyone was all right but knew they had to stop this monstrous fish. Duf, when he saw the rope to the trunk floating on the water, pulled on it. There was nothing but a small piece of wood attached to the other end. Looking up the river, he saw the creature had gone under the water again.

"Be ready!" Asim yelled. At that moment, Jubly was floating toward him facedown. Both he and Lanee grabbed her, turning her over. There was a large, sharp piece of wood sticking out from her chest.

"She is alive," shouted Lanee, feeling her heartbeat. The blood was dripping out of the wound, and she was unconscious.

Wooly was close to them. "Can you float her to the bank to Zollo?" Asim asked him.

"I will." As he swam, he kept Jubly's head above water, being careful.

They watched the creature come back up. It stopped to turn back and head toward them, swimming on the top of the water. Its large mouth open was still to scoop up anything. Duf could see Pooly with one of the children, trying to swim to the bank on the other side. The creature's massive teeth were shining in the sunlight, heading straight towards them. Duf, seeing the danger, moved toward the creature, grabbing his club tight. With one swing, he hit the beast hard under the tip of its mouth. The whole body of the creature seemed to shake enough to change its direction, making it safe for Pooly and the child to swim to safety. A significant amount of water spewed from its mouth, enough to push Duf back three lengths in the water. Swimming forward, Tyron had now joined with Lanee and Asim on one side of the creature. "Seems like old times again." He was smiling.

Each one had their swords ready; Stone, Lube, and Duf were all on the other side of the beast.

"Can you see if there is anyone still floating?" he shouted to Stone.

"Don't think so," shouting back.

"Let's kill this fish!" Asim yelled.

Each one of them lunged at the beast. Most of the blades were slicing, not able to penetrate the thick skin of the creature, and it dived back under again.

"Stay ready," he shouted. They could see where it turned and was heading back again. Asim seemed in its pathway, but this time, he was willing to gamble. He dived under, right when the creature's enormous head and was almost on top of him. Coming back up as fast as he could, he drove his sword up deep into the creature's neck. The force ripped his sword from his hands. The beast wounded, flinched hard, diving under again. Asim moved out of the way, although he was caught by its giant tail; it flipped him back a short distance in the water. The others were still trying to strike a blow when it passed. Swimming upstream underwater, it turned once again, swimming back at them. Asim seemed to be the target again, who, this time, was without a sword; he could see his blade stuck deep in the creature's neck, entering up into its mouth when it approached. It rose high into the air, diving at them once again. Duf had swum forward, smashing it hard with his club, again enough to turn it away. This time, Tyron and Lanee were both ready and lunged at the creature, plunging their swords as deep as they could into its neck. Stone and Lube were next, striking hard into the neck of the beast when it passed. They could see blood trailing from the creature now, knowing it was hurt; it tried one more turn, but having trouble, it floated away down the river.

"I think we won this battle," said Asim. "But I lost my sword! We will need to regroup to ensure that everyone is on the other side now and no one is missing."

Asim and Lanee swam back to the bank, where Wooly had taken Jubly. Zollo and Wooly were attending to her, and the child was sitting close to him.

"How is she?" asked Lanee.

"She is good," said Zollo. "The piece of wood is out, and we stopped the bleeding, just putting on a makeshift bandage. She was awake but drifted off again."

"Wooly and Lanee, help me float Jubly to the other side. Zollo, you take the child."

All three were careful when floating Jubly to the other side of the river.

"We are all together now. Is there anyone not here?" Asim was asking Radel.

"Speak up now," shouted Tyron, "if you're missing."

"Fool," said Lanee, "this is serious."

Radel shouted in a thankful voice, "We have the thirty-four boys."

"Thank heaven," said Tonas. "That was close."

"Seems everyone else—" She stopped in midsentence. "Benson is missing! Has anyone seen Benson?"

Asim stood up after sitting to gain his strength back. "Who was next to Benson?"

"I was," waved Anson, "but when that creature came at us, we were all pushed separate ways. I lost track after that."

"Did anyone see him after this attack?" Everyone was quiet.

Asim walked over to the children who were on the log when the creature attacked, but they could not remember. He talked to Radel, Tonas, and Toya. "Help comfort them. They seem to be in shock. Maybe we should light a fire."

"We need to check the river for him. This is what we will do. We will split up into four groups. Two groups will swim to the other side of the river. It should be safe, one upstream and the other downstream. Same for the groups on this side. Lanee, we will go with Boben. We will cross and go downstream along the riverbank on the other side. Tyron, take Anson and Mup and go downstream on this side of the river. Stone, take Tig and Wooly. You will cross the river with us and go upstream. Lube, take Wilt and Pooly. You will go upstream along this side of the river."

Asim swam across, and Stone followed. The two groups that were on the other side had already begun to look for Benson. Having parted, they went their respective ways.

"Hope we find him," said Boben, ready to go.

"We will find Benson," Lanee assured him with a confident voice.

They continued to walk along the side of the bank. Asim could see Tyron a little ahead of them on the other side; he was pointing to something in the water. Asim could not see anything until he moved up on top of the bank for a better view. Then, he could see the massive trail of blood in the water; it was thick. He knew they hurt the creature.

But still, there was no sign of Benson as he looked out along the river bank.

"This is not good at all," said Lanee, keeping her eye on the bank and surrounding bushes.

Asim could see they were approaching where the river meanders again and would flow around the bend.

"How far should we go?" asked Lanee to Asim.

"Up around the bend of the river. There are lots of jagged rocks. They could have tangled his body."

As they rounded the bend, Asim again could see Tyron pointing again. This time, he could see the giant buru stuck between two large rocks on their side of the river.

"Is it dead?" asked Boben.

"It looks like it. We will know when we are closer." Asim waded out; it seemed as if the creature was dead. He waved Tyron over. Tyron swam across, leaving Mup and Anson on the other side for now.

"Is it dead?"

"I think so. I will grab my sword back," Asim said.

"Try to be careful around that thing." Lanee was watching him.

He waded over and started to pull his sword out. The creature's head suddenly reared, causing Asim to fall backward into the water with shock. Tyron had his sword out ready; the beast had no energy to do anything more. Lanee was almost in tears, laughing at Asim.

"Not funny." He was shaking his head, lying in a pool of water!

"Oh, I'm sure it was." Tyron chuckled with a grin on his face.

Asim was trying not to laugh. "We will need to put it out of its misery. It will just lay here and die anyway."

Tyron climbed up on the side of the large rock until he was at the same level as the upper part of the beast's head. It had stopped moving again; nothing was moving at all. Everything was quiet and motionless; he stood on top of the creature, ready to plunge his sword deep into the creature's head, when he thought he heard a voice. "Did you say something?" He was looking down at them.

"No," Asim said. "Just do it so that we can leave."

Must be the river water and the air in my ears, he thought. This time, he brought the sword down hard into the creature at the back of its head. The beast never moved; it stayed motionless.

It must have already died, he thought. "Help," came a voice this time. Tyron was sure of it now.

"Did you say anything?" He looked at Asim.

"No! Why do you keep asking?"

"I heard a voice."

"Woo, is the creature's ghost talking to you," Lanee said in a mocking voice.

"I heard a voice," insisted Tyron, more defensive now.

Everyone listened intently; no one heard anything.

I could be hearing thing. He thought.

Then there it was again. "Help me."

"This time, I heard something," shouted Boben, who had moved further along the creature's body.

"There," quipped Tyron. "I'm not the only one now."

Asim was listening intently. "We hear nothing at this end."

"Move closer to Boben," Tyron asked.

There it was again. "Help."

"I heard something," said Asim. "It is from inside the buru, I believe."

"That will be a first time? A talking buru." Lanee giggled.

Asim went back and retrieved his sword; he looked at it and kissed it. "I thought I lost you."

Lanee looked at him. "Would you do that for me if you lost me?" she asked.

"Maybe," he said, smiling. "You know I would."

She smiled.

Asim went around the creature's belly, taking his sword. He stuck it into the beast. There was a muffled scream from inside. He stopped. Tyron had climbed down and joined them.

"Do you think Benson could be in there?"

"Strange as that sounds, there is something in there." Asim put his sword away and pulled out his dagger. Following suit, they all helped him stab into the Buru's stomach.

"Oh, Lord," said Lanee. The smell was turning her nose up as she stared at Asim.

"It's a little unbearable," said Tyron, using one hand to cover his nose now. They had cut away a large square between them, continuing to dig into the flesh.

"Hoping we reach something soon." The more that they dug away, the less muffled the voice seemed. They cut deep into the side of the buru.

"I can almost stick my whole body in here," said Tyron, stabbing again at the flesh.

Suddenly, Asim heard, "STOP!" It was loud as he pulled his dagger back out.

"Hold on, everyone," he shouted. They all stopped cutting the flesh out, putting his blade in slowly. Asim twisted, then heard a voice, "I am right here."

"I can hear you."

"Is that you, Asim?" came the voice.

"Benson?" shrieked Lanee.

"Lanee?" the voice came back.

Asim had cut a hole now, and Benson stuck his hand out.

"Stay back as far as you can," said Asim, holding his dagger ready. "I will cut this area out."

"I am back," shouted Benson as Asim took his dagger and sliced the flesh back until the hole was large enough for Benson to crawl out.

He stuck his nose out first.

"Yes, that's Benson," jested Tyron. "I would recognize that nose anywhere." Benson stuck his head out next, then his arms. At that point, Asim and Tyron grabbed him and pulled him out.

"What in the stars above!" said Asim. "How did you end up in there?"

"And how can you stand the smell?" asked Lanee, still turning her nose up.

They were all in the river, trying to wash the smell from their bodies and help Benson at the same time.

"I was swimming back up on top of the water after being pulled under when that thing came back again. I was swept up by the water and wood into the beast's gaping mouth. At first, being under the water, I thought I would drown, but it soon subsided, and then I was shaking like a leaf. I was so scared."

"What was it like in there?" asked Lanee.

"It was dark. I could see nothing. Then I kept sliding, I guess going down to its belly."

"Glad you are still alive." Boben seemed relieved.

"We all are glad," said Asim. "I'm not sure how we will all tell this story."

"This has to be the funniest thing." Tyron laughed. His laugh was so infectious that soon everyone was laughing.

"We need to go back," said Asim. "Are Mup and Anson still on the other side?"

"Here," said a voice from behind them.

"Both of us swam over. We did not know what was happening." They were both hugging Benson. They talked and laughed all the way back.

"We must cross the river again," said Lanee.

"I think it might be all right this time," said Tyron. "Unless big bad Father Buru comes along," and he let out a laugh.

"I will hurt you, fool." She swung to hit Tyron's arm. He dived into the water to slip away.

"Come on, children," Asim laughed.

"You are next," she said, laughing.

As soon as they reached the other side, they gathered together. The other three search parties were back from searching earlier. Asim, Tyron, and Lanee went to check on Jubly. She was doing much better under the care of Toya and Radel. She was sitting up with her chest and shoulder bandaged. Everyone gathered around Benson.

"Where were you?" asked Tig in a concerned voice.

"You won't believe me if I tell you."

Benson told the story later. The children were in awe, especially when they listened to him describe the fish that swallowed him.

"Now that's a story to tell your children and grandchildren," Lanee laughed; they all had fun at Benson's expense. He didn't seem to mind.

Chapter 38

GOING HOME

ll right, everyone," Asim shouted. "Let's settle back into the same order as before." Looking out, he saw a mist forming over the water.

"That's scary." One of the children was trembling.

"You are right," Asim agreed, "but I hear something coming that is even scarier. Run, everyone! Run for the cover of the trees." A loud screech sounded close to them.

Everyone took off running when the sky blackened and there was a stiff breeze that blew. Asim grabbed the small boy running toward the forest.

"What is it?" shouted Boben.

"A cockatrice. Don't look back. Just run." Even Jubly was trying to run with a little bit of help from Toya. Duf grabbed her up as they headed for the trees. Asim picked up another of the children straggling behind, carrying two now. Most were diving behind the tall trees as best they could; Asim was the last to run into the forest. Just as he did, they felt the wind and dust as the large cockatrice landed by the riverbank with a tremendous thud.

"We must be quiet," he whispered.

The cockatrice looked around, then made a move into the water, taking a drink. Returning to the bank, it slowly looked around before it flew off.

"That was close," Asim exhaled. "We don't want to fight with them again. Let's try this. Fall back into the same order and be as quiet as we can."

"Stone and Lube, go on ahead and try to find a good place for us to camp. Soon it will be dark. Nothing needs to go wrong," he said to Lanee and Tyron.

"I hope we have had our fill of excitement," said Lanee.

"Camping down tonight. We can start out early in the morning."

That night in the forest, it seemed quiet except for the odd screech from the mountains. Stone and Lube had found them a place to camp as they all settled down. The moon was shining through, making small light beams in the camp. Asim sent out guards. Toya, Wilt, Mup, and Pooly went in four directions that night.

"Are you feeling good after your workout today?" Asim asked Zollo.

"I think I feel better still," Zollo smiled. "I'm about ready for that wrestling match!"

"Maybe tomorrow?" Asim laughed.

"You know I will take you," Zollo smirked, then he laughed.

Asim patted his head, laughing with him. "I hope so. I hope you can."

He had Stone, Lube, Tyron, and Duf join him in sleeping closer to the children, giving them a more secure feeling. The children, playing in the moonbeams, found it easier to relax after the day they had.

Morning came upon them, it seemed. They all made their selves ready for the journey to the village. The sun was out, shining early this day, starting the day with a dazzling light show as the sunlight bounced off the leaves and branches. It sparkled like tinsel as it danced across the ground. Asim had a good feeling about this day. *Maybe we will have a calm walk through the forest*, he thought after a while of walking.

Tonas came to him. "We are close to the outskirts of Tress," he said to him. Asim knew it would not be long before the children would be back home. Tonas was feeling overwhelmed to bring all the children home, knowing it was more than an achievement. "I know that this all could never have happened without you." He was smiling inward and outward.

"Not just me," said Asim. "It took all of us together."

Suddenly, he felt a slap on the back; he did not need to look; it had to be Tyron.

"How is this beautiful day going?"

"So much better now," Asim said. They could see the smoke billowing up into the sky, rising from the chimneys of the houses, drifting into the heavens. He looked at Tonas's face, and he could see tears rolling down his cheeks, and looking over at Spen, who was fighting with his pouch, trying to drain out the last dregs. That made Asim smile. Boben was playing with his brother when he stopped and ran over to him.

"This is an enjoyable day," he sighed. "But I am a little sad."

"Why?"

"I think I know now what it means to be brave. Some villagers did not come back. As we faced the enemy, I feel sad for them this day, for they were brave to give their life for what they believed."

"I understand," said Asim. "But just like you, each one chose to walk their pathway. Remember this: some friends walk the path and stay steady, and some friends walk the path and fall off along the way. But we need always to be happy to know our friends were once on that pathway with us!"

Boben was crying for the lost friends, and Asim put his arms around him.

"I don't know how we can ever repay you and the others." Boben shook his head.

"You already have." Coming to the village, some villagers had already seen them. Someone had gone back as they were ringing the bell. People were rushing out of their houses, some from the fields nearby. Mothers were hurrying out to find their children.

"Too many tears," whined Tyron. "This is making me cry."

"The big bad robber." Lanee let out a laugh as she smiled at him.

"No, the big bad warrior now." He laughed. Lanee and Asim laughed with him. Some children were running to their parents; it was a sight in the village square. It seemed as if everyone was running in every direction. There was hugging, screams of joy and laughter, kissing, and the pleasure of the father lifting their children high in the air. Some of the younger girls came and kissed Asim, Tyron, and the other warriors. It was a beautiful reunion; Tonas, Spen, and Boben were champions for the day. Asim and the other warriors stood back a little.

"Oh no, you don't!" Tonas grabbed Asim and Lanee and pulled them to the middle, returning for Tyron and the others. "This is your day," he shouted. Villagers were shaking hands, some hugging to make everyone welcome. They were setting up a pig to roast in the square. Tonas stood up on the steps and rang the bell; everyone quieted down to listen.

"I want you to know," he shouted. "These are the bravest men and women you will ever meet. We would never have rescued the children if it were not for these brave warriors." The villagers cheered. "Make them welcome and open your hearts to them as they did for us." Now, they were mobbed with more handshaking and hugging.

"The tavern is open. No charge for our brave warriors," the bar owner shouted. Food of all kinds was being laid out.

This is just amazing, Asim thought. Tyron and Lanee joined him in the tavern. There, of course, at the bar was Spen, taking the tankard from his mouth with foam now all over his face. All three laughed at him.

"I don't think you will ever change," said Lanee. Spen smiled and shook his head; the others had moved in from outside. Tonas and Boben joined in, and Asim grabbed a tankard in a long line already filled for them. He raised it high in the air.

"I want to raise this tankard to all of you," Asim shouted, looking at Tonas, Spen, and Boben. "You all left out as villagers and came back as brave men, and I have been proud to spend this time with you. This was all for the children." They all drank and cheered. "On this extraordinary journey with all of you, I am pleased to celebrate with you now."

Tonas raised his tankard. He coughed to clear his throat. "In fairness," he said, "I want to thank each one of you. You did not even know us, but you all put your lives at risk for us to bring our children home. I don't know if we could ever thank you enough. We owe you so much."

"Another tankard of ale," shouted Asim, "and we will consider it paid." He laughed as they all laughed and cheered. It was another night of fun, laughter, ale, and singing for them.

Spen shouted, "I will drink to that," right before he fell off his chair. "I'm all right," they heard from the ground. That brought the loudest cheer of the night.

Early the next morning, everyone in the tavern was slow to rise. Asim, Tyron, and the others all settled for baths and clean clothes, as did Lanee and the ladies. They had a good breakfast before starting out; the whole village was out early to see them off, even the children.

"You are all our champions," said Tonas.

Spen was taking a sip from his full again pouch. "I love y-you-all," he blubbered.

"It won't be the same without you," Asim said to Spen. "You had made us laugh, even when we were down."

"Please stay safe," Boben said.

"We will miss you all," said Asim as they started out to leave the village. "Tonas, we will be back someday. And Boben, look after your brother. You will make a great warrior someday."

Tyron grabbed Spen. "Bye, little drunk man," They all hugged as they left.

"Anson, we will have you back to Bendo and your camp. That will be our first stop." Anson looked at Asim.

"Where will you go after that?" he asked.

"To the west!" Asim smiled. "There is trouble I heard about in that direction."

"Well, I have talked it over with Benson, and we would very much like to stay with you—that is, if you don't mind two old broken-down dwarfs hanging around?"

It overwhelmed Asim. "We have grown attached to you; I would be happy if you and Benson stayed with us."

"The others still want to go back."

"We are heading to the dwarf camp. We will still need to be careful. We don't need to run into Swank!"

"You know," Asim shouted toward Lanee's direction. "before we started this last journey. We were going to the west, toward the land of Ghant, to see about the rogue elephants. A lot of strange things are happening in that distant region, so I hear!"

"Well," said Lanee, who was staring at him, "sounds like you will need protection." She smiled. "However," she emphasized, "can we please stay clear of any rivers?"

Everyone laughed.

"No guarantees." Asim laughed. "But you know if we can stay clear, I will."

Arriving at the dwarf camp, Asim spoke to Bendo and apologized for not bringing them all back.

"They all knew what was at stake," said Bendo. And Asim received his blessing to take Anson and Benson with them; they again had a small celebration at the dwarf camp. They were drinking and eating once more.

"I think I can become used to this." Tyron smiled, having fun.

Leaving Tig, Pooly, Wooly, and Mup the next morning was a sad affair as they left out again, heading on their trek westward.

******

"What did they do next?" one of the children in the classroom asked the teacher.

The children were absorbed in the story that Saon Jestin was telling them.

"Yes!" the other children shouted. "What happened next?"

"Well," Saon said, "that's another story for another day."

THE END.
FOR NOW.

9 781958 751145